THE ENFORCER

The Taskforce Series
Book Three

Marliss Melton

Cover and Book design by eBook Prep
www.ebookprep.com

June, 2014
ISBN: 978-1-61417-615-2

ePublishing Works!
www.epublishingworks.com

ACKNOWLEDGEMENTS

Everyone says that writing is a solitary occupation, but I have to disagree. My books are a product of a large group effort, and THE ENFORCER is no exception. Oftentimes, contributors don't even realize that they've added a key ingredient to making my story sparkle. My gratitude overflows to everyone who participated in this production, from its earliest inception to its final publication. Special recognition is reserved for my friend and lead editor, Sydney Baily-Gould, without whom I would never have figured out this story's ending, let alone written a story fit for reading. Thanks also to Rachel Fontana, a reader-turned-writing-expert, who taught me how to "show" more and "tell" less. Hats off to all of my wonderful Beta readers, Cindi, Cyndi, Suzy, Susan, Barbara, Bobbie, Penny, Lori, and Nicole. Your sharp eyes eliminated zillions of typos and errors, ensuring enjoyment for other readers. Thank you to Mark Goodin for helping me grasp Dylan's political philosophies and to Officer Chris Lyons and Deputy Larry Lineweaver for advising me on police and law enforcement matters. And, finally, thanks to April Martinez, my cover artist, and to Judi Fennel, my formatter, for putting the icing on the cake. I could not have completed this feat without any of you!

"I ask, sir, what is the militia? It is the whole people except for a few public officials."

~ *George Mason*

CHAPTER 1

Stepping off the Amtrak at the train station in Harpers Ferry, West Virginia, Special Agent Tobias Burke spared a distracted thought for the station's architecture. The building, a relic of the Victorian Era, stood quaint and well-maintained. Someone with questionable taste had decided to paint it maroon.

Milly, his bomb-sniffing Labrador, tugged him toward the luggage being tossed out of the train's underbelly. As she snuffled inquisitively at the bevy of suitcases, Toby picked out his army-issue duffle bag and slung it over one broad shoulder.

The bag matched his battle dress uniform and the black gel bracelet embossed with *Never Forget*. He'd strapped on his old military watch and the boots he'd once worn to trudge across Afghanistan. In combination with his shaggy hair, the ensemble made him look like a veteran drifter—just the illusion he wanted to create.

Pushing out of the train station, Toby headed for the Civil War era buildings teetering on the façade of the crimson-leafed mountain in front of him. The small historical town of Harpers Ferry looked in danger of sliding into the rivers that converged below, especially if it were to rain too hard. Fortunately, a bright October sun warmed the top of Toby's dark head and only one fluffy cloud floated in the light blue sky.

As he skirted the parking lot for Milly to relieve herself, the hairs on Toby's nape began to prickle. Was he being watched already? His gut burbled with unexpected nervousness. He had battled extremists in Afghanistan and, for the past six years as a member of the Special Response Teams in the ATF, he'd exchanged fire with gun-traffickers on the streets of Washington D.C., so why would lunch with a West Virginia militia leader so much as elevate his pulse?

Then again, Captain Dylan Connelly wasn't your average, everyday militia leader. Her work in Mortuary Affairs with the U.S. Army had left her with a raging case of PTSD. Her anti-government essays and civil-rights-violations protests made her the FBI's top suspect in the bombing of Defense Secretary Nolan's car the month before. The bombing had left the Secretary dead, but FBI had yet to prove her culpability. If she was guilty of murder—and they were pretty sure she was—Toby was bound to find out.

Searching the nooks and crevices of the town before him, he hunted for the eyes that were no doubt watching him. The shops and sidewalks teemed with tourists taking advantage of Columbus Day, hiding the source of his disquiet. Keeping a sharp lookout, he proceeded toward the designated meeting spot— Private Quinn's Pub, a dog-friendly eatery.

The hostess standing on the wooden deck beamed down at them. "Just the two of you?"

"We're joining the Connelly party."

"Oh, yes, they're waiting for you. Follow me."

As Toby rounded the corner of the building, a silvery set of eyes alighted on him, sending a jolt of awareness clear to his toes. She'd been watching him from the back of the L-shaped deck where the shadows had kept her concealed. Her rich auburn hair, pinned into a bun, contrasted sharply with her milk white skin. Her striking eyes seemed to see straight through Toby's guise, unsettling him. The size of her dark-skinned companion did little to reassure him, as that man pushed to his feet.

"Tobias Burke?" His deep voice resonated in the open space.

"Yes, sir." Toby extended a hand, but the giant ignored it.

"Terrence Ashby, Executive Officer of the Second Amendment Militia," he intoned with formality. "This is Captain Dylan Connelly," he added, gesturing to his leader.

Do I salute? Toby opted for a respectful nod. "Pleasure, ma'am."

"Welcome." Looking chagrined by her XO's pompous formality, she fixed her gaze on Milly. "Who is this?" she asked, extending a hand to the black Lab.

"Her name's Milly," Toby said. "She's a service dog, though, not a pet."

The leader abruptly drew her hand back.

"I was diagnosed with PTSD," Toby lied. "And Milly keeps me on an even keel." He had to have some excuse for bringing his bomb-sniffing dog with him. Claiming Post Traumatic Stress Disorder was meant to give them something in common.

Except that Captain Connelly did not acknowledge her diagnosis.

"Please, have a seat," she said.

Drawn to her pleasant voice and the way her lips

moved when she talked, Toby dropped into the chair
next to hers. If the rumor about the leaders was true,
then they made an odd-looking couple. The executive
officer was as broad and dark as the captain was slight
and fair. At least they wore civilian clothing in lieu of
militia garb, which would have made them stand apart
from the tourists and locals even more.

"Have you heard from Ken Larsen lately?" he asked
to break the ice.

Larsen, who'd also served in the Army, was a
common acquaintance and Toby's ticket to an
interview.

"Not since he called to recommend you," Lt. Ashby
answered.

"Ah," said Toby, trying hard to send the captain a
warm smile. His gift for charming women had made
him the Taskforce's obvious choice to play the
informant. If she had, in fact, masterminded Secretary
Nolan's murder, Toby would surely find out—but
probably not today. Her piercing scrutiny kept the
muscles in his neck tight, and Lt. Ashby's daunting
presence made flirtation all but impossible, for now.

Spying the captain's purse on the floor between
them, Toby directed Milly's nose toward it. "Sit," he
said, but Milly responded only to his subtle gesture.
Sniffing at the purse, she *then* sat, signifying she
smelled gunpowder.

Just as Toby suspected, the militia leader was
packing heat.

As the waiter neared, he pulled kibble from his
pocket and quietly rewarded Milly for her discovery.

"Hey, Cap'n. Hey, XO." The waiter smiled at the
militia leaders while glancing curiously at Toby, who
snatched up his menu to scan the offerings.

"How's your wife doing, Nathan?" he heard Captain
Connelly inquire.

"She's three days overdue and miserable," the waiter replied.

"Tell her to hang in there. It can't be long now."

Her sincere advice wrested Toby's attention from his menu. A wry smile had transformed Dylan's merely pleasant features into a vision of loveliness. A kind, caring light shone from her crystalline eyes. Surprise rooted Toby to his seat.

"Thanks. I'll tell her that," Nathan said.

Seeing Toby's attention off his menu, Dylan added, "I'll have your crab soup and two hush puppies, plus another coffee."

"And I'll take the Reuben," Ashby interjected.

"And you, sir?"

Toby had barely glanced at the menu. "I'll have the Reuben, also."

"And to drink?"

The list of ales on tap tantalized him, but he ordered a Coke, seeing as how the others weren't drinking.

Silence fell over the table as the waiter walked away. Milly broke the spell by laying her head on Dylan's knee.

The captain went perfectly still.

Toby laughed at her uncertain expression. "Okay, you can pet her if you want to," he relented. "She obviously likes you."

With a fleeting smile at him, she smoothed long, graceful fingers over the dog's glossy head. He tried to imagine her nimble-looking fingers assembling the bomb that had blown up Nolan's car. Components of the bomb had been traced to a hardware store just outside of Harpers Ferry, and the FBI had lifted bomb-building material off Dylan Connelly's property. Still, that evidence alone was not enough.

"What makes you want to join my militia, Mr. Burke?"

The softly spoken question reminded Toby of his objective. "I'd still like to serve my country, ma'am. I used to be an Army Ranger before the PTSD thing, which is pretty much behind me now. Matter of fact, I turned down a wrestling scholarship so I could become the best the military had to offer."

Her auburn eyebrows quirked as she glanced up at him. *You're the best?* she seemed to ask.

"I served three back-to-back tours in Afghanistan. It's not that I miss the war, but I'd still like to feel useful."

She gave a thoughtful hum. "How long have you been out?"

"Two years." Actually, his last six tax returns showed he worked for the ATF, but he'd spent the last six months on loan to the Inter-Agency Counterterrorism Taskforce, whose job it was to support the whole alphabet soup of government agencies. In this case, he was charged with finding evidence for the FBI. Not that Dylan Connelly needed to know that.

"And what have you done since leaving the Army?"

"Construction jobs mainly; some security work." His service record had been altered just in case she looked it up. "But it's not the same as protecting the country. We've got terrorists lurking around us and corrupt politicians leading us astray. I'd like to help change that."

Her X-ray eyes seemed to see straight through his fabrications. "How familiar are you with the Constitution, Mr. Burke?"

Fortunately, as most militias based their beliefs on a strict interpretation of the Constitution, he was ready for that question. As he rattled off the first few lines, her elegantly curved lips lifted with approval.

"What's the Second Amendment to the Bill of

Rights?" she quizzed.

"A well-regulated militia, being necessary to the security of a free state, the right of the people to keep and bear arms shall not be infringed." Any ATF special agent worth his salt had that amendment memorized.

"Do you believe in the Second Amendment, Mr. Burke?" She regarded him intently.

"Absolutely." Toby had no beef with peaceful militias acting in support of law enforcement. However, those who called themselves "patriots" while plotting to undermine the federal government were terrorists in his book, and he'd do whatever it took to stop them. "Plus, I know a lot about weapons and tactics," he added, thinking he could be a little more persuasive. "I can train your soldiers to be fierce fighters, prepared for almost any challenge."

At his remark, her gaze fell with feminine appraisal to his hands lying loosely on the tabletop. Sexual awareness sparked without warning, sending heat surging to his extremities as their gazes collided. But then the waiter appeared, sweeping dishes piled high with food onto the tabletop and breaking the spell.

The aroma of French fries distracted Toby from his mission. Famished from his morning travels, he sank his teeth into his sandwich, only to freeze with a mouthful as he noted Dylan Connelly's head bowed in prayer. Lt. Ashby eyed him reprovingly. A second later, the captain looked up and started eating, and Toby was free to chew again.

As they ate in silence, her smooth brow remained furrowed. Toby could feel himself perspiring. He had to be doing something wrong for her to withhold her immediate acceptance. He'd never worked this hard before.

After several sips of her soup, she laid down her

spoon, dabbed the corners of her mouth, and said, "What made you leave the service, Mr. Burke?"

Sadly, the answer to that question was a true one, and just the thought of it soured the food in Toby's mouth.

He reached for his Coke to wash it away. "My platoon was hunting down a suicide bomber." He scratched the bristles on his cheek, recalling the dry air, the blistering heat. "In a village outside of Kandahar, we finally caught up to him. We had orders to shoot on sight, so we hid ourselves, waiting. Then he finally came out, dressed like a woman and carrying a baby."

Dylan's pupils seemed to shrink. "How did you know it was him?"

"Well, we ID'ed him by his shoes. Since he'd fled empty-handed and was passing himself off as a woman, we figured it had to be him. Our sniper would tap him with a headshot and the kid wouldn't get hurt." Toby swallowed hard to counteract his sudden queasiness. "Turned out, that was his cousin's house, and he'd left himself a one-way ticket to paradise inside." The scene flashed through his mind making him shudder. "They both blew up."

Dylan went perfectly still, her face chalk-white.

With a muttered apology, Toby looked down at his half-eaten sandwich. Dredging up the horrors of war wasn't how he got his kicks, but they had to have as much in common as possible if he was going to learn her darkest secrets. "I was diagnosed with PTSD not long after that and removed from active duty," he summed up.

In the quiet that followed, he realized Dylan's pupils had expanded again. A sheen of moisture coated her ivory skin and her chest rose and fell in sync with the pulse hammering at the base of her slender neck.

Mission accomplished. He'd triggered her PTSD with just a simple story.

And to think that a woman so susceptible to adrenaline rushes was carrying a weapon in her purse, while her sidekick radiated the protectiveness of a presidential secret service agent.

Toby fought to relax his facial muscles to keep his contempt from showing. It was none of his damn business what kind of strange, co-dependent relationship these two had. But if they were up to no good, he sure as hell was going to put a stop to it.

Perhaps sensing Dylan's distress, Milly put her head on the leader's lap.

Traitor, Toby thought, though he was secretly impressed with her acting ability. He'd trained her to be a bomb-sniffing dog, not a therapy dog, but she managed to fool Dylan, who returned Milly's steady stare as if in a trance. With a shaky breath that gave him a brief glimpse of full breasts beneath the baggy sweater, she reached for her coffee and took a quick sip.

"Well." She cleared her throat, and Toby jerked his attention upward. "I'm sorry you've come all this way for nothing, Mr. Burke," she said on a firmer note. "I hope you understand that there's nothing personal about my decision, but I don't take in soldiers with mental or emotional disorders. I just can't afford the liability."

Toby's jaw came unhinged. For a stunned moment, he just stared at her, unable to accept her decision. *Isn't that the pot calling the kettle black?* he wanted to scoff, except a comment like that would reveal the fact that he'd read the FBI's extensive case file and psychological profile on her. Other organizations, like the National Security Administration, had been keeping tabs on her phone calls for months. ATF had flown surveillance drones over her property to assess her training facilities. Pulling together agents and resources from all of those organizations, the Inter-Agency Counterterrorist Taskforce had been tasked with proving her culpability. It had never occurred to Toby that he might be turned away, especially considering the skills he brought with him. Desperate to persuade her otherwise, he considered his next move.

The FBI's profile on Dylan had delved into her reverence for her ancestor, John Brown, the abolitionist whose raid on Harpers Ferry had sparked the Civil War. This morning, with that pearl of information in mind, he had donned a certain T-shirt as a last-resort measure.

Pulling back the edges of his jacket, he exposed the white letters emblazoned on the black cotton. Then he reached for his drink and emptied it, giving Dylan time to read the words printed across his muscular pecs. Over the rim of his glass, he watched her eyes widen as she scanned the message.

Lowering his glass, he smothered a burp and rose to his feet. "Well, I'm sorry to have wasted your time, if that's how you feel, ma'am." As he pulled a worn, leather wallet from his pocket and slapped a ten-dollar bill on the table, Milly moved away from Dylan's chair, dragging her leash behind her.

"Good-day, Cap'n." He tossed off a sharp salute. "XO." He saluted again. Then gesturing for Milly to heel, he swiveled smartly on his boots and stalked off, all the while praying he would hear Dylan call him back.

She'll change her mind, he assured himself. She just needed to think about what his shirt said.

Dylan watched Tobias Burke saunter past the railing

with a swagger that conveyed undiminished confidence in the wake of her rejection. His crooked half-smile could not disguise the dangerous aura he exuded as a result of his military training. The U.S. Army Rangers had conditioned him to hold his head high, his shoulders back. Her trainees would follow a man like Burke to the ends of the earth.

"You sure you should've let him go?" Terrence Ashby echoed her churning thoughts on a note of disapproval.

She drew her lower lip between her teeth. "I can't get a read on him," she said in defense of her decision.

That was true enough, but that wasn't what had made her chase him off. It was the ease with which he'd brought back the disturbing images of severed body parts. Thank God she'd never had to match up the scattered pieces of a child.

"I think we could've used him," Terrence persisted. "I won't be around forever, you know."

His words plucked at her heartstrings even as they wrested her attention to his rigid countenance. "Don't say that," she pleaded.

"You know it's true. Who's going to take my place?"

She swallowed hard at the wrenching reminder that she would soon lose her dearest and only friend. Tearing one of her hushpuppies in half, she stuffed the morsel in her mouth and chewed it without tasting. Terrence was right, of course, but..."I don't know. I don't trust him," she said. The memory of the FBI's suspicions made her extra cautious.

Or maybe it was just herself she didn't trust.

Tobias Burke hadn't been at all what she'd expected. It was true he'd evoked disturbing memories of the war, but apart from that, he'd made her feel unsettled, tumultuous—even excited. Thank

God for his dog or she would have stammered like a schoolgirl under his dancing, ocean-blue gaze. And those hands—they were exquisite, strong yet sensitive. Combined with his sexy smile, his presence had kept her enthralled and therefore fully in the present, until he'd agitated her PTSD by bringing up that story about the poor child.

It was easier just to send him away than it was to examine her reaction to him.

Terrence's chair groaned as he leaned back and folded his arms in palpable disagreement. No words were needed to make Dylan regret her quick decision.

Her right temple throbbed. She closed her eyes and rubbed it absently. She had always trusted Terrence's intuition, especially in times like this, when her own mind was so confused and unreliable. Besides, given her XO's diagnosis of incurable, stage-four leukemia, time was running out on her most trusted friend, and she could use a soldier with Burke's expertise and obvious physical prowess to take his place. So what if he was as emotionally unstable as she was? She had PTSD, herself, and still managed to function as a physician and a well regarded leader. And despite what she'd told him, her militia was filled with less-than-stable individuals.

"Let's go find him," she decided.

They both left money on the table, enough to cover the bill and the tip. Departing the pub, they climbed into Dylan's old Chevy Suburban, which was parked across the street. Because of his prosthetic leg, Ashby let her drive. Neither of them spoke as Dylan pulled a U-turn, guiding the gas-guzzler through Lower Town where the Potomac and Shenandoah rivers converged under a high bridge.

Tobias Burke wasn't lingering around the Swiss Miss ice cream shop or the Coffee Mill, or even at the park down by the water. Dylan turned up High Street, throwing the gear shift into a lower gear to fight the steep grade as she drove back up the mountain.

And then she spied him sitting on the stone wall adjacent to the road, and her pulse ticked upward. He sat with one foot up on the wall, the other dangling by his dog, looking like he was waiting for her. Had he been?

Dismissing the absurd thought, she eased up on the gas and slowed to a stop, lowering her window. His widening smile gave rise to an unmistakable warmth spreading through her body.

"You'll have to cut your hair immediately," she announced, employing her sternest voice to combat his weakening effect on her. "And shave that scruff off your face."

"Not a problem." He leapt nimbly off the wall.

"And you will address me as ma'am or Captain Connelly," she informed him, elevating her position to maintain her distance.

"Yes, ma'am." He picked up his bag and grinned at her.

She had the feeling she was being mocked but let it slide. "Well, get in the car, then, unless you have somewhere else to stay."

Without another word, he crossed to the SUV, opened the rear passenger door for his dog and climbed in after her, sitting right behind Dylan.

As she gunned the engine to get them moving again, she glanced in the rearview and caught him looking pleased with himself.

"Don't get too comfortable, Mr. Burke," she warned him, tightening her grip on the wheel. "I'm taking you in on a trial basis, only. If you prove unstable or unbeneficial to the militia in any way, I'll have to let you go. Am I clear about that?"

"Crystal, ma'am," he replied.

She re-fixed her attention on the road, wondering what it was about him that made her body thrum with awareness. He had better not be more trouble than his T-shirt suggested with its provocative message, NICE BOYS DON'T CHANGE HISTORY.

CHAPTER 2

—◆—

Ten minutes outside of town, Captain Connelly swung her SUV off the country road onto a gravel driveway. It was here where she trained her militia, on what used to be a family-run apple orchard. Toby drew an appreciative breath. High-altitude photos from the ATF's drones didn't do the property justice. The thirty-acres of rolling fields lined with apple trees and framed by thickets of ash, sumac, birch, and sweet gum could have graced the cover of *Country Living Magazine*.

Rocks pinged the underside of the Suburban as it barreled up the long driveway. Through the burnished leaves of century-old trees, sunlight glanced off a shiny metal roof of what the Taskforce had surmised was a nineteenth century farmhouse. The roof was clearly new. The paint on the home's exterior had been scraped right down to the original clapboard siding in anticipation of a fresh coat. Not a single weed grew around the broad front porch supported by brick pillars. Lush hedges gave way to freshly raked grass.

A sleek cat lounged on one of the porch's rockers,

prompting Milly to quiver on the seat next to him, but Toby's eyes were on the humans. One man stood at the height of a ladder, his girth blocking the rungs as he made his descent. Another straightened out of a chair and folded his arms across his chest. A third man, who was missing his right arm, rounded the corner of the house from the rear. A silhouette appeared behind the screen door. How many more were there?

Dylan braked in the yard and killed the engine. Lt. Ashby pushed out of the SUV to open her door, but Dylan beat him to it. As the three men in the yard pulled themselves into smart salutes, Toby eased out of his seat, leaving Milly in the car for the moment.

"At ease, gentlemen." The captain's voice conveyed mild frustration with their formality. Their not-so-friendly gazes fastened on Toby as she turned to introduce him. "I've brought us a senior operations sergeant," she announced. "Everyone, this is Tobias Burke, former Army Ranger."

Toby took note of the rank and title she'd conferred on him—senior operations sergeant. *Perfect.*

"You can let Milly out," she added, seeing the dog still in the car. "Milly is Burke's service dog," she added, "so don't coddle her."

The black Lab leapt from the car and padded up to the strangers wagging her tail.

"Sergeant Burke, this is Ivan Ackerman," Dylan said, leading Toby toward the whipcord thin, greasy-haired man sneering at him. "Ivan is our supply NCO."

Toby and Ivan exchanged curt nods.

"Next we have Sergeant Gil Morrison, former Marine Corps artillery expert. He's our weapons NCO."

Morrison stepped toward Toby, and a grin split his

broad face as they shook hands. "I like to blow shit up," he divulged under his breath.

Okay, then.

"And this is Chet Lee, our communications NCO." The man whose right hand was missing proved to be of Asian descent. He offered Toby his left hand, instead.

"First or second battalion?" Lee asked, pinning him with a hard look.

"Seventy-fifth, actually," Toby admitted. "I drew an assignment with USASOC."

A grin supplanted Lee's glare. "Army Special Ops. Nice!"

As they pumped hands, Toby took another look around. *Is this it?* Were there just three non-commissioned officers, plus the captain and her XO? he wondered.

"Chet's wife cooks and cleans for us," Dylan stated as if reading his mind. He glanced toward the screen door, and the shadow disappeared. "I trust you'll fit right in," she added confidently.

"I'm not sharing my room," Ackerman tossed out, belying her words.

"You can sleep in the barn, then, Sergeant," Lt. Ashby thundered, "if that's your attitude."

"I don't need a room," Toby said to ease the tension.

Dylan sent him a quick frown. "Don't be ridiculous. But the bedrooms are all taken, so you'll have to sleep in the attic for now. I'm afraid it gets chilly up there."

"Attic's great." In fact, it suited his purposes perfectly.

"Sergeant Ackerman." She addressed the rebellious entity firmly. "Kindly fetch a bedroll for Sergeant Burke from Supply."

Ackerman made a sour face before stalking toward

the shed, and Toby swallowed a chuckle. It amused him how seriously the men all took their roles. The so-called "Supply" was probably just some musty corner of the barn where Ackerman was headed. He wondered what else was stockpiled in there.

"Follow me," Dylan requested, leaving him no time to speculate.

Removing Milly's leash, he followed Dylan to the door.

Watching the dog make a beeline for the snoozing cat, Dylan said, "She's not going to run away, is she?"

"No, ma'am. As long as I've got treats, she'll stick close." He patted his breast pocket.

"I see." Pulling the screen door open, she led him into her sanctum. A cool hush and the scent of cinnamon followed him down the hall, past a formal living room and dining room, both clearly unchanged from her parents' era, to a post-and-beam great room that took up the entire rear portion of the house. A kitchen with a stone chimney and eating area filled the space on one side and a gathering place-turned-command center occupied the rest.

Several maps with push-pins used for demarcation hung on the walls, and an easel stood with hand-written notes on it—but there were no computers of any kind in sight. Like al-Qaeda, Dylan's militia operated low-tech, with no online presence to speak of, making it impossible for NSA to keep tabs on her remotely. As far as they knew, she didn't even own a cell phone—probably true since she'd demanded that Toby surrender his own on the way here.

He'd lied, of course, and said he didn't have one.

"This is where we spend our time when we're not working or training," she said, observing his reaction.

The clanking of pots drew his attention to the Asian woman in the kitchen who was scrubbing dishes.

"This is June, Chet's wife. She and Chet live in the guest house." She gestured to a building in the back that might have once been an outdoor kitchen. "You'll appreciate her culinary talents soon enough."

June shot him a shy smile, which he answered with a wink that made her turn quickly back to the dishes.

Captain Connelly's lips pursed at the overly-familiar gesture. "Follow me," she commanded, retracing her footsteps and heading for the stairs.

As she ascended ahead of him, her loose-fitting cargo pants pulled taut around her thighs, outlining a well-toned backside. *She's a suspect, not a woman,* he reminded himself. But he couldn't keep his hormones from kicking in like heat-seeking missiles hot on her trail.

"There are four bedrooms on this floor," she said, pausing at the height of the steps to look back at him. "Three men share a common bathroom." She showed him the door, laying a hand on the schedule posted on the wall beside it. "Each man gets ten minutes in the morning and ten minutes at night to himself. You can go before or after."

Toby glimpsed outdated fixtures and a warped countertop beyond the cracked door.

"Did you grow up here?" Getting to know her better was the name of the game, though he already knew the answer.

"I did." Her tone did not invite more questions.

He tried anyway. "You got any brothers and sisters?"

"No."

"Big old house for a family of three."

Ignoring his comment, she headed toward the end of the hall. Through a partially opened door, Toby caught sight of what had to be the master's suite. Dark walnut furniture and a pair of petite combat boots told him she had taken over her parents' bedroom. She opened the door next to it, revealing a steep set of stairs leading to the attic.

A low ceiling forced him to stoop as he joined her under the eaves. The exposed brick of the house's two chimneys stood at either end of the long, cool space, both flanked by casement windows that admitted just enough light for him to see that the attic was cluttered with boxes, old furniture, even a used guitar.

"You can sleep in this space over here." Dylan picked up a box and moved it out of the way. "You'll probably want to sweep before you lay your bedroll—squirrels and all. I'll have one of the men bring up a broom."

"Little dust never hurt anyone," he assured her, hoping the squirrel comment proved to be a joke.

She wiped her hands on her thighs. "It's not exactly insulated from the cold, but the heat rises through the floorboards, so I don't think you'll freeze."

"No ma'am. Compared to the Hindu Kush in winter, this is downright cozy."

Her expression froze at the reference to the mountains in Afghanistan.

Her job in the Army—to collect bodies from the battlefields, ID them, and send them home in flag-draped boxes—was among the most gruesome in the military. He wondered why, given her anti-government sentiment, she'd even joined the Army, let alone agreed to perform such difficult work. Mortuary Affairs personnel suffered a higher rate of PTSD than any other specialty in the military. Pity pricked him briefly.

"Ackerman ought to be up with your bedroll soon," she said, oblivious to the questions running through his mind. "Take your time and settle in. We have a briefing every weekday in the command room *precisely* at seventeen hundred hours. Since today's a holiday—Columbus Day—" she added, in case he didn't know, "we're holding our meeting an hour earlier."

He almost rolled his eyes at her unrelenting military-speak. "Yes, ma'am."

"We'll inform you of our policies and regulations then," she added, heading for the stairs. Halfway down, she stopped to add over her shoulder, "Oh, and don't let Sergeant Ackerman get your goat, Burke. It's not *you* he's angry at."

"Yes, ma'am." Was she a military leader or a camp counselor?

The door at the bottom of the stairs clicked shut. Ackerman would arrive with the bedroll soon, but the bastard probably wouldn't knock. Toby tossed his duffel bag in the cleared corner and shrugged out of his jacket. Retrieving the tiny cell phone hidden in the lining, he sent his Taskforce lead a quick numerical text—2990—signifying that he was in. Then he stowed his phone back in the special pocket in his jacket before shoving his jacket deep inside his duffel bag.

He then prowled around the attic. The space was packed with relics of Dylan Connelly's childhood. He imagined he could learn a lot about her from searching through the boxes. Plus, he'd be sleeping right above her bedroom, close enough to keep tabs on her at night.

He moved to the nearest window. This hawk's eye view of the grounds suited his purposes perfectly.

The squeaking doorknob alerted him to Ackerman's approach. Boots thudded up the stairs. Toby turned in time to catch the sleeping bag and pillow lobbed at him, one right after the other.

"That's the last time I'll be doing you any favors."

Ackerman glared up at Toby, clearly expecting some kind of reply as he backed down the steps slowly.

"Love you, too, man," Toby called. He couldn't help himself.

"Fuck you," Ackerman snarled up at him.

"Let's hold off until the second date," Toby suggested.

"Funny guy." Ackerman's gaze dropped to the message on Toby's T-shirt. "Real fuckin' funny," he added stomping off.

What the hell's his problem?

Toby set up his bed under the window. He flicked his wrist to check the time. The meeting wouldn't start for another hour. He had plenty of time to walk Milly and get a feel for the property.

No one prevented him from leaving the house. With Milly at his side, they performed an initial reconnaissance. The house had been built in the 1880s but it was slowly being renovated. Just as he suspected, the outdoor building, once an old kitchen, had been converted to a guest cottage for Chet and June.

Toby made a circuit of the apple orchard while heading for the large red barn designated as "Supply." The broad double doors stood securely locked. He gestured for Milly to sniff at the crack, and it came as no surprise when she sat. This was where the FBI had found bomb-building components—pipe and copper wires, but no gunpowder, strangely enough.

The barn also housed the arsenal used by her militia: dozens of M-16 rifles. Good thing she kept it securely locked.

He rewarded Milly with a handful of kibble, and together they returned to the farmhouse.

Captain Connelly stood on her porch holding a mug of what smelled like fresh coffee as she watched him through narrowed eyes.

"Nice property," he said in an attempt to avert suspicion.

"We're all waiting for you, Sergeant," she said impatiently.

He checked his watch again. Two minutes to five. She was one of *those* people.

Venturing into the command room, he realized why arriving early was a good idea. The XO and the NCOs had nabbed all the good chairs for themselves. Toby wasn't about to share the love seat with Ackerman, so he toted a chair in from the kitchen, where June Lee puttered about preparing supper. As he sat down, Dylan pulled several stapled pages from a briefcase.

"I'm going to keep this meeting brief," she said, distributing the handouts all around.

Toby looked at his copy. Given the URL at the top, the printout had come straight from an anti-government website he was already familiar with. The title read *Fusion Centers Violate Civil Rights.*

"Last Friday, I brought up the issue of fusion centers," Dylan said, offering him a bit of background information. "The Feds have spent millions of dollars installing and running them. Allegedly, they exist to promote the sharing of threat-related information between the federal and local law enforcement. But, according to a subcommittee investigation, not a single terrorist threat has been uncovered as a result of their inception. Instead, the Feds were telling local authorities what books were being read by the Muslims in their community, which is a clear violation of those citizens' First Amendment rights."

Toby felt like a fish out of water. He glanced up to see a stain of indignation suffuse Dylan's porcelain cheeks. Seeing her reach for her coffee, he wondered if she fueled herself on caffeine to maintain her energy levels.

"The nearest fusion center is in Woodlawn, and the next meeting of law officials there is November 9th. I'd like to propose that we picket that event. We have two weeks to mail out educational brochures and to make signs. I'd like your feedback on this."

One by one, the militia leaders pledged their support for the proposed protest.

Toby waited for the other shoe to drop. That was it? The militia was planning a peaceful protest, complete with brochures and signs? Was there no shooting involved? No targeting of federal law enforcers? *So, what gives?*

"Very well," Dylan continued, unaware of his thoughts, "then we'll iron out the details as that date approaches."

Stepping toward the easel, she put down her coffee cup to flip through the sheets of bound paper until she came to one labeled *CPX.* Toby guessed that stood for Command Post Exercise.

"In regards to this Saturday's CPX," she said, "we'd discussed holding physical readiness evaluations, but I'm thinking of substituting training of some kind, specific to the skills Sergeant Burke can teach us." Her crystalline gaze flickered to Toby. "Since he's new and needs to be brought up to speed, I'm going to release the rest of you so I can educate him. Does anyone have any immediate concerns?"

The former Marine who liked to blow shit up put his hand in the air.

"Yes, Sergeant Morrison?"

"We're low on ammunition, ma'am. I need you to order more clips."

"Of course." She nodded at her XO, who was already jotting himself a note. "Anything else?"

Toby harbored dozens of questions, but he kept

them in check. It would look suspicious to voice them so early on.

"No? In that case," she said, addressing just the NCOs, "kindly return to your work while I orient our newest member."

With a glare at Toby, Ackerman pushed to his feet and followed the other sergeants out of the room. Lt. Ashby stood up and limped to the filing cabinet, where he pulled out three sheets of paper and surrendered them to Toby, one at a time.

Toby skimmed the first sheet, entitled *The Defender's Creed*.

I accept and understand that human predators exist. Criminal or terrorist, they take advantage of our civilized society to prey upon the weak. They represent evil and must be confronted and defeated. His eyes fell to the words with righteous indignation and superior violence, and a shiver chased up his spine.

"Read it, believe it, and live it," Ashby commanded with gravity. "Our Creed is what gives each man and woman in the SAM purpose."

Just like in the Rangers Regiment but with vigilante flair. *Got it.* Toby nodded.

Next, Ashby handed him a copy of the Constitution of the United States and one of the Bill of Rights. "You will carry these with you at all times in the backpack you will be shortly issued. These pages constitute the core of our beliefs."

"Yes, sir." Toby glanced over at Dylan, who'd gone to stand by the window, her back to both of them as she drained what was left in her cup.

"There are some terms you need to know." Ashby hobbled toward the easel. He flipped to a clean page, picked up a marker, and scribbled *FreeFor*. "The FreeFor, or freedom forces are the overt participants

in a CPX." He pointed at Toby. "You are now a
member of the FreeFor."

The marker squeaked as he scribbled *OpFor*.
"These are the oppositional forces opposed to the
objectives of FreeFor. They may be individuals, but
more often they are governments, state, federal, and
foreign."

And servants of the government, like Nolan. And
me.

As if privy to his thoughts, Dylan turned her head
and pinned him with an Arctic stare. Toby fought to
mask his discomfit. God, if she knew he was, in fact, a
servant of the OpFor, who knew how she would
react?

"Our main objective," she announced turning from
the window to approach him, "is to rebuff the federal
government's natural propensity to oppress the
people." The sway of her hips heightened his
awareness of her subtle curves. "The alphabet soup of
government agencies—FBI, CIA, NSA, DEA—you
name it, have spied on, harassed, and ruined the lives
of individuals deemed to be enemies of the state, all
under the guise of preventing crime and halting
terrorism."

Toby swallowed hard before muttering his
agreement. From her burnished hair, still caught up in
a bun, to the earnest glint in her eyes, she reminded
him of a flame of indignation. But she couldn't be
more of a cynical individualist if she tried.

"Our daily routine looks like this." She ticked off
the information on her slim fingers. "Reveille sounds
at oh-five thirty, every day except for Sunday. We PT
for forty-five minutes, shower, and eat. You'll earn
your keep here by completing projects around the
compound. This facility is not a charity. Since I'll be
away at work on weekdays, you will answer to Lt.

Ashby while I'm gone. Upon my return, we convene here for the evening briefing. Dinner follows immediately after. Lights out is at twenty-one hundred. Saturday is the CPX. On Sundays you may sleep in and relax or leave the area, if you so desire, but I encourage all my soldiers to attend mass with me."

"Yes, ma'am." She didn't give her leaders much time to reflect on what the hell they were doing with their lives, did she?

Her cool gaze darkened as it slid to the curls at the nape of his neck. "I promised you a haircut, Sergeant," she recollected. She sent a thoughtful look at June Lee, who was busy whisking sauce into a bowl. She looked over at the wall clock and back at Toby's curls.

He could tell what she was thinking—that she wanted his hair shorn before dinner, which meant she'd probably end up doing it herself.

The mere thought of her wielding a sharp instrument near his neck made his testicles draw up. Yet, here was his chance to lay the groundwork for a special kind of relationship—one that entailed confiding secrets.

"Have a seat on the back porch," she invited, waving a hand at the rear door, thankfully unaware of his thoughts. "I'll be out in a minute."

"Yes, ma'am." Ashby, who was absorbed in tidying the filing cabinet, didn't even look his way.

Toby got up and returned his chair to the kitchen. Milly followed him out onto the screened-in porch, where she plopped down in the last remaining patch of sunlight.

He sat uneasily at the outdoor table and surveyed the tidy yard, rimmed by a hedge of azaleas. In the center, stood an old brick well, newly-renovated and topped with a fresh coat of paint. Off to one side, stood a child's outdoor playhouse, freshly painted with its own flowerbed out front. Beyond that, a dry-rotted tire swing hung from a massive weeping willow.

A gentle breeze, redolent with the scents now coming from the kitchen, stirred the tire. He pictured Dylan as a child, pumping her legs to get higher, her red hair streaming.

A minute later, she joined him, flicking on an exterior light and shutting the door. In her hands she held a pair of sharp-looking scissors, a towel and a spray bottle. Toby's nerves jangled.

"You might want to take your shirt off," she suggested, laying those items on the table next to him.

He braved the rapidly cooling air to pull off his T-shirt. Self-consciousness speared him as her gaze dropped to his thickly muscled shoulders. Her eyes affected him like ice against his skin. Most women liked what they saw, but if she did, she didn't show it. She frowned at the tattoo on his upper left arm.

"What is this?" Her light touch felt like the flick of a whip.

"It's the 75th Ranger Regiment distinctive insignia."

She picked up the towel and shook it out. "I thought the Ranger symbol was a skull over crossed rifles."

Toby shrugged. "That's one of them. I'd feel like a pirate with a skull on my arm."

"You look like a pirate with this ridiculous hair." She draped the towel across his shoulders, and Toby held the edges together as she spritzed his mane with the spray bottle.

Then she attempted to draw a comb through it.

Every tug affected him like fingernails on a chalkboard. The pleasant aroma of coffee emanated off her clothing, underlain by the scent of clean linen.

She reached for the scissors, which gleamed like twin blades in her hand, and he tried not to flinch. "I can trust you, right?"

"A doctor should always be trusted."

He wondered at the cryptic reply. "You're a doctor?" he asked, though he already knew her occupation.

"A physician." She pulled on a lock of hair and snipped it off. "I work at the VA Medical Center in Martinsburg."

Silence fell between them, and Toby started to feel like a cat being petted. As she stroked her fingers through his hair, snipping as she went, he fell into a semi-hypnotic state.

"What do you think about doctors taking bribes from pharmaceutical companies?" she inquired out of the blue.

He roused from his pleasant stupor to ponder the question. "You mean accepting purchase-incentives to use their products?"

"Bribes, purchase-incentives, what's the difference? A doctor gets four free rounds of golf for prescribing a drug that's not adequately tested. Does that sound ethical to you?"

"Not when you put it that way."

"Well, I work with a doctor who's been playing a lot of golf lately."

Snip, snap. She was working herself into a state of agitation. Maybe if she drank less coffee, she'd be more relaxed. He could feel her fingers shaking. The edge of the blade grazed his ear, and Toby flinched.

"Sorry." With a guilty look, she began to check her work. "Almost done," she assured him.

"Great, just...take it easy," he invited. He gestured to the dog sprawled and snoring at their feet. "Gotta live life the way Milly does."

Hearing her name, Milly lifted her head to study them through luminous and intelligent eyes.

"I've read about therapy dogs," Dylan volunteered.

"You should get one," he suggested, regretting his words the instant he heard her indrawn breath.

"Are you implying that I have PTSD?" she demanded, stepping back.

Well, duh. Her condition was so obvious that he couldn't bring himself to deny the accusation, not even to protect his position as the new guy. "Sorry, but it's fairly apparent when you've been through it."

Whirling so that her back now faced him, she laid the scissors slowly on the tabletop.

A tense silence filled the enclosure.

"Your hair's short enough for the clippers, now," she told him, dropping the subject like he'd never brought it up. "You'll find them in under the sink in the bathroom upstairs. If you need help, Morrison's a decent barber. June Lee will tidy up out here." Snatching up the spray bottle and the scissors, she fled the porch, leaving him to his own devices.

Toby looked at Milly, who put her head on her paws with a long-suffering sigh.

"Don't say it," he grumbled. Pushing to his feet, he removed the hair-dusted towel.

He'd thought it would be a simple matter to *develop* Dylan Connelly—to use the word his team lead had supplied. Toby hadn't met a woman yet who didn't respond to his easy-going charm. But the militia leader wasn't like any woman he had ever tried to flirt with. She was so preoccupied by political matters and civil rights concerns that he had to wonder if she even saw him as a man at all, let alone a prospective confidant.

This job is going to be a little harder than I thought.

CHAPTER 3

At dawn the next morning, Dylan stepped out of her house and drew up short as she spied the solitary figure bathed in the silvery light, waiting for the others to join him. Tobias Burke had beat all of them to morning PT, and given Milly's labored breathing as the dog padded up to the porch to greet her, he'd even walked his dog already. Recalling her humiliation yesterday, she harbored no desire to find herself alone with the hunk, not before downing her morning coffee.

The man was too appealing by far, not to mention disturbingly astute.

Bending at the waist, Dylan paused to pet Milly's head—anything to delay joining Tobias in the yard.

"Morning, ma'am," he called, removing her choice to ignore him.

"Hello."

She'd seen for herself at supper that he'd buzzed the rest of his hair just fine, with or without Morrison's help. This morning, the spiky strands were mussed from sleep, and the strong jaw he'd shaven smooth had already grown new stubble.

The flutter in the pit of her stomach annoyed her as she determined whether to stay where she was or to find something else to preoccupy her. What was it about the man that unsettled her at such a visceral level? She had thought herself immune to animal attraction.

None of her NCOs or militia members had ever dared to mention her struggle with PTSD. It was their faith in her that kept her going. Tobias's insight left her feeling transparent. It crippled her confidence. Would he follow her leadership knowing what a wreck she was?

"You're up early," he persisted, forcing her to stop petting Milly at the risk of looking rude.

"I don't sleep much," she admitted, joining him in the yard.

"Might want to switch to decaf, at least in the afternoon," he suggested.

She wasn't about to defend her habit of drinking coffee all day long when it gave her the energy to combat her lack of sleep. "How was the attic?" she asked, changing the subject abruptly. "Did you freeze?"

"No ma'am. It was perfectly comfortable in the sleeping bag. Thanks again for taking me in. I have a sense of purpose, now."

"Hmm." He must have sensed her doubts about him.

In all fairness, aside from commenting on her PTSD, she had no real complaints—yet. He'd projected an upbeat outlook at the supper table, deflecting Ackerman's nastiness with humor and deferring to the rest of them. She managed a small smile. "Then you'll have no complaints about the workout this morning," she said sweetly.

His white teeth flashed in the gloom. "No, ma'am."

His exuberance teased a smile out of her. She

quickly masked it as light poured out of the house and three men tumbled into view. At the same time, Chet Lee rounded the building from the guest cottage. The NCOs fell into place next to Burke, while the officers squared off to face them.

Terrence Ashby got them moving. "Jumping jacks!" he bellowed. Hampered by his prosthetic and fatigued by his illness, Terrence oversaw the routine more than he participated in it. Dylan, who craved the endorphins, lived for exercise. Fifty jumping jacks preceded a series of stretches and core-conditioning exercises.

Terrence's voice boomed in the quiet yard. "High knees!"

Over the stamping of their feet and the huffing of their breaths, Dylan heard a rooster crow. If not for that distinct sound and the smell of wood smoke wafting from the fireplaces in the county, she could almost close her eyes and pretend she was back in Afghanistan, leading PT in the barren yard outside the MACP. In her mind, her specialists—her boys—were still alive, ribbing each other, telling dark-humored jokes.

What do you call two dead guys hanging in your closet? Curt and Rod—get it? Curt-n-rod?

"Pushups!" Ashby announced, snatching Dylan out of the past. They all dropped belly-down onto the cold, damp grass. The sun edged higher to illuminate their sweating faces. Most of them had shed their jackets, including Tobias, whose broad shoulders made her think of the tattoo on his upper arm. He'd chosen a shield over a skull. She liked that about him.

Intercepting her stare, he shot her a grin, and she promptly looked down at the grass.

Down. Up. Down. Up. With each depression, the scent of fertile soil and wet grass filled her lungs. The dirt under her hands made her think about her boys, all buried deep beneath the earth, while she remained above, still alive…for what?

Sergeant Burke's baritone startled her from her reverie as he cut off the others' groans. "Come on, guys. We got this. Easy day."

They had fifteen more pushups to go to get to fifty. He joined Terrence Ashby in belting out the count. "Thirty-eight, thirty-nine, forty, forty-one…"

Sergeants Morrison and Lee chimed in, latching onto Burke's enthusiasm. Dylan, whose own arms had started burning, added her own voice. Only Ackerman refused to count, but then he was barely even doing pushups.

"Fifty!" they chorused, scrambling to their feet with a sense of accomplishment.

Dylan's gaze fell to Tobias's broad chest and the message on his red T-shirt.

I'D LIKE TO APOLOGIZE IN ADVANCE FOR WHAT I'M GOING TO SAY LATER.

A rusty chuckle scraped up her throat and escaped her parted lips. Catching her eye, he sent her a quick nod, and she realized that was his way of apologizing for his PTSD comment, yesterday.

"Burpees!" Ashby shouted, reclaiming her attention.

With muttered curses, the men dropped into a plank position, but Tobias kept them motivated as he called out the count again. Dylan fought to keep her eyes off him.

His charisma, even more than the skills he could teach them, made him an asset to the militia. Was it possible that he might want to take Terrence's position?

Hope for the future, so long absent, pulsed through her bloodstream, keeping her from drifting back into the past.

"Two miles!" Terrence called as their calisthenics came to an end. He consulted his watch, preparing to time them. "On your mark."

Dylan pointed out the running course to Tobias. "Follow the path."

"Go!" Terrence pushed a button, and they all took off, Dylan at the lead.

Down the hill and along the perimeter of the open field she raced, her warmed muscles accommodating her with ease. Dew glimmered like droplets of liquid mercury under the ever-brightening sky. The chilly air nipped at her ears and cheeks. Her hair, caught up in a ponytail, whipped back and forth in rhythm to her graceful strides.

Running was her refuge. When she ran at top speed, her memories could not keep up, and so she pushed herself to stay ahead of them—free of pain—if only temporarily.

She could hear her NCOs falling behind, as usual, even though they dared one another to overtake her.

The running course split at the tree line. A right turn would take her to the firing range, only used on Saturdays. Dylan bore left, running parallel to the forest. Normally, by the first mile marker, she found herself running all alone—in a still, peaceful setting where the drum of her heart and the patter of her feet were her only company. But today, someone was gaining on her fast, and she didn't have to look back to know who it was.

Innately competitive, she lengthened her stride.

But it was no use. By the time she turned uphill in the last half mile to the house, she could hear Tobias gaining on her. With her calves screaming and lungs burning, she gave up the pretense of being able to outrun him.

He pulled alongside her, shooting her a gamey

smile. "Damn, you're fast," he huffed.

The compliment took some of the sting out of being overtaken. He was obviously giving it his best effort. "You run pretty fast yourself."

"Used to be a lot faster. This is good for me."

There he was, kissing up to her again. "Beat you to the finish," she tossed out, shifting like an engine into an alternate gear.

With a muttered curse, he surged forward to meet her challenge.

Their sawing breaths and pounding feet silenced a twittering cardinal. It lit out from a dogwood tree as they tore up the slow grade to the back of the house. Ashby stood by the willow tree, poised to call out their times.

Accelerating at the last instant, Dylan defeated her newest NCO by two seconds and beat her personal best record by seven.

Walking in circles with her hands clasped at the back of her head, she gasped for breath. Tobias doubled over, hands propped on his knees, his chest heaving. He glanced up suddenly, caught her watching him, and grinned. A sense of camaraderie washed through her, sending her into confusion.

As he turned away, calling encouragement down to Sergeant Lee, Dylan studied him covertly. She liked his enthusiasm, his natural leadership. She liked more than that, only she wasn't ready to admit it.

"Come on, brother," Burke called, encouraging Lee, who tackled the incline with his only arm pumping furiously. Tobias held out his hand for him to slap as he crossed the finish line, well ahead of his colleagues. Sergeant Morrison huffed up the hill twenty seconds later, and Sergeant Ackerman trotted up dead last.

"Twenty   minutes   and   ten   seconds,"   Ashby

announced on a disgusted note. "That's pathetic, Sergeant. You're supposed to beat your last time, not add to it."

Ivan Ackerman's hands balled into fists. Sensing his volatility, Dylan chimed in, "You'll pick up the pace next time, won't you, Ivan?"

"Yeah, sure," the supply sergeant muttered. "I'm coming down with something." He hacked up some phlegm, beating his chest to prove it.

"We'll all beat our times on the next run." Tobias Burke's dancing eyes swung in her direction.

Dylan frowned at him. How the hell was she supposed to run any faster than she had?

He countered her dismay with a wink that made her jaw drop. *He did not just wink at me.* Horrified, she glanced at the others to see if they'd noticed. Thank God, no one had. Next time they were alone, she'd take him to task for his insubordination.

Or maybe she'd take the high road and let him off the hook as she'd done with Ackerman. In good time, they'd all settle into the roles they were meant to fill.

At least she hoped that was true, especially for her.

An hour later, Dylan climbed into her Chevy Suburban with a travel mug of fresh coffee and drove off in the direction of the Martinsburg Medical Center. Ivan Ackerman went with her.

"For counseling," Sergeant Morrison explained as they watched the Suburban disappear. Lt. Ashby had ordered them to paint the front of the house. "Ackerman has more issues than most."

Toby turned toward the ladder. "Why, what happened to him?"

"From what I heard, he was on leave from the service, visiting his family over Christmas. His wife and daughter went shopping at the mall and were killed by a thug who opened fire."

Toby stared at him aghast. "No shit."

"True story."

"Damn." Dylan had tried telling him not to judge Ackerman too harshly. In Ackerman's world, predators were everywhere, even at the mall. No wonder he'd joined her militia.

"Sergeants Morrison and Burke!" Lt. Ashby's stentorian voice carried easily across the yard. "Get to work."

All morning and into the afternoon, Toby stood at the height of a ladder, coating window frames with paint so thick it went on like glue. The sun shone warmly on his back. A lone fly buzzed around his head. On a ladder not too far away from him, Sergeant Morrison rolled the chiffon-colored paint over the scraped old clapboard with desultory sweeps. What Morrison failed to accomplish in work, he made up for in gossip.

"You know, I used to be a patient over at the veterans hospital," the artillery expert divulged in the middle of his running monologue.

Toby glanced over in surprise.

"I'd been going to Martinsburg for years, trying to find relief from Gulf War Syndrome, which I got in the first Gulf War. You know, bone aches, lethargy, the whole nine yards. I used to pop a dozen different pills a day, and it didn't make a lick of difference. Matter of fact, I got worse. Started having heart palpitations. Then these black outs would hit me out of nowhere." He spit a wad of phlegm into the rhododendron below him. "Can't keep a job when you pass out for no good reason. I used to head up security at a software development company in Kearneysville."

"Oh, yeah?" Toby picture Morrison in a blue

uniform wearing a gun in a holster that went across his pot belly.

"Yep. Liked it, too, but I was sicker'n hell, and when I keeled over one night, they fired my ass the next day." Morrison moved his roller to a new area.

Toby mumbled his condolences. For a while, they painted in silence.

"After that, I could see the writing on the wall." Morrison picked up right where he'd left off. "I applied for disability and couldn't get it. I was gonna lose everything to Gulf War Syndrome, and the VA didn't give a rat's ass. To hell with it, I thought. Next time I went to the hospital I told them, 'Give me a new doc who'll fix me, or I'll take my complaints to the media.' That's the day I met Cap'n Connelly and, if I say so myself, she's a sight for sore eyes." He waggled bushy eyebrows at Toby. "She takes one look at my records and turns white as a sheet. I'll never forget that look on her face."

"Why? What was in your records?" Toby prompted.

Morrison paused for dramatic effect, dragging his roller through the pan of fresh paint. "It was all those pills I was on—experimental drugs. She said I was lucky they hadn't killed me. She put me through a detox program, and in a week or two I felt like myself again. Except, by then, the bank had taken back my house. When I found myself evicted and jobless, she gave me work and a place to live. Damn fine woman, Cap'n Connelly." Morrison spat on the bush a second time.

Toby ground the bristles of his paintbrush into the grooves of the frame. Was it possible to be both a saint *and* a terrorist? He glanced over at Morrison, who'd lapsed into thoughtful quiet.

"I take it you were the first one here?" The FBI had neglected to ask these kinds of questions when they interrogated Dylan last month.

"Oh, no." Morrison shook his round head. "Cap'n Connelly brought the XO home from the war with her. He was the first man here."

"You mean they served together?" How was that possible? Records showed Ashby was a helicopter pilot.

"Well, yes and no. The XO was an aviator. Used to fly the Cap'n from the Mortuary Affairs Collection Point and back. That was her job—collect the dead from the field, identify 'em, clean 'em up as best she could, and ship 'em home. Used to be called Graves Registration back in my day."

"Why do you think she did it?" Toby probed, eager to have his questions answered.

"Penance," the former gunny sergeant answered.

"What?"

"It's like this: The only way Cap'n Connelly could afford med school was if Uncle Sam footed the bill. For the cap'n, that was like making a pact with Satan himself. But, hell, it was either that or be stuck with a lifetime of student loans. Still, it bothered her conscience. So to keep from feeling like she'd compromised her beliefs, she volunteered for the worst assignment a physician could get—to command a MACP. In other words, penance."

"Sergeant Morrison!" The deep voice bellowing up from ground level nearly startled Toby off his ladder. "Less talk and more work will get the job behind you."

Lt. Ashby had caught them gossiping again.

Gil Morrison rolled his eyes and kept right on layering the same wood he'd been painting for the past half hour. Toby, meanwhile, had finished his last window frame on this side of the house.

The XO shaded his eyes against the sun and

inspected Toby's work. "Nice job there, Burke. Once you've cleaned your brush, march to the head of the driveway and fetch the mail from the box."

"Yes, sir."

"Then you're free to relax until the briefing. Morrison, you have one hour to go. Work faster."

Toby dabbed his last touch of paint on the window frame, climbed down the ladder, and doused his brush in turpentine. Calling Milly, who sat in the yard watching the cat, he headed up the driveway toward the mailbox, glad for an excuse to breathe fresh air instead of paint fumes.

The gravel crunched under his feet, and the farmhouse fell further behind him. Milly loped along next to him, her mouth wide open, tongue lolling in an unmistakable doggy grin.

"You like it here, huh?" Toby's gaze swept the rolling terrain. The gnarled apple trees growing in rows for acres in either direction had just dropped their yield for the season. Rotting apples pebbled the ground for as far as the eye could see. It's a shame, he thought, to let the harvest go uncollected. But the birds and squirrels sure as hell enjoyed it.

It was hard enough to envision Dylan training a militia here on this untarnished landscape bathed in autumn hues. He couldn't wrap his head around her plotting the demise of the Defense Secretary. But given Nolan's passionate support of Syrian military intervention and Dylan Connelly's equally virulent articles opposing involvement, she certainly had a motive for wanting him dead.

An American flag fluttered on the picket fence at the head of the driveway. Toby's stride broke as he regarded it. Was she a patriot or a terrorist? Her ancestor, John Brown had killed five pro-slavery southerners before raiding Harpers Ferry armory in the hopes of sparking an antislavery insurrection. By modern standards, that would have made him a terrorist. And yet, he was still upheld by many to be a hero for civil rights.

With a shrug, Toby popped the mailbox open and pulled out a handful of mail. Signaling for Milly to retrace her steps with him, he turned back toward the house, sifting through it as he went.

There were two envelopes, one containing a bill for the landline phone that NSA had already tapped into and the other containing a letter from the Director of the Martinsburg VA Medical Center. Curiosity tempted him to slit the latter open, read it, and seal it shut again, but postal mail, unopened by the recipient, was inadmissible in court, and Dylan was due home at any moment.

He strolled back to the house, laid the mail in the command room and dashed up to the attic to swap his paint-splattered T-shirt for a fresh one. Hearing the sounds of Dylan's return, he headed to the first floor to claim a decent seat in advance of the briefing.

He had just shut the attic door when Dylan's voice, carrying from the command room, made him stop in his tracks. Her odd tone and Ashby's soothing answer prompted him to halt Milly and eavesdrop on the landing.

"I can't lead the briefing today." Dylan's words, uttered in a shaken voice, reached his ears clearly. "This letter's giving me a headache."

"I'll take care of the briefing." By contrast, Lt. Ashby sounded as steady as a rock.

"I told you the director was too spineless to reprimand Hendrix," she said bitterly.

So she'd read the letter from the director, Toby surmised. It sounded like a response to her complaints about her colleague, the one taking bribes from pharmaceutical companies.

"You were right," Lt. Ashby agreed.

"I just can't accept this!" Fury colored her voice, shortening her syllables. "I refuse to turn a blind eye to his malpractice."

"Just calm down," the XO soothed. "There's nothing you can do."

"Of course there is. I can stand up to the both of them." Her footsteps grew louder on the oak flooring as she stalked toward the stairs. "Tell the men I've got a migraine," she pleaded.

Wiping all expression from his face, Toby released Milly and started down the steps just as Dylan rounded the banister. Her eyes flew wide as she caught sight of him.

He pretended not to notice. "Afternoon, ma'am." He stepped to one side, throwing up a salute, which she did not reciprocate. Biting her lower lip, she fled past him without a word. Consumed with curiosity, he watched her disappear into her room.

Lt. Ashby's unmistakable tread galvanized Toby into motion. He continued down the stairs, intercepting the XO's harried look as that man passed him en route to the door. "Have a seat in the command room, Burke," Ashby muttered. "I'll be in with the others in a minute."

"Is she going to be okay?" He tossed out the question on a whim.

Ashby froze and swiveled around to face him. "Of course," he answered with a forced smile. "This happens from time to time."

It was just as Toby thought. She was as unstable as a one-legged pirate walking a tightrope. Good thing she had a reliable XO to keep her militia up and running whenever she lost her balance and fell.

* * *

Dylan rolled onto her back and stared unseeing at the dark ceiling.

Both her alarm clock and the inky darkness in all three of her windows informed her that she had hours to go before Ackerman blew his horn for reveille. This was what she got for drinking coffee so late in the day. The caffeine kept her brain humming, preventing her from catching up on lost sleep. She inevitably woke up still tired, in need of more coffee. And so the cycle continued.

Her eyes burned, and she closed them, remembering the dream that had wakened her minutes before. A shiver traced her spine. Was the dream born out of helplessness or was it an omen? She'd been stuck in a hospital room, her arms trapped against her body, wearing a straightjacket. Doctors and nurses streamed in and out, whispering in hushed tones as they examined her, but none of them would answer her questions or speak to her directly.

There's been a mistake, she'd tried to tell them. *I'm a doctor, not a patient.* They'd returned her words with looks of disdain or pity. But no one would acknowledge her statements.

Then one of the nurses whispered to another, *She's crazy.*

I'm not! Unstrap me and I'll prove it! She'd struggled to free herself until the one who'd maligned her jabbed a syringe deep into her arm, and Dylan had gasped awake, her heart pounding, her body drenched in sweat.

It was just a dream, she assured herself, but then the words of the letter from the director flashed into her thoughts, and humiliation boiled in her.

The letter was real; the dream just a figment of her imagination. A single tear slid from Dylan's left eye and trickled into her hairline. *Maybe I am crazy.*

That was certainly the gist of the director's message. His words, which she had memorized, spilled over like a toilet backing up.

I have found no evidence to substantiate your claim of prescription abuse by your colleague. In fact, I am concerned that the spreadsheets and copies you forwarded to my office are, in fact, forgeries. The production of such forgeries is a violation of West Virginia's Code of Law, Section 46-5-109. In light of your uniformed service to this country, I will abstain from taking legal action against you, provided your allegations desist. I ask with utmost respect that you consider whether your diagnosis of PTSD has left you with unfounded paranoia.

In one violent move, Dylan vaulted out of the bed.

Peeling off her sticky nightshirt, she threw it down onto her quilt. She shivered in her underwear, pawing through her dresser drawers until she found a pair of sweatpants and a hoodie from the University of Virginia, where she'd earned her medical degree. Sliding socks over her cold toes, she jammed her feet into her sneakers and laced them tightly.

Then she stepped into the hall, taking great pains not to disturb those sleeping in the rooms next to her. Except for the snores of sleeping men, the hall was silent. Avoiding the floorboards that squeaked, she made her way down the steps, crossed to the front door, and slipped outside.

The need to run—to cast off the weight crushing her chest—fueled her heartbeat as she leaped off the porch into the cold, dark yard. The instant her shoes touched the grass, she broke into a sprint, galvanized by humiliation and oppression and righteous indignation.

Biting cold nipped at her ears and stung her eyes, as she chased the running course down the frost-covered slope toward the trees. If she could run forever, she would never stop.

Veering off the path, a mile from the house, she slowed to a walk to enter the sanctity of the forest. As she caught her breath, a belated sob convulsed her lungs. She let it out, desperate for relief from the pressure that pounded in her head. A rash of sobs followed, shaking her so violently that she fell to her knees on a brittle bed of sticks and leaves.

Why am I still here, Lord?

How many times over the past twelve months had she asked that question?

You should have taken me, and left my boys alive.

CHAPTER 4

Lying flat on his back in his sleeping bag, Toby raised an arm to check his watch. Ackerman wouldn't blow the bugle for another two hours, but Dylan had been up and stirring in the room below his. For a while, he'd ignored the restless noises, determined to sleep. But then he'd thought he'd heard the screen door at the front of the house squeak shut and a flurry of footsteps cross the yard.

Why would Dylan leave the house at this ungodly hour?

He sat up slowly so as not to disturb Milly sleeping next to him. Levering himself to peer out of the window over his head, he spied a shadow streaking down the moonlit hill like an apparition in flight. Christ, what was Dylan thinking?

As she disappeared from view, he sat a moment, thinking. Perhaps she made a habit of running alone at night. All the same, he felt he ought to let Lt. Ashby know.

Toby slithered out of bed, and Milly raised a sleepy head. *Stay,* he signaled before tiptoeing down the stairs with stealth that belied his broad build.

As he stepped into the hall, his gaze slid toward Dylan's open door. Darkness lay beyond, a chamber of sleeplessness and nightmares bad enough to make her flee. The other doors remained shut, muffling the snores of three sleeping men.

A golden opportunity—one too good to pass up—presented itself, unexpectedly.

Toby slipped into her room and closed the door. He stood a moment to study the layout. Faint moonlight gilded the ornate headboard of an old bed, a walnut bureau, and a matching vanity. The open book by her bed drew him nearer. He picked it up, turned it over, and by the light of his watch, read the title: *John Brown Still Lives!: America's Long Reckoning with Violence, Equality, & Change.* The pages had been earmarked and passages heavily marked.

Struck by her complexity, he laid the book back down, next to the Bible and a rosary, along with a framed photograph of her elderly parents.

As he turned to the bureau, a pale rectangle drew him straight to the letter that had thrown Dylan into a funk yesterday. Finding the envelope open, he drew out the letter with a steady hand and once more used his watch to scan the contents. The message confirmed his assumptions regarding the subject. But the director's closing comment made him wince on Dylan's behalf. *We ask with utmost respect that you consider whether your diagnosis of PTSD has left you with unfounded paranoia.* Ouch. That had to have hurt.

And now she was outside in the dark and cold, trying to run from the director's humiliating—though possibly accurate—remark.

He put the letter back and turned to the door. The sight of Dylan's purse hanging from a hat rack elevated his pulse. Eager to discover what weapon she carried, he lifted the flap. The gleaming butt of a .357 Magnum caused his eyebrows to shoot up.

Jesus. No micro-sized pistol for this woman. The revolver was large and lethal looking. Not only that, but she carried a full box of Speer, Gold Dot .38 special, 135 grain ammo in the same pocket. He closed the flap and looked around. *Anything else?*

A ghostly object lay across her quilt. Curious, he crossed to the bed to pick it up and realized he was holding Dylan's nightshirt. Lifting it to his nose, he inhaled a blend of woman, coffee, and sundried cotton. *Nice.* The pleasing scent strummed a protective chord inside him.

He couldn't just leave her out there, distraught and alone.

On the other hand, wouldn't he appear too astute going after her? *Play your cards close to the vest*, he reminded himself. Hell, he even owned a T-shirt with that message on it.

Dylan Connelly was a grown woman, not a child. If she wanted to run around at night on her own property, who was he to stop her?

Ignoring the seed of doubt rooted in his mind, he returned to the door, where a peek and a listen assured him he could slip upstairs unnoticed. Reveille would sound in less than two hours, anyway. How much trouble could she get into on her own before then?

Back in the attic, he squirmed into his bedroll for a little more shuteye. It felt like he had just lapsed into slumber when the bugle squawked.

Fuck. Did Ackerman really play the horn that badly or did he do it on purpose?

Rising a second time, Toby slipped on his shoes, grabbed his jacket, and made his way downstairs, this time with his dog.

Dylan's still-open door filled him with concern. The

thump of Lt. Ashby's crutch heralded that man's trek to the bathroom, on which he had first dibs. Seeing Toby at Dylan's door, the XO stopped in his tracks.

"Captain Connelly's not here," Toby announced.

A crease appeared on Ashby's forehead. He edged Toby aside to peer into Dylan's room himself.

"I think I heard her leave a couple of hours ago," Toby admitted.

Ashby's eyes flashed with apprehension. "That's none of your concern," he growled, but he thrust his way into the bathroom with haste, betraying his desire to discover where Dylan had gone. Toby was several steps ahead of him.

Remembering her nightshirt, he darted into her bedroom to retrieve it. Then he headed for the stairs with Milly on his heels.

Ear-aching cold socked him in the face as they slipped outside. That hadn't been just moonlight silvering the lawn earlier; it was frost. She'd picked a hell of a night to go out running.

Kneeling on the porch, he held Dylan's nightshirt up to Milly's nose. The dog had never been trained as a scent dog, but the concept was similar to sniffing out explosives. Who knew? It might just work. "Seek," he urged, giving her the signal he'd seen rescue workers give their canines.

Milly stared blankly back at him.

He put the nightshirt to her nose again. *Seek,* he signaled. She sniffed it for the longest moment then looked up at him. There seemed to be a flash of recognition in her eyes before she turned and hopped off the porch—only to squat beside the nearest azalea bush.

Toby groaned. He stuffed the nightshirt into the pocket of his jacket and eyed the path down which Dylan had disappeared hours ago. With a sigh, he started toward it. But then he stopped when he realized Milly was just standing there watching him walk away.

He gestured for her to join him. Icy dew seeped through his sneakers, numbing his toes as Milly turned her back on him, ambling toward the rear of the house and waving her tail like a flag. *What the hell?*

Chasing after the Lab, Toby caught up with her at the door of the playhouse he had noticed on his first day. Either the militia stored weapons in the little building, or Milly had located Dylan. Hope vied with skepticism as he tugged on the rusty door latch. As it swung outward, Milly tried to dart inside. He edged her aside and stuck his head and shoulders in.

Just enough light pierced the gaps between the planks to illumine Dylan's red hair. He crawled into the musty space and saw that she was curled up in the corner, her forehead resting on her knees, motionless.

Please be alive. Stretching out a hand, he lightly touched her arm and felt her shivering. *Thank God.* "Ma'am?" If she wasn't hypothermic, it'd be a miracle. "Captain, wake up." He gave her a light shake.

Dylan roused to consciousness reluctantly. As she cracked her eyes, brittle pain gripped her body, keeping her immobile. Her thoughts returned to the dream where she'd been bound in a straightjacket. *What if it wasn't a dream?*

The silhouette of a man loomed over her, and she flinched away from him. Her head struck a wall, and the familiar feel and smell of the enclosure in which she sat delivered her to reality.

She had stopped by her playhouse on her way back from the woods. In search of happy memories, she had crawled inside and fallen asleep.

"You okay, ma'am?"

Sleep beckoned her back into its numb embrace, but pain kept her conscious. Sergeant Burke's concerned words focused her attention on the uncontrollable shuddering of her body. Every muscle quivered in a locked position. The cold had seeped into the marrow of her bones. "Hy-hypoth-thermic," she stammered, recognizing the symptoms and fighting her lethargy.

Beneath her heavy eyelids, she watched him struggle out of his jacket. In the next instant, he slung it over her, and heat enveloped her like sunshine. "We've got to get you out of here."

She tried to cooperate, but she couldn't seem to move.

That was no deterrent to Tobias. Planting a foot under his hunkered body, he wedged an arm behind her back, another under her bent knees, and scooped her out of the corner and through the narrow door. In the next instant, he swung her high above the ground, lifting her against the wall of his chest. With her head lolling on his shoulder, she saw that the sky was shot with silver. The rooster on the neighboring farm crowed.

"I should w-walk," she protested, her speech as slurred as a drunkard's. He started for the back of the farmhouse, where all of the lights were on. She couldn't let the others see her like this! "I have to walk," she repeated.

But Tobias ignored her, heading doggedly for the screened-in porch. "You're the doctor, ma'am. You know the best thing you can do is stay curled up. Let my heat warm you."

It was impossible not to. His thermal energy burned through the cotton of his T-shirt like flames from a bonfire. With a compulsive need to huddle closer, she looped both arms around his neck and hugged him hard. "I can't be seen," she said through clenched teeth.

The edges of his eyes crinkled as he sent her a smile. "Don't worry, ma'am. The XO's the only one who knows you're missing. We'll sneak you in past the others. Do you know if the back door's locked?"

He made her feel like a naughty teen, sneaking into the house after curfew. "There's a k-k-key hidden behind a loose brick."

"Show me," he said, shouldering his way onto the back porch.

Her hand shook like a leaf as she pointed to the brick in question.

"I gotta put you down," he said regretfully. "Think you can stand?"

"Yes." Except that she couldn't even feel her legs.

He released her carefully, letting her slide down the front of his thighs. The journey over his hard contours revived every nerve in her body. All too soon, her feet touched the concrete floor. Her legs now burned with a numb fire, but her knees buckled, leaving her no choice but to hang on tight.

He anchored her against him with a powerful arm. "You good?"

His resonant voice seemed to vibrate inside her. How long had it been since a man had pressed her to him like this? It felt so wonderful. Desire, as unexpected as it was unwanted, had her clinging to him shamelessly. "Yes."

Her attention slid to his chiseled lips, then to the cleft on his square chin, and then the message on his broad chest.

"Contrary to popular belief," she read aloud, drawing back and pulling it taut over his pecs, so she could read it better in the dim light, "no one owes you anything."

"That's right." He tugged the loose brick from the wall, transferred it to his left hand, and retrieved the key hidden in the space behind it. All without letting her go.

Dylan felt like she'd been hit over the head. How true. Her thoughts expanded. No one owed her a damn thing. She would have to right this wrong herself.

The lock gave a click, snapping her out of her trance. "Think you can walk?"

She shivered convulsively. "I think so."

"Wait." He caught her arm as she started to push the door open. "I hear men on the stairs. Wait until they go out front."

Inside the house, at least two pairs of shoes tramped down the stairs. The front door thumped shut.

"Now." Tobias opened the door for her.

She tried to walk but her legs felt like Jell-O. "Guess not," she admitted with a helpless grimace.

He roped her to him with an eager smile and half-carried, half-escorted her through the command room toward the lit foyer, and to the stairs. Terrence Ashby's halting descent had Dylan squirming free. She reached for the newel post to keep her balance.

"There you are." Terrence was moving down the steps as fast as his prosthetic allowed. His gaze went from Dylan's pale face to the oversized jacket she wore. He shot Sergeant Burke a probing look.

"She's fine," Tobias assured him before Dylan could explain. "She'd fallen asleep in the little house out back."

Terrence placed a large hand over her ice-cold one and squeezed it with palpable concern. "You could have frozen to death." He hobbled closer, forcing Tobias to give up his ground as he cupped a hand under her elbow. "I'll help you upstairs. Then you can call in sick today, which you probably will be, anyway."

"Wait." She needed to give Tobias back his jacket. The cold rushed back into her bones as she shrugged it off.

He reached into the front pocket as she surrendered it, pulling out some balled-up fabric with a sheepish look. "Milly used this to find you."

Her nightshirt. "Smart dog." She tucked it out of sight, perturbed to think that Tobias had handled it.

"I'll lead PT today," Tobias offered on his way to the door.

Terrence nodded. "You do that, Sergeant."

Disappointment swirled through Dylan as Tobias let himself out, taking his warmth and sexy swagger with him.

She squashed it ruthlessly. A militia leader had more important things to consider than the chemistry between her and her newest NCO. It was just like the message on his T-shirt said: No one owed her anything—not because she had a medical degree, not because she'd served five years in the Army, and not because she was a disabled veteran.

If she wanted to stamp out injustice, she had to take the bull by the horns and fight for it the way her ancestor John Brown had.

Toby relaxed back into the armchair he'd secured in advance of the other NCOs. Once again, he'd finished his designated job before anyone else, giving him time to scrub the flecks of paint from his hair, change his clothes, and still get the best seat in the command room. As the others tramped in, vying for a place to sit, Toby studied Dylan surreptitiously.

She looked like hell on the heels of her misadventure. And even though she'd called in sick on Ashby's advice, it was obvious she'd downed coffee all day instead of sleeping. Dark circles ringed her bloodshot eyes. Her hair, while glorious in hue and texture, hung down her back in an untidy ponytail. As she scribbled two words on the easel, underlining them three times, Toby's scalp tightened. *Ambush Tactics.*

What the hell was this about?

He glanced at the XO, who was leaning against the desk, arms folded across his massive chest, looking tense. Dylan's frenetic behavior clearly worried him.

Glancing sharply at the clock, Dylan jammed the lid back on her marker and swiveled toward the men. "Shall we start?"

The innate authority in her tone made the men fall quiet.

"Good. Let's recite *The Defender's Creed*, then."

In one voice, they launched into what Toby had discovered was a ritual for them. Having merely glanced over the papers given to him on the first day, he pretended to mutter along under the XO's watchful eye.

"...I accept that I am a pariah among some of my countrymen, and a quaint anachronism to others. I will not hold their ignorance against them. I will win, or die trying. I swear this creed before God, my family and my fellow citizens."

Toby tried not to squirm.

When the recitation ended, Dylan gestured to the easel. "I've made a decision in regards to Saturday's CPX." She swept a silvery gaze over her leaders. "I know all of you have experience with ambushing enemy combatants. Some of you have even been ambushed by the enemy." Her gaze rested briefly on Sergeant Lee. "But, as a former Army Ranger, Sergeant Burke has undoubtedly had the most training in executing an ambush. Am I right?" she asked him.

Toby's mouth went dry. He acknowledged her supposition with a shrug.

"That's why I'm going to ask him to devise our training schedule for the next two CPXs. I want all of us, including our civilian soldiers, capable of capturing high-value targets without spilling a drop of blood or destroying personal property."

An excited hush filled the room. Toby's mind spun as he grasped what it was she was saying.

She paced before them carrying her coffee mug. "I've decided that the only way to stamp out corruption is to confront the perpetrators with our disgruntlement and to make them fear reprisal if they don't change their ways. So we abduct them. We transport them to some secret location and we give them the bottom line. Once we're satisfied that we've been heard, we let them go. If their behavior doesn't change, we re-capture them and reiterate our demands."

She was flipping crazy. Toby glanced at the others' pleased expressions. Correction, *all* of them were crazy.

"I repeat. We will not draw blood or destroy property," she said severely. Her eyes shone like silver plates. "*We* are not the aggressors. We are the voice of the people who abhor injustice and demand righteousness." She thumped her coffee mug down on the desktop.

"Hear, hear!" Morrison and Lee said at the same time.

"Sergeant Burke."

Toby prayed his incredulity wasn't stamped all over his face. "Ma'am?"

"Can I count on you to teach us what we need to know?"

Oh, he knew what they needed to know. As an agent with ATF's Special Response Teams, he grabbed targets on a regular basis, but they were arms smugglers and drug dealers, not just people who failed to live up to his expectations. "Maybe I need to understand the mission better." His Taskforce lead would want details.

"I just explained the mission." Her brisk words held a thread of annoyance.

"True, but there's a lot to consider. I'd need to assess the enemy composition and disposition. How many in number are there; will they have weapons? What's the terrain like?"

"I'll supply you with that information in good time."

Back off. Tell her what she wants to hear. But he couldn't shut himself up. "What's to keep your targets from going straight to the authorities and filing a complaint?" he demanded. She did realize abduction was illegal, right?

To his surprise, Dylan relaxed. She sent him the look of a woman with a perfect poker hand. "The Sheriff of Harpers Ferry is a member of our militia," she informed him with a touch of condescension.

Really? The Taskforce would be interested to hear that.

"And so is the Sheriff of Martinsburg. I'm not ignorant, Sergeant Burke. I don't take risks without thinking them through."

Toby felt his face heat. Gesturing that she'd won her argument, he locked his jaw so as not to say anything else that might arouse her suspicions or make her irate. *Just listen*, he told himself.

"Who are we grabbing first?"

Sergeant Morrison gave voice to Toby's most pressing question. Toby's money was on Hendrix, the doctor that had made Morrison sick.

Dylan's lovely lips pursed. "I'll let you know that once I think we're ready. We have a lot to learn before we can execute the event I have in mind."

Her gaze slid back to Toby. "So, what do you say, Sergeant Burke? Are you with us or not?"

Was that an ultimatum, or was he just imagining that it was? With every soldier in the room awaiting his reply, Toby signified that he was game. "You're the boss." Working for the Taskforce, he had immunity, so what did it matter to him what she did, except that it put a tight feeling in his chest to picture a phalanx of Feds hauling her and her band of merry men off in handcuffs.

Toby used the light of his phone to illuminate the packed up memories as he sifted through the boxes in the attic, hunting for information that might point to Dylan's true nature.

Was she a terrorist, or wasn't she?

So far, all he'd found were family albums depicting a small but happy family and a stack of high school records showing her to be a brilliant student, even the senior valedictorian. She'd been named most likely to succeed in her yearbook. Delving farther back into her past, he'd come across dolls and a plastic doctor kit; drawings of horses and mountain vistas—in short, nothing to suggest that the young Dylan would grow up to be a militia leader, let alone a murderer.

With the house too quiet to proceed without drawing notice to himself, Toby sat on an old, three-legged stool and texted his team lead. The light of his phone illumined the eaves of the attic as he brought Ike Calhoun up-to-date on Dylan's plan to abduct individuals with whom she felt she had a bone to pick—her mostly likely target being the doctor at the

VA Medical Center in Martinsburg.

She wants me to train her leaders and soldiers so they can pull it off. He finished texting and hit the send button. Then he waited to see if Ike would reply tonight or wait until the morning.

With a tired sigh, Toby relaxed his head on a two-by-six that ribbed the attic. A deep snore permeated the floorboards, coming from the direction of Lt. Ashby's room. Dylan's room, on the other hand, lay still and silent beneath him. He pictured her sound asleep in her bed, overcome by exhaustion, her hair loose and flowing across the pillow, her sweet-smelling nightshirt tangled around her hips.

The memory of her curves sliding over the front of his body kept him warm despite the chill. Under her frumpy sweat suit, Dylan Connelly was all sleek, toned muscle and soft curves. Her breasts without the benefit of a bra were fuller than they'd looked—he'd received that pleasant surprise when she'd cuddled against him.

And then there was the way she'd looked at him. He'd seen that look of awareness in many a woman's eye. There was no mistaking he could rock her world and vice versa if it ever came to that. Hell, if Ashby hadn't crossed their path, he'd have stolen a kiss to warm her from the inside out and left her with something to really think about.

The thought flooded him with mixed feelings. As enticing as kissing Dylan might be, was it fair to seduce a woman as mentally and emotionally vulnerable as she was? It just didn't seem…ethical.

The phone in his hand emitted an electric shock, in lieu of a buzz. That was how it got his attention when it was buried in his jacket. Toby glanced down at Ike's reply message, and his heart sank.

We need details, the team lead had texted. Work

your magic on the leader.

In other words, keep up the sweet talk and the flirtations. *All right, then.*

In spite of his misgivings, Toby tingled at the thought of pursuing Dylan in that way. Usually it left him faintly nauseated to pretend an attraction he didn't feel, but this time that was not the case. He didn't doubt he could eventually worm his way into Dylan's bed, and if that was what it took to get her to confide in him, he'd gladly do it. The only thing that bothered him was the need for deception.

Still, duty was duty. If she could terrorize civilians who failed to meet her code of expectations, who was to say she couldn't blow up a car with someone in it? A little probing might lead to uncovering some dark, ugly truth about her.

So be it. He couldn't waste time debating the morality of his actions. After all, he was a servant of the people, sworn to defend them, even those whom Dylan disapproved of.

Deleting any record of his text, he hid his phone back inside his jacket and stuffed it deep into his bag.

CHAPTER 5

Dylan stalked out of the VA Medical Center in Martinsburg in a foul mood. Wasn't it bad enough the director hadn't believed the evidence she'd sent him? Wesley Hendrix must covered his tracks, eliminating the data had tried to use against him. Or had the director simply chosen to ignore the obvious, preferring to call her paranoid, instead? Given the looks of loathing she'd received today from Dr. Hendrix and the whispered comments of the staff, the director had made no secret of her complaints. No doubt he'd also divulged her documented struggles with PTSD—perhaps hoping Hendrix would be forgiving toward her if he knew.

Hah! The bastard had made certain she'd gotten grounds in her coffee this morning; he'd stolen her prescription pad and given her the most irascible patients.

What a hell of a day!

With her long strides eating up the sidewalk, Dylan reminded herself that she would have justice in the end. In a bid to soothe her agitation, she lifted her face to the warm October sun and breathed the sweet mountain air as she headed toward the parking lot. As her gaze lit on her Suburban, the sight awaiting her brought her to a sudden halt. It was covered in white spray paint.

"No." Her heart fell as she rushed toward her vehicle to assess the damage. The word CRAZY had been sprayed in bold letters across the passenger side doors, driving an arrow straight through her heart. This wasn't just haphazard graffiti. With a heavy step, she rounded the front of the car to eye the driver's side. BITCH.

The blood roared in her ears. Her heart raced. Wesley Hendrix had done this—or probably just paid some young orderly to do it. *Asshole*. She clutched her purse to her side, seeking the reassuring weight of her .357 Magnum against her hip. The desire for revenge rose up in her with volcanic force.

She pictured Wesley Hendrix at his office window now, spying on her dismayed reaction, hoping she'd do something so rash that even the spineless director would be forced to fire her. Imagining his look of horror when she thrust her gun in his face, she whirled and stormed back into the building.

One moment she was out in the parking lot, the next, his office door beckoned at the end of the hall. The blood roared in her ears, drowning out the small voice inside whispering doubts. Her temple throbbed, sending shards of pain into her right eye. Her heart threw itself against her breastbone. Bathed in a cold sweat, she reached into her purse, anticipating his terror when she threatened him.

Dylan, stop! The warning seemed to be shouted from a great distance. *What are you doing? Stop and think!*

Heeding it, she slowed her step, staggering toward the wall and sucking in air to clear her fogged mind.

Several nurses and an orderly paused in their sundry activities to regard her curiously.

She looked around. *How did I get here?*

Dear God, was she seriously about to burst into Hendrix's office and shove her gun in his face? A wave of nausea had her clutching the handrail.

"You feeling okay, Doctor Connelly?" The face of one of the nurses swam before Dylan's eyes.

"Yes, Leigh," she whispered. "Just a little dizzy from skipping lunch."

But she wasn't fine. She'd reacted violently to Hendrix's nasty prank. And in her blind rage, she'd almost killed the man.

Licking her dry lips, Dylan released the rail and tottered down the hall toward a different office, one she used to visit weekly after returning from Afghanistan. Leigh watched her with worried eyes as she knocked on Doctor Kevin Richardson's door.

Dr. Richardson's work with traumatized veterans had made him a national hero. He'd served as a psychiatrist on the front lines. He knew what soldiers had seen, the horrors they'd endured and still carried with them. Thanks to him, hundreds of soldiers had turned from the brink of suicide to live productive lives again. He and Dylan attended the same church in Harper's Ferry, Saint Peter's Catholic Church.

"Come in."

Drawn to the comforting rasp of his pack-a-day voice, Dylan pushed into his office.

Locking eyes with her, he rose up slowly from behind his desk. His thick salt-and-pepper hair, always mussed from raking his hands through it, stood straight up. Concern wreathed his forehead over the plastic rimmed glasses he wore. "Why, Dylan," he said with surprise as she sagged against the closing door. "Is everything all right?"

She shook her head, unable to speak, yet.

"Come in. Come in." He left his desk to draw her into the room, his hands large and gentle. "Have a seat," he said, leading her by the elbow to one of the two plush chairs that faced his desk.

"Can you see my car through your window?" she croaked as she sank into a chair.

With a puzzled look, Dr. Richardson went to the window and tabbed his lowered blinds.

"Someone took a can of spray paint to it," she said when he didn't speak. "Dr. Hendrix, no doubt," she added, lifting a hand to her forehead as it started to throb again.

The blind gave a *pop* as Kevin released it. A grimace of compassion firmed his lips as he turned to face her. "You're sure it was Wesley Hendrix?"

"Of course it was Hendrix. He knows I've got a bone to pick with him. He even knows I complained to the director."

"Did you?" Dr. Richardson looked dismayed.

"Yes."

He sent her a sad smile. "And did anything come of that?"

Bitterness swirled inside of her. "No." With a flush of humiliation, Dylan described her letter from the director.

The psychiatrist clicked his tongue in commiseration. "I'm so sorry, Dylan." He rounded his desk to sit on the edge of it, immediately in front of her. "Can I get you something? A cup of coffee, maybe?"

She would love a cup of coffee, but considering how late it was in the day and how badly she needed to sleep, she declined with a shake of her head. "I have to admit to something," she whispered, peering up from under her massaging fingers.

His brow puckered. "Yes?"

"A minute ago, I wanted to kill him. I think I could've killed him."

His frown became a quizzical smile. "With your bare hands?"

Dylan laughed despite herself. "No." She pulled the purse she clutched onto her lap, reached inside it, and pulled out the revolver. "With this."

At the sight of her snub nosed Magnum, he closed his eyes and sighed. "Is it loaded?" he asked steadily.

"No."

"Well, then you wouldn't have killed him," he said, opening his eyes again.

She dug in her purse a second time and produced a box of bullets. "Are you sure?"

He slowly shook his head. "Oh, Dylan. I thought we'd moved past this. You still carry your revolver everywhere you go?"

Shame choked her reply. With a jerky nod, she put the gun and bullets back inside her purse. This was an issue that had preoccupied them during her rigorous therapy the first half of the year. The gun was her security blanket. For a while, he'd succeeded in getting her to leave it at home, but as their sessions ended, she'd gone back to carrying it everywhere.

A weighty silence filled the office. If Dr. Richardson thought her a public menace, he had every right to break with patient confidentiality and report her behavior, which would, essentially, cost her job.

She swallowed down the emotions strangling her and asked, "Are you going to report me?"

He very slowly shook his head. "Of course not. I'm going to help you. Why don't you start visiting me again, say once a week until we resolve this lingering issue?"

Pain lanced her chest at his gentle suggestion. She

had thought she was coping well with her PTSD until Tobias Burke had picked up on her diagnosis. The fact that she couldn't recall storming back into the building just now informed her plainly that she was still a danger to herself and to others. "Fine," she whispered.

"How are you sleeping these days?" he asked, plucking a prescription pad from his pocket.

"Not well," she admitted. She forbore to mention her coffee habit, which she had just decided to kick. "I had an awful dream the other night."

"Tell me about it," he offered.

A chill coursed through her as she relayed her dream about the straightjacket. "Am I crazy?" she asked him. "Do other people think I'm crazy?"

"Who wouldn't be a little crazy after what you've seen?" he joked.

She sent him a humorless smile.

"Let me write you a prescription to help you sleep."

"I just need to cut out the caffeine," she protested.

"That's not enough. And you'll never fully heal if you're constantly exhausted."

She knew he was right; she just detested taking medicine. "Something mild," she agreed.

"Of course." He scribbled something on the pad, tore off the first sheet, and gave it to her.

"I've never heard of Hipnosedon," Dylan admitted after reading it.

"It's a mild hypnotic. What day would you like for us to meet? How about Tuesday at four? That's the same day you bring in Ivan for his session."

"That'll work," she agreed.

"Good." He sent her an encouraging smile. "I'll see you next Tuesday then."

"Tuesday at four," she confirmed, rising on knees

that still jittered.

"And Dylan," he added, straightening and laying a hand on either of her shoulders. "Stay as far away from Hendrix as you're able," he advised.

"I intend to."

"That's the spirit." He gave her shoulders a squeeze and let her go.

The crush of gravel under a heavy vehicle tore Toby's attention from the training in the yard.

At last, Dylan was back from work—a full hour after their evening briefing was due to start. Lt. Ashby's unspoken worry had spilled over to the men, making them quick to lose focus and turning Toby's directives on strategy into a waste of time.

He wondered where the hell she'd been.

Shading his eyes against the setting sun, he studied the Suburban's approach. What on earth? It looked like a whole flock of seagulls had shit all over her car, only seagulls didn't live in the Blue Ridge and they couldn't spell the word BITCH. "Holy hell," he muttered as she pulled up in front of them. Someone had defaced her Suburban with a can of spray paint.

The men stared dumbfounded at the graffiti, clearly unable to fathom such disrespect. Ashby's expanding chest made him look like an irate, silverback gorilla as he crossed to her door to pull it open.

Dylan killed the engine and slipped out of her seat, dragging her purse behind her. To Toby's surprise, she appeared composed as she faced her protective XO.

"What happened?" He gestured at the vandalism. "Who did this?"

"It doesn't matter, Terrence." Her firm voice and eye contact made him back down immediately. "Just get rid of it," she requested, hastening toward the house. Her eyes met Toby's briefly, conveying private pain.

"Well, you heard her," Ashby snarled at the men as they all watched her walk away. "What are you waiting for? Let's get started."

Toby chased them into the barn.

"Rubbing compound, terry cloth, and turpentine," Ashby barked, flipping the light switch to illumine the sizeable interior.

Toby had determined that the locked closet housed the M-16 rifles noted by the FBI. The other walls were lined with shelves and a workbench with tools displayed above it. Sergeant Ackerman kept "Supply" as neat and tidy as any facility in the military. Thanks to the cat, any rodents that might have taken up residence were long gone. As Ackerman located the goods they would need, Lt. Ashby tore a terrycloth towel into strips and thrust one at Toby.

"I want every fleck of paint scrubbed off this vehicle before supper," he thundered quietly.

They returned to the yard to tackle the monumental task. Pink clouds streaked the sky as they labored, and the air turned sharply colder. The smell of stir-fried beef wafting from the house prompted Toby's stomach to rumble. After an hour, they'd managed to remove all but the most tenacious acrylic. The Suburban's already lackluster paintjob now looked patchy, but at least the words were gone.

The screen door thumped shut, and Toby lost his focus as Dylan made her way toward them. She'd changed into cargo pants and a gray sweater, and had let her hair down. Even as tense as she had to be feeling, she moved with lithe grace.

"Not bad," she said, assessing their progress. "Here, try this acetone on those stubborn spots." As she handed Lt. Ashby a bottle of nail polish remover, her pale eyes flickered toward Toby. "Walk with me, Sergeant Burke," she ordered, unexpectedly. "I want to hear what you accomplished today."

Pleased to be singled out, Toby gave Morrison the rag he was using and fell into step beside her as she turned to follow the running course.

"You cut me slack on the run this morning," she accused.

"Nah, I was sore," he lied, matching his step to hers. "Couldn't keep up."

"Liar." Leaves from the trees swirled around them, crunching under their feet and muffling the voices of the others as they continued down the hill toward the tree line. In another thirty minutes, it would be dark. The multi-hued sky and the sweet aromas of grass and leaves evoked a romantic atmosphere. Toby felt like reaching for her hand.

"Seriously, I was sore. I'll beat you on the run tomorrow, though." He sent her a challenging smile.

"Tomorrow's the CPX," she reminded him. "You won't be racing me. You'll be running with the soldiers, inspiring them to keep up."

"Ah." He looked forward to it, to seeing her interactions with the civilian soldiers. What did they see when they looked at her?

"So, tell me what you did today to assess our strengths and weaknesses."

He'd assumed she would get the details from her XO and not skip over the chain of command, but this was better. It afforded them a moment alone together. He quickly summarized each NCOs' capabilities in regards to military strategy and technique.

"Assuming we perform the classic L-shaped ambush, I would put myself and Morrison in the assault group," he suggested, "with Lt. Ashby and Sergeant Lee in the position of support fire. Ackerman shouldn't interface with anybody, so I'd keep him in an observational capacity. Of course, you'll want to change your radio frequency for the ambush."

Dylan gave an earnest nod. "Yes, good. This is exactly the kind of input I need."

Toby seized his chance to learn more. "It's only a broad stroke," he argued. "I need more details so I can plan accordingly. I don't even know who we're ambushing or where."

"I told you." Her voice hardened subtly. "You'll have that information soon enough, and it won't change a thing. An L-shaped ambush is ideal. Your designations are spot on."

"Okay, then." Her tone informed him that he'd get nowhere by pressing her. If she hadn't brought him along to hash out details, then why'd she ask him to walk with her at all?

Silence fell between them, and the sky darkened to mauve, seeming to reflect Dylan's somber mood. Studying her profile, Toby glimpsed an expression of unguarded sorrow on her face. And it occurred to him, with an unexpected wave of pity, that she'd brought him along for comfort—not that she would ever admit it.

He snuck a peak over his other shoulder. They'd arrived at the tree line and followed the running course, so that the house now blocked them from the inquisitive eyes of her men. There was no better time to work his magic, as his team lead called it. Catching Dylan's elbow in a light grip, he swung her around to look at him.

Her eyes widened with wariness. "What?"

"You want to talk about who did that to your car?"

Startled silence answered his question. "Not really." Her voice was stilted, unreceptive.

"You must have some idea," he persisted. "Was it

that doctor you had issues with, the one who almost killed Morrison with all those meds?"

She drew an audible breath. "How do you know about that?"

"You mentioned him the other day. Plus Morrison can talk," he added with a wry smile. He peered at her more closely. "You sure you're okay? You have every right to be shaken, you know. That was a pretty personal attack."

"I'm fine." She tried maintaining eye contact and failed. "I've already talked to someone, and…I'm fine," she repeated. Coiling her arms around her body, she drew a sharp breath. "Why are we discussing this?"

"I'm sorry." She had to be freezing. "Here take my jacket." He started to unzip it.

"No, keep it. I'm warm enough." But her gaze had caught on the bit of T-shirt he exposed. "Does your shirt say something today?" she asked before he could zip it back up.

With a sheepish grin, he parted the halves of his jacket.

She leaned in, squinting through the shadows to see. "Let me drop everything and work on your problem," she quoted. Her jaw dropped and her eyes flashed with indignation. "You wore that because of me!" The accusation was fraught with amazement.

"I hope you're not offended."

The corners of her mouth twitched as she waffled between amusement and annoyance. Amusement won out and she laughed. "I can't believe you own a shirt for every occasion. It's insane."

As before, on the deck at Private Quinn's pub, her smile transformed her face completely. Suddenly she was young and lovely. "I wish you'd do that more," he commented.

"Do what more?"

"Smile."

The corners of her mouth fell even as her eyes widened.

He didn't give her time to backpedal. "Do you know what I see when you smile?"

"What?"

He stepped closer, holding her gaze captive. "I see who you really are." Amazingly, he didn't have to work hard to find the words to sweet-talk her. They rolled effortlessly off his tongue, probably since he was being completely honest, for a change.

In the stunned silence that followed, he could hear a cricket chirping in the grass beneath their feet. A bird twittered in the trees behind them.

"Sorry." He grimaced and shoved his fingers into the pockets of his jacket. "I don't know where that came from. I'm not trying to be insubordinate or anything, but you work so hard to hold everyone else together. What about you? What about your happiness?"

Bravo. Suddenly, it was like he was standing off to one side watching his own performance, along with Dylan's reaction.

Damn, you're good, Toby. Judging by the look on her face, his remark had struck gold. *You manipulative son of a bitch.*

Dylan couldn't find her voice. Protocol demanded she rebuke Tobias for his impertinence. How dare he speak to her on such a personal level? But his words had stripped off her façade as militia leader, and, for the life of her, she couldn't seem to slap it back on.

"Don't get me wrong." He bent toward her, pitching his voice lower. The velvety timbre soothed the pinpricks of agitation needling her skin. "I think what you've done for the soldiers here is a good thing. You've given them a sense of purpose, someone to lean on. But who's taking care of you?"

Where was he going with this? "Why would I need taking care of?"

"Come on, now," he chided her with a wry and sympathetic smile. "I know from Morrison that you used to retrieve the fallen. Let me tell you what. You wouldn't be human if the things you've seen didn't get to you sometimes."

A lump swelled in Dylan's throat, lodging her cool retort as a vision of her boys lying broken in their coffins panned across her mind.

Tobias's hands came out of his pockets. Stepping closer, he lifted them slowly, cautiously to her face. The breath evaporated from her lungs as his warm and lightly callused hands cupped her cheeks.

"It's okay to lean on people." His dark gaze, nearly the same color as the cobalt sky, searched her face before sliding toward her mouth. "If you want to lean on me from time to time, that's okay, too." In the next instant, he lowered his head, startling her with a swift, sweet kiss that left her lips tingling.

Taking in her stunned response, he slowly dipped his head again, giving her time to pull away before his lips settled snugly over hers, thawing her from her frozen state with a deft, warm, unthreatening kiss.

Like melting wax, Dylan's lips softened then parted, allowing his tongue to glide against hers, filling her with an intimate knowledge of his taste, his texture. He intrigued. He intoxicated. Parting her lips wider, Dylan sought more, rolling up on her toes in a tribute to the woman buried deep inside.

Fill me. She coiled her arms around his neck and kissed him until her head swam. *Fill me with your light and warmth and laughter.*

And he did, kissing her with such gentle skill that it stripped away her captain's guise and left her nothing but a woman utterly at the mercy of her own desire.

So this was how it felt to be alive. She'd forgotten. The bloodbath that had ended her career had robbed her of the memory. But it rose in her anew, like a resurrected Lazarus. She reached for the quenching beauty with all her heart, wanting to hold it close.

Her pebbled nipples grazed the sturdy fabric of his jacket. Desire traveled in a slow burn along her neural pathways. She ached to touch his skin, but his jacket and clothing formed a frustrating barrier.

Slowly, lingeringly, Tobias lifted his head and ended the magic. Fresh air cleared Dylan's head. The reality of their embrace speared her consciousness, and she guiltily jumped back.

"My fault." He was quick to take the blame but sounded not at all repentant.

Dylan wedged her tingling hands under her crossed arms, whirled away, and stalked blindly along the path skirting the tree line.

What just happened?

Her mind scrambled to make sense of that kiss. Sergeant Burke had crossed the line, but so had she. Worse than that, she'd sucked him in like a black hole. God, how humiliating!

Glancing back, she ascertained that he was following. Yes, and much closer than she'd thought, not having heard his footsteps. Adrenaline spiked her pulse. She'd almost forgotten that he used to be Special Forces. He must have been a stealthy fighter, a masterful tactician.

"You don't have to worry that I'll say anything."

His softly spoken promise was meant to reassure her, but to Dylan it sounded smug. She spun around to face him. "I am your commanding officer," she bit out, swiping her own hair out of her eyes. "What just happened between us was a complete breach of protocol. It *cannot* happen again."

Her firm reproach would have made any of her other soldiers back away.

Tobias looked down at his boots. A devilish glitter twinkled in his eyes when he looked up again. "Well," he drawled, clearly measuring his words, "if we were *actually* in the service, ma'am, I'd have to agree with you. But we're not. No matter how much you pretend for the sake of the others, you're as much a civilian as I am."

His logic undermined her authority completely. At the same time, a weight seemed to lift off her shoulders. She *was* a civilian. For a second time in just minutes, he'd left her with nothing to say.

"I don't see anything wrong with us getting to know each other better." He sent her an appreciative and appraising look.

Squelching the pleasure evoked by his words and his obvious interest in her, Dylan clung to her righteous anger. "Our discussion is over, Sergeant Burke. Kindly go back and help the others," she commanded.

He tipped her a disappointed-looking nod and turned away, but his stride remained confident.

Watching him walk away, Dylan's knees shook. She would never accept his offer to lean on him. To do so would make her appear weak to the others. Yet there was a certain truth to what he'd said. She *was* human, and the gruesome atrocities she'd seen did get to her sometimes.

When he disappeared from view, she turned and walked blindly toward the light pouring out of the kitchen.

Alive. A fragment of her earlier exhilaration clung to

her, still, lightening her step as she approached the rear entrance.

Hidden behind a spruce tree at the corner of the house, Toby paused a moment to compose himself before rejoining the men.

Dylan's clean cotton scent, the memory of her unexpected passion left him fully aroused. He'd been right about their chemistry. For the first time on any of his undercover assignments, his body hummed with the anticipation of deepening their relationship. He wouldn't have to pretend with this one.

At this rate, it wouldn't be long before Dylan divulged all her secrets. He had that effect on women, whether he found them attractive or not. Women confided in him. It was a gift he had, not that he actively exploited it, but he found it extremely useful in his line of work. And until now, he'd never felt a lick of guilt for leading them on, not when the information he gleaned took arms dealers and drug smugglers off the streets. Not when he rarely followed through with his flirtations.

But this was different.

Dylan wasn't like the conniving hustlers who looked out for their own interests first and screwed everyone else over, even their own families. Dylan did what—in her own quixotic mind—seemed right. In that sense, she was honorable.

And possibly the most vulnerable woman he had ever known.

What's more, he was starting to like her—a circumstance that privately concerned him. Because, chances were, he would be called to testify against her when her case went to trial. And, damn, he would feel like shit for using her confessions against, her especially if he did find his way into her bed, which was where their connection was leading. For once, the prospect thrilled him.

CHAPTER 6

Fog blanketed the landscape on the morning of the CPX.

The pearly veil was so dense at zero seven hundred hours that Toby could scarcely make out the cars and pickups lumbering onto Dylan's property and parking on either side of the driveway. The sheer number of civilian soldiers tramping toward the front yard suggested that every one of Dylan's sixty-odd members promised to be in attendance.

Given the business and confusion, Toby opted to keep Milly in the house and out of harm's way. Wearing the camouflaged gear that he'd been issued the previous night—woodland patterned BDUs, a large pack, and an olive-colored beret with a red patch that went over the forehead—he made his way to Supply, where Second Amendment Militia soldiers scribbled their names on the attendance ledger. Helping himself to a steaming cup of coffee from the dispenser provided by June Lee, Toby watched Gil Morrison issue M-16s from the unlocked closet. Every soldier received two spare clips.

Toby blew on his scalding coffee to cool it off.

That's a lot of ammo. In the hands of sixty-some soldiers, it was enough to cause some very serious damage.

He glanced at the ledger, waiting for the opportunity to snap a picture of it—not with his cell-phone, which would remain buried in the lining of his jacket, but with a tiny digital camera disguised to resemble an Army Rangers Regiment pin. He'd affixed the pin to the collar of his jacket this morning, counting on Dylan to view it as a symbol of his prowess, not as a violation of dress code. The Taskforce wanted the names and faces of her civilian soldiers to run through their terrorist database on the off chance that they'd find a match.

At last, Morrison stepped away from the table for a moment. Toby laid his coffee down, leaned over the ledger and, with a pinch of his finger, snapped several photos of the entries in it. Then he tossed back his coffee, crushed the cup, and pitched it in the trash on his way to the yard.

Given her irrational plan for people like Hendrix who failed to share her point of view, Dylan was bound to end up in jail sooner or later. He needed to accept that probability and live with it. Using his thumbnail, he switched the pin from camera to video mode while approaching the throng in the yard. An atmosphere of merriment hung over the crowd as they milled about, waiting for the officers to join them.

Made up of predominantly young and middle-aged men, plus a few tough-looking women, the militia vied for standing room. Greeting one another with good-natured humor and slaps on the back, they struck Toby as little more than grownups looking for an excuse to play war.

He approached the nearest knot of soldiers and introduced himself. Receiving words of welcome, he moved to the next group to receive more of the same. The sense that he was being watched had him scanning the crowd until his gaze intersected with that of a steely-eyed loner. Taking in the man's square jaw and the scar hashing his upper lip, Toby ventured toward him. This man wasn't like the others.

"Morning." Toby tipped him a nod. "I'm Tobias Burke, the new senior operations sergeant."

"Cal Fallon, Sheriff of Harpers Ferry." The sheriff stuck out a hand.

"Of course." They shook, one hard clasp and a quick release.

Toby made certain the pin on his lapel had an unobstructed view of the man's face, scar and all. "Captain Connelly said there was another sheriff in the militia." He glanced around. "Where is he?" The thick fog concealed several of the soldiers standing at the back of the yard.

"Hooper? He's around here somewhere." But Fallon kept his attention fixed on Toby, and when Toby looked back, he found the sheriff studying his pin.

"You wear that for a reason?"

The challenging question made Toby's pulse kick. The sheriff was versed in surveillance; maybe he could tell that the pin was actually a camera. "Pride," he said with a shrug. "I served in the 75th Ranger Regiment."

The sheriff's eyes narrowed. "What years?"

Shit. He was supposed to be the one asking questions, not the other way around. Rattling off his practiced lie, he could only hope that Homeland Security had been thorough in altering his service record.

"I'm a former Ranger myself," Fallon announced, unsettling Toby further.

He forced a laugh. "No kidding? What years?"

The Sheriff had left the service before Toby even went in, a fact that eased his worries only slightly. "Bet you saw a lot more action than I did," Fallon surmised.

"More than enough." A layer of sweat formed under Toby's jacket. He couldn't wait to shrug it off, but he couldn't yet, not until he'd filmed the rest of the militia members.

"There's Hooper." The sheriff pointed to a thick-set man with a handlebar mustache.

"Thanks. I think I'll introduce myself." Toby walked away, feeling Fallon's eyes on his back.

Sheriff Hooper of Martinsburg proved to be less of a threat.

"Excellent," he exclaimed as Toby introduced himself. "Captain Connelly must be thrilled to have you on board," he added pumping Toby's hand.

Toby wasn't so sure about that. Since their kiss last night, she'd scarcely said two words to him.

"At-ten-TION!" Ashby's booming voice snuffed the yammering in the yard and replaced it with silence. "Fall into line for muster and inspection!"

With a shouldering of packs and a rustling of dead leaves, soldiers scrambled to sort themselves into neat rows, about ten men deep. Toby followed the example of the other sergeants and positioned himself at the head of the last line. Standing the butt of his M-16 on the ground, he clasped the muzzle like the others. Silently, with just the barest scuffling feet and clearing of throats, they watched Lt. Ashby open the screen door and announce: "Commanding officer of the West Virginia Second Amendment Militia."

Dylan stepped onto the porch, and elbows shot out as everyone present saluted. With a sense of surrealism, Toby saluted right along with them. Dylan paused on the porch to survey her troops from a distance. In the misty light it wasn't easy to read her expression, but Toby thought he'd seen that look of exasperation on her face before. It was her XO who insisted on the formality, not Dylan herself.

With an eloquent return salute, she freed them to lower their arms to their sides. Then she stepped off the porch with her graceful, loose-limbed stride, and Toby's gaze drifted to her honed thighs. She wore the same woodland patterned BDUs as her militia, as well as the hallmark beret on her head—only hers was burgundy, and it had a gold star on a green patch reminding him of the Czechoslovakian paratroopers. The suspicion that she'd bought the berets wholesale from Eastern Europe nearly made him snort out loud.

The head covering topped a thick French braid that kept her hair under disciplined control. With just a slash of gloss on her lips and not a drop of makeup, she managed to captivate every eye in the regiment as she paused to run a maternal gaze over her army.

How many men, besides him, were admiring the way her camouflage jacket outlined her curves?

"Good morning," she finally called out.

"Good morning, ma'am!" the legion chorused.

"We have a full regimen in store for you today." She clasped her hands behind her back and began to pace. "For six months to the day, we have withstood threats to individual liberties. You know what they are—tyranny, corruption, illegitimate force, and apathy, to name just a few." She turned and covered her own tracks. "We have trained to respond to an attack or emergency propagated by the Oppositional Forces. Until now, our mission has been a purely defensive one. Yet, I believe that our passivity makes us guilty of the very apathy that we abhor."

She paused in her pacing to fix her crystal gaze on her troops. "It is not enough to protest corruption. Our forefathers fought for their freedoms, and so must we, before they are wrested away. The time has come to take more offensive action."

A bad taste filled Toby's mouth as an expectant hush fell over the yard. She really was crazy. And completely serious about her intent to frighten civilians into seeing the world her way.

She folded her arms across her chest. "Our creed clearly states that illegitimate force and illegal violence must be met with righteous indignation and *superior* force. It states that we should learn new skills and techniques with firearm or blade, so that we can hit our enemies hard, fast, and true."

He realized she was quoting directly out of The Creed, which he now had mostly memorized.

Her pale gaze zeroed in on Toby. "In the next few weeks, our newest staff member, a former Army Ranger, will be refining our skills and turning us into an effective strike force. Everyone, say hello to Sergeant Burke."

"Hooah, Sergeant Burke!" the militia shouted.

Toby turned toward the crowd, forced a smile, and waved.

"Lt. Ashby, do you have any announcements?" Dylan turned toward her XO, who stood respectfully behind her.

"No, ma'am," he said grimly.

"In that case, Lieutenant, kindly proceed with the inspection and the march."

Inspection required each NCO to examine the pack of every soldier in his line. Those who'd failed to fill their canteens with water, who didn't carry three-days' worth of rations, a flashlight, extra batteries, ammo, a first-aid kit and a gun-cleaning kit, *plus* the paper copies of the U.S. Constitution and the Bill of Rights were made to drop and do thirty pushups. Only one soldier in Toby's line failed to meet the mark. Toby recognized him as the waiter, Nathan, from Private Quinn's Pub.

"Wife had her baby yet?" he inquired.

"Not yet, Sarge." Nathan looked upset with himself for having left his canteen empty.

Toby let the oversight slide. Lacking water to quench his thirst would be punishment enough. This wasn't real combat training, where an empty canteen could mean the difference between life and death.

"Suit up!" Lt. Ashby called as inspection came to an end.

Soldiers shrugged on their packs.

"Atten-TION. Right FACE!" the XO bellowed.

Everyone swiveled toward the running course.

"Forward MARCH!"

Just like soldiers in the Civil War, they tramped down the hill in formation, matting the dew-damp grass beneath their many boots. The sun had edged high enough to burn away most of the fog. Toby watched Dylan hustle toward the head of the pack. At the tree line, the troops veered right, away from the running course toward the shooting range Toby had yet to see in person.

"Pick it up!" Lt. Ashby shouted. Every man, with the exception of the XO himself, broke into a jog, with Dylan in the lead.

The land rose, the trees on their left thinned. They ran for a mile over rolling hills before coming to a rocky outcrop. On the other side of the outcrop stretched a large field, which Toby recognized from the drone photos as Dylan's shooting range. Sandbag bunkers edged one side and black-and-white bulls-eyes standing at intervals lined the other.

By now his line had disintegrated as out-of-shape soldiers fell behind. He focused his attention on motivating the stragglers. By the time the entire militia reached the range, many of them were red-faced and out of breath.

Toby led his squad toward a sandbag bunker. There, he ordered them to drink water, sharing a sip from his own canteen with Nathan. Next, he ordered them to clean their guns, to lock and load. It was all so oddly familiar.

And then the fun began. Not that Toby wanted to be enjoying himself. But as the quiet countryside crackled with the *rat-tat-tat* of semi-automatic gunfire and his squad competed against Ackerman's to accomplish the most hits, he found himself cheering on his men, adjusting their grip and stance to improve their aim. Pretty soon, his squad led the rest in direct hits.

"You want to practice, ma'am?" he asked, catching Dylan's eye as she paused to watch his team shoot.

"Oh, no. Thank you."

He stepped closer to her, pitching his voice low so the others couldn't hear it. "A true leader leads by example," he told her with a challenging smile. "Come on. Take a shot." He nodded at her revolver, which she carried on her hip in lieu of an M-16. Truth was, he wanted to see how dangerous she was.

Biting her lower lip, Dylan looked like she would rather clock him in the head with her revolver than shoot it. Her chin came up in response to his challenge, confirming Toby's suspicion that whatever reservations she might have about firing a weapon, the last thing she wanted was to appear ineffective in front of the troops. "Fine, I'll give it a whirl."

Watching her set her elbows on the sandbags, thumb off her safety and set her sights on the bulls eye at the other end of the field, Toby could see why she hadn't wanted to show off her skills. She really didn't have any. Her form was bad. Her aim was off. But then again, she'd served with Mortuary Affairs units, not on front lines—at least not while a battle was raging.

Crack! A chip of plywood went flying off the corner of the target, and Toby's eyebrows shot up. Well, well, she'd actually hit the mark.

"Bravo," he called, applauding her effort and saving her from further embarrassment. "Well done."

Her cheeks turned pink as she put her gun away and pushed wordlessly past him.

Later as the shooting progressed and his squad emerged victorious, he sensed her approving gaze on him and it ratcheted his self-awareness. Shooting doubled his testosterone levels. Firing in front of Dylan turned him on.

But then she put him in charge of the ambush training and suddenly, he became too busy to notice her noticing him. Each NCO drilled his squad according to their role in the L-shaped ambush. Ackerman's squad practiced concealment and using alternate radio frequencies to communicate. Sergeant Lee's squad practiced providing support fire, while Toby and Morrison's squads enacted their role as the assault group.

Dylan neared Toby's group just as he was illustrating how to grapple a target into submission without causing bodily harm.

"Sergeant Burke, I want you to take down the target on our first ambush," she informed him when he rolled to his feet.

He just stared at her. So now *he* had to do the dirty work?

"You already know how." She gestured to the soldier whose face he had rubbed in the dirt. The man looked thoroughly humiliated. "It'll save us time and ensure success."

He was still mulling over the role foisted on him when the CPX ended. Collecting their packs, they formed loose lines and tramped back to the farmhouse to turn in their rifles. But then, instead of leaving, the soldiers toted coolers from their vehicles, and everyone flopped down in the front yard for a picnic, while June Lee served lemonade from a giant, glass dispenser.

Toby chugged down his drink while wishing it were a tall bottle of ice-cold lager. There were sixty-odd soldiers in the yard and not a single beer can in sight. Not only was Dylan the enforcer of her forefather's liberties, but she was also, apparently, a prohibitionist.

If I weren't working undercover, I would be so gone, right now. He'd had his fill of the militia life; he wanted to be a normal citizen again.

Thank God, tomorrow was his day off. Of course, he'd have to rendezvous with his colleagues at the NCTC. But after that, he was going to his apartment to do laundry, kick back with a few beers and watch football. The prospect of looking up one of his regular playmates teased his imagination briefly.

But it was really Dylan who aroused him, he realized, watching her pick her way across the yard. She paused here and there to share a word with her soldiers, to lay a concerned hand on them. Strands of her hair had worked loose from her braid, framing her face in fiery tendrils that drew attention to her sweet smile. God, she was pretty when she smiled.

As loony as she was, it was hard to imagine her plotting Secretary Nolan's demise. He'd found nothing yet to suggest her innocence or her guilt, which meant that his undercover job was far from over. He might have the day off tomorrow, but he'd be back tomorrow night for another whole week of insanity.

If he didn't want to be here a month or more, he needed to take this relationship to the next level, tonight.

With her back against her headboard, Dylan read from her Bible taking comfort in the words of Matthew. Out in the hallway, the bathroom door swung open, claiming her attention. Stealthy footfalls headed toward the attic, telling her that Tobias Burke was done showering. She'd left her door intentionally ajar, hoping to waylay him on his way to bed. "Sergeant Burke," she called.

He filled her open door with his bare shoulders, and her mouth went dry. His chest was completely bare and breathtaking. He wore plaid pajama pants, and his hair was damp and spiked.

"Ma'am?"

"Please, come in," she requested, setting her Bible aside. She remained seated as he edged into the room. His ocean-blue gaze held hers captive. When he closed the door unexpectedly behind himself, her heart kicked into a gallop. She froze in astonishment.

"What?" he asked as if he hadn't just shut the door, giving them all kinds of privacy.

The lamp beside her bed cast just enough of a glow to highlight his raised pectorals and the rippling muscles of his flat abdomen. A mat of dark hair fanned between his dusky nipples, narrowing to a line that ran toward his naval, disappearing past the waistband of his low-slung sleep pants. Dylan's head swam. She'd forgotten what she even meant to tell him.

If you want to lean on me from time to time, that's okay, too. The inference that he'd like to deepen intimacies kept her pinned to the bed like a fearful virgin, even as it brought a warm flush to the surface of her skin. Recalling his perfect kiss the other night, she found she had no desire to eject him from her room just yet.

"You wanted to ask me something?" he prompted, looking completely at ease with himself.

She finally remembered what it was. "You didn't look pleased to be tasked with the take-down of the target. Is there something about the mission you object to?"

His faint smile disappeared. Thick lashes obscured his eyes for a moment as he glanced down at her threadbare rug. "Not at all," he said flatly.

He was lying. The concern that he might leave her militia after proving so useful propelled Dylan off the bed. Drawing her robe about her, she searched for loyalty in his dark-blue gaze as she approached him, but it was hard to concentrate on just his face with his chest so broad and bare, the dark thatch of hair so distracting. "I hope you're not questioning your decision to join the militia," she said, revealing her sudden worry.

"Not at all," he assured her, his gaze falling to the gaping edges of her pink velour robe.

"Will you come to church with me tomorrow?" she pleaded. If anyone could inflame his willingness to battle injustice it was her priest, Father Nesbit.

Her question wrested Tobias's gaze upward. "What time?"

"I like to attend the early service at oh-eight hundred."

"Hmmm."

His less-than-enthusiastic answer made her wonder which he deplored more—the early hour on his day off or the destination. Did he not believe in God?

"Please," she added, persuaded that his attendance

would assure his commitment.

His sexy mouth quirked. "Tell you what," he said in a gruff voice that had an immediate tingly effect on Dylan's nipples. "Why don't you give me a reason to confess my sins, and then I'll go?"

She was still making sense of his words when he hooked an arm around her waist and pulled her gently but forcefully into his arms. Her indrawn breath filled her head with the scent of soap and clean man. His naked chest, like warm silk beneath her fingers, caused them to unfurl. As soon as her palms made contact, she longed to explore further.

And that was her excuse for offering him her lips. His eyes glinted with triumph as he ducked his head. With little restraint, this time, he covered her mouth passionately, slipping his tongue between her welcoming lips, and conveying the determination to possess her completely.

Dylan's mind went blank. The worry of what it would cost to be caught fraternizing evaporated. The delectable feel of his lips melded to hers, his tongue delving, his aroused male flesh branding her thighs preoccupied her every thought. Desire pooled low in her belly spreading to her extremities like a drug, so that her body felt heavy, her head light.

The belt at her waist went slack, and cool air wafted up under her nightshirt as he gathered it in his hands. His palm, warm and slightly calloused, grazed her thigh, her hip, and her waist, drawing a trail of gooseflesh behind it. Her heart thudded in anticipation as he closed in on her left breast and gently palmed it. A moan escaped her as he rolled her nipple between his thumb and forefinger, eliciting a spark of pleasure both there and below.

Her back hit the wall. At some point, Tobias had turned them around without her realizing. He pressed her against it, kissing her unceasingly. She buried her fingers in his thick, damp hair, responding to him mindlessly, only half-aware that his other hand had found its way beneath her gown. It breached the elastic waistband of her panties to rake the trimmed curls at the juncture of her thighs. She broke the kiss and gasped in surprise. "You shouldn't."

But he did. Gazing intently into her eyes, he slid a finger into the moist cleft within her curls, seeking the silky nectar seeping there and using it to coat the nub that swelled at his touch. She closed her eyes against a torrent of pleasure, her protest silenced.

What they were doing was wrong, and yet, when she clutched his shoulders, it was only to draw him closer, not push him away. Dear Lord, how could something so illicit feel so good? Her thighs quivered, her chest heaved as tongues of pleasure lapped at her.

"Let it happen, beautiful," Burke whispered against her lips. Then he plundered her mouth with a kiss that mimicked the actions of his clever fingers, and...

Oh, God. She had never been so conscious of her femininity, especially when he thrust a finger into her aching center, covering her mouth to absorb the cry that issued from her throat.

Yes!

He added a second digit and thrust again, using his thumb now to tease the pulsing knot that ruled her pleasure.

"Burke!"

He spoke against her lips. "Call me Toby."

But she was unable to speak again. She came in a rush of pleasure so powerful and pure it brought tears to her eyes as she rode his thrusting fingers until the episode ended, right where it had begun.

Tobias's burning regard bespoke of a hunger that kept her heart beating irregularly. But, instead of pressing his advantage, he withdrew his hand reluctantly. A bittersweet smile tugged at one corner of his mouth.

"Don't look so horrified," he said, straightening her nightshirt almost tenderly and retying the sash of her robe as she weaved on her feet, too overcome to speak. "Think of it this way. Now I *have* to go to church to repent for my sins." He gave her his patented wink, dropped a lingering kiss on her slightly parted lips and let himself out of her room.

A second later, Dylan heard him climb the stairs to the attic. Still, she couldn't bring herself to move. She throbbed in places she hadn't given a thought to in over a year. Her knees jittered. Despite what she knew she ought to do—banish that aberration from her mind forever—she relived every intimate detail of it, savoring every forbidden pleasure.

Alive!

But then chagrin burned her face as she considered what an easy conquest she must have seemed. *I ought to be ashamed of myself.*

Only, it wasn't shame that made her insides quiver. It was the unholy thought of Tobias possessing her with his entire body. With a moan, she covered her hot face with her hands and squeezed her eyes shut. Thank God she was headed to church tomorrow, so she could atone for her sins.

Toby lay back on his bedroll staring at the patches of moonlight as they floated across the attic's eaves. He ought to be feeling smug at his accomplishment. He'd made Dylan Connelly orgasm in less than five minutes. And yet, despite his own throbbing hard-on, he felt strangely upset with himself.

What for? It wasn't as if he'd forced himself on her. Having read her subtle willingness, he'd taken decisive action, following his standard operating procedure: arouse the target and then back off. The technique practically guaranteed that the woman made the next move. It had to be that way. Perceiving herself to be in control, she was likelier to share her secrets in a timely fashion, and he didn't want to be here any longer than necessary.

Still…He felt mildly ashamed.

Initiating the information game had never bothered him before. Nor had it concerned him whether the women he'd seduced—mainly discontented housewives and girlfriends of small arms traffickers—found out that he'd used them to get to the truth because they'd all been tramps. Not one of them held a light to Dylan Connelly.

Oh, shut the fuck up, he told the poetic voice inside him.

The fact of the matter remained that he was here to do a job. Whatever it took to discover the truth, he would do it. He just couldn't help thinking what a hypocrite he'd be sitting in church with her tomorrow.

CHAPTER 7

Seated near the front of St. Peter's Church with the pews full behind him, Toby wondered if the stained-glass eyes of saints and martyrs were making his nape prickle, or if everyone seated behind them was remarking his presence and speculating.

A casual glance back informed him that many of Dylan's militia members attended church here. Men from his own squad acknowledged eye contact with a nod, including Nathan the waiter, whose shell-shocked expression suggested not only that his wife had finally given birth but also that he'd witness the entire event.

The Sheriff of Harpers Ferry, seated in the rear pew, sent him a hard look. Toby gulped and looked away. Now that man made him nervous.

At Dylan's nudge, he devoted his attention on the priest moving into the pulpit, his voice echoing under the chancel with its ribbed vaults as he intoned, "In the name of the Father, the Son, and the Holy Spirit."

At those words, Dylan relaxed into the pew, her knee brushing Toby's thigh and jolting his senses. Lt. Ashby sat on her left side, all four NCOs on her right, with June Lee all the way at the end. Toby counted himself lucky that he got to sit next to Dylan, even though her touch had him replaying her sweet surrender in his arms last night. He ignored the priest's sermon until he heard Syria being mentioned.

"Reading the headlines of *The Washington Post* this past year, my heart has bled for the Syrian people," the priest admitted.

Toby focused on him abruptly, surprised to being hearing a politically-based sermon.

"I have watched their struggles to overthrow the current regime, to no avail," the priest admitted. "I have wept as Bashar Assad has countered their efforts with the brutality of Satan himself, shelling cities into rubble, inflicting chemical warfare on the very people he ought to be protecting. Yet regardless of my empathy for the plight of Syria, this morning's headlines disturb me even more: 'Five Thousand Marines to Lend Support to NATO.' I ask myself, is this the beginning of another long war?"

Father Nesbit laid claim to a pleasantly bland face. There was nothing remarkable about his appearance or his stature, but his conviction held his audience captive.

"When we hear of atrocities perpetrated on the innocent, our hearts cry out for justice. How can we not lend a hand to a people striving for democracy? How dare we turn a blind eye to the starvation and deprivation of women and children? Look to history and to the Bible and you will find the answer."

He smoothed the pages of the thick book in front of him. "One of our scripture readings this morning comes from the Book of Isaiah. 'God shall judge between the nations, and shall decide disputes for many peoples; and they shall beat their swords into plowshares, and their spears into pruning hooks;

nation shall not lift up sword against nation, neither shall they learn war anymore.'"

He looked up. "Did you hear that? God shall judge. God shall mediate. Not the United States of America. We have only to look to Iraq and Afghanistan to see what happens when we take that mission upon ourselves. What happens is war, and war is *always* wrong."

Dylan's rapt expression reminded Toby of the anti-war articles she had written and published online. She and the priest obviously saw eye-to-eye on this subject.

"But look at the numbers, you argue. Over sixty thousand dead; two hundred and fifty thousand are homeless and in need of food. Surely the Church understands the need for war in the face of such desperation. The answer is, no! Not in the case of Syria. Not if you abide by the Just War Doctrine, which the church has upheld since its founding and uses to determine whether war is the only possible solution to resolving conflict."

He began outlining the four conditions of the Just War Doctrine, while illustrating that, in the case of Syria, not a single condition had yet been met.

Toby gritted his teeth. Sending in Marines to lead the NATO-initiated force was the only right thing to do, in his opinion. It was clearly a situation of act now or pay later.

A sheen of sweat shone on Nesbit's high forehead. "And let us not forget what war has done to our own fighting men and women—" he added, his blue eyes straying toward Dylan, "—who've returned home in coffins, without limbs, and with broken hearts and broken minds."

Toby stiffened. *What the hell?* Had the priest just implied that she was crazy? Of course, he'd had the same thought himself but…

"Rather than send soldiers abroad, we would be better off looking to our own brokenness." Nesbit glanced back down at the Bible. "As the apostle Paul writes in his letter to the Romans, 'Then do what is good, and you will receive Christ's approval, for he is God's servant for your good. But if you do wrong, be afraid, for he does not bear the sword in vain.' Amen."

"Amen," muttered a subdued congregation.

In the prayers and the sacrament that followed, Toby squirmed, willing the service to be over. He wondered if Dylan inherited her anti-war sentiment from Father Nesbit, or vice versa? Did she dread the prospect of war enough to kill those who acted in support of it?

Time would tell. Right now, he just wanted to be with people like himself and enjoy his only day off. With relief, he sang the closing hymn, earning a startled look from Dylan, who appeared to be impressed by his singing voice. No sooner was the benediction uttered than he broke for the door, pushing past the others to make his escape.

Dylan quickly caught up to him. "Come meet Father Nesbit." Putting a light hand on his arm, she steered him toward the line of parishioners waiting to shake the priest's hand.

With envy, Toby watched the other NCOs slip around the priest and make their escape. "I need to catch my train," he reminded her.

"It'll take five minutes."

At last, it was their turn. "Dylan!" The priest greeted her with a broad smile and both hands outstretched. His blue eyes jumped to Toby. "And who's this?" he asked, with a welcoming smile.

Dylan made the introductions. "This is Tobias

Burke, my newest NCO. Father Nesbit was a friend of my parents," she told Toby. "He baptized and confirmed me."

"I've heard good things about you," Nesbit said, proving that the gossip mill was alive and well in Harpers Ferry. The priest lowered his voice conspiratorially. "I hope my sermon didn't offend a former Army Ranger. In no way did I mean to denigrate the efforts of our brave fighting men and women."

"No problem." The feeling that he was being watched tickled his nape again. He had to get the hell out of here. "Sorry to rush off, but I have a train to catch."

Dylan excused his rudeness with, "My men look forward to their day off." Together, they climbed shale steps to the tiny lot uphill where they'd left her SUV. There, all the NCOs except for Chet Lee, who took off with his wife in his own car, hovered around the Suburban, anxious to leave.

As Dylan fished her car keys from her purse, Toby glimpsed the butt of her pistol still tucked inside and his pulse ticked upward. Christ, did she take it everywhere she went, even into church?

"It's open."

Raising the back hatch, Toby strapped on Milly's service vest, grabbed up his jacket and his duffle bag now full of dirty laundry, and called the dog out. Turning to Dylan, he found her watching him. "Well, see you tonight," he promised.

Her quartz-colored eyes reflected doubt. "I'll pick you up," she offered unexpectedly. "What time does the train get back?"

"Five fifteen," he said, forgetting to use military time.

"I'll meet you at the station, then," she promised,

looking tense.

"Okay. Thanks." With a wave at the men who'd already climbed into the Suburban, he headed toward the shale steps that would take him to the street below. He could feel Dylan's eyes on his back.

He hadn't managed to prove her guilt yet, but in one week's time, he had her eating out of the palm of his hand, exactly as the Taskforce had needed him to do.

Where, then, was the satisfaction he normally felt at such an accomplishment?

Tobias's disappearing head filled Dylan with a panicky sense of loss.

In just one week's time, he had brought her back to the world of the living. Before that, she'd just been going through the motions. She had used the militia's creed to infuse her life with purpose, the noise of the firing range to subdue her PTSD. But it wasn't until Tobias Burke first smiled at her that she'd started to anticipate each waking day.

He wasn't like the other NCOs, all of whom ascribed to her political and religious views—or pretended to. She wasn't even sure why he'd joined her militia. Maybe he just wanted to relive his glory days as an Army Ranger. He certainly didn't seem to care that the liberties their ancestors had fought so hard to secure were under threat. And yet...he drew her like a moth to flame.

"Come have some coffee, Dylan," called a voice from the front of the church.

Forcing a smile, Dylan shook her head and waved. "I'm sorry. I have to go now." She longed to mope in solitude.

Just then, a train clattered over the trestles that spanned the merging rivers. That would be Tobias's Amtrak nearing the station, and he would arrive just in time to board it. But would he come back? That was the question.

With a heavy heart, she slid behind the wheel of her SUV feeling like the sun was already sinking on her new dawn.

The usual bustle and confusion in Washington D.C.'s Union Station was distinctly absent on a Sunday morning. Toby and Milly hopped down from the train into a hush interspersed with the sounds of hissing hydraulics and leisurely footsteps.

Following a handful of backpackers who'd ventured off the Appalachian Trail in Harpers Ferry, Toby guided Milly to the subterranean levels of Union Station where they boarded an Orange Line Metro train bound for West Falls Church. From there, they took a cab to the National Counterterrorism Center in McLean. All the while the hair on the back of Toby's neck prickled, making him suspect a tail.

But whenever he searched for the source, he saw no one. Evidently, Dylan's paranoia had rubbed off on him.

The National Counterterrorism Center buzzed with activity seven days a week, twenty-four hours a day. Analysts from thirteen different agencies worked in the Operations Center without ceasing. As Toby crossed from one side of the room to the other, scenes of an ongoing firefight in Syria unfolded on the giant screen overhead. Several analysts called greetings to his dog. Everyone knew Milly by name; Toby they usually ignored, except to smirk at whatever message he was wearing on his T-shirt. Today he'd dressed for church in a pale blue button-down, so no message.

A set of stairs conveyed him to offices on the second level, including the boardroom where the Taskforce convened on a weekly basis. Comprised of a handful of agents pulled in from various agencies—the FBI, ATF, DEA, and NSA to name a few—the central mission of the Taskforce was to lend support to Homeland Security in general, by placing informants in suspected terrorist cells in and around the D.C. area. Dylan's militia was one such cell.

Toby pushed his way inside only to find that the team lead and his two colleagues had already beat him to the meeting. They all glanced up from a long table to remark his entrance.

Jackson Maddox, a light-skinned African-American FBI special agent, sent him a smile. The black-haired stranger studied him intently, and Ike, the team lead, with closely-cropped, prematurely silver hair, glanced pointedly at the wall clock. "You're late," he grated.

Toby wished he was wearing his T-shirt that read CHILL, except Ike Calhoun, a former Navy SEAL, didn't know the meaning of the word. Rumor had it he only relaxed when he escaped to his cabin in the Blue Ridge Mountains.

Ike made terse introductions between Toby and the stranger. "Burke, this is Special Agent Hamilton, on loan to us from DEA."

Hamilton stood up, proving to be well over six feet tall. His hand swallowed Toby's as they exchanged a handshake. Black hair, dark eyes, and strong cheekbones testified to American Indian heritage. "Call me TJ," he offered.

"Tobias Burke. This is Milly," Toby added, when the man's dark eyes shifted to his dog.

"Enough small talk," Ike interrupted.

Toby took his seat. "How's Lena?" he asked Jackson, ignoring the team lead's determination to get right down to work.

Jackson's gray-green eyes, startling pale against his dusky skin, glinted with satisfaction. "Excellent."

"Glad to hear it." Jackson had met Lena the previous year while posing as an ex-convict in a prisoner reintegration program. The journalist who'd threatened to expose his investigation had ended up becoming his wife.

Not that something like that could ever happen to me, Toby mused. Dylan wasn't exactly wife material.

"And your wife and baby, sir? How are they?" he asked, continuing to frustrate Ike, who'd become a father to a bouncing baby girl last February.

"Good." For a moment, it seemed that was all he was going to say when he added gruffly, "Ariel can stand up already."

Fatherly pride colored his voice. "No kidding," Toby exclaimed. "She'll be dating before you know it," he ribbed, earning a cold stare. He knew he was crazy to shake the bars of Ike Calhoun's cage but, just once, he'd like to see the man lose his cool.

"What's your gut feeling on the militia leader?" Ike clipped, putting an abrupt end to the small talk.

Toby touched his jaw as he considered where to start. "Well, she's a little off her rocker," he conceded. "And she's definitely a strict constructionist when it comes to interpreting the Constitution." He brought them up-to-date on her plans for the peaceful protest at the fusion center in Woodlawn. "She views oversight on the part of the federal government as a breach of First Amendment rights."

"What's her position on the impending war with Syria?" Ike inquired.

"She hasn't brought it up, but her priest has. You should've heard him in church this morning."

Jackson coughed to cover up a laugh. "You went to church?"

"Just this morning," Toby affirmed. "And it didn't collapse, burn down, or sink into the river. But seriously," he looked back at Ike. "She's known the priest all her life. If she's responsible for the bombing, he could well be the motivating force behind it."

"What's his name?"

"Arthur Nesbit." Pulling the church bulletin from his rear pocket, he handed it to Ike, who flipped through it.

"Tell me about the militia members who live with her," Ike requested, laying down the bulletin and transferring his fingers to his laptop. "Who are they and what are they like?"

One by one, Toby described Dylan's NCOs and then her executive officer, Terrence Ashby.

"Ashby used to fly the choppers that carried the dead she recovered. He and Dylan have a history that's not spelled out in their records. I'll get to the bottom of it eventually. All I know is that he'd lay down his life for her if he had to."

Ike reflected a moment. "Look into that, will you?" he requested of Jackson.

"Yes, sir." Jackson scribbled himself a note.

"Did you bring the surveillance material?"

Toby grubbed in the pocket of his duffel bag, found the clean sock in which he'd stowed the Ranger pin, and pulled it out. Releasing the tiny memory card from the port in the back, he handed it to Ike, who pushed it into a gadget connected to his laptop. With a tap of the key, Ike accessed the image files and projected them on the wall screen at the other end of the table.

Ten minutes later, they'd captured twenty-two faces to run through their Terrorist Identities Datamark Environment. Toby's picture of the ledger provided them with a list of names, as well. If any of Dylan's soldiers happened to be known terrorists, it would strengthen the FBI's case against her.

Toby caught the team lead's eye. "Any word yet on whether the pipe and the wires found on her property match the components of the bomb?"

"Not yet," Ike clipped. "The tests are complicated. You got anything else for us?"

Toby pulled *The Defender's Creed* from his bag, unfolded it, and slid it toward Ike, who skimmed the contents. "Like I said, Dylan uses the militia to enforce the Constitution and to frustrate those who violate it, and that's pretty much the extent of it."

Ike's green-as-grass eyes jumped up at him. "What do you mean by pretty much?"

Toby deliberated how much to say. It felt strangely disloyal to Dylan to reveal her plans to Ike; after all, they had nothing to do with the FBI's investigation. "She's making plans to teach certain individuals a lesson. Those failing to live up to her standards might find themselves abducted, taken to a strange location, and told to change their ways—or else. It's harmless, really. Kind of like of like Robin Hood stealing from the rich to give to the poor."

Ike regarded him dubiously. "How's that?"

Toby tried to explain Dylan's high standards. He mentioned her colleague's penchant for prescribing experimental medication and how irate it made her. "He's probably her first target."

Ike's chair creaked as he sat back in it. "You call that harmless? Kidnapping is a felony offense," he pointed out.

"Not if the local sheriffs participate and refuse to make an arrest." Toby tipped a nod at the laptop where they'd just uploaded their images into the database.

Ike drummed his fingers on the tabletop. "Find out more," he finally ordered, pinning Toby with a hard look. "I want to know how much influence this priest has over her. Is she as preoccupied with Syria as he is? What else is on her mind besides punishing the local scum? I want her spilling out her guts to you. Is that clear?"

Oh, the pressure. "Yes, sir."

Across the table, Jackson's long stare told Toby that he could read his mixed thoughts. TJ Hamilton sat as still and quiet as a deep pool.

"Anything else, sir?" Toby inquired. "Would you care to lobotomize me?" he teased, hoping to startle Ike out of his seriousness. "Donate my gonads to science?"

Ike shut his laptop with a snap. "Maybe later," he retorted, unfazed by Toby's offers. "We'll meet again next week, same time, same place. If the results come in on the pipe or any militia members come up hot, I'll text you."

Toby nodded and hoped not to get a text from Ike at all.

Jackson started putting his notes away.

Zipping up his laptop bag, Ike headed for the door. Halfway out, he paused and looked back. "Good work so far, Burke," he said. And then he disappeared.

Toby and Jackson shared a look of astonishment. Maybe fatherhood was mellowing Ike, after all.

TJ spoke for the first time since their introduction. "You're drawn to the suspect," he stated, in a tone that conveyed no judgment whatsoever. "But you don't know if she's guilty," he added thoughtfully.

The provocative speculation invited confidence, only Toby balked at having his thoughts and feelings analyzed. The suspicion that Hamilton might be psychic had him shutting out the man completely. "Either way, she's a nut," he retorted. "I never said I liked her," he added irritably.

"Hey, what are you doing for lunch? I'm sure Lena

would love to feed you." Jackson's offer swept aside the tense moment.

"Laundry followed by a nap," Toby answered. Suddenly, he wasn't in the mood for company. "Sorry, Stonewall, but I'm worn out."

In a nod to the famous Civil War hero, General Andrew Jackson, Toby had called Jackson Stonewall from their very first introduction.

Jackson's shrug conveyed his understanding. "Maybe next week," he suggested, pushing to his feet.

TJ Hamilton followed his example, rising with silent, fluid grace.

As the two men headed for the door, Toby gathered his stuff together. Hamilton laid a hand on his shoulder as he passed him. "Take care," he said.

The words sounded strangely like a warning.

"Later, Toby," Jackson called and, together, the two men departed, leaving Toby to his perturbed thoughts.

Damn it, he *did* like Dylan Connelly. It was never good to like the suspect.

Milly sat up and whined, sending Toby an anxious look. She probably had to pee.

"I need a beer," Toby mumbled.

Dylan hugged herself against the chill seeping through her coat as she searched the emptying passenger cars for Tobias. Several tourists disembarked, commenting on the delightful dimensions of the train station. Behind them, Sheriff Cal Fallon hustled toward the parking lot without acknowledging Dylan, but, then again, the sheriff was a busy man.

She glanced at her watch and consulted the posted train schedule. This was definitely the train Tobias Burke was due to return on, yet he was nowhere to be seen.

Her worry that he would not return was morphing rapidly into reality. Disappointment hollowed her belly as the hope that he would help her lead the militia in the next calendar year slowly died.

The boarding platform emptied. The train gave a hiss of releasing brakes as it prepared to continue its trek to Pittsburg. The conductor shouted out, "All aboard!" Dylan was just about to turn away, utterly distraught, when Milly bounded out of the third car. At the other end of her leash, Tobias Burke half leapt, half-fell out of the train, just as the doors were closing.

Relief made Dylan's head spin, but why was he stumbling?

Recovering his balance, he sent her a slow smile that buoyed her spirits and then he lurched in her direction. Had he hurt himself? The scent of alcohol wafted toward her as he halted in front of her. Milly bumped Dylan's hand with her head, but astonishment kept Dylan from returning the canine's greeting.

"You're drunk!" she accused. Her spine stiffened. Did he have nothing better to do on his day off? Were the clothes in his duffle bag even clean? Or had he frittered away his time completely.

"Had a couple of beers on the train," he conceded, grinding the ball of one hand into his left eye. "Fell asleep," he added, blinking at her.

Grubbing in her purse for a stick of gum, she thrust it at him. "I can't have a drunk in my militia." She whirled on him and started to march off.

With reflexes that startled her, he caught her elbow and swung her back around. "Whoa, there—a drunk?" His tone conveyed affront.

"A drinking man," she amended.

He cocked his head at her, and she held her breath, concerned by his reaction. Was he a mean drunk or an easy-going drunk? She was about to find out.

"Know what your problem is?"

His unruffled tone relieved her. "What?"

"You're too uptight, Captain. I had a couple of beers on the train and then I fell asleep. That doesn't make me a drinking man." He popped the gum into his mouth and started chewing. "You should try it some time. Might loosen you up a bit."

She bristled at the implication that she was tight-laced. "Have you any idea what liquor does to the human liver?"

"A drink a day is good for you," he insisted.

The Journal of Modern Medicine actually agreed with him, but guns and liquor didn't mix, which was why she maintained a zero tolerance policy in her militia. Plus, he'd admitted himself that he'd had more than one. "Even so, what kind of message would that send the others bringing you home in your present state?"

He shrugged his agreement. "Fair enough," he said breezily. "So we'll take a walk first," he suggested, and a gleam entered his eyes.

The prospect of a walk, a chance to spend some time alone with him, dissipated her annoyance. "We could do that," she conceded.

Whirling, she led him through the station and into the emptying parking lot. They stowed his bag in her Suburban and turned toward town on foot. Harpers Ferry lay cloaked in shadow with only the highest chimneys and the tops of trees lit by the setting sun.

"Which way?" Tobias inquired when they reached the street.

"Uphill." She pointed in the direction of the Appalachian Trial. In silence they climbed a series of lumber steps to High Street, then the steep shale steps to Church Street, where they passed Saint Peters

Church, climbing an ascending path that was a portion of the Appalachian Trail, where it briefly paralleled the Shenandoah River.

As steep as the trail was, this portion was paved. A railing on one side and intermittent lamps kept hikers from falling to their deaths, not that the trail was open at this time of night. The National Historical Park was closed to hikers after sunset, which was exactly why Dylan had come this way. They wouldn't be seen together by locals prone to gossip.

Alone with Tobias Burke. What am I thinking? Prospects danced before her, pitched by an imagination brought to life in his presence.

Milly panted to keep up, but Tobias remained as stealthy and athletic after a few beers as he was sober. As they passed the ruins of the Episcopal Church, he slanted her a grin that put an effervescent feeling in her stomach.

The path grew ever steeper. "You're not going to push me off a cliff, are you?" he teased.

"Don't tempt me."

His baritone chuckle made her feel as light as a feather. *He came back.*

The river flowed quietly below them. The air smelled sweet and cool. It had been ages since she'd climbed to this spot. As the only child of elderly parents, she'd explored it many times, but always on her own. Walking with a man and his dog felt strangely intimate. She couldn't insist on her authority, out here. She wasn't his commander when there was no one to see them. She was just an ordinary woman with no greater concerns than whether her companion would try to steal a kiss.

She mocked herself. You want him to, don't you?

When he caught up her hand unexpectedly, her pulse kicked. She ordered herself to pull away, but the tender restraint with which he cradled her fingers made her recall the way he'd touched her the previous night, unleashing such sweet pleasure. In comfortable silence, they plodded the steep path to an ever-higher altitude.

Zigzag steps carved out of the mountain conveyed them to the pinnacle. There, the giant boulders she had climbed upon in her youth stood spotlighted by the setting sun. Piggybacked on the largest boulder was a flat slab of rock held aloft by four sturdy pillars.

Tobias stared at it. "What's that?"

"Jefferson's Rock." She gestured. "Our founding father stood right there in 1783, and later he wrote that the view was worth a voyage across the Atlantic."

"Let's see if he was right." He dropped Milly's leash, signaling for her to stay, and tugged Dylan toward the monument.

"No, we can't. It's a monument now. You're not allowed to stand on it."

"You're such a rule follower. Who's going to see?"

"It's dangerous," she added, halfheartedly resisting.

"I won't let you fall."

His confidence prompted a snort of irony as he scrambled up the toe-holds in the worn shale, dragging her with him onto the first large boulder. "You're the one who's inebriated," she reminded him.

"Am I?"

Inebriated or not, he seemed certain of himself. Dylan clung to his hand, leery of the edges. Stepping onto the forbidden platform, he pulled her up alongside him, where the view kept the breath wedged in her lungs. Tobias's arm stole around her, keeping her secure as she sent her gaze past the steeple of her church toward the bridge that spanned the merging rivers.

The amber remnants of a sun now gone from view

gilded the purple mountains that rippled off into the distance. Closer in, where the rivers met, the lights of the town and the bridge twinkled on the water's surface. She could hear the Shenandoah River sliding leisurely past the rocks below.

Without warning, Tobias broke into song in the velvety baritone that had taken her aback that morning. The familiar song heralded the view while setting a sentimental tone.

"John Denver," she said, identifying the original artist. "He died in a plane crash."

Tobias clicked his tongue. "Don't go sucking all the joy out of the moment," he reproved. "Denver didn't die. His music lives forever. Just listen to the breeze and you'll hear him singing."

She listened. A puff of cool air ruffled the dry leaves all around them, and Tobias picked up where he'd left off, singing softly, reverently about both the ancientness and the youth of the mountains.

She joined him on the refrain, in a voice rusty from disuse. This particular song of Denver's was practically the state anthem. Unaccustomed tears moistened Dylan's eyes as she reflected on the beauty of West Virginia, her home from birth.

A sweet comfortable silence fell between them. Toby drew a deep breath and let it out again, inviting her to relax against him. "This view is most definitely worth the voyage," he declared.

Her throat tightened. She'd taken a voyage of her own—a long and painful detour—when she'd left for Afghanistan four years ago. She hadn't realized how blessed she was to be home again; how grateful she was to born an American, where, despite the corrupt government's attempt to wrest them away, the Constitution guaranteed her certain liberties.

Tobias turned her in his arms to face him and her

innards cartwheeled as she beheld his crooked smile. "Are you a mountain mama?" he inquired.

She shrugged. "My mother's people were miners, so, yes, I suppose I am." His solid warmth made her want to stay in this very spot, bantering with him, all night.

He lifted his hands to the bun at the back of her head. One by one, he plucked loose the pins that kept her hair in a tight knot. Silky skeins slipped through his fingers giving rise to pleasant shivers.

"This is who you really are," he said as her hair fluttered loose in the breeze.

He'd said that the other night when he first kissed her, too. She wasn't so sure who she was. But it didn't seem to matter, not when he tipped her chin up with his fingers and gave her the kiss she'd been craving since he first got off the train. His lips plied hers, teasing them apart. He'd discarded his gum on the trail somewhere, but his mouth still tasted of spearmint with a trace of beer that was not at all unpleasant. Dylan coiled her arms around his shoulders and crushed her breasts to his chest, all too willing to be seduced again.

"I thought about you all damn day," he grated, moving his lips to her throat where he besieged the tender skin there.

The confession thrilled her though she wondered at his half-angry tone. "Is that a bad thing?"

"You tell me." He kissed her harder, his tongue seeking every corner of her mouth as if the answer lay hidden there. His hands, warm and skilled, found their way beneath her coat to squeeze her bottom, pulling her hips against the proof of his manifest desire.

I want him, she acknowledged. In fact, if he asked her to lie down right here on this stone where Thomas Jefferson had once stood, she'd be sorely tempted.

Just then, Milly growled below them, and Tobias tore his lips from Dylan's to search the forest. "Someone's coming," he whispered.

Following his gaze, she spied the orb of a flashlight bobbing toward them.

"The park ranger," she replied, both alarmed and annoyed by the interloper's timing.

"Yep." Tobias leapt off the flat rock and scooped her off it. She slid down the front of his body—a poor substitute for what might have been. With a hand around her elbow, he helped her off the larger boulder.

The light came closer. "You there," called an authoritative, yet familiar voice. "No one's allowed to stand on the monument. And what's more the park is closed."

Dylan blinked against the invasive light. Ah, yes. Corbin Harrison, a member of her militia, worked for the National Park Service.

"Oh, sorry Captain," Corbin said recognizing her simultaneously. "I didn't realize it was you." He directed his flashlight at Tobias. "Sergeant," he acknowledged stiffly.

"No reason to apologize," Dylan said. "We were in the wrong and hoping to catch the view before the sunset. We're leaving now."

"I'd better escort you. It's even steeper going downhill," Corbin insisted.

"Thank you. We'd appreciate that." Truth to tell, she would rather push Corbin off a ledge for ruining such a special moment, but since he'd caught them fraternizing, the gracious thing to do was to agree to his escort in the hopes that he would keep his conclusions to himself. In a town this small, word was bound to get around.

The prospect stole a portion of her contentment.

As they descended the path back to her church and the steep shale steps toward Lower Town, the consequences of Dylan's actions started drifting down like particles of debris in the aftermath of an explosion.

She'd loved every second of her stolen interlude with Tobias—loved it far too much. Her reliance on him was fast becoming an emotional need—an addiction even more unhealthy than her love of coffee.

On Church Street, they parted company with Corbin. By the time they arrived back at the train station, Dylan had arrived at a painful decision. As appealing as Tobias was, as much as his presence made her feel alive and joyous again, her reliance on him for her emotional well-being posed a danger to her.

Yes, he had come back tonight, which gave her hope that he might agree to be her new XO, when Terrence's illness forced him to step down.

But, in her heart of hearts, she knew Tobias Burke had not returned out of a sense of commitment to the SAM, or even to her. So, why had he returned at all?

From the day they'd met, he'd been harder to read than most people, and that was still the case. He didn't need her the way the others did. He might claim to require a service dog for his PTSD, but she'd never seen him display signs of that disorder. According to Morrison, who'd talked at length with him, Tobias had earned a college degree, which meant that he could go anywhere, do anything.

For now, he had chosen to play war with her militia and to help them to be better soldiers. But how long would that last? The novelty of being in a militia was bound to fade, and when it did, Tobias would head off for the next adventure awaiting him.

She'd spent a year putting the pieces of her shattered self back together. How stupid could she be, putting her faith in someone who was bound to walk away?

Dylan, you idiot.

She'd lost her boys in one fell swoop. She was going to lose Terrence Ashby sometime soon. Tobias's departure might just be the straw that broke the camel's back. She'd hovered too close to losing her mind not to realize that the point of no return lay closer than she cared to admit.

For her sanity's sake, she had to think of him as just another one of her NCOs. He could stay for as long as he chose, but she would keep him at arm's distance or pay the consequences later.

Something had happened, and he had no idea what.

Toby studied Dylan as she drove them home. Apart from Milly's panting, silence filled the interior of the vehicle. Dylan's grip on the wheel and the firm line of her mouth suggested that she was having second thoughts about what had almost transpired up there on Jefferson's rock.

Well, damn.

Ike's demands that he figure her out had made him push too hard, too fast. And now she was regretting it. The demands of his job were eating at him, too. Torn between the need to pick Dylan's brain and defend her radical philosophies, he'd downed one too many beers which, in turn, had skewed his judgment. If she changed her mind about letting him get closer, it could only be his fault.

"You okay?" he asked, a tad worried now. If she shut him out completely, he would fail the Taskforce, meaning—if she really was a terrorist—she would get away with murder a little longer.

The wheels of the SUV jiggled through a pothole she didn't see. "Fine," she answered.

But she obviously wasn't. Several seconds ticked by and the silence thickened.

At last, she cleared her throat. "Sergeant Burke," she said, addressing him in the voice she used when speaking to her soldiers, "I have to ask you never to kiss me again. In fact, in the future, when you speak to me, kindly do so with company present."

Double damn. He'd really screwed up. "Look, if I said or did something wrong, I didn't mean to—"

"It's not you," she assured him, her tone thawing slightly. "It's me. I'm not...I'm not able to involve myself. I can't—" She shook her head..

Well, shit. He sat back in his seat and stared at the dark, winding road ahead of them. The emptiness he was feeling had nothing to do with failing to meet Ike's expectations. He'd preyed on Dylan's vulnerabilities and now he felt bad about it. Emotional frailty like hers required a protective barrier and he'd crashed right through it, leaving her no choice but to pull away.

And if she pulled away, he might never determine whether she had masterminded Nolan's death or not.

"I understand," he said wearily, knowing he would have to double his efforts just to get back to where they'd been the night before.

At his words, he noticed Dylan's grip on the steering wheel slowly relax. "Thank you," she whispered.

Was that regret lacing her tone? God, he hoped so, and not just because the Taskforce was counting on him. He enjoyed getting to know her better. The more layers he peeled back, the more layers he discovered, the more interesting she became. He didn't want to have to back off now.

CHAPTER 8

Dylan slit her eyes at the sound of the bugle squawking.

Was it morning already? The sleeping pills Dr. Richardson had prescribed for her made her feel as though she'd just closed her eyes. She would rather tumble back into the dream still fresh and warm within her mind of Tobias making love to her on Jefferson's Rock. With a throb of regret, she reconsidered her decision to distance herself emotionally.

Yes, it was the wisest thing to do. She couldn't rely on a drifter for her happiness, not after putting herself back together again, piece by little piece. Terrence's impending decline was enough of a horror to face without worrying that Tobias Burke would break her heart.

Kicking off her covers, she rolled out of bed to prepare for morning PT. For her own welfare and for the good of the militia, this was how it had to be.

Toby came to a horrified halt as he entered the kitchen. The scent of June Lee's specialty, Korean ribs, wafted from the oven, but his attention was fully captured by the scene he'd walked in on following a full day's work.

"What did you just do?" he demanded of Dylan, forgetting for the moment that he wasn't to speak to her without another person present. She'd just returned from the hospital, and it was nearing time for the evening briefing.

"What do you mean?" she answered, her eyes opening wide.

He glanced from Milly's rapidly waving tail to the hand Dylan hid behind her back. "You just fed her something," he accused. "I told you she's a working dog. Food is a motivating tool. You can't just feed her for no good reason."

Ruddy color bloomed on Dylan's cheeks. "It's just a milk bone," she protested, pulling her hand out from behind her back to show him. "And I didn't give it to her yet."

"How many have you given before today?" he demanded.

"Just…a few."

He tried masking his dismay. After all, the motivation for rewarding therapy dogs was probably different than it was for bomb-sniffing dogs, and Dylan could look that up in no time at all, causing her to call Milly's ultimate purpose into question.

"Well," he said, modulating his voice to keep from sounding as annoyed as he felt, "you should have asked me first."

"Sorry." Her cooler tone told him plainly that she didn't see what the big deal was.

But it was a big deal. Lots of his own time—months, to be precise—had gone into training Milly to sniff out explosives. By giving her random treats, Dylan had just ruined Milly's motivation and sent her specialized training straight down the drain. Why should she work for food when she could get food for free by appealing to Dylan? But since she was supposed to be a therapy dog, kicking up a fuss over milk bones made him look like an ass. "No worries," he assured her. "Just...no chicken bones—you know, she could choke."

"Yes, I know that," she said in a stilted voice.

"It was sweet of you to think of her," he added lamely.

She visibly bristled at the word *sweet*.

"But if you don't limit the treats, she'll get fat," he added, supplying one more reason for his protest.

"Fine," Dylan assured him. Keeping the last treat firmly in her grasp, she patted Milly's head with her free hand and said, "Sorry, no more today, love."

Watching the exchange, Toby could feel his resentment leaving him. Dylan had taken a real liking to his dog, which, in his mind, made her less likely to be a terrorist. He decided, right then and there, that when his undercover job was over, he was going to leave Milly as a consolation prize for Dylan, a token of his mixed feelings for her. Not only had Dylan and Milly bonded from the start, but Milly would need a lot of work after this holiday if she was ever going to be a reliable working dog again.

"Almost time for the briefing."

Dylan's cool comment brought him sharply back to the present and to Dylan's determination to treat him as just another one of her NCOs, despite the magic they had shared last night.

With a nod of acknowledgement, he went to throw himself down in one of the armchairs. It wasn't like he'd never been told by a woman to back off, he reminded himself. As recently as six months ago, a blonde whose butt he'd pinched in Grogan's Irish Pub had slapped him silly. In his own defense, it had been Saint Patrick's Day; he'd had a few; and she wasn't wearing any green.

But, for some reason that had nothing to do with the Taskforce's expectations, Dylan's sudden rejection stung. It stung more than it ought to, which meant that TJ Hamilton had apparently hit the nail on the head. He *did* like the suspect.

He liked the way she moved as she crossed the command room to take a map off the wall. She carried it to the easel and pinned it in place, her movements charged with purpose. Regarding her more closely, it struck him that she still looked energized, even on the heels of a long day. She'd beat him on the run again that morning and put in eight hours of work, and yet her eyes were still bright with intent, even without the benefit of her signature mug of coffee. Since when had she kicked that habit?

The entrance of the XO and NCOs interrupted Toby's speculations.

"We have a lot to discuss, so let's get started," Dylan said briskly, urging them with a look to take their seats. "As I reminded our soldiers at the CPX, our creed states that it's our moral imperative to meet illegitimate force with righteous indignation. And so we will. Tonight, I will present my plans for confronting a certain evil."

Toby drew a bracing breath. *Here we go.* This was where Dylan crossed the line from upholding her right to bear arms to disregarding the law by brandishing those arms against other civilians. If she could browbeat Hendrix, what made him so sure she hadn't murdered Nolan, after all?

Crossing to the easel, she jabbed a finger at a spot on the map. "The Martinsburg Medical Center lies here." Snatching up a red marker, she circled the area.

"Dr. Hendrix lives here in a neighborhood called Shenandoah Junction. He leaves work at eighteen hundred hours and drives this route to get home." Her red marker squeaked across the map.

"If we set up roadwork right here—" she tapped the map, "then we can reroute him onto this rural road where we ambush his vehicle, cuff him, and blindfold him."

Toby slowly raised his hand into the air. *Don't say anything!* he ordered himself, but he just couldn't keep his mouth shut.

"Yes?" A hint of annoyance colored Dylan's voice.

"How do we make it look like we're doing roadwork?" Perhaps, if he tried, he could throw a wrench into her plans.

"One of our soldiers works for the department of transportation," she informed him. "He operates a van and two work trucks and has offered us use of all three vehicles."

She had more resources at her disposal than a queen bee had workers.

"Once we grab Hendrix," she continued, turning back to the map, "we drive him here." She circled an isolated area, just off the rural road. "This is Ron Baker's house. Baker is the big guy on Morrison's squad," she interjected before Toby could raise his hand again. "He has a windowless basement and no neighbors. We take Hendrix there and lay out our demands—no more doling out pills that make vets sick. We rough him up a bit, give him some solitary confinement in which to consider his sins, and then we let him go. If and when he turns to law enforcement, Sheriff Fallon won't find any leads. Are there questions?"

Three pairs of hands shot up in the air. "Yes, Sergeant Ackerman."

"We gonna beat his ass or what?"

Dylan's auburn eyebrows snapped together. "I said rough him up, not beat him up. Our lesson is more psychological than punitive." She pointed to the next man. "Sergeant Lee?"

"When is this going to happen?"

"Sometime in the next two weeks. Our volunteers will require training, as will we." Her gaze rested briefly on Toby, informing him that the training schedule would be up to him.

Lt. Ashby, who'd been silent up till then, issued a low groan.

Dylan regarded him sharply. "Terrence? Did you have something to add?"

He shook his head. "No, ma'am," he said in a strained voice.

She regarded him an instant longer then turned her head toward Toby. "Sergeant Burke."

"Yes, ma'am?"

His overly enthusiastic tone made her blink. "I'll need you to reconnoiter the area with me and Lt. Ashby—perhaps on Wednesday, as I'll be working late tomorrow. I need you to fine-tune the details of the ambush. Also, if you know of any interrogation techniques that would intimidate but not hurt Hendrix, I'd welcome your input."

Toby wanted to point out all the things that could go wrong with her plan, but given how unreceptive she'd become to him, he didn't dare press his luck. "Yes, ma'am."

She frowned at his gusto before running her gaze over the others. "This mission is still in its planning phase. We'll sketch in the details as the week progresses and train our volunteers this Saturday during the CPX. If word of our intent leaks out, then our plan will fail. Corruption will win the day. We

must retain the element of surprise—" Her glacial
eyes rested briefly on Ackerman,"—and speak about
this to no one outside our circle. Is that clear?"

"Yes, captain," the men chorused, all but Lt. Ashby
who suddenly doubled over, clutching one side of his
body.

"Terrence!" Dylan dropped to her knees in front of
his chair.

Toby surged to his feet while the other men gawked.

"Talk to me," Dylan ordered, her initial panic giving
way to practiced calm. She checked the XO's pulse.
"Where's it hurting?" she asked him. "Here?" She
slipped a thumb under Ashby's large hand and
pressed it into his stomach, prompting a groan of
agony.

Watching her work, Toby couldn't help but respect
her competence. Appendicitis was his first thought,
but Dylan's reaction conveyed that his attack was not
unexpected. She slowly sat back on her heels. "We
need to get you to the hospital," she determined,
grimly.

"No." Lt. Ashby vehemently shook his head. "No.
There's nothing they can do."

"They can moderate your pain," she insisted,
confirming Toby's suspicion that Ashby had a
condition she was well aware of.

"You can do that for me just as easily," he ground
out.

"What's wrong with him?" Ackerman blurted,
earning reproving glares from the others.

Dylan ignored him. In a demonstrative moment, she
caught Ashby's face in her hands and peered into his
eyes. "Tell me when you think you can make it up the
stairs. Or would you like us to set up a bed in here?"

"Upstairs," he grated, clearly humiliated.

Christ, Toby thought, wondering just how bad it

was. Did Ashby have advanced-stage cancer or something? Dylan remained calm and collected, but he could read the man's prognosis in the rigid set of her jaw, and pity welled within him.

"I'll get you something for your pain," she murmured, weaving as she pushed too quickly to her feet. Toby shot out a hand to stabilize her, but she shook him off and hurried toward the stairs. The four remaining men stared at their XO with silent worry.

Ashby craned his neck to look up at them with pain-glazed eyes. "It's T-cell Leukemia. I've had it for a while. My liver and my spleen swell up. They'll go down again," he insisted, but there wasn't much conviction in his voice, nor mention of any cure, Toby noticed.

Ackerman shifted in his chair. Morrison swiped a hand over his eyes and muttered his condolences. Lee looked down at the floor. Toby heard himself speak up. "What can we do to make it easier?"

Ashby clenched his fists and let out a harsh breath. "Protect the captain," he grated harshly. Pain gripped him suddenly, preventing him from saying any more. "The Feds...they're trying to frame her for murder. They don't like free thinkers like Dylan."

The man's words gripped Toby by the throat.

Protect Dylan from the Feds? A wave of guilt kept him rooted to the floor, unable to move, unable to offer Lt. Ashby so much as a reassuring word.

Dylan rushed into the room with tablets in her hand. She pushed them into her XO's palm. "Burke, go fetch a glass of water," she requested.

He shook himself out of his trance and went to do her bidding.

Dylan staggered out of Terrence's dark room with a crick in her neck. If his digital clock could be trusted, it was three in the morning. She'd fallen asleep in the armchair across from his bed where, thanks to the sleeping pills Dr. Richardson had prescribed for her, Terrence finally slept.

She needed as much rest as she could get if she hoped to make it through the coming day. Calling in sick was not an option, not when she and Ackerman were scheduled for counseling. Besides, she'd missed a day at work just last week. The best she could hope for was a few hours' rest before the sun came up. And if Ackerman dared to blow his bugle at oh-five thirty, she'd personally kill him.

Keeping Terrence's door cracked so she could hear him if he needed her, she drifted down the hall in a sleepy daze, only to pull up short as a shadow rose up the wall beside her door, whipping her heart into a trot. The vision of Tobias's broad shoulders did little to calm her startled senses. He'd been sitting with his back against the wall, like a sentinel.

A beam of moonlight slipped over his face, illuminating his worried expression. "How's the XO doing?" he asked before she could take him to task for scaring her.

"Better." She steeled herself from responding to his presence, but her blood already flowed faster. Her dulled wits revived.

"I'm so sorry, Dylan."

His genuine sympathy closed the distance she strove to keep between them. Misery and sorrow clogged her throat, making speech impossible. She groped for her doorknob intending to flee into her room and shut the door in his face.

"Hey." His hand, warm and comforting, curled around her arm preventing her escape. "You don't have to deal with this alone," he said.

Yes, she did. She reminded herself that Tobias was

bound to leave eventually. But when he stepped closer, folding her tenderly into his warm embrace, his comfort proved too consoling to reject.

Her weary head dropped on its own accord against his broad chest. His powerful arms enfolded her, making her feel safe and secure. The fullness of her impending loss tore into her like shrapnel, weakening her further. Hiding her face against the soft cotton of his T-shirt, she concealed the tears that flooded her eyes in a warm gush.

"Shhh." He smoothed circles into the small of her back. To her relief, he didn't offer up empty platitudes. He let her cry silently in his arms, her tears forming a wet patch on his T-shirt. When her eyes finally stopped leaking, she raised her head to pull herself together and realized he had moved them into her bedroom, without her realizing.

She couldn't remember the last time anyone had seen her in such a weakened state. "I'm sorry," she muttered, pulling away.

"Don't apologize," he told her curtly. With a hand still curled around her elbow, he led her to her bed and pulled back the blankets. "Time to sleep."

Why did he have to be so kind? Considering him through the gloom, she peered more closely at the message on the dark T-shirt he was wearing. In the shadows she could just make out the white lettering: TOUGH TIMES DON'T LAST; TOUGH PEOPLE DO.

The words had her standing straighter. "I can put myself to bed, Sergeant," she informed him. She better had, before he took advantage of her.

"Whatever you say, Captain." In a deliberately insubordinate gesture, he wiped a late tear from her cheek, then swiveled on his toes and padded toward her door.

"Tobias." She'd said his name without meaning to.

He stopped and looked back, hope flaring in his eyes.

Her body ached for the fulfillment of her dreams. But Terrence was sick, and she was all but broken. It would do her no good whatsoever to set herself up for more heartbreak. "Good night," she whispered.

He grimaced. "'Night," he replied. Her door opened and closed, and he was gone.

Kevin Richardson's salt and pepper hair looked as though he'd run his fingers through it countless times that day, which was probably the case. After all, his patients at the Martinsburg Medical Center were distraught and war-torn vets, who'd come to him for healing, just as Dylan had many months ago. The man had been counseling soldiers with PTSD going on thirty years. Clearly, the job hadn't gotten any easier.

Leaning forward in his seat, he laid a gentle hand on Dylan's knee, interrupting her monologue about how much Terrence meant to her. "Dylan," he said, "There's nothing you can do."

His simple words, uttered in his smoker's voice, were not what she wanted to hear.

She looked pointedly down at his long fingers, causing him to remove his hand and sit back.

An aching silence filled his office. The pressure in Dylan's chest expanded like a helium balloon being overfilled. It cut off her airways. Her chest felt like it would surely split open, the pressure was so severe. A sticky sweat filmed her skin. PTSD sucked. Ever since the fateful night she'd collected her boys' bodies off the battlefield, she had felt this way off and on. God in heaven, she could not face the loss of another person close to her! But, of course, she had no choice. Terrence was dying.

"You've known of his condition for months," Kevin Richardson reminded her, his words like fingernails on a chalkboard. "That will make his passing easier to deal with."

She doubted it, but she gave a jerky nod just the same in the hopes that he would change the subject. A wave of exhaustion rolled over her. Given the angle of the sun's rays slanting through his blinds, their session was probably over, anyway. It was time to return home where she was needed.

"Try to focus on the positive," Dr. Richardson urged. "I mean, just think about it." He sat back, folding his arms across his chest as he eyed her with pride. "A year ago you were a body of torment and self-doubt, weighing all of ninety pounds. Now, you're a strong, beautiful, and respected leader. You've given others like you a clear sense of purpose. Day by day, you make the world a better place. This is recovery, Dylan!" He dropped his arms and leaned forward. "Give yourself some credit. The only thing you still need to work on is learning to leave your revolver behind."

She heaved a heavy sigh.

"We'll work on that next time." He cocked his head and raised his eyebrows. "Did you bring it to work today?"

Her face grew hot. "It's locked in my desk, in my office," she muttered.

"That's okay." He sent her an encouraging smile. "One step at a time. Right now I'm more concerned with the way you're managing your stress."

Dylan rubbed her temple. It had to be apparent she wasn't managing her stress well at all.

"Tell me about your plans your militia is making to right certain wrongs." Behind the lenses of his glasses, the doctor's hazel eyes glinted with concern.

Dylan's tired brain drew a blank. What was he talking about? But then it came to her that Ivan Ackerman, who'd had his session earlier in the day, must have mentioned the militia's plan to target Dr. Hendrix. *Damn it all, he was supposed to keep mum about the militia's intent!*

"Don't worry." Dr. Richardson seemed to read her anxious thoughts. "Your secret is safe with me, but I have to tell you that I don't condone your plans. The FBI already questioned you in regards to that bombing in D.C. You have to know that they're keeping an eye on you at all times," he added anxiously. "Are you sure that teaching Hendrix a lesson is the right solution?"

Dylan felt her patience wearing thin. "What am I supposed to do? Let his abuses go unchecked like the director has? Should we all be passive citizens and let selfish jerks like Hendrix do what they want? No, we should take a stand against it!"

Her impassioned reply brought a wry smile to his lined face. "You have a point," he conceded.

Ten minutes later, Dylan left her counselor's office. Seeing Ivan Ackerman sprawled on the bench by the double glass doors, she took her time collecting her purse and her coat from her own office. And then went to wake him up.

"Ivan." His even snores masked the sound of her tentative voice.

She cautiously nudged his toe with her foot and he jumped like a startled squirrel, lunging at Dylan with a feral cry and wild eyes.

She startled back. God, is that what I look like when I'm caught off guard?

Ivan's harsh breathing filled the quiet corridor. His craze-glazed eyes cleared by degrees. Considering what had happened to his wife and daughter, Dylan couldn't blame him. "It's okay," she soothed, giving him time to compose himself.

Only it wasn't okay, was it? Ackerman had PTSD, just like she did. And for him, it would never be okay again, no matter what kind of outlet for his pain her militia offered him.

The same was true for Terrence. His wife had divorced him while he was in the service. He'd lost his right leg and his job as a helicopter pilot. And now leukemia would take his life. There was nothing okay about any of it. "You ready?" she choked out.

"Yeah."

Wrestling with her unwieldy emotions, Dylan led the way outside. As she drove them home, she mulled over the consequence she would impose on Ivan for violating the code of silence her NCOs were sworn to uphold. As much as she pitied him for the loss of his wife and daughter, it was vital that her leaders be circumspect. Otherwise, the militia's endeavors would fail. He would have additional chores, she decided. His Sunday leave would be revoked.

Luckily, his big mouth had caused no lasting harm, since Dr. Richardson—in spite of his disapproval—had promised to be circumspect. Still, it might be wise to advance the operation to an earlier date before Hendrix got wind of her intent.

The 31st of October—Halloween—fell on Thursday of next week. Hendrix was about to get tricked.

According to Toby's phone, the text from Ike Calhoun had arrived just before noon. As Toby was working outside without his jacket on, it went overlooked until sunset when he dashed up to the attic to change his shirt for Wednesday's supper. He had spent the day sawing and laying oak planks to replace the rotting ones on Dylan's porch. Swapping out his dusty T-shirt for a fresh one, he checked his cell phone on the off-chance that he'd received a message, and, lo and behold, he had.

Pipe is a match.

His heart seemed to stop as he stared at the cryptic phrase before resuming its beat with a heavy thud. A match? He stood there, struggling to grasp the ramifications for Dylan. What would happen to her now?

Withdrawing to the farthest corner of the attic where his voice was least likely to be overheard, he placed a furtive call to his team lead.

After two days of misery, Lt. Ashby still lay in his bed just under Toby's feet. Dylan, who'd arrived home early from work, was likely fussing over him right now. Tonight was supposed to be the night they reconnoitered the place where she hoped to ambush Hendrix, but those plans may have gone out the window with Terrence's illness. He sure as hell hoped they had.

Ike answered on the first ring. "Home plate."

"What's this mean?" Toby murmured, not bothering to encode his speech. Was the FBI en route to Dylan's compound, even now, all set to arrest her?

"It means the pipe found on her property came from the same manufacturer as the one used in the bombing. That's still not enough to implicate her."

Toby breathed a silent sigh of relief. "Why not?"

"Arco Iron Works produced hundreds of yards of that same piping last year."

"What about the surveillance pictures? Anything come up on the Datamark Environment?"

"Negative. None of the militia members are known terrorists."

Toby briefly closed his eyes. "Okay. Thanks." Thumbing the call to a close, he returned his phone to its hiding place. Without sufficient evidence to convict, the FBI wouldn't arrest Dylan, which meant she was still in the clear—for now. But what were the odds it was just a coincidence that the pipe found on her property and the one used to bomb Nolan's car came from the same manufacturer?

With doubt re-rooted in his mind, he went back downstairs for supper and saw that not only had the evening briefing been canceled, but Dylan was postponing her meal to stay by the XO's bed.

The four NCOs ate their burgers and beans in gloomy silence. Taking advantage of Dylan's absence, Toby decided to question Ackerman. "So, Ivan, I was talking to Captain Connelly the other day and she mentioned that the FBI found a pipe in the barn, and they seized it thinking it was evidence for something."

The table fell quiet, and four sets of eyes, including June Lee's, regarded him curiously.

Toby plowed ahead. "She has no idea where that pipe came from. You're the supply sergeant. Any thoughts?"

Ivan's deer-in-the-headlights stare immediately aroused Toby's suspicions. The man knew exactly what Toby was talking about.

"Well, yeah, I think so." Ackerman shrugged and looked down at his foot. "I found the pipe lying in her yard one day. Thought it might come in handy, so I stuck it in the shed."

"You sure about that?"

Ivan laid down his fork abruptly. "Sure I'm sure," he said, pushing back his chair and getting up for seconds.

Noting the others' curiosity—no doubt they wondered why Toby even cared, he let the subject drop. But Ackerman's guilty reaction raised more questions than answers. Where had the pipe really come from? Had Ivan planted it in the shed? Why the hell would he do that unless he was Nolan's killer?

"Captain's gotta be hungry by now," Morrison commented in a clear attempt to change the subject.

"I'll go relieve her so she can eat," Toby offered. Excusing himself, he rinsed his plate and dashed upstairs to check on Dylan. The first thing he saw when she answered his light knock was her bloodshot eyes.

"Your supper's waiting downstairs," he said, "I'll watch him for you while you eat."

"I'm not hungry."

He edged through the opening, lightly grabbed her by the arms, and forcibly but gently ejected her from the rom. "You need to keep up your strength, ma'am. The men are waiting for you. Go on."

She opened her mouth to protest then closed it with a snap. "Disinfect your hands," she ordered, whirling toward the stairs.

Rubbing hand-sanitizer into his hands, Toby sank into the armchair next to Ashby's bed to listen to the XO's uneasy snores. Doubts circled him like Indians surrounding a wagon train.

What if Ackerman had conspired *with* Dylan to target the Secretary of Defense? That would also explain his agitation when Toby brought up the FBI's investigation. Toby scrubbed his face with his clean hands. Why was he so reluctant to believe in Dylan's culpability?

Protect the Captain. Lt. Ashby's words played like a broken record in his mind. The Feds...they're trying to frame her for murder.

From Toby's perspective as a government agent, that was absolutely false. Why would the FBI intentionally frame her? They wouldn't. And yet their preconceived notions about her as detailed in her psychological profile may have predisposed them to believe in her guilt. Maybe that pipe was simply from the same manufacturer as the one used in the bomb, and the fact that Dylan had it on her property was pure coincidence.

Recalling the look of guilt on Ackerman's face, Toby tended to doubt that. Which meant that Dylan was either guilty or someone really was framing her.

Dylan forced herself to linger in the kitchen. Sharing words with the men, she assured them that they always had a home with her, regardless of Terrence's prognosis. After they'd eaten dessert and cleaned up, she put together a tray for her XO and carried it upstairs, hopeful that he'd at least take a bite. The pain meds had robbed him of an appetite, not to mention that they upset his stomach.

When she entered his room, she found Terrence sitting up in bed, chuckling over something Tobias had just told him. In her joy, she almost dropped her tray. "Look at you!" she exclaimed.

His crutch, now propped next to him, suggested he had used it to make his way to the bathroom. Tears of relief pressured her eyes as she quickly laid the tray aside and touched a hand to his forehead. His fever was gone. "You must be feeling better."

"I am better," Terrence insisted.

"The swelling responded to the Retrovir," she marveled, feeling a great weight lift off her shoulders. She sank weakly onto the end of the bed, grappling with her emotions, highly conscious of the peculiar way Tobias was looking at her—almost like he'd never seen her before.

Terrence picked a baby carrot off his plate and crunched it between his strong teeth. Pleased to see him eating, she ignored Tobias's scrutiny and kept her eyes on Terrence, who picked up his burger, took note of her rapt stare and said, "You two aren't going to sit here watching me all night, are you? I thought we had plans this evening to reconnoiter the area where we're grabbing Hendrix."

Dylan shook her head at him. "*You're* not going anywhere."

He shrugged. "Who says I intend to? Take Sergeant Burke with you."

Dylan continued to ignore Tobias. "I'm not leaving you alone tonight," she insisted.

Terrence took a bite out of his burger. "I'll be fine," he insisted around a mouthful. "Take Burke and go. The others will keep an eye on me."

Dylan glanced at Tobias, who was keeping unusually quiet. Leaving Terrence in his sickened state felt wrong. But then again, if Hendrix's abduction was going to take place next week, she had a lot to do by way of planning. The militia couldn't afford to be careless.

But did she dare venture out alone with Tobias, especially in her present vulnerable state? Perhaps some other NCO ought to tag along as chaperone. But Ackerman had already proven himself a liability, Morrison talked too much, and Chet Lee preferred spending his evenings with his wife. That left her and Tobias reconnoitering the countryside alone.

Her palms moistened at the prospect of him seeking to deepen intimacies between them.

Be honest, Dylan. You hope he will.

From the corner of her eye, she considered him as he pushed to his feet, arched his back and stretched. "I guess I'll get ready then."

Drawn to the message on his green T-shirt, she couldn't resist reading it.

ALL OPINIONS ARE WELCOME, BUT MINE'S THE ONLY ONE THAT COUNTS.

In this particular case, that much was true. She couldn't coordinate her plans for Hendrix without Tobias's input. If he made a move on her tonight, she would have to find the strength to resist him.

CHAPTER 9

"This is where we'll set up our road crew," Dylan explained, stopping the Suburban at the intersection of Route 20 and Rigby Road. The roads divided the dark countryside into the shape of a cross. This late in the evening, the land lay quilted in dusky shadows that clung to the memory of sunlight.

Milly panted in the back seat relieving the silence as Tobias frowned at the inverse cones of their headlights, saying nothing. He struck Dylan as distant and preoccupied. Her concern that he might try to seduce her seemed depressingly unlikely.

"John says his road crew will be filling potholes," she explained, hoping to rouse his enthusiasm. "You can see some right up there. Whenever cars pull up, he'll wave them through—all but Hendrix's gold Taurus, which he'll put behind a detour van. The van will lead him this way." Accelerating, she turned left onto Rigby Road. "Then one of John's trucks pulls out behind them and Hendrix is boxed in."

Out the corner of her eye, she saw Tobias fold his arms across his chest. She thought he might finally say something, but he didn't.

"I need you to tell me the best place to assault his vehicle," she reminded him. *She* wasn't the expert at ambushing; *he* was. And if he didn't start contributing soon, her plans would never be realized.

Rigby Road, even more rural than Route 20, was barely wide enough for two cars to pass. Deep ditches hemmed them in on either side. "With Ackerman's squad stopping traffic at the other end," she rambled on, hinting at her desire for feedback, "there shouldn't be any witnesses to what happens next. Very few people actually live down here."

The road curved to the right.

"Here," Tobias finally said, and she braked abruptly.

She described what would happen next. The assault team, wearing ski masks, would swarm out and surround Hendrix's car with weapons drawn.

"What if his door is locked?" Tobias's curt tone conveyed disapproval. "Then I'll have to break his window."

"Right." She hadn't thought of that.

"So much for no damaged property."

Ignoring his cynicism, Dylan reviewed the way they would cover the target's head with a sack, place him in the van, and drive him to Baker's. "What should we do with his car?" she inquired. "Take it all the way to Baker's place?"

"No. Park it somewhere out of sight, not far from here. You don't want leave tire tracks from Hendrix's car on Baker's property."

"True."

They found a deserted hunting track just up the road. Tobias lapsed back into silence, making Dylan want to demand what the hell his problem was. Except she didn't want to argue with him, not with her emotions so highly charged, her self-control so tenuous.

Two miles later, they turned down Baker's driveway. The dairy farmer sat on his porch smoking a cigar. Coming out into the yard to greet them, he saluted Dylan and offered Tobias a handshake. Patting Milly on the head, he led them all toward his cellar, accessed via doors at the foundation of the house.

Milly refused to descend the narrow stairs. Wading into the cold, musty cellar, Dylan could see why Milly was too spooked. Even blindfolded, Hendrix would sense the creepy atmosphere. If any basement was haunted, this would be the one.

Baker snapped on a naked light bulb and gestured to the metal pillar supporting the home's central crossbeam. "You can cuff him to that."

Envisioning Hendrix bound and gagged and whimpering in fear, Dylan reckoned this wouldn't be a lesson he would easily forget.

"Who's going to talk to him?"

Tobias's terse question canceled out her satisfaction.

"Obviously, you can't do it," he pointed out when she just looked at him. "He'll recognize your voice."

She had planned on letting Terrence have a go at him, since his voice was by far the most intimidating, but if Terrence wasn't up to it, then who?

Hendrix could identify Morrison and Ackerman, both former patients of his. Lee's voice was too soft-spoken. "I need you to do it," she realized out loud. When his jaw hardened, she quickly added, "I'll tell you exactly what to say. I'll even write it down for you."

Without another word, Tobias turned and exited the cellar, signaling his noncompliance. Mumbling an apology to Ron Baker, Dylan chased after him.

Tobias and Milly were both in the car by the time she jumped into the driver's seat and hauled on her seatbelt. Too unsettled to speak, she started the engine, backed up, and drove off Baker's property. At the first stop sign they approached, she braked abruptly and gripped the steering wheel, unable to withhold her thoughts. "If you have something to say to me, Sergeant Burke," she bit out, "then why don't you just say it?"

Milly whined. Toby opened his mouth to talk, snapped it shut again, and shook his head. "Not a good idea," he said.

"What is it, exactly, that you object to? If it's stamping out corruption, you joined the wrong militia."

"It's not that," he said flatly.

"Oh, really? I've seen your expression when we recite the *Defender's Creed*. What are you even doing here if you don't ascribe to our beliefs?" With emotions that were already raw, she braced herself for his answer.

Please, don't leave me.

"Look, I believe in a citizen's militia," he told her dully. "What you've done for the locals is all good. I've told you that."

"Then what haven't you told me?" He'd been holding something back. From the day they'd met, she'd sense that about him. The fear that he would abandon her now, with Terrence so ill, squeezed her chest making it hard to breathe. He'd been a breath of fresh air. How would she move forward without him?

He pinched the bridge of his nose. "I'm just wondering if you've really thought this thing with Hendrix through, that's all."

She'd mulled it over for months. "Of course I have."

"Have you?" He turned and frowned at her. "We're talking about a forced abduction with the use of firearms. That's two felonies, Dylan."

This again? "Not if the police are in on it," she reminded him. "Plus the weapons will be loaded with blanks. I told you, no one's getting hurt."

He gestured with a hand. "You can't guarantee that. How do you know one of your civilian soldiers won't bring his own ammo just for the thrill of it? How do you know Hendrix won't have a heart attack? Hell, he could even die down in Baker's basement, and then what?"

"That isn't going to happen!" she protested. In an effort to rein in her runaway temper, she jammed down the accelerator and peeled out of the intersection, heading for Route 20.

"You're a doctor," Tobias persisted. Now that she'd pried him open, he wouldn't shut up. "You know that stress can prompt a heart attack. Don't you see how quickly this plan could blow up in your face? And where will you be, if and when it does? You'll either be riddled with guilt for inadvertently killing him or sitting your ass in jail along with the rest of your followers."

A vision of Wesley Hendrix having a heart attack speared her with sudden doubt. He was a middle–aged male, not in the best physical condition. Stranger things had happened. Damn it, why was Tobias undermining her confidence when she'd been so certain this was the way to go?

"Doesn't that worry you?" he pressed.

Mostly it just pissed her off. She whipped her face in his direction. "You think I'm scared of going to jail?" she raged. "Do you really think I care about what happens to me?" The hoarse, stricken quality of her own voice made her clamp her mouth shut. She hadn't meant to reveal how flat, how meaningless her life was without *The Creed* to give it purpose. All of her hope for the future had ended on the day her boys were taken away. She had no right to be happy when they were dead. The militia life was just a charade, a game she played to give her life direction.

Whether she was imprisoned in the end made no difference.

Well, hell, Toby thought, recoiling at Dylan's words. If she held her freedom in such low regard, then maybe she *had* bombed Nolan's car. The evidence certainly pointed to her guilt.

But his gut refused to believe she'd killed anyone. In the fractured starlight that illuminated his surroundings, he could see tears sparkling in her eyes, suggesting that she did, in fact, care.

"Where does it end, Dylan?" he demanded as she drove like a bat out of hell through the countryside. "What if Hendrix refuses to change his ways? What will you do to him then—kill him?"

She cast a horrified look at him. "Of course not!"

"Who's next after Hendrix?" he persisted.

"I don't know. Whoever betrays the people they've sworn to protect!"

"And would that include elected officials pushing us toward war with Syria?"

Her knuckles shone white against the steering wheel. "So, you've heard about the FBI's suspicions. Is that what this is about? Why would I have bombed the Defense Secretary's car? That's ridiculous."

"I've read one of your anti-war essays. I saw it online. It's pretty obvious that you'd oppose a war with Syria." There. He'd revealed that hand of cards, at last.

She cast him a baffled look. "I don't know what you're talking about," she said on a half-hysterical note. "I've never written any anti-war essays."

"Find me a computer with Internet access and I'll

show them to you."

"I'm telling you, I never wrote anything like that!" she shouted, losing her cool completely.

Milly barked, scolding her for shouting.

Struck by her vehemence, Toby filed away Dylan's denial for later pondering. "Forget that. My point is where does this vigilante business end? How far up the food chain do you go?"

"What the hell does it matter?" Suddenly, the Suburban began to drift from one side of the road to the other, back and forth.

"Dylan, focus," Toby warned, as they crossed the yellow line.

She didn't even seem to notice that they were now driving in the oncoming lane.

With a quick push of his thumb, Toby shook off his seatbelt. But he was too slow. Even as he slid across the bench seat, the driver's side tire dropped onto the opposite shoulder. He grabbed the wheel, fighting to pull the vehicle back onto the pavement, but the back tire followed suit, and the six thousand pound SUV lumbered down into a ditch. In the back, Milly lost her footing as it lurched up the other side, heading straight toward a line of sumac trees.

"Shit," Toby cried, throwing a leg over Dylan's to stamp down on the brakes. The SUV swerved to a shuddering halt, just yards short of plowing into the tree trunks standing in their path.

The dog bounced off the rear seat and recovered.

Dylan roused with a gasp. "Oh, God!" she cried, staring at the trees in shock.

"You almost killed us," Toby stated, half angry with her, but mostly with himself.

She clapped both hands to her face. "I'm sorry. I'm so sorry!" she cried before bursting into tears.

"Shhh. It's okay." The excess of adrenaline dumped

into his bloodstream left his extremities tingling. "Here, trade places with me," he invited. Freeing her seatbelt, he hauled her up and over his lap before moving to take her place behind the wheel. Taking a moment to let his pulse settle, he threw an arm over Dylan's shoulders and pulled her gently against him.

"I'm sorry," she cried again.

"It's not your fault." He could see it clearly now. Once again, he'd pushed her too far.

For a long moment, they just sat there, breathing in and out and clearing their minds. Dylan finally wiped her face and sat up straight. "That's what you call an episode," she informed him.

"I know. I've been there, remember?" The words made him wince because they weren't exactly true. He'd never had PTSD as bad as hers was. "It's my fault. I shouldn't have grilled you like that. I just…I just want to know what makes you tick. What happened to you to make you think your future doesn't matter?"

Maybe he was unwise to pry, having pushed her too far already. She went perfectly still at his question, so still that he could hear the crickets chirping in the grass outside. "You don't have to talk about it if you don't want to," he quickly amended. "But if you think it would help to talk about it, I'd like to listen."

A cold sweat still enveloped Dylan from head to toe. Nausea roiled in her as she pictured how close she'd come to killing both of them, and the dog, too. The last thing she wanted to do, on top of the stress she was already feeling, was to relive the past. But having nearly dragged Tobias down with her tonight, she owed him an explanation as to why she lost it sometimes.

"I used to collect the fallen," she admitted,

smoothing the tremor in her voice. "That was my job with the 54th Quartermaster Company, which consisted of me, the commander, and four enlisted men—Staff Sergeant Ruiz, Sergeants Shroeder and Mackenzie, and Private Victor Giglio. Those were my boys," she explained, grief strangling her momentarily.

With dread, she peered into the past, praying it wouldn't suck her in again. "On December 8th of last year, we flew out to Korengal Valley. Four Marines had been killed on reconnaissance there. Terrence Ashby was our pilot, along with a co-pilot named Griggs. There'd been reports of insurgents in the area, so we were eager to collect the Marines and get back to camp."

She found her purse on the floor mat and set it on her lap. Pretending to fish out a tissue, she fingered her revolver to calm her jittering nerves. "Being protective of me, Staff Sergeant Ruiz told me to stay in the helicopter because of the threat. There were four of them and four fallen men; I wasn't needed on the field. So, I started to prep the cabin while they headed out with body bags. That was when the first IED exploded." She gasped as the memory of the percussion rippled through her.

Tobias squeezed her shoulder, keeping her in the present.

"I thought we were under attack, but we weren't," she continued. "The Taliban had rigged the bodies with explosives. When I looked outside, I saw that Mack and Schroeder were injured. The next thing I knew, I was outside, running through snow to get to them. It was Terrence who saved my life. He tackled me to the ground right as a second IED exploded, then a third and a fourth. The noise was deafening. Debris pummeled us. When I looked up, Giglio and Ruiz were dead. Terrence was writhing in pain, his anterior tibial artery severed by shrapnel, blood everywhere.

"Griggs helped us back into the chopper. We had orders to pull out at once. The insurgents had heard the explosions. They were coming back. We had to evacuate, leaving my boys behind."

She pressed the tissue to her leaking eyes. She hadn't shared so many details with anyone else—not the Army's investigative team, not even Dr. Richardson. It came as an unexpected relief to bring Tobias into her nightmare. "Eighteen hours later, the area was deemed secure. I walked out of the infirmary to join the second recovery team."

"Oh, Jesus," he whispered. "You went back."

She stiffened. "What was I supposed to do, let someone else pick them up?"

"No." He rubbed her arm absently. "No, I understand your reasons."

"I loved my boys. I should have died with them that night, but I didn't." There, she'd said it. "I brought them back to camp, and I fixed them up as best I could. Giglio and Ruiz had died right away—I could tell from their injuries. Mack and Shroeder might have lived if the Taliban hadn't riddled them with bullets."

"Fuckers," Toby growled, giving voice to her own thoughts.

The memory of trying to dignify their disfigured bodies brought on another wave of nausea. "I tried to make them look nice."

"Christ," Toby whispered. Crushing her against him, he pressed his lips to her temple.

There was nothing sexual about his touch. It was solace in its purest form, a balm to her wounded soul.

"I accompanied them all home, drove across the country to attend four funerals, to meet the families, offer my regrets."

He rocked her gently back and forth.

"That was it for me. I couldn't go back after that."

"Who the hell could have?" he countered.

"I never did fulfill my obligation to the Army for paying for medical school. But they agreed to forgive the debt, providing I worked at a VA Hospital after becoming a civilian."

"So, Uncle Sam has a benevolent side," he pointed out.

An aching, honest silence filled the SUV, broken only by the soft panting of the dog in the back.

Tobias suddenly tipped his head forward, catching her eye in the shadows.

"You know, you're story beats mine, hands down. It's honest-to-God the worst war story I've ever heard," he admitted.

She gave a humorless laugh.

"But, believe it or not, Dylan, your life is still worth living."

She closed her eyes in protest.

"Do you think your boys wanted you to die like that with them? Hell, no. That's why they left you in the chopper. They wanted you to be safe and live a long, happy life."

Only when Tobias was with her did she even remember what happiness felt like.

He heaved a sigh. "Tell me more about these boys of yours. I want to see them in my head."

Her eyes opened wide at the unexpected request. No one had ever asked her to talk about her boys—not even Dr. Richardson. With a poignant smile, she described each man's idiosyncrasies, weaknesses, and special talents, wrapping it up with Schroeder. "He was the one who kept us laughing when things got so gruesome we couldn't keep food down. He had a repertoire of gruesome jokes. Sometimes…without him around, I wonder if I've finally lost my mind," she admitted, baring her greatest fear.

Tobias shook his head. "No, you haven't."

She slanted him a weak smile. "You sure about that?"

He kept silent a minute. "What do you think your boys want from you?"

The question left her disoriented. "What do you mean?"

"I'm just wondering if you feel like you have to do something for them."

She searched his inscrutable expression. "Like what?"

"Well, like, do you head up the militia for them or for yourself?"

"For myself," she said decisively. "It's part of my therapy, learning to tolerate the sound of gunfire and to cope with stressful situations. It's also a family tradition. My father commanded the SAM in the early 90s, my grandfather before that."

"All the way back to John Brown?" His eyes glinted with humor.

"You know about that?"

"Morrison," he said.

"What about you?" she demanded. Here she was, baring her soul to Tobias while his motives remained murky. "Why'd you really join my militia? I want the truth this time."

He looked away, out into the darkness. "The truth?" he asked mildly.

"Yes."

A lengthy silence followed, raising her anxiety.

At last, he looked back at her. "Well, at first, I just wanted to relive my time in the service."

That was exactly what she'd thought.

"But now I'm here because I want to get to know you better."

Her heart flip-flopped and her eyes widened as he twisted in his seat to trace her jaw with a fingertip. Was he seriously coming on to her?

"You're an amazing woman, Dylan." He gazed deep into her eyes. "Don't let anyone tell you otherwise. Not even yourself," he added.

She licked her dry lips, wishing he would kiss her. "Okay," she agreed.

"You're going to live a meaningful and fulfilling life, you understand me? I know you miss your boys and you feel guilty that you're here and they're not."

A painful knot formed in her throat.

"But you need to put that behind you and start living your life to those guys."

As a tribute. Her heart felt suddenly too large for her chest. How noble that sounded. Maybe he was right. She'd been focused on the past for so long now—on her loss, her pain. But the present wasn't all about the past. It also included the future, where anything—anything—remained a possibility.

"I'll think about it," she agreed. Her eyes stung with tears she couldn't shed. Why hadn't anyone said these words to her before? "Thank you."

He laid a finger over her lips, silencing further words. "Don't ever thank me."

His abrupt change in tone made Dylan blink.

"Now—" he removed his arm from around her shoulder. "Put on your seatbelt, sister. Let's get you home so you can rest. No, no, this seatbelt," he said, showing her the one in the center of the seat, right next to him.

Content to be coddled, Dylan snapped herself in as she watched Tobias maneuver them skillfully away from the trees. He drove them through the ditch and back out onto the road. Exhaustion weighted her eyelids as they sped toward home.

"Close your eyes," he offered, and she tipped her head gratefully against his shoulder, stifling a yawn.

He hadn't kissed her tonight. And yet she felt more at peace with herself and with the future than she had in a long, long time.

Relying on road signs and his innate sense of direction, Toby made his way toward Dylan's farm, while replaying her tale of horror in his mind.

No wonder Terrence Ashby was so devoted to her. What she had done that night—going back to retrieve her boys, honoring them by escorting each man home, was nothing short of heroic. She had survived hell on earth. Little wonder she was stuck with PTSD.

Given all that she'd endured, it was a miracle she hadn't lost her mind completely. Maybe she had written those anti-war essays, maybe she hadn't. How could war be anything but an anathema to her? She had every reason for wanting Secretary Nolan dead, considering his determination to go to war. Except that Dylan would never, ever have blown him up, not after having seen what bombs did to the human body.

Dylan Connelly was many things, but a murderer she was not. He knew that now, just as surely as he knew his own blood type.

Then why did three anti-war articles with her name on them exist on an anti-government website? And why had the FBI found a length of pipe on her property matching that of the pipe used to bomb Nolan's car? A hair-raising possibility lodged itself like a splinter in his mind.

What if Terrence was only partially right, and it wasn't the FBI who was trying to frame Dylan but someone else?

As he coursed Dylan's driveway, the thought took root and sprouted into an ugly weed. Given her position as leader of a militia and her mental and emotional instability, she made an ideal scapegoat. A protective wave rolled through him.

To hell with finding evidence to prove Dylan's guilt. She was innocent. And only a coldhearted bastard would let her pay the cost of another man's crimes. If it was the last thing Toby did, he would find the coward responsible for the bombing and bring him to justice, clearing Dylan's name once and for all.

Considering everything she'd been through, it was the least he could do.

CHAPTER 10

The flames of a large bonfire leapt in the back yard, snaring Dylan's attention as she guided her Suburban into its usual parking spot. The long, grueling work week was over—with Wesley Hendrix none the wiser about what was coming down the pipe for him. The prospect of finally putting him in his place ought to be filling her with satisfaction. Instead, no thanks to Tobias Burke, now all she could think of was Hendrix having a heart attack.

Speak of the devil. There he was tossing a stick onto the fire, so handsome and vibrant that the pressures of her work and of the impending operation seemed to disappear at the sight of him. Scrambling out of her car, she hurried around the house to gauge what was going on.

She found her leaders sitting like Indian chiefs around the fire—each in his own folding chair. Sparks floated from the tips of the flames toward a periwinkle sky. Tobias looked up to intercept her wondering gaze. The slow smile he sent her made her skin feel prickly.

"At-ten-TION!" Terrence called, spying her

approach.

"Stay seated," she ordered, keeping the men in their seats while she greeted Milly. Rubbing the dog's ears, she absorbed the preparations made in her absence. The picnic table had been carted off the porch into the grass. June Lee had laid out paper plates, napkins, potato salad, and sauerkraut on it. A pan of polish sausages stood next to long skewers that were obviously meant to go in the fire. "What's all this?" she asked, consulting her mental calendar.

"Oktoberfest," Sergeant Morrison sang out.

"Wiener roast," Ackerman chimed in with enthusiasm.

Dylan waited for Tobias to say something. His crooked little smile told her this was his idea. None of her leaders had ever thought to have fun before he came along. Concealing her pleasure, she moved toward Terrence to assess his health.

"How are you feeling?" she asked, kneeling next to his chair.

"Very well."

His complexion still struck her as sallow, but the contentment on his face and the fact that he had made his way outdoors consoled her.

"This was Sergeant Burke's idea," Terrence added, confirming her guess.

"I'm glad he thought of it," she admitted, glancing at Tobias briefly. Ever since their close call on Wednesday night, his behavior seemed different. There was a softness, a tenderness in his regard that made her heart flutter and made her thoughts harken back to what he'd told her—that he'd returned to her militia to get to know her better. At the same time, he seemed to radiate an implacable determination. What was that about?

"Figured we could hold our briefing out here just as

easily as indoors," he remarked with a shrug. "Shouldn't let the mild weather go to waste." He gestured to the message on his yellow T-shirt: TIME IS PRECIOUS. WASTE IT WISELY.

Dylan chuckled. "The weather is mild," she agreed, realizing it was warm enough for them to sit outside without wearing jackets. She herself would never have considered something so spontaneous as to gather and eat outside. The sweet smell of burning wood—of sassafras and cedar—reminded her of hiking trips with her father. The stress that she had toted around all week slipped farther away.

"Well, then," she added brightly, "let's get the briefing over with so we can eat." Claiming the empty chair between Terrence and Tobias, she looked around at the men's expectant faces, all glowing in the firelight, and discovered she had no desire whatsoever to talk about Hendrix. But Saturday's CPX was now just forty-eight hours away, leaving her with little choice.

Diving in, she reviewed the plan in detail, adding that she would hand pick ten volunteers from the militia on Saturday, giving them first right of refusal. That way, each NCO would have three men assisting them in their contribution to the ambush. Sergeant Burke would get the fourth man. After the inspection and the march tomorrow, the NCOs could pull aside and train their volunteers for forty-five minutes each while the remaining soldiers practiced at the firing range, as usual.

"I'm sure you have questions," she added, having gone over the details quickly, "but I'll answer them tomorrow. Right now, I'm famished and I'd like to eat."

Whooping with enthusiasm, the men shot to their feet to snatch up skewers and sausages. Dylan called

June Lee outside to join them in the feast she had so thoughtfully assembled. They carried their plates to the fire, scooting their chairs close so they could roast their wieners as they started in on the potato salad and sauerkraut.

Tobias nudged Dylan's foot with his boot. "You slept in this morning," he commented with a teasing light in his dark eyes.

She had missed morning PT for the first time ever. Dylan pointed at Milly, whom Tobias had let into her room at midnight. Who'd have guessed that eighty pounds of Labrador in the bed could chase off her recurring nightmares? "It was Milly's fault," she insisted, spooning up her potato salad. "I couldn't hear the bugle over her snoring."

He sent her a slow smile. "You're welcome."

Chagrined by her lack of graciousness, Dylan added quickly, "I was going to thank you."

One dark eyebrow arched over the other. "Waiting for the proper place and time?" he asked quietly.

The implication that he'd like to be thanked with a kiss flustered her into breaking eye contact. Desire cascaded through her veins to pool in her belly. As she grilled her dinner, she reconsidered her circumstances. If Toby had returned to get to know her better, then keeping him at arm's length might be all it took for him to leave again. Yielding to their attraction, on the other hand, might just get him to stay.

Her insecurities protested. Deepening her reliance on Tobias while Terrence was succumbing to his illness would surely be a foolish measure. If Tobias left her when Terrence finally passed, how would she cope?

And yet, to rebuff Tobias meant depriving herself of his company when she craved it above all else. She should invite him to her bed. A slow-moving heat blazed through her at the enticing thought.

"There's only one thing missing with this food."

Sergeant Morrison's muttered comment dragged Dylan's attention from her inner tug-of-war to the conversation taking place on the other side of the fire pit.

"Beer?" Sergeant Lee guessed with a guilty glance at Dylan.

Morrison nodded dolefully. "I'd give my right arm for a can of Miller Light right about now."

"Or a bottle of Yards pale ale," Tobias suggested.

"Amstel's better than all of 'em," Sergeant Ackerman insisted.

"What's wrong with hard apple cider?" Dylan interjected, becoming the object of five pairs of eyes.

"You got some?" asked Sergeant Morrison hopefully.

"Possibly, if it's still any good. It's been fermenting for three years now."

"Let's try it," Ackerman enthused.

"I'll be right back." Excusing herself, Dylan slipped into the house through the back door. In the kitchen, she dug around in the cavernous pantry before finding what she was looking for: a case of the hard cider her parents used to bottle and sell, most likely still good, thanks to its original potency. Blowing the dust off two bottles, she carried them outside, poured the cider into plastic cups and distributed them.

"To the leaders of this militia," Tobias called out as he accepted his cup. "To Captain Connelly and Lieutenant Ashby."

"Hear, hear!" chorused the other NCOs.

Dylan caught Terrence's dark gaze and lifted her glass to him. A rush of gratitude to Tobias for making her XO feel honored had her blinking tears back as she tipped the cup against her lips. Cider, sweet and heady, filled her mouth and warmed a path down her throat. "Not bad," she murmured, pleased that it had kept its quality for so long.

"Not bad?" Morrison smacked his lips. "It's the best I've tasted."

"I'd drink this over beer any day, ma'am," Sergeant Lee concurred.

Dylan glanced at Tobias for his reaction. He had taken a sip and was frowning at the amber liquid in his glass. "Your parents bottled this?"

"Yes."

"Here at this orchard?"

"Of course."

He lifted a quizzical gaze and asked, "Why don't you harvest the apples anymore?"

Dylan searched herself. "It's a lot of work for one person."

His eyes trekked over the others. "You're not exactly alone," he pointed out.

Taking a second sip, she considered his point. "I'd have to start all over," she demurred. "The machinery was broken down and hauled away when my father died. My mother couldn't handle the harvest on her own."

Terrence shrugged his broad shoulders. "So you invest in new machinery," he said in his deep and certain voice. "It's bound to be more efficient and cost-effective than the old stuff, anyway."

"Heck, if you could bottle cider like this, you'd be pulling in a profit in no time," Morrison predicted. "I'd like to be a part of that venture."

"So would I," said Ackerman.

"You can count me in," Chet Lee agreed.

Clearly, the alcohol was going straight to their

heads. "Farming is a tough business," she insisted, recalling all the hours in her childhood that she'd devoted to working in the orchard.

"Something to keep in mind, though, down the road," Terrence insisted.

Dylan tucked the possibility away for future consideration. Who knew what she would do with herself after…after Terrence died?

Tobias leaned toward Dylan's ear, preventing her emotions from taking a dive. "I think I saw an old guitar up in the attic. Mind if I go get it?" he inquired.

She turned her head to assess his seriousness. The guitar he referred to had been her father's. "I don't know if the strings are any good."

"I think they are," he said, with confidence that implied that he'd already ascertained as much.

She shrugged her compliance. "Go ahead and fetch it." She knew he could sing. How well could he play?

A few minutes later, firelight gleamed on the lacquered surface of the acoustic guitar as Tobias strummed it softly. He'd taken the time to dust it off. The sky became a star-spangled dome, and Tobias Burke was strumming tunes that her father used to play on the car radio when he took her on his house calls to neighboring farms. His velvety baritone stirred her admiration and drew compliments from the others as he started singing classic rock songs.

He paused to appeal to the others. "Come on, you guys. Sing it with me."

In one raucous voice, they joined him in the chorus.

Dylan added her own voice, surprised to find the words still remarkably intact in some dusty corner of her mind.

They came to the refrain, belting out lyrics about what it meant to be American, drinking whiskey like today might be your last.

The chilling reminder of death blew Dylan's thoughts briefly back in time. Her boys used to sing like this in the MACP—only they sang country music, not rock. The past started to bleed into the present, but the sound of her father's guitar brought back the happy years of her youth, keeping her PTSD at bay.

"Here's another classic," Tobias announced, in the mesmerizing voice of a performer. The chords of a Beatles song rippled off the six-string.

With every passing minute, Dylan relaxed deeper into her chair, content to listen. The lyrics about a deep, cold winter being thawed by the spring's sun, resonated somewhere deep inside her. The worst was now behind her; hope and happiness lay before.

When that song ended, he announced a song by Bruce Springsteen, brought the volume to an intense thrum, and stared into the fire as he crooned out the tale of a young man desperate to posses the girl next door. The message of simmering lust made Dylan's heart beat faster.

By the song's end, she had made up her mind. Tobias Burke might not hang around forever. At any time, he could pack up and leave taking his warmth and smile with him, and there was nothing she could do about it. But if she just took a chance, then she would have a memory of them together that she could keep forever.

Tonight, she would give herself to him.

Toby had just laid his head on his pillow when the door at the bottom of the attic stairs opened and closed quietly. He'd been the last one to shower, the last soul in the house still awake at quarter to eleven. But someone was creeping up the attic steps and, given the daintiness of the ascending footfalls, he could guess who it was.

Blood rushed straight to his groin, propelled by a rush of anticipation that overruled his conscience. Knowing Dylan was innocent, there wasn't any need to seduce her, other than his own throbbing desire to claim her for himself.

His mouth turned dry as her burnished head crested the floorboards. Wearing her silky night robe, her hair loose and tumbling over her shoulders, she looked nothing like the tense militia leader he had met on Columbus Day nearly two weeks ago. He sat up slowly.

"I hope I didn't wake you," she whispered.

"Not at all."

"Milly was hogging the bed, so I thought I'd try sleeping here, with you."

Sure, right. They were going to sleep.

Reaching out, he deliberately tugged the sash at her waist causing the two halves of the robe to part. The exposed swathe of creamy beneath let him know she wasn't wearing anything else. To his delight, she shrugged her shoulders and the robe skimmed down her body to pool at her feet, taking all of the air from his lungs with it.

"Should I leave?" she asked.

"Hell, no." He jerked down the zipper of his bed roll and tossed back the corner. "Come on in."

The contrast of her cool, silky skin as she squirmed in next to him brought a groan to his lips.

"You sure about this?" A vision of her curled up in the dollhouse flitted through his mind. Was he preying on her vulnerability?

"I'm sure." Full breasts pillowed his chest as she looped an arm over his shoulders.

"What happened to forbidding me to kiss you ever again or even speak to you without company present?"

"I figured we broke half of those rules last night; might as well break the other half."

He grinned at her logic. "Works for me."

Her sweet breath touched his face before she pressed her lips fervently to his, communicating her explicit desire that he take everything she had to offer. Not only did it silence his doubts for good, but sent blood roaring past his eardrums. Conceding to her unspoken orders, he stroked his tongue deep into her mouth and kissed her thoroughly.

The impulse to ravish her rode him like a world-class bull rider. He'd wanted her for so long now; it would be so easy to plunge ahead. But while she wasn't exactly virginal, his instincts assured him that her sexual experience was limited. And considering the certainty that one day, soon, she would regret having given herself to him, the least he could do was show her as much consideration as he could muster.

Tearing his lips from her sweet, untutored mouth, he nuzzled the shell of her ear. He lathed the hollow behind it with his tongue, scraped his teeth lightly down the swan-like length of her neck toward her collar bone. Levering himself up and over her, he invited her to scoot into the center of the bedroll, where moonlight fell across her breasts like a sheer, silvery scarf, illuminating the pale globes and the rosy tips of her puckered nipples. *Fucking beautiful.*

He bent his head, nuzzling her impossibly soft skin. His day-old bristles made her gasp and catch his face in her hands. Circling her nipples with his tongue, he delighted in their velvety texture and the way they puckered and extended as he blew cool air across the moist peaks.

Dylan's spine arched. With a soft moan, she spread her thighs, opening up to him like an evening primrose. He dragged his mouth over the curve of her ribs, across the plane of her belly to her naval, pausing to foreshadow his intent by swirling his tongue around it.

She squirmed, her skin already hot to the touch. Digging her nails into his shoulders, her body language conveyed both trepidation and excitement.

"It's all right," he whispered. "Just relax, sweetheart."

With a shuddering exhalation, she released the tension in her body. As her thighs went lax, he settled between them, sweeping his palms up her runner's legs, from her ankles to her inner thighs. He took his time familiarizing himself with her contours, brushing his stubbly jaw through the crisp curls of her woman's hair. Her fresh-linen scent could not disguise the perfume of her arousal.

"Tobias!" she gasped.

He speared his tongue between the plump swells determined to wring every ounce of pleasure possible from her. Her hips jerked upward. Cupping her tight buns in his hands, he circled her silken folds with his tongue then centered his assault on the knot there until she whimpered softly. On target, he thought with an inward smile.

Dylan fought to keep her moans of pleasure from carrying through the floorboards to the rooms below. Never, *never* in her entire life had she experienced the sensations Tobias was unleashing. Goosebumps ridged every inch of her skin. She was certain he could feel them against his palms which cradled her cheeks, lifting her against his hot, wicked mouth as if she were a feast and he a king, determined to enjoy a full-course meal.

He stabbed his tongue into her opening, and her inner muscles convulsed, greedy for more. He flicked the nub of her clitoris and the world spun off its axis. Any second now, she would climax helplessly, but that wasn't what she wanted.

"Stop," she cried, grateful when he actually paused to raise his dark head.

"Take me now," she commanded, her heart pounding with the enormity of her request. "Now," she repeated, sinking her fingers into his short hair and tugging his resisting body up and over hers.

His larger form loomed over her, and the moonlight frosted his chiseled features and powerful upper body. Trepidation trickled through her. Could she do this? If she wanted a memory to carry with her into the future, then yes, she could.

Delving her hands beneath the waistband of his boxer-briefs, she encircled his erection with a shaking hand. "It's been years," she heard herself admit.

He nodded, seemingly incapable of speech as she slid her hand lower to cup the soft sac below.

"I'm not on the pill or anything," she tacked on, appalled that she hadn't considered that earlier.

Her words seemed to shake him from a trance. "I have a condom." He groped for his duffel bag and pulled one out. Tearing into it, he sat back to cover himself while she watched, expectant but somewhat apprehensive.

When he once more covered her body, his sex hung hot and heavy against her thigh. Their breaths merged. Dylan braced herself to receive him as he fitted his powerful frame against her softer one, guiding himself to her opening. He kissed her, pressing gently into her tightness. Suddenly, he drew back to send her a thoughtful look.

"What?" Was there something wrong with her?

"Let's do this a different way," he suggested. "You on top."

"Me?" Doubt shot through her.

"That way you'll be in charge." He eased off her, rolling to one side as they traded places.

Worried she'd make a fool of herself, Dylan settled over him, straddling his hips. He pulled her to him, flinging the sleeping bag back over them to cloak them in warmth. She could feel his heart thudding swift and strong beneath her breasts. Cupping her face in his hands, he kissed her leisurely. The seductive dance of his tongue rekindled her mindless yearning. With gentle hands, he urged her to sink slowly down on his tumescence.

Dylan's senses clamored as she took him, one inch at a time until—just as she doubted her capacity to take anymore—their hips collided. Now, they were completely joined. She shuddered in amazement and with fulfillment. *Tobias is a part of me now.*

Through heavy-lidded eyes, she studied his reaction. A sheen of sweat glistened on the thickly muscled contours of his torso. His eyelids looked heavy, his jaw tight. An impulse to drive them both to madness had her rocking her hips frantically now, in a feverish mission to burn up into a bright ball of flame.

"Please," she gasped, wanting more, though she couldn't possibly handle it.

But then his clever thumb sought and found the center of her pleasure, and there it was, the treasure she was looking for. All it took was the barest friction to send her flying over the precipice.

Biting back her cry of rapture, she rode his bucking hips through a soul-shattering climax. Tobias gave a growl of repletion and bowed beneath. As he slowly stilled, she collapsed against him, every muscle in her body spent.

A minute passed as they caught their breaths, as their heartbeats slowed to a more restful tempo.

Tobias recovered first, tucking in his chin to study her face in the dark. Dylan rested her head on her forearms and absorbed the satisfaction glimmering in the ocean depths of his irises.

"You okay?" he asked. His obvious satisfaction gave way to uncertainty—she'd never seen him look uncertain.

She queried the languorous warmth spreading through her. "I'm good." She would have to be a poet or an artist to describe the fulfillment she'd just experienced, and she was neither.

His small smile held just enough wickedness in it to assure her that he was good, too. "Next time, I'm on top," he promised.

The implication that he intended and expected to have her again—at his mercy next time—wasn't lost on her. Her pulse quickened at the sensual warning.

"I'm up for that," she retorted breezily.

"I'm sure you are, but I won't be for a while. Besides, it's late, and you need all the rest you can get."

His practical words prompted a pang of rejection. "Are you kicking me out of your bedroll?" she asked in disbelief.

"It's for your own good," he assured her. "If you stay here, neither one of us is going to get a lick of sleep, I can promise you that. Tomorrow's the CPX. You need your rest."

She didn't want to think about the CPX and all the drilling that was still required to ensure that Thursday's operation went according to plan. If anything, she suffered an impulsive urge to scrap her plans for Hendrix entirely, but, of course, she couldn't. She had set events into motion, and now she had to see them through.

"Fine," she grumbled, her annoyed tone bringing

out a chuckle.

Scrounging for willpower, she separated their still-joined bodies, and felt immediately empty.

"Dylan." He clamped a gentle hand on her thigh as she reached for her robe. "If it makes you feel better, next time we do this, it'll be in your bed, and you can throw me out."

The thought of him in her bed, taking her every which way to Sunday, made her shiver with anticipation. "If you behave, I might actually invite you," she quipped with a saucy smile.

His answering grin flashed in the dark. "You know I have a hard time behaving."

"Uh-huh." Threading her arms through the sleeves of her robe, she tied it primly around her waist. Then she dropped a lingering kiss on his lips, before pushing to her feet. Tobias obviously didn't realize that endorphins were still spilling into every cell of her body, making her anything but tired. She could make love to him all night, but he had obviously not picked up on that.

"Goodnight," she whispered, turning toward the stairs. A smile tugged at her mouth as she returned to her room.

Now, that was an experience she would *never* forget or regret.

CHAPTER 11

The Indian Summer continued into the next day, making the CPX a warm and sultry one. The exercise unfolded as it always did—first the inspection, then the march, then shooting practice. Halfway through it, the NCOs took turns up at the house training the volunteers on mission-specific tasks. Training on site would have been preferable to the mock-up in the yard with John's trucks and Chet Lee's car serving as Hendrix's car. But activity of this sort on Rigby Road on a Saturday morning would certainly have drawn attention.

Shading her eyes against the sun, Dylan watched Tobias work with the assault group. The smell of trampled grass and dry leaves surrounded her as she watched the soldiers exit the van and truck and descend on what was supposed to be Hendrix's vehicle. Tobias ordered them to move faster. He was timing them.

A light breeze ruffled the leaves of the large elm tree. The fluttering sound made her recall what Tobias had told her about John Denver's music. *You can hear it in the breeze.* She really could. Back in her youth, she'd spent much of her time outdoors, feeling at-one with nature. The war had robbed her of that satisfaction, but now it seemed to be back. After months of feeling, tasting, and seeing nothing, her senses seemed to have come awake overnight. Thanks to Tobias and the magic they had shared last night.

Focus, Dylan. If the mission on Thursday went awry, she'd never forgive herself. But try as she might, plotting Hendrix's humiliation brought far less satisfaction than pondering when and where she and Tobias would find time alone together. His broad shoulders, his encouraging voice and the heat that flared in his eyes whenever their eyes met kept her in the moment, and more alive than she'd been in months.

At noon, the civilian soldiers packed up their possessions and their lunches and departed, leaving the compound strangely quiet but littered with napkins and wrappings. Dylan and her NCOs tidied up the yard together.

She had just chased down a napkin that was blowing across the grass when she looked up to find Terrence limping toward her. "Let's take the rest of the day off," he suggested.

Dylan's mouth dropped open. The garbage sack in her left hand hit the ground. "I don't think I've ever heard you say those words," she marveled.

He nodded and thinned his lips. "Time's running out for me. I've got a bucket list."

Guilt banded her rib cage. "Of course." Here, she was so preoccupied with her own desires that she'd pushed Terrence's imminent demise to the farthest recesses of her mind. "What would you like to do? Just name it. Parasailing? Swimming with the dolphins?"

"Bowling," he said, loudly enough for the others to

hear.

They glanced over, their faces alight with the prospect of doing something new.

"Bowling," Dylan repeated, dubiously.

"I used to be a championship bowler," Terrence confessed. "There's a bowling alley right in town."

Dylan saw Tobias glance at his watch. "The sooner the better, so we can beat the evening crowd," he called out.

Sensing a conspiracy, Dylan looked back at her XO. He'd gotten through the CPX without appearing fatigued or in pain. "Are you sure you're up to it, Terrence?"

"I'm sure," he said.

Dylan sighed. "Very well, but we're taking two cars in case you need to come back early. Can you drive your car, Sergeant Lee? That way June can join us."

He beamed at her. "Yes, ma'am."

Dylan swept an eye over the yard. Only one napkin still lay amidst the fallen leaves. Her doubts over the impending operation were forgotten as a tingle of enthusiasm buoyed her spirits. She crossed to the trash bin and tossed the bag inside. "What are we waiting for?"

An hour later, they were lacing up their bowling shoes and testing out bowling balls. The scent of pizza and beer wafted from the refreshment counter. A few zealous bowlers had beaten them to the alley. Balls rumbled down lanes and scattered pins with loud crashes.

Tobias leaned toward her ear to shout, "Who says you have to go to a shooting range to hear loud noises?"

She searched his inscrutable expression. Was this the new therapy for her PTSD?

In the middle of the first game, he asked permission

to buy a pitcher of beer. "For all of us," he explained.

Dylan glanced at the hopeful looks on her leaders' faces. "Just one pitcher," she allowed.

Tobias dismissed himself briefly then poured drinks all around. They each drank half a glass as they finished the first game. Tobias proved a formidable bowler. Only Terrence led him consistently by several points. "You're really good, Terrence," Dylan told her XO.

"Used to be excellent," he replied, collapsing in a chair and rubbing the spot where his prosthesis attached to his leg.

Dylan emerged from the first game with a moderate score and a strained wrist from using too heavy of a ball. "I don't know if I can play again," she demurred as they prepared to start a second game.

"I'm out, too," Terrence called on a note of defeat.

Dylan swiveled toward him. Reading pain in the set of his jaw, she kicked herself for not noticing earlier. "I'll take you home," she offered ignoring the others' disappointment.

"We just started," Ackerman whined.

After a brief protest, Terrence gave in to her insistence. While he struggled to put on his own shoes, she went to return their bowling equipment. Out of the corner of her eye, she saw Terrence start to stand, saw the blood drain from his face. With a cry of alarm, she rushed toward him, but Tobias was already there, catching him from falling and bolstering him up.

Dylan reached them in under a second.

"I'm fine," Terrence insisted. Beads of sweat glimmered on his brow. "Just worn out is all."

"Can you walk?"

His dark eyes slid from her worried face to Tobias's grim one. "I don't know," he muttered with humiliation.

"I'll go back with you," Tobias offered. He shot Dylan a challenging look even as he toed off his bowling shoes.

Ten minutes later, they were back in the Suburban returning to the farmhouse. Terrence mumbled an apology and Dylan tersely cut him off. An odd tension charged the interior of the SUV as she sped toward home. Mixed emotions roiled in her.

Had she really thought she could enjoy a carefree evening, like she wasn't any different from anyone else her age? She'd forgotten how to relax, how to have fun. And soon she would lose the one person who'd been to hell and back with her, who understood the trauma she'd endured because he'd been by her side through it all. How was she supposed to get on with her life when the past continually dragged her down?

She wished Tobias could just sweep her away from it all—the way he'd swept away her nightmares by giving her Milly to sleep with. If anyone could teach her how to play, how to have fun again, Tobias could.

Milly greeted them at the door as they entered, Tobias on one side of Terrence and Dylan on the other. Together, they helped him up to the bathroom and then to his bed. To Dylan's surprise, he promptly kicked her out.

"I told you, I'm just tired. I'm taking my pills and going to sleep."

Tobias had already left the house to walk Milly. Dylan closed Terrence's door and crossed through the quiet upper level to her bathroom, where she showered and washed her hair.

Brushing her teeth minutes later, she assessed her wide-eyed reflection in the mirror.

Who am I?

The militia leader who had looked back at her for six months looked different, somehow. She pictured herself as someone else—the owner of an apple orchard.

The house seemed so quiet without the other NCOs around. Was Tobias back yet? She strained her ears for the sound of him up in the attic. Hanging up her damp towel, she slipped on her nightshirt and left the bathroom intending to read in bed. The sight of him half-sitting, half-lying across her bed, shirtless and shoeless, his hands clasped behind his head in a posture of supreme male confidence, drew her up short.

"Took you long enough," he drawled as she stood there gaping at him.

"Does Terrence know you're in here?" she whispered, aghast.

"He's snoring so loudly that his door is shaking."

"Oh." The realization that they were, for all intents and purposes, very much alone and in her bedroom took her by storm, making her head spin and her heart race.

"Come closer," Tobias commanded, holding her gaze captive as she took tentative steps toward the bed. Without warning, he rolled to his feet, grabbed her around the waist, and tossed her onto the center of the mattress, flat on her back, before coming down on top of her.

Dylan stifled a squeal of laughter.

"All day long I wondered if I'd ever get time alone with you."

The suspicion that he'd choreographed the evening's events entered her thoughts briefly even as she thrilled at his confession. At least she wasn't the only one obsessing. "We still need to be discreet," she warned.

"So no screaming," he agreed, his eyes dancing like waves on the ocean. He tickled her ribs, eliciting a gasp and a choking sound as she fought not to laugh.

"Stop it!" She slapped his hand away. "You play dirty."

"I know I do. Want to see?"

Breathing fast, biting her lower lip, she felt like she was standing on a precipice about to throw herself over it. "Yes," she daringly replied.

In the next instant, he was kissing her with primal passion, stealing her breath away and making his intent so clear that she moaned and arched toward the hard length of his body. He nudged her knees apart, swept a hand up under her nightshirt, and pushed it higher and higher until he exposed her heaving breasts.

Fastening his mouth on one taut peak, and then the other, he sucked and licked and gently bit the tingling nubs until she thought she'd go out of her mind with want. She dug her nails into his back, raked her fingers through his hair and thrashed helplessly beneath him.

She'd known it would be like this—like a mad reckless ride on a powerful stallion.

Tearing his mouth from her breasts, he nipped and grazed his way toward the epicenter of her quaking body. His skilled tongue lapped and lathed, spiking her pleasure to new heights. At the same time, he reached up and pinched a nipple and that was all it took for Dylan to climax, helpless beneath his teasing onslaught.

But he gave her no reprieve. Her inner muscles were still convulsing with aftershocks of pleasure when he released the zipper on his jeans, pushed them past his hips and buried himself in one smooth stroke inside her. Covering her mouth, he caught the animal cry that issued from her mouth into his. Kissing her deeply, he retreated and filled her again.

Dylan closed her eyes, riding the storm with abandonment. It was just as she'd imagined—even better. Words she'd never dreamed of saying trembled on the tip of her tongue. If he weren't ravishing her mouth, she might have said them out loud.

Tobias lifted his head without warning. His entire body stiffened and he withdrew from her suddenly.

"What?" she cried, crashing back to reality.

"My fault," he huffed, grinning like a kid. "Got carried away and forgot about protection."

Groaning because she'd also forgotten, Dylan watched him extract a condom from his back pocket. He flipped over and jackknifed, shucking off his jeans and boxers in one athletic movement. His erection, jutting upward, beckoned her touch. Dylan stretched out a hand and stroked him, causing him to still with an indrawn breath. Squirming closer, she looked to him for permission.

"Oh, hell, yeah," he told her.

With a smile for his gusto, she lowered her head, traced the smooth head of his sex with her tongue. The salty-sweet taste of her own arousal excited her. With a muttered curse, he gathered her hair in his hands and watched her treat him like a Popsicle.

"Better stop," he growled after a minute. "Lie back." Twisting onto his side, he wrestled her to the mattress, so that she lay on her back. "Behave," he said, sheathing himself with the condom.

Her own husky laughter echoed in her ears, reminding her of something from her distant past.

Tobias's eyes crinkled at the corners but his expression was a picture of mock seriousness as he looked over at her. "Now, remember. No screaming. Make a sound and I'll spank you."

She tingled at the threat. "Sure you will."

"You want to find out?" He hooked one of her legs in the crook of his arm, tipping her hips up to receive his possession.

Possession. There was no other word for it, Dylan reflected as he surged into her.

He pistoned his hips, riding her with such intent that she had to bite her lip to keep from uttering unladylike encouragement. In spite of her efforts, a word broke from her lips.

He stilled in amazement. "God *damn* you are hot," he commented.

"Don't use God's name in vain," she scolded.

"You're right. Sorry." He withdrew from her suddenly, prompting a gasp of regret. "Oh, don't worry," he said, shifting his weight. "We're not nearly done yet."

Goosebumps rippled up the backs of her thighs.

"Up on your knees," he instructed. "Face the headboard."

Following his directions, she was rewarded by the feel of his hands on her waist, his magical lips on her shoulders. Kissing the sprinkling of freckles there, he nuzzled her neck until she hummed in pleasure.

"Hands here and here," he said, lifting them to the top of the mahogany headboard, placing them well apart. "How old is this bed?"

She could scarcely think. "Like a hundred years." Her heart galloped with anticipation.

"Hope we don't break it." He scooted up behind her. The hair on his chest tickled her back. She arched her spine, inviting him nearer, turning her head to send him a pleading look.

He slanted his mouth across hers in the same instant that he entered her. The bed creaked as their bodies came together. The headboard groaned as they pushed and pulled in a mindless quest to get deeper, closer. Dylan wished herself nowhere else in the world but where she was, being claimed by the one man who'd brought her back to life.

Their joining became feverish, desperate. The headboard clanked.

Tobias released one of her hands to reach between her thighs. As he had the other night, he brought her quickly to crisis. His sensual touch, paired with his hips ramming her from behind, hurtled her into an unprecedented climax. His final retreat and plunge seemed to wring pleasure from her very soul.

The first sound she made when she could catch her breath again was a sob. They collapsed onto the pillows in a tangle of limbs. Tobias lifted his head so he could search her face. "What's wrong, baby?" he asked, as tears blurred her vision.

The endearment only magnified the feeling that she'd just been reborn.

"Nothing." She shook her head, afraid that if she said another word she would start weeping and not be able to stop.

She'd never considered herself a sentimental person. Anger and fear—those were her bosom companions. Those were the emotions she grappled with on a daily basis, not tenderness or wonder or this terrifying sense of fragility. Fresh tears brimmed in her eyes, embarrassing her by leaking out to slide down her face.

"Hey," he crooned as he carefully separated their lower bodies, sweeping aside the used condom. He rolled her toward him, so that they lay face-to-face, sharing the same pillow. "I didn't hurt you, did I?" He gathered her protectively against him.

She shook her head vehemently. "No. It's not that." But she couldn't have said what it was.

His expression struck her as uncharacteristically grave, almost…tortured.

"I'm fine," she assured him.

A moment of silence fell between them, an opportunity for words to be spoken, if she knew what to say.

Tobias was the first to break it. "I want you to know something."

"What?" Her imagination caught fire.

"I've never known anyone like you," he said, straight-faced.

Her heart trembled, but she sought to make light of his remark. "Really? And you've been with—" she shrugged, "hundreds of women, so that's really saying something, huh?" she teased.

"Dozens," he corrected with a leer. "But, yes, that is saying something."

Dylan broke eye contact lest the happy glow inside her became too apparent. A man like Tobias would run the other way if he felt in the least bit smothered. The thought of him leaving gutted her.

"So," she said, desperate to change the subject, "do you think we woke up Terrence with the ruckus we made?"

Tobias grimaced. "I think I might have ruined your reputation, Captain."

Her face flooded with heat. "I don't think he'd mind too much," she assured him. "He doesn't show it, but I think he likes you."

"I like him, too," Tobias admitted, lowering his gaze. "He's a good guy."

A lump swelled in Dylan's throat giving rise to fresh tears. She blinked them back.

"How much longer does he have?"

She regarded him in amazement. "You never tiptoe

around forbidden topics, do you?"

"Don't see the point," he said with a shrug. "How long?"

She swallowed hard. "I don't know. A month, maybe a little more, maybe less."

Tobias's jaw jumped. "Okay," he said sadly.

The sound of the front door thumping shut and the thud of footfalls in the entryway made them freeze. Milly pushed up off the floor and looked at the door. Dylan tightened her hold on Tobias.

"Sleep with me tonight," she whispered, risking rejection by baring her need for him. "As long as you're the first one up, which you always are, who's going to know?" she reasoned.

"Tomorrow's church," he retorted with a devilish smile. "If I stay here tonight, you're going to have a lot to repent for."

Her extremities tingled at the sensual warning. She lifted her lips to his. "You promise?" she whispered.

"Swear." He squeezed her backside. "Let me get rid of this condom and I'll be right back."

With a sigh of contentment, she let him go.

Toby stepped into the adjoining bathroom and quietly shut the door. He took a look around. Dylan's bathroom was all porcelain fixtures and outdated floral wallpaper. It smelled like her—like clean linen. Avoiding his reflection in the mirror, he dropped the used condom into the toilet, flushed it and ran a washcloth under hot water. He didn't have to see the look on his face to know that something profound had just happened.

He'd become deeply emotionally involved with the FBI's top suspect in the Nolan murder. *Way to go, bro.* Using the washcloth, he wiped himself clean.

In his own defense, he hadn't been able to help

himself. Dylan was a one-of-a-kind woman, a truly unique and complicated soul. She'd intrigued him from the start. Whatever she did or said seemed to touch him somewhere deep down, in a place where he'd never been touched before. No woman—suspect or otherwise—had *ever* made him feel this way.

If he thought about why that might be true, it would send him into some dark, tortuous maze from which he would emerge with his thoughts completely tangled. The best thing to do was not to think at all, but just clap on blinders and get back into the bed with Dylan, letting himself enjoy more mind-blowing, spine-tingling sensations without over-analyzing them.

He rinsed out the towel, dried his hands, and went to do just that.

CHAPTER 12

———— ◆ ————

A muffled voice announcing that the metro train had stopped in West Falls Church roused Toby from a sound sleep. Milly was licking his hand, trying to tell him something. It took him a minute to recollect where he was and what he was doing. And then he realized they'd arrived at their destination, and she was telling him to get off. Toby leapt to his feet, snatched up his duffle bag, and headed for the open doors with Milly fighting to keep up.

The cold air on the outdoor platform brought him more sharply awake. As he urged Milly to climb the unmoving escalator, Toby reconsidered his upcoming meeting with the Taskforce lead. What could he say to convince Ike that Dylan was being framed when all evidence suggested otherwise? If the culprit responsible for the bombing succeeded in framing her, then—God forbid—Dylan might disappear into some prison or hospital somewhere, never to emerge again.

Every cell in his body rebelled at the thought. He simply couldn't let that happen.

Crossing the covered walkway spanning the tracks, he emerged on the other side, only to be assailed by the sense that he was being watched—the same as last week.

He scanned the area, seeing nothing but a quiet drop-off zone and a virtually empty parking garage, all standing under a damp, cloud-covered sky. What the hell was going on? He couldn't see a soul paying any attention to him, so why was his sixth sense jangling?

Remaining vigilant, he waved one of the three taxis out of the queue, ordered Milly into the back seat, and dove in after her. He supplied the driver with the address to the NCTC and sat back, keeping an eye on every window for signs of a tail.

Great Falls Street, which became a four-lane highway, conveyed only a few cars toward McLean this Sunday morning. The handful of drivers appeared to be headed to and from church. Glancing over his shoulder, Toby noticed a taxi pacing them at a distance. It followed them two and a half miles, all the way to the turn-off to the NCTC, only to continue past when Toby's taxi turned in.

"This is good." Toby paid the driver and got out at the head of Tysons-McLean Drive. He stood a moment on the shoulder, shivering in the cold, waiting to see if the taxi retraced its route and came back. When it didn't, he shrugged and walked up the short, curved road to the National Counterterrorism Center.

As with the previous week, analysts inside the Operations Center greeted Milly, ignoring Toby, as they passed along the back of the room toward the elevators. Toby hit the button for the second floor and checked his watch. Today, he was five minutes early. Dylan had trained him well.

Regardless of his timely arrival, the Taskforce lead and Special Agents Maddox and Hamilton had *still* managed to beat him to the boardroom. All three looked up from the long table as Toby pushed his way inside. "Morning," he called, unable to summon a smile.

Jackson's astute gaze didn't waver. His old friend couldn't tell just by looking at Toby that he was sleeping in Dylan's bed, could he?

"Have a seat," Ike said, nodding at the chair that Toby had occupied the previous week. "We were just reviewing a report forwarded to us by the Department of Cyberspace. At their request, the Russians surrendered satellite images of Dylan Connelly's Suburban parked one block from the site where Secretary Nolan's car exploded."

Toby's stomach dropped. How could that be? "How can they tell for certain that it's her car?"

Ike Calhoun leaned back in his own seat and raised a silver eyebrow at him. "The rear fender is bent. The images don't lie."

"That doesn't mean she drove it there. People close to her have access to the keys," Toby insisted, though he'd never seen anyone but Dylan drive her vehicle. He'd intended to lay the groundwork for his suspicions first, not toss them out there right away, but Ike had put him on the defensive. "I think she's being framed," he blurted unceremoniously.

When a weighty silence followed his declaration, Toby sucked in a deep breath and plowed ahead. "Think about the pipe found on her property," he said. "According to the supply sergeant, it was lying in the yard one day and he just stuck it in the shed, thinking it could come in handy later. If you consider the number of civilian soldiers who drop by on a weekly basis, any one of them could have tossed the pipe out the window of his car. Plus, there's something else that doesn't add up. Dylan denies ever having written any anti-war essays, and I believe she's telling the truth."

The team lead's eyes narrowed. "Are you sure her memory is intact?"

Anger flickered in Toby briefly. "There's nothing wrong with her memory," he said through his teeth. "She's emotionally damaged from a tragedy she witnessed and took part in, but she's not insane."

Ike's measuring look informed Toby that he'd taken note of his defensive tone. He glanced at Jackson. "Make a note to research her essays further. We ought to be able to pull up a domain name that tells us where those essays were uploaded." He looked back at Toby. "Who would frame her?" he demanded.

Toby exhaled. At least Ike seemed to be considering his theory. "Anyone who wants to avert suspicion. The militia already has an anti-government reputation. Add to that Dylan's emotional instability, and you've got yourself a readymade suspect."

Not even a glimmer of Calhoun's private thoughts showed in his expression. "Any idea who you might be talking about?" he paraphrased.

Is he mocking me? Toby deliberately held his gaze. "No, sir. Have you researched the priest?"

Calhoun looked pointedly at Jackson, who thumbed through his notes and said, "Arthur Alan Nesbit, born in 1943 left seminary in 1968 to serve as an Army chaplain. He worked in mobile hospitals in the Vietnam War for the next five years, during which time he earned two purple hearts for valor under fire." Jackson glanced up. "Looks like he came by his anti-war sentiment honestly. I asked several former parishioners if they thought him capable of killing for his beliefs, and they all said no. There's nothing in his record to suggest otherwise—no history of arrests, no protest marches, no bombing of abortion clinics, nothing of any radical nature whatsoever."

Toby wasn't so sure. Sitting in church that morning next to a sleepy Dylan, he had listened to Nesbit preach a sermon on grace while letting his imagination run amok. The only good thing about Nesbit *not* being a suspect was that Dylan adored the man. It would be a true blow to learn that the priest was using her to conceal his actions.

Almost as bad as finding out that the man sleeping in her bed was, in fact, a federal agent, noted the voice of his conscience.

Ike caught his eye. "Director Bloomberg wants to make the arrest," he announced.

Toby's heart stopped beating. "What? No." He shook his head.

"He thinks the evidence is sufficient to convict her."

Toby pictured Dylan's reaction to finding herself under arrest for a crime she didn't commit. Something like that might send her off the deep end. "Give me one more week," he implored. "Let me find out who would frame her like this. I swear to you, someone with a political agenda is hiding behind her militia."

An uncomfortable silence fell over the table. Ike broke eye contact to consider the report under his hand. He drummed his fingertips on the tabletop. "We'll take a vote," he decided. "Who's for giving Burke another week?"

Jackson Maddox and TJ Hamilton both raised their hands. Ike's eyebrows climbed, but he shrugged in acceptance of being overruled. "All right," he said, shutting the folder of the latest report and freeing Toby to breathe again. "You've got one week."

Despite his relief, Toby's stomach remained knotted. If he couldn't prove Dylan's innocence, she would be arrested and sent to trial. God knew how she'd handle something that traumatic.

Half an hour later, he exited the mammoth building with a heavy step. As if in response to his worsening mood, the sky had darkened and was now spitting cold flecks of rain. A gust of wind had him pulling up the collar of his army jacket as he led Milly past the clanging flagpole toward the parking lot. His gaze locked in disbelief on a man sitting on one of the cement blocks in front of the building. Recognizing the hawk-like features of the Sheriff of Harpers Ferry, Toby's blood abruptly thinned.

The sheriff caught sight of him, stood, and headed directly toward him. Toby slowed his step. He felt suddenly like prey.

Oh, shit.

Cal Fallon approached with his hands in his pockets and a snarl on his scarred lip. For several seconds, they assessed each other in electrical silence.

"You followed me," Toby accused.

"You lied to us, you son of a bitch," Fallon said at the same time.

Envisioning the entire investigation swirling down the drain, not to mention Dylan's deep disillusionment when she learned from the sheriff who Sergeant Burke really was, Toby opted to be fully honest with the lawman. "You need to know that Dylan Connelly is a suspect in the Defense Secretary's murder."

Fallon's expression grew thunderous. "Tell me something I don't know. But if you think Dylan's a murderer, then you don't know her like we do."

"Relax," Toby countered. "I *know* she didn't do that. Unfortunately, there's evidence that suggests otherwise." He glanced around, relieved to find that they were still alone.

"What kind of evidence?" Fallon demanded.

"That's classified. The bottom line is if I can't figure out who is framing her, she's going to face trial for a crime she didn't commit."

The scar on Fallon's lip turned bone white. "Who would frame her?" he demanded.

"I was hoping you'd know that." Briefly, Toby considered whether the sheriff himself might be the culprit. At the moment, he didn't have much choice about including the man in his investigation. "Look, someone's using Dylan to cover up their own agenda, and I can't protect her unless I'm on the inside. Please. I need you to protect my identity. She'll discover the truth sooner or later." He quailed at the thought. "You don't need to be the one to destroy her faith in me."

Steely gray eyes drilled into Toby's. "All right." Fallon folded his arms across his chest. "I'll keep your business to myself for now." His eyes narrowed. "But if you Feds try to pin a crime on her that she didn't commit, I swear to God, you'll wish you never crossed my path. I will raise holy hell on national television. I will personally ruin you for fucking up her life any more than it's already fucked up."

Clint Eastwood in *Dirty Harry* had nothing on this guy. Toby felt a grin coming. "I'll hold you to that, Sheriff," he replied. Noticing the taxi lurking at the far side of the lot he asked, "Is that your ride?"

Fallon followed his gaze. "Yep."

"Do you have an hour or two? I'd like to pick your brain some. How about lunch?"

Fallon looked like he'd rather dine with the devil than with him.

"You know better than I do who Dylan's enemies are," Toby explained.

Fallon's mouth curled with scorn. "Good luck there, son. Pretty much every filthy politician and legislator despises her."

"Maybe together we can whittle down the list.

Finding the culprit may be our only way to keep her out of jail."

At the mention of jail, Fallon seemed to blanch. "Fine," he muttered, waving at the distant taxi. As it started slowly toward them, he added, "Just so I make this clear, I'm doing this for Dylan, whose father was a well-respected man in our town. I don't like Feds and I never will."

Toby had to hold back a smile. "I appreciate your candidness," he replied. He'd take honesty like Fallon's over the backstabbing habits of government agents any day.

"Why, Dylan!" Father Nesbit's face lit up with pleasure as he opened his kitchen door. She stood on the stoop of the rectory in a cold drizzle. "Come in, please. What brings you to my humble abode in such inclement weather?"

Dylan slipped into his warm kitchen with relief. The familiar smells of chamomile tea and burnt toast assailed her nostrils. "I'm picking up Sergeant Burke at the station at seventeen thirty," she said, shaking out of her army-issue trench coat. "I thought I'd drop by and visit you first."

"I'm so glad you did," he insisted, taking her coat and draping it over a chair. "Let me make you some tea."

"No, that's okay. I don't have much time. I'd rather just talk."

His brow creased with concern. "Well, of course, my dear. Take a seat, then."

They sat across from each other at his scarred dinette table, where he laid a blue-veined hand over her chilled fingers. "Something's bothering you. What is it, my child?"

Dylan averted her gaze. Her throat tightened and her

stomach churned. Discussing her inner life had never been easy; it was harder still when there was a man involved.

"Something's changed," she said, speaking quickly to keep her emotions from overtaking her words. "Sergeant Burke joined my militia, and things have been different ever since."

The priest sent her a searching look. "Different good or different bad?" he asked.

"Good." She drew a bracing breath. "Wonderful, in fact," she added, flicking him a look to gauge whether he grasped what she was saying.

His expression of dismay hit her like the rain that started pelting the window over the sink.

Dylan tugged her hand free and fisted it in her lap. "I know Tobias seems aloof and skeptical in church," she added, making excuses for him, "but outside of church, I assure you, he is warm and helpful and *very* capable. He puts a humorous spin on everything." She smiled as she thought about his T-shirts. "When he's around, I find that I'm not living in the past anymore."

"That's wonderful," Nesbit said, but his tone lacked full conviction.

Dylan tried again. Her parents were dead. This man was her last connection to them and to the wisdom they might have imparted if they'd lived longer. "I've begun to question whether I should lead the militia any longer," she confessed.

Bushy gray eyebrows rose toward Nesbit's sparse hairline. "Go on," he encouraged.

Dylan sighed. She realized it was his blessing that she craved. "I nominated myself for a leadership position because I needed a reason to live, and the militia gave me that. Plus, supposedly, all that gunfire and the public protests raise my anxiety threshold."

He nodded his understanding. "Those were all good

reasons."

"But now I picture myself doing other things—like tending the orchard, perhaps, and harvesting apples the way my parents did."

To her relief, his blue eyes crinkled with delight. "I think that's a grand idea." He beamed at her.

"You do?"

"I do. Your parents would be so pleased."

Her eyes stung with relief. "Thank you."

"As for this young man you speak so highly of..."

She held her breath, waiting for the other shoe to drop.

"Just be careful," he advised. "Move slowly. Don't do anything too rash, dear Dylan. Remember that your heart is still terribly vulnerable."

His words filled her with childlike fear. "Yes, father."

She wished she'd sought out his counsel sooner, though she wasn't sure it would have made any difference. She'd been drawn to Tobias as recklessly as a moth was drawn to flame. Having already invited him into her bed, it was too late to be careful now, even knowing that she relied on him for her present happiness.

What would happen if he didn't return on the train tonight? That was still a very real concern—though after the passionate kiss he'd stolen in secret after church, that was hard to envision.

"You're right." Her hoarse reply was scarcely audible as the rain outside drummed the building. Still, the familiar whistle of the incoming train, sharp and clear, managed to pierce the sounds of the downpour. "That's him arriving now." She stood up abruptly. "Thank you for speaking to me, father."

He popped up and reached for her coat. "Any time, my child. Any time at all." He helped her to put it on.

Dylan stepped from the cozy kitchen into a chilly deluge. Icy droplets hit her scalp and raced down her neck into the collar of her coat, making her shiver as she negotiated the treacherous steps to the street below.

By the time she rushed into the station, the passengers were already stepping from the cars. Tobias stood on the platform, holding his duffle bag and Milly's leash, clearly searching for her. His contagious smile widened as he caught sight of her. The impact of his intelligent gaze made her knees tremble as she approached him. Her spiraling joy had her fixing her attention on the dog.

Too late, father, she thought, bending to greet Milly first. With a dose of dismay, she realized she'd fallen irrevocably in love.

"You look more like a movie star than a militia leader."

Tobias's compliment startled her attention upward. It took her several seconds to recollect that she'd worn a skirt and applied makeup for the first time in months, in the hopes that he'd say something just like that. She felt herself blushing.

"Thank you. And aren't you remarkably sober," she retorted with a smirk.

He pretended to flinch. "Ouch."

Out of the corner of her eye, she spied Sheriff Fallon hustling from the train to the parking area, just like last week. "All set?" she inquired briskly. Spinning on the balls of her pumps, she marched ahead of Tobias, through the small station toward the exit.

Before she could push out into the rain, he caught her by the arm and spun her back into his embrace. The arm banding her waist kept her plastered against him, where his enticing scent and familiar heat rushed into her senses, undermining her determination to remain strong, invulnerable.

"Not in public," she protested, noting that his gaze was focused on her mouth. Her traitorous body, relishing the solid feel of him, tingled in anticipation.

"It's no secret that we're seeing each other, Dylan," he remarked.

She drew back slightly. "What?"

"Thanks to Corbin, the park ranger, everyone knows. You don't have to be stand-offish."

"I am not stand-offish," she protested. She'd been trying to take her priest's advice and distance herself a little.

"Angry, then."

"I am not angry!"

"Good because you're kind of scary when you're angry." Laughter sparkled in his navy eyes. "I think it's the red hair."

Dylan felt the corners of her mouth wobble. He'd managed to undermine her distancing efforts in just seconds. And now all she wanted to do was be alone with him in some very private place—the consequences be damned.

Through the glass-paned doors, she peered at the Suburban standing in the pouring rain. "On the count of three?" she suggested.

They counted together. "One, two, three!"

Despite the mad dash through the downpour, they managed to get soaked. At last, Milly was stowed in the rear and they were seated up front with the heat blasting, shivering and grinning at each other.

"Well, that went well," Tobias remarked, shaking water droplets from his hair. "If it were warmer outside I'd make you dance in the rain with me."

A vision of them dancing in a summer downpour with their clothes plastered to their bodies filled her with yearning. Would he still be a part of her life by summertime? The odds were slim, in her opinion. All she had was here and now.

Determined to make the most of it and to keep whatever part of him she could, she reached out and seized his wet jacket, while sliding to the center of the bench seat. "Make love to me," she commanded, cringing slightly as the L-word passed through her lips.

He bestowed a kiss so blistering that it curled her toes and made her throw a leg over his thighs. Then he lifted his head abruptly. "Slow down, there, Captain," he rasped.

Holding her face in his hands, he smoothed back the wet tendrils sticking to her cheeks. For a breathless moment, he studied her face in the semi-darkness. The train in the station gave a prolonged hiss and a brief whistle. Then it rumbled away.

Dylan tried and failed to fathom Tobias's expression. "Make love to me," she reiterated with slightly less assurance this time.

"Oh, I will," he promised. "Just not here. If you find a deserted road on the way home, I won't protest."

Needing no more motivation to start driving, Dylan pulled away, sliding back behind the wheel to tug on the gear shift and started driving. She knew just the place for a stolen moment.

By the time she nosed the Suburban down the rutted track leading to an abandoned farmstead, she was trembling with expectancy, her panties as wet as the rest of her. In the midst of a dark pasture, with heavy raindrops making music on the roof of the car, she braked, doused the lights, but kept the motor running in order to heat the vehicle.

Tobias unbuttoned her damp blouse, unhooked her bra and slid a hand up under her skirt. "I've never seen you in a skirt before," he said, breathing hard. "You should wear them all the time to show off your gorgeous legs." He drew her panties slowly down them.

Dylan's chilled skin grew feverish at the compliment. "It's hard to lead a militia in a skirt," she replied.

"So drop the militia," he quipped.

Of course, he had no idea she was already considering doing just that, but with his blessing, the idea seemed to have more merit than ever.

With rising anticipation, she freed the erection straining against his zipper, rolled up on her knees, hiked her skirt, and sat in his lap. As she kissed him, she funneled her hands under his long-sleeved shirt, loving the warmth and breadth of his furred chest. Pushing Father Nesbit's advice to the back of her mind, she tipped her hips so that that the head of his sex nestled her opening. The need to feel him deep inside her goaded her to sheathe him in one desperate stroke. Tobias's gave a helpless groan. Crushing his lips to hers, he kissed her deeply.

"Tobias," she cried against his mouth. Rolling her hips, she rode him with abandonment, unable to get enough.

I love you. I never thought I'd love anyone or anything again. But I love you.

Through a fog of passion, Toby remembered the condom in his wallet. *Son of a bitch.*

"Have to stop a minute, sweetheart," he protested hoarsely. God knew he didn't want to stop. It felt like heaven what she was doing to him. Her ass cheeks filled his palms like cool, velvety globes, and every time she ground her hips against his, she engulfed him in tight heat and catapulted him closer to heaven. But it was bad enough that he couldn't tell her who he was; he didn't need to impregnate her on top of everything else.

"Stop." He caught her by the waist, lifting her reluctantly off him. "Just give me a second."

Straining to reach the pocket of his jeans, he found what he was looking for, tore it open with his teeth and started to cover himself. Dylan finished the job for him, her touch sure and delicate. He wondered how he'd ever imagined those tender fingers building a pipe bomb.

"Hey," he said, catching her against him as she assumed her dominating stance.

"What?"

Even in the dark, her hair shone like a fire's embers. Her lips glistened, moist and swollen from his kisses. She looked so aroused and so beautiful that he wanted to kill the motherfucker using her to cover up his own twisted agenda.

"I'm here for you," he said, wishing he could simply be candid with her, striving to say something, anything that would reduce the blow she was bound to experience when she found out who he really was.

"For how long?" she demanded, gripping his shoulders. Her short, blunt nails dug into his deltoids.

His heart ached to offer her assurance. But as long as she was still a suspect, as long as he was working undercover, that confession would have to wait. "As long as you need me," he swore.

With a whimper of what sounded like relief, she crushed her lips to his while guiding him back into her silky warmth. She proceeded to love him with all the depth of feeling he knew she kept locked inside for fear of being hurt.

Her head fell back and her full breasts, dangling like ripe fruit before him, enticed him to suckle her beaded nipples.

His climax started out as a simmer that bubbled harder and harder until it flashed to a boil. Just when he feared he would spill over prematurely, Dylan gave a keening cry and drove herself down on him, consuming him so completely that he came close to blacking out. *Christ.*

She fell limply against his chest, where he could feel her heart thudding out the same frantic tempo as his was. Their torsos, damp with sweat, stuck together.

He wrapped his arms around her and held her tenderly. Emotion closed a noose around his throat.

I'm so screwed, he thought. I am so fucking screwed.

Dylan sank into the plush chair in Dr. Richardson's office and regarded his kind, overworked face with relief. The doubts and uncertainties that had been building in her all week needed an outlet, and Dr. Richardson provided a listening ear.

"I saw you at church on Sunday," he remarked, collapsing into the chair adjacent to hers. "Did that nod you sent me mean that you left your pistol at home?"

"Yes, it did," she answered.

"Good for you."

Her momentary pride immediately evaporated. "But I'm still bringing it to work," she admitted.

He grimaced at the short-lived victory and ran his fingers through his already-mussed hair. "Ah, well. It's still progress." Hazel eyes contemplated her for several seconds through the lenses of his glasses. "You look different today," commented with a quizzical air. "I can't put my finger on it."

She felt different, like she'd been given a whole

new lease on life. *I'm in love.* Only, she couldn't just come out and say that. For one thing, it compromised her professionalism. For another, he would likely only pity her or, even more likely, caution her as Father Nesbit had.

"Have you reconsidered your plans for Hendrix, perhaps?" he asked hopefully.

Dylan blinked at the reminder that Wesley Hendrix's abduction was scheduled to occur in exactly forty-eight hours. In fact, she'd given so little thought to the impending operation that it came as a shock to realize how fast that time was approaching.

Cancel it, urged an inner voice. The desire to do just that flickered like a stubborn little flame inside her. She argued against it: *Hendrix deserves to be punished and humiliated.* But Tobias's disapproval of her use of psychological force carried weight. She didn't want him leaving her militia in disgust.

"I'm thinking about it," she admitted. "Actually, there's something else I want to discuss."

"Of course." He looked intrigued. "What is it?"

Dylan drew a deep breath. "Remember how you encouraged me to lead the militia, saying it would mitigate my PTSD?"

"Yes, I do, and I would say that it has helped tremendously."

"It has," she agreed. "It put me into tense situations that resolved peacefully, and that has definitely lowered my anxiety threshold."

Dr. Richardson gave a deep nod. "That's the beauty of Prolonged Exposure Therapy. It works."

"Yes, it does. In fact, it's worked so well that I don't feel like I need the militia to give me a sense of purpose, anymore."

The psychiatrist's expression turned quizzical. "Well, that's wonderful, Dylan."

"I'm actually considering other pastimes."

He blinked several times. "Such as?"

"Well, like tending the orchard the way my parents did, selling apples and bottling cider."

The crease on Richardson's forehead deepened. "Are you thinking of abandoning the militia altogether?"

The word *abandoning* pricked her conscience. Aside from leaving the Army, which she'd only joined because they'd paid for her medical degree, she'd never abandoned any project in her life.

"Not necessarily, but elections are coming up for next spring, and I thought, perhaps, I'd remove my name from the roster and let someone else lead. I know I wouldn't be very effective without Terrence, and I'm not sure…" Momentary grief strangled her voice box. "I'm not sure he'll survive the winter."

Richardson heaved a sad sigh. "Is he declining that rapidly?"

"He's rallied lately," she replied, swallowing the knot in her throat. "But I don't know how long that'll last."

"It sounds as though you've come to better terms with his illness, at least," Richardson noted in his raspy voice.

That was only because Tobias distracted her from her loss and pain. "Perhaps," she conceded. "So what do you think about my stepping down?"

The psychiatrist stroked his chin, and a far-away look entered his eyes. "When are the elections?"

"In December," she told him.

The crease reappeared on his forehead. "Change is a tricky thing, Dylan," he mused. "If it isn't accomplished in increments, it can cause a relapse." He eyed her with concern. "You wouldn't want to lose all the ground you've covered."

Considering what a mess she'd been a year ago, Dylan shook her head. "No, of course not. I just wonder if I've outlived my usefulness as a leader, that's all."

"You're a wonderful leader. I'm sure you haven't outlived your usefulness." He cocked his head to one side. "Something must have prompted this desire to spread your wings and test the air. What could it be? Do you know?"

Dylan gnawed her lower lip and weighed the wisdom of bringing up Tobias. Her private and self-reliant nature balked at mentioning him at all. What they shared was still a secret in her mind—despite Tobias's teasing assurance that the whole town already knew.

Dr. Richardson's hazel eyes glinted. "It wouldn't have anything to do with a certain sergeant I saw sitting next to you in church, would it? I hear you've become quite an item."

Dylan's breath caught. Had the rumors spread all the way from Harpers Ferry to Martinsburg, twenty miles away? More likely Ivan Ackerman, whose session came immediately before hers, had brought the gossip here directly. Annoyance and then chagrin pinched Dylan's cheeks. She had thought she and Tobias were being discreet. Evidently not.

The doctor sat back, looking thoughtful. "It's all right, Dylan. You're entitled to happiness, and I can see that this man makes you happy." But he sounded more perturbed than pleased by her romantic relationship.

Dylan glanced at her watch, eager to get home and spend time with Tobias and Milly. Dismissing the thought that, one day, she might be bawling right here in this office in the wake of their abandonment, she started to collect her things. "I suppose I should get going."

Minutes later, she left her counselor's office, confused as to whether she was making progress or not. Through the glass doors at the end of the hall, she spied Ivan on the stoop smoking a cigarette. He noticed her coming and quickly snuffed it out.

"Since when did you start smoking?" she demanded, pushing through the door to scold him.

"I just bummed one." He hung his head in that cowed manner of his that made her regret her sharp tongue.

"Don't let me catch you at it again," she warned. She gestured toward the Suburban. "Let's go."

She was just about to back out of her parking space when the devil himself, Dr. Wesley Hendrix, stepped out of the hospital building en route to his own car. As always, just the sight of him stirred her indignation. The angle of his blond head communicated arrogance. As he headed for his car, his haughty gaze scanned the parking lot and intercepted Dylan's narrow-eyed glare. He sent her a disdainful smile.

Just wait, she thought, gripping the steering wheel so hard her knuckles ached. In forty-eight hours he would realize he was just as helpless as the trusting veterans who came to him for healing and walked away with prescriptions for drugs that hadn't been adequately tested. Whether they lost their hair, gained or lost weight, or got sick to their stomachs didn't seem to matter to Hendrix, so long as the perks from pharmaceuticals kept coming.

If I don't put an end to it, who will? Dylan asked herself.

In spite of Tobias's disapproval, she had to go through with her plans.

CHAPTER 13

———————◆———————

Toby turned his head on the pillow and studied Dylan's profile in the dark. The light of a waxing moon shone upon her closed eyelids, but the uneven rise and fall of her breasts beneath the blanket betrayed restless thoughts.

"What's on your mind, beautiful?" he asked her.

Her eyes flew open and she turned her head to look back at him. "How'd you know I wasn't sleeping?"

"Because you snore when you sleep."

"I do not!"

"Shhh." He covered her mouth with a hand even as he chuckled at her indignation. God, it was fun to tease her.

She was the one who insisted that they had to keep their voices low, the same way they had to keep the bed from squeaking, all to maintain the pretense that they weren't sleeping together. Toby let her think that the others remained clueless, but because he worked day in and day out with the men, Toby knew that *they* knew. Still, Dylan had her pride and he respected that.

"What's keeping you awake?" he asked, removing his hand.

She gnawed on her lower lip, the one he couldn't stop kissing because he loved the curve and shape of it.

"Is it your plans for Hendrix?" he pressed. "Because, if I were in your shoes, I'd be having second thoughts."

She heaved a sigh, then squirmed onto her side to face him. "Yes," she admitted. "Do you think we've covered all the bases?"

"Not by a long shot. But I have an idea." He came up on one elbow. "And I want to run it by you."

"What kind of idea?"

"Cal Fallon and I crossed paths on the train last Sunday."

She blinked. "Yes, I saw him get off at the station right after you."

"He and I talked about dealing with Hendrix, just the two of us alone, so that you and the militia wouldn't have to get involved."

"Seriously?"

Was that wonder or resentment coloring her tone? "Dylan, we both think you could get into trouble seeing as how the Feds are already watching you. At the same time, Hendrix deserves to be taught a lesson. What if Fallon and I took care of that for you?" He held his breath, awaiting her reaction.

"How would you do that?" Her remote tone gave him no indication as to which side of the coin she'd land on.

"Cal said he could get his deputies to set up a routine traffic stop on a busy road. When Hendrix got in line behind the other cars, we'd jump in wearing masks and make him drive to a remote location where we'd read him the riot act."

Her eyes grew shiny. "You'd do that for me?" she asked softly.

The question, spoken with gratitude, made him squirm. "Of course."

"Why?"

Was she fishing for a declaration of his feelings for her? "To protect you," he whispered, tracing the delicate outline of her jaw with his thumb. If she were caught kidnapping, Ike might renege on his offer to give Toby more time, and Toby needed all the time he could get to find out who was framing her.

"From whom?" she asked, puzzled.

If he knew that, he'd be sleeping like a baby right now. Any one of Dylan's many enemies might be framing her. But he couldn't afford to reveal how much he knew about the FBI's investigation, so he teased her, instead. "Well, from yourself, of course."

She play-punched him in the ribs, and he grabbed her wrists, rendering them useless. "See what I mean? You're dangerous." He pinned her beneath him, pressing her down into the mattress. "Please say you'll let us help, Dylan," he begged. "It'd make me feel better."

Her furrowed brow betrayed mixed feelings. "What will our volunteers soldiers think if I cancel the op?"

"Who cares what they think?" he retorted. "Making Hendrix pay for his sins is the objective, right?"

She stiffened at his terminology. "I'd rather he just changed his ways but, yes, I guess." She drew a deep breath and let it out again. "Fine. Okay, I'll let you and Fallon handle him."

"Seriously?" He grinned at her in relief.

"Just promise me you'll scare the crap out of him."

"I promise. I've got plenty of experience along those lines," he assured her.

"And you'll tell him exactly what I want you to say."

"Down to the word," he assured her.

"Thank you," she whispered on a note so gracious and naïve that concern bit into him as he brushed her hair from her face and gathered her into his tender embrace. Unless he found out who was hiding his political agenda behind her militia, she wouldn't be thanking him again—that was for sure.

Dylan entered the cafeteria at the medical center with a healthier appetite than usual. Grabbing up a tray, she pushed it briskly along the narrow counter, selecting a tuna salad and a dish of peach cobbler from the offerings. A quick glance around the large room showed it to be scantily populated. She'd been so busy all morning that her lunch break had been pushed back to mid-afternoon. Everyone else had eaten—everyone but Doctor Richardson, whom she spied at a table next to the window, finishing his lunch.

Sending him a nod, she took a seat at a table nearby and started eating. She was just digging into her tuna salad when the faint odor of cigarette smoke had her looking up to find Dr. Richardson easing into the chair across from hers. "Late lunch?" he inquired, clearly just dropping by for small talk.

"Yes, I'm famished." She used that excuse to take another bite.

"It's been a busy morning," he observed. For a while he watched her eat, and she wondered when he would get around to bringing up Hendrix.

"I don't suppose you've reconsidered your plans?" he asked with an apologetic smile.

Dylan glanced about to make certain no one else could overhear. "Actually, I have," she admitted.

His dark eyebrows shot up. "You have?" He sagged back into his chair with visible relief.

"A couple of my men will handle the matter

discretely," she explained.

"Oh." He appeared briefly disappointed before offering a shrug of acceptance. "Well, as long as you're not directly involved, that should keep you out of trouble," he observed. "All the same, it wouldn't hurt to stay at work where the nurses and staff can vouch for your presence. That way, if Hendrix takes his suspicions to the director, you'll have a solid alibi."

It had been a while since she'd reviewed her patients' records, which she liked to do from time to time, so why not? Besides, what would she do at home but wait for Tobias to get back so she could quiz him? "I'll think about it," she promised.

"Please do. And wish me luck tonight." Kevin Richardson grimaced as he pushed to his feet. "I'll be chaperoning my niece's Halloween party."

"Are you dressing up?"

"Oh, yes. My brother's loaning me his big bad wolf costume to scare off the teenage boys."

Envisioning Kevin as the big bad wolf, Dylan chuckled.

"Better get to my two o'clock appointment." He sent her a parting wave and walked away.

Gratitude rose up in her as she watched him leave. Her psychiatrist had brought her from the brink of despair to her present state of satisfaction. He'd reduced her PTSD to manageable proportions and provided a safe haven to which she could return whenever she felt herself backsliding. She owed him her life, truly.

But then she thought of the revolver locked even now in her office, and the illusion that she was fully healed disappeared like a desert mirage. The only time she'd managed to go anywhere without it was to church last Sunday. Until she felt safe at work, as well, she still needed her therapist. And when Terrence passed and if Tobias moved on with his life, regardless of his promise to stay, she would need Dr. Richardson even more.

So much for a complete recovery, she thought, her appetite dwindling.

"You're sure everyone got the message?" Tobias stood over Chet Lee, who sat at the desk in the command room poring over the roster.

Chet gestured to the landline phone on the desk in front of him. "I had to leave a message for three people. The only way to know for sure if they got the message is to keep calling until they pick up."

"I need you to do that for me." The last thing Toby wanted was for random militia members to be combing the countryside, looking to participate in an op that had been downsized.

Chet rolled his eyes. "Fine." He reached for the phone.

Toby clapped him on the back. "You're the man."

As Chet started tapping out a number, Toby crossed to the window to peer outside. Evening rapidly approached. The overcast sky promised to blot out the light of the stars and moon without threatening rain. That was good. He put a hand to the window pane. It was going to be cold, though. He didn't want Hendrix freezing to death before the police "located" him in his car.

At the tramping of footsteps, Toby turned to see Gil Morrison and Ivan Ackerman enter the command room with long faces. When Dylan had announced her plan to alter the operation at last evening's briefing, only Lt. Ashby had seemed relieved by her decision. The other NCOs, Morrison and Ackerman especially, had moped about, looking disappointed.

"Why isn't the cap'n back from work?" Morrison asked, peering around.

"She's working late," Toby reminded him. Her decision to remain at the hospital was a smart one, giving her a solid alibi should Hendrix's complaints reach the ears of the FBI.

"You getting ready to head out?" Ackerman's surly tone betrayed his jealousy.

Toby glanced at Chet, who murmured quietly into the phone and hung up, only to dial another number. "In a bit. Sheriff Fallon's going to pick me up at five-thirty."

Morrison folded his arms across his protruding belly. "Make sure you get your point across," he cautioned. "Hendrix is an arrogant prick. He deserves every ounce of humiliation you can inflict on him."

Toby had plenty of experience dealing with scum just like him. "Don't worry. He'll get what he deserves."

Truth was, he was more interested in finding out if Hendrix had uploaded the anti-war essays with Dylan's name on them. Ike had texted him the startling news earlier today: Experts at the NCTC had confirmed that the anti-war essays supposedly authored by Dylan Connelly had been uploaded to the Internet from an IP address located within the VA Medical Center in Martinsburg. While that fact implied that she'd written them, the FBI's writing analysts had compared them to a thesis Dylan had written back in medical school, and the styles proved substantially different. She hadn't penned the anti-war essays, after all, giving Toby's theory credibility. Someone wanted the world to think that Dylan Connelly loathed the prospect of military intervention in Syria, enough to murder its staunchest advocates. Maybe it was Hendrix.

Given the man's contempt for Dylan, it was possible, right?

Except that would be too easy, and Toby knew it. He doubted he'd find Secretary Nolan's killer tonight. The most that he could do was remove Hendrix from Dylan's private hit list, making her seem a little less crazy, even though he liked her just the way she was.

Dylan returned to her office from the restroom and found a cup of steaming coffee sitting on her desk. The sticky note under it read, *A pick-me-up from the nightshift nurses. Enjoy!*

She bit her lip as she regarded the offering. She had all but kicked her caffeine habit, limiting herself to just one cup a day, in the morning. But how could she let a tall cup of coffee go to waste? And when she picked it up, savoring the warmth in her hand, the aroma of a mocha latte wafted from the sip hole, undermining her intention to march back into the hall and give it away.

What the heck. She'd probably get more done if she jolted her system with a little caffeine. If she ended up not being able to sleep as a result, she'd pop another of her prescription sleeping pills. Having only ever taken one, it wasn't like she'd be abusing medication.

Taking her first sip, she found the coffee just the way she liked it—sweet and chocolaty. With a sigh of contentment, she sat down at her desk and logged into her computer. As she accessed her patients' records, she tried not to think of Tobias and Sheriff Fallon holding Hendrix up at gunpoint. A part of her wished she was there to manage the operation.

Focus, she told herself, peering at her screen. Her patients' treatment and recovery reports had been typed up by a medical transcriptionist. She made a point of reviewing them monthly in order to spot any developing trends. Reviewing treatment was tedious work, but the well-being of her patients mattered more than the time required.

Twenty minutes later, the screen began to blur. Dylan sat back, rubbed her eyes, and opened them again. It wasn't just the print on her monitor that was blurry, she realized. With a stab of concern, she cast her eyes about the office and realized her eyes were failing, in general. Suddenly, the walls of her office began to ripple like the surface of disturbed water. What on earth? Had she forgotten to eat? Was she having some kind of physiological reaction linked to her PTSD?

Perhaps she just needed fresh air. She tried to stand up, but the floor seemed to swallow her feet like quicksand. She couldn't move them. Frightened, she collapsed back in her chair and clutched the arms. *What do I do?*

Call for help. As she reached for her desk phone, her hand caught the side of her half-empty coffee cup, knocking it over. Lukewarm liquid seeped across her desk in a murky rivulet. A sudden suspicion trickled through her consciousness just like the coffee sliding over the edge of the desk and dripping onto the carpet.

I've been poisoned.

That was her last thought before her body pitched forward and her temple struck the corner of the desk with a thud she didn't feel. The room tunneled to black.

"Scoot over."

"W-what?" Wesley Hendrix cried. One minute, he'd slowed to a stop behind what looked like a roadblock on Route 20. The next, two masked giants had materialized out of the dark, startling him out of his skin as they ripped open his car doors and jumped inside, one in the seat beside him, the other behind. The snout of a pistol gouged the back of his skull, making his heart jump into his throat. In the same instant, cold metal closed around his right wrist, shackling him to his steering wheel.

"You heard me," growled the man in the passenger seat. "Back the fuck up, now, and drive the other way." He jammed the automatic shifter into reverse, saving Wesley the trouble.

"Okay, okay." An unmistakable rush of warmth informed Wesley that he'd lost control of his bladder. His coordination appeared equally impaired as he depressed the accelerator and the car lurched backward. I could crash in the ditch, he thought, attracting the attention of the officer at the roadblock.

"Don't even think about it," grated the man beside him. Clamping a powerful hand on the steering wheel, he overcame Wesley's half-hearted intention, tugged the shifter into drive, and in a voice that raised every hair on Wesley's body, grated, "Drive."

Wesley took off in the direction he'd just come from. "What do you want?" he squeaked, accelerating reluctantly. A glance in the rearview mirror didn't show any cops coming to his rescue. "If it's money, you can have whatever's in my wallet. Just don't hurt me." His voice broke on a fearful note.

"Shut up," both assailants said at once, in identical tones of disgust.

"Turn right up here," said the one next to him.

Wesley read the sign for Rigby Road and swallowed hard. There were hardly any houses down Rigby Road, just the local dump. Why would they direct him this way?

They drove another mile without a soul in sight, not even a hint of light from a window.

"Slow down," ordered the man up front. "Turn left

here."

Wesley slowed. As he turned onto a rutted track, he recognized it as the spot where his Uncle Dan had taken him hunting when he was just a kid. Dan had gutted a deer right in front of him, amazing Wesley with the quantity of intestines crammed into one animal. A chill of foreboding swept over him, as he guided his Lexus down the bumpy track. He wasn't going to end up like the deer, was he?

"Stop," said the man beside him.

Wesley braked to a stop and that man jammed it into park. At the same time, the assailant prodding Wesley's skull with a pistol banded a thick arm around his neck.

"Oh, God!" Wesley sobbed, clawing ineffectually at the arm that constricted his airway.

The man next to him held up a spray can and shook it. "You know what this is? It's spray paint. We're going to paint your car for you."

"No!" Wesley had bought his Lexus just last year.

"Your protests won't do you any good, asshole," the stranger retorted, shaking the can menacingly. "What words would you like us to write on the side? How about crazy bastard?"

Comprehension flooded Wesley, bringing with it a wave of relief. These were men from Dylan's militia. They were avenging her for what he'd done to her Suburban, nothing more. That conniving bitch! When they were finished with their mischief, he'd accuse her publicly and have her arrested.

"But before we defile your car, how about we give you a taste of your own medicine?"

The man shook what sounded like a full pill bottle and set it on his dashboard.

"I'm sure you've heard of Elypsia, since you prescribe it all the time, even though it hasn't been adequately tested. Why is that, Hendrix? Are you enjoying the kickbacks from the drug companies pushing you to prescribe it, even though it hasn't been thoroughly tested?"

Uncertainty threatened Wesley's returning confidence. Apparently, this wasn't just about Dylan's car. "So what?" he wheezed. The drug earned him the equivalent of a hundred bucks per prescription, but he wasn't paid in cash, making it perfectly legal to accept the drug companies' incentives.

"So maybe you should familiarize yourself with the side effects," the stranger countered, picking up the bottle again and unscrewing the cap. "I'm sure you're aware that Elypsia causes vomiting and disorientation and sometimes even hallucination and death."

Wesley's blood ran cold. "Don't," he croaked, suddenly certain that they planned to overdose him.

Leaning closer, the stranger skewered him with a stare that made Wesley's bowels churn. "Is there anything else you've done that you'd like to confess to? The truth could save you an awful lot of suffering."

Wesley cast his thoughts wildly about. "I don't...know what you mean. I did that to Dylan's car, but that's it. I swear."

"Have you put her name on anything you've written?"

"Like what?" Wesley stammered, not understanding.

"Essays protesting our involvement in Syria."

"I don't give a shit about Syria," he insisted.

The man's eyes resembled dark blue marbles. "Hold his head back," he said to the man in the back.

"No!" Wesley cried. A gloved hand landed on his forehead, slamming his head back against the seat. The pressure around his throat disappeared as his jaw was pried open. With his free hand, he tried to pull away the hands that controlled him but he lacked the strength.

Pills tumbled into his mouth, one after another. Gloved fingers pushed them down his throat, making him gag. Wesley tried coughing them up, only to find a water bottle jammed between his teeth. He had to swallow to keep from breathing water and the remaining pills slid down his esophagus. How many all together—six, seven, eight?

God, he could feel the initial effects already. His head began to swim. The sounds outside the car became magnified.

The cuffs disappeared from his wrists. His car doors opened and closed, and suddenly the assailants were gone. They didn't even spray paint his car the way they'd threatened. But instead of feeling relived, Wesley felt strangely abandoned. Here he was, alone in the woods and helpless to save himself.

Any moment now, the full effects of the pills would hit him, predisposing him to frightening hallucinations. Fear burbled in his stomach and his mouth watered, warning him that he was about to vomit in his Lexus if he didn't get the door open, only his muscles refused to respond.

Oh, God, how could this have happened to him? He was the doctor, not the guinea pig.

Cal Fallon circled the lit parking lot at the VA Medical Center in the police cruiser that they'd hidden close to the spot where they'd abandoned Hendrix.

"Where the hell is her Suburban?" Toby asked, not seeing it in any of the three sparsely occupied parking lots.

"Maybe she already left," the sheriff suggested.

"She said she'd stay until she heard from us." And since they hadn't had any luck reaching her on her office phone, they'd decided to come tell her in person.

A tingle of apprehension feathered Toby's spine. "I'd like to run inside and ask if someone saw her leave. You mind waiting for me?"

"I'll park and come in with you," Fallon replied. As he pulled into a spot beside the entrance, his radio crackled with the announcement that a white male had been found in his vehicle, overdosing on drugs.

Toby and the sheriff shared a quick smirk and got out. As they cruised into the lobby shoulder to shoulder, they caught the startled eye of the receptionist. She laid her pen down on the counter and divided an anxious look between them. "Can I help you, gentlemen?"

Toby put her at ease with his most charming smile. "Busy evening?" he inquired.

"Not too bad, actually." She spared a glance at Fallon's hard face before looking back at Toby.

"I'm looking for Dr. Connelly," he divulged. "I didn't see her car outside. Do you know if she's still here?"

"Let me check for you." She reached for her phone and pressed a number. "Hi, Leigh. Did Dr. Connelly leave for the evening, do you know?" She listened for several seconds. "Oh, great. Thank you." She looked up at Toby. "The specialty care nurse says she's still in her office."

He smiled his thanks. "How do we get there?"

Following the woman's directions, he and Cal cruised a long hallway, accompanied by the smell of antiseptic and the faint pulse of heart monitors. They arrived at a nurse's station, where a chubby blonde nurse pointed them down a shorter hall with plaques on all the doors.

Toby located the closed door marked *Dr. Connelly*. Silence followed his brisk knock.

"See if it's locked," Fallon suggested.

Toby turned the doorknob and the door swung open, revealing a lit but empty office.

Sharing a puzzled look, they went back to the nurse's station.

"She's not there, Leigh," Toby said, glancing at the woman's name tag. "Are you sure she didn't leave? We didn't see her car outside."

"She wouldn't have left without checking out first," the cherubic looking woman assured him. "Let me see if she's in the restroom."

"Thank you." Toby's temple started to throb.

When Leigh returned with a baffled look, he asked her, "You mind if we search her office?"

With a glance at the sheriff, she said, "I suppose that's okay."

Toby and Cal returned to Dylan's office and stood a moment looking around. Her computer hummed beneath the desk. Toby clicked her keyboard and the screen saver popped up on her monitor.

Fallon ran a finger over the desk's laminate surface. "This was just cleaned," he noted. "Not a speck of dust or even a fingerprint in sight."

"Maybe the cleaning service does that." If so, they'd missed a wet spot on the carpet, under one of the chair's wheels. Toby knelt to touch the stain, carrying the scent to his nose. "Coffee," he said with relief. "She must have spilled some on herself and gone home to change her clothes."

"Without checking out?" Fallon looked dubious. "I'll call her at home," he offered, snatching his cell phone off his hip. "Maybe she's there already."

As the sheriff placed his call, Toby crossed to

Dylan's closet door and opened it. His gaze froze over the coat she'd worn to work that morning, still hanging inside. Recalling what she'd told him about leaving her purse, with the .357 Magnum inside it, locked in her desk, he went to look for it. Every drawer of her desk slid open, and not one of them contained her purse, or the revolver.

Over the quickening thud of his heart, Toby listened to Fallon telling whichever NCO had answered that they were looking for Dylan.

"She's not there yet," Cal relayed, putting his phone away.

Toby directed the man's attention to the coat hanging in the closet. "Her coat's still here. Why wouldn't she have worn if it she took off?"

Cal shrugged. "Maybe she just forgot."

"I don't think so." Something didn't feel right.

The sheriff apparently agreed. "I'll put out a BOLO on her car," he offered, snatching up his phone again.

Toby swallowed hard. What the hell was going on? Dylan wasn't supposed to get into trouble while he was still around to protect her.

Dylan resisted the familiar dream. *Not again.* She couldn't move her arms at all. They felt like they were pinned against the sides of her body, too heavy to lift. It's just a dream, she told herself. If she could just wake up, it would be over.

Hearing voices spoken not too far away, she focused on the sound, using it to pull her out of the well of lethargy. One voice in particular made her heart clutch with a desperate need to make contact.

She surfaced, gasping for air to clear her thoughts. *I'm awake.* Then why couldn't she move? It was only supposed to be a dream, yet her arms were still too heavy to lift, her body scrunched into what felt like a dark, narrow space.

The last time she'd roused to an environment like this, she'd been sleeping in her little playhouse in the backyard, and Tobias had rescued her from near hypothermia, tossing his coat over her. *Tobias!* With a burst of adrenaline, she realized that was the voice she'd just recognized.

Working her jaw and her irresponsive tongue, she fought to articulate a cry for help. *Save me.* Only the feat proved impossible. She couldn't get her voice box to vibrate. All she could manage was a whimper. *Where am I?*

Her head hung heavily from her neck. Her eyes felt as if they'd been sewn shut. The only appendages on her body that she could move at all were the tips of her fingers. She curled them, feeling carpet under her hands. Something crinkled against her palm—a candy wrapper, she decided.

If her woolly senses could be trusted, she was sitting in a container of sorts, so severely medicated that she couldn't move. But that made no sense. And the weight pulling her down into unconsciousness was too great to overcome. In despair, she gave up, letting lassitude pull her back down into a deep, dark void.

Toby sat up straighter in the passenger seat of Cal Fallon's cruiser. Did the mailbox up ahead of them look just like Dylan's or was he losing his mind? "Wait, what are we doing?" he demanded as Cal began to slow down.

"I'm dropping you off." That fact became evident as Cal turned down Dylan's driveway.

"What?" Toby glanced at the digital display on Cal's dashboard. It read 1:30 A.M. "Granted it's late, but we can't just give up now. Dylan's still out there, somewhere. I'm not going to sit on my ass at home when she's possibly hurt or injured—"

"Son," Cal interrupted him with a tired but patronizing air, "we've driven down every road in the county looking for her. I've got five patrol cars out doing the same thing. Best thing you can do right now is get some rest while you wait for a phone call."

Toby's ears burned. "Are you shitting me?"

"Look," Cal growled, "if you want to borrow Sergeant Lee's car and continue your search, then you go right ahead. But my advice to you is to leave this matter up to the Sheriff's Office. If she's out there, we'll find her. In the meantime, she needs you to be where she can reach you."

The sheriff had a point, but it chafed Toby to give up so soon. Light blazed out of every window in Dylan's farmhouse, a beacon in the dark night. The silhouette of Lt. Ashby's head and shoulders filled the pane of his bedroom window. With a mutter of thanks to the sheriff, Toby jumped out of the cruiser and sprinted for the front door, running into Ivan Ackerman who paced restlessly up and down the hall.

"Did she call?" Toby asked.

"Nope." Ackerman shook his head and stared at his feet.

As Toby shut the door behind him, the sound seemed to echo through an empty house. "Where is everyone?"

"Morrison and Lee are out looking for her. The XO's upstairs sitting at his window."

Disappointed to learn that the only available car was already in use, Toby recognized that he had no choice but to head upstairs and talk to Lt. Ashby. He found the man snoozing in a seated position, his head supported by one of the chair's wingbacks. Apparently sensing his presence, Terrence slit his dark eyes and looked up at him. "You didn't find her, yet."

It wasn't a question. Toby heaved a heavy sigh. "Do you have *any* idea what could have happened to her?" he asked. If anyone knew Dylan's deepest, darkest secrets, it was her closest friend.

"None," the XO replied, his face wreathed in equal parts worry and pain. "This isn't like her. Something bad has happened. I'm certain of it."

The words enveloped Toby in icy dread. He concealed his reaction by fetching a blanket to drape across the XO's belly, tucking it in around him so he could keep up his vigil without freezing. "Can I bring you anything?" he asked.

"No," the giant replied, his eyes drifting shut.

Toby's own eyes trekked toward the window. Nothing lay beyond but the shadowy yard, barely lit by a cloud-smothered moon. The fear that something insurmountable had happened to Dylan raked his spine. Helplessness shuddered through him. And all he could do was wait for news and then react.

CHAPTER 14

The electrical shocks emanating from the cell phone buried in Toby's secret pocket had him leaping straight up out of the love seat where he'd sprawled at approximately five in the morning, an hour after Gil and Chet dragged themselves through the front door, baffled, defeated, and worn out.

A sweep of the brightly lit command room showed him to be alone. He pulled his phone out of the hidden pocket and scanned Ike's numerical text. It was code for "Call in."

Toby's stomach lurched. He would rather walk barefoot across hot coals than tell Ike Dylan had disappeared. Then again, Ike might have already heard rumors through the law enforcement grapevine.

With a groan of dread, Toby tucked his phone away and zipped up his jacket. Calling Milly to join him, he headed out the front door. Dylan's car remained notably absent. The dog bolted past him to pee beside the elm tree. Brisk morning air cleared the cobwebs from Toby's mind as he started down the running course.

Normally at this time, they were all up and

exercising. Without Dylan, the well-oiled machinery of her militia had ground to a halt. The land around her house seemed to have fallen under an evil spell, one that had sucked the life out of the once-glorious leaves, leaving them brown and brittle on the dead grass. Even the song birds were mute.

Reaching the bottom of the hill, Toby waded into the woods until he could no longer see the house. He pulled his phone out a second time and speed-dialed his boss.

"What's up?" he asked, his gut churning.

"Tell me Dylan Connelly was with you all last night," Ike exhorted.

The urgency in the former SEAL's voice hit Toby like a slap in the face. "Why?" He braced himself for bad news.

"General Treyburn was shot to death coming out of a Halloween party in Loudon County at 11 P.M. last night."

Toby widened his stance to keep from staggering backward. Loudon County lay within twenty miles of Harpers Ferry. And General Treyburn was a member of the Joint Chiefs of Staff, as passionate about military intervention in Syria as Defense Secretary Nolan had been.

Christ. Someone was knocking off supporters of Syrian involvement, and they were hiding behind Dylan and her militia.

"Unfortunately, she wasn't with me," Toby admitted. "She's been missing for the past eight hours." With reluctance and self-censure, he explained how she'd disappeared out of the hospital, taking her vehicle and her purse, but not her coat.

"You said she owns a .357 Magnum?" Ike didn't sound at all interested in the details of Dylan's disappearance.

Toby braced himself for more bad news. "Why?"

"Treyburn was shot with Speer, Gold Dot .38 special, 135 grain ammo. That's the kind a Magnum would take."

It was also the same brand of ammo that Dylan carried in her purse. Toby kept the phone to his ear. Every thud of his heart rocked him on his feet. "Listen to me, Calhoun," he grated, his blood pressure soaring, "Not only is Dylan incapable of killing another human being, but I've seen her fire her weapon at the shooting range. She's way too lousy of a shot to hit a moving target. Last night she disappeared. Someone abducted her and used her pistol in order to frame her. I'm telling you, she's being set up! I'm the one here. I can see what's happening."

"Maybe so, Burke," Ike admitted on a slightly softer note, "but the evidence is overwhelming. When she shows up, you can expect the FBI to drop by and question her. Unless she has a fool-proof alibi, they're going to charge her with Treyburn's murder."

"No." Denial ripped through Toby with the force of a volcanic explosion. "God damn it, sir, I don't even know where she is right now!"

"Why didn't you advise me that she was missing?" Ike's biting question let Toby know that he'd get no support from him now. "You say she's being set up," the team lead persisted, "but where's the proof? All the evidence so far points to her guilt. I have no way of keeping the FBI from charging her with either Treyburn or Nolan's murders."

Both? Toby ground his molars together. "I'll find the proof," he swore. But right now, he just wanted to find Dylan. Without waiting to see if Ike had anything else to say, he ended the call with a jab of his thumb and a virulent curse. Slipping the phone back in his jacket, he called Milly to return to the house with him.

He was just pushing through the front door when the landline phone started ringing. The sound galvanized him into tearing down the hall and snatching up the receiver with a breathless, "Hello?"

"Tobias?"

The sound of Dylan's frightened voice nearly brought him to his knees in relief. "Where the hell are you?" He winced when she audibly hesitated. "We've looked everywhere for you, baby," he tacked on more gently.

"Something happened," she whispered. "I don't understand…"

Her fear and confusion made him want to reach through the wire and comfort her. "Talk to me, beautiful." He swallowed against a dry throat. "Where are you right now?"

"In my office. I just woke up and found myself sleeping at my desk."

Tobias pictured her empty desk chair and kept quiet. She clearly didn't realize he'd swung by the hospital on impulse last night. Why would she lie to him? "After taking care of Hendrix, Fallon and I looked for you at work," he stated, in a neutral voice. "You weren't there."

Silence. "What do you mean I wasn't there?"

"Your office was empty, your purse and your car were gone. You weren't there, Dylan. Where'd you go?" A hint of accusation colored his tone in spite of his faith in her innocence.

"Where'd I go?" She seemed confused by the question. "I didn't go anywhere."

Is she lying to me? Had he allowed himself to be blindsided by her seeming wholesomeness that he couldn't see her for who she really was? A vision of her coat, hanging in her closet edged aside the suspicion. Why wouldn't she have taken it with her if she'd gone out, considering how chilly it had been? And when had she ever been anything but honest with him? He had to give her the benefit of the doubt.

"Tobias?"

If someone at the hospital had published essays in her name, then that same someone could have stolen her purse and her car. Maybe they'd even drugged her so that it looked like she'd left. He couldn't believe anything less.

"Dylan, listen to me." He could hear the distinct thump of Terrence's crutch, now, as the XO made his way to the restroom upstairs. "I want you to go straight to the lab there at the medical center. Have them take urine and blood samples and screen them for toxins."

He heard her draw a shaky breath. "But I don't take drugs," she stated.

He nearly smiled at her righteous tone. "I know that, honey. But something happened last night, and I think you're going to be implicated. We need to know if you were drugged."

"What? What happened? Tell me."

"I'll tell you when I get there. In the meantime, go straight to the lab and don't talk to anyone. Tell the lab techs that you need the results right away."

"Okay." She sounded frightened and confused.

"One more thing. Is your purse there with you?" he inquired.

He heard her pull her desk drawer open.

"Yes, it's right here."

"What about the Suburban? Do you see it in the parking lot?"

He heard her get up and cross to the window. "It's parked right where I left it. Where else would it be?"

When he hung up, he'd get Fallon and Hooper—

whoever had jurisdiction—over to the VA Medical Center, ASAP, to scour her vehicle for fingerprints. "Okay, don't go anywhere. Go get those tests run. I'll have Chet drive me over. I'll be there soon."

He could hear some of the men moving around upstairs now. They'd all want to be the first to get to her, to collect her and bring her safely home.

"I just don't understand what happened," Dylan murmured in an anguished voice. "Why don't I remember anything?"

He could tell that her disorientation was genuine. "I don't know, beautiful, but the tests will help us figure it out."

The only way she could be lying to him was if she were also lying to herself. Was it possible that PTSD had spawned schizophrenia, giving rise to some kind of split-personality disorder? If so, she could become someone else entirely and then have no recollection of her actions.

God, he hoped that wasn't the case. "I'll be there soon, babe. Go do what I said. Don't waste any more time."

"Okay." She remained on the line for several more seconds as if there was something else she wanted to say. But then the phone clicked in his ear.

Toby fished Cal Fallon's business card out of his wallet and dialed the sheriff directly. Both the Taskforce lead and the FBI were convinced of Dylan's guilt. But Toby knew that the law enforcement officials at the local level vehemently believed in her innocence, and he wanted them on his side.

Shivering on a bench at the edge of the hospital parking lot, Dylan watched Sergeant Hooper's forensic expert clean up the charcoal-colored dust he'd left behind from fingerprinting the steering wheel and door of her Suburban. He'd lifted and bagged a couple of hairs found on her car seat. Now he was swabbing the entire dashboard and gearshift with a Q-tip.

At the far end of the lot, the sun's rays climbed up the trunks of the trees, and the lot itself began to fill with cars as the morning shift arrived for work. Dylan herself was expected to meet with patients in just one hour, but according to Tobias who'd left a voicemail on the director's line, she was taking the day off. Dr. Hendrix had yet to show up for work, which meant that he would be absent, also. A lot of patients were about to have their appointments canceled.

Rubbing the tender spot on her temple, she watched Tobias and Sheriff Hooper put their heads together to discuss her circumstances. Something had happened last night, but no one wanted to tell her what. The look on Sheriff Hooper's face when she surrendered her Magnum and box of ammo had put a cold feeling in the pit of her stomach. What if someone was dead and she looked guilty—just like last month after the car bombing in D.C.?

Then again, considering the results of her urine test, how could she be guilty of anything?

She'd tested positive for benzodiazepines, a broad class of psychoactive drugs that produced sedative, hypnotic, and amnesic effects. Perhaps if she'd taken the sleeping pills she'd been prescribed by her psychiatrist, she could understand why there'd be benzos in her bloodstream, but she'd only taken one sleeping pill over a week ago.

That being the case, there was only one way benzos would have shown up in her bloodstream: the coffee she'd been given last night as a so-called gift from the nursing staff had been laced—with what, exactly?

Only the blood test could determine that, and the results weren't available yet.

But surely the urine test would exonerate her of any wrongdoing. She couldn't have harmed a soul last night, let alone have driven her car somewhere to perform a nefarious act, not if she was drugged.

A squealing of tires wrested Dylan's attention to the police car circuiting the parking lot and braking to a stop next to Tobias and Sheriff Hooper. The driver's tinted window lowered, and Sheriff Fallon joined the first two men in what appeared to be a tense discussion. Since the topic no doubt pertained to her, Dylan rose from the bench to approach the trio. The time had come to demand answers. As she drew nearer, she could hear their voices, low and fraught with urgency. The tail end of Tobias's words reached her ears, "…up to us to prove her innocence."

He caught sight of her and quickly cut himself off. "Almost done here," he assured her with a strained smile.

Dylan looked past him at Sheriff Fallon's scowl. The man looked like he'd been chewing on gravel and had the stomach ache to prove it.

"I want to know what happened last night," she demanded, including all three men in her request. "What am I being accused of this time?"

"I'll tell you on the way home," Tobias promised, reaching for her elbow.

To her surprise, Sheriff Fallon deliberately raised his tinted window and peeled off without another word, leaving rubber marks on the asphalt and her mouth hanging open in astonished hurt.

"Come on, honey. Let's get you home," Tobias repeated.

Huddling deeper into her coat, Dylan allowed herself to be drawn toward her Suburban. The cold in the pit of her stomach had started to spread through her entire body. Foreboding underscored her racing thoughts with the worry that a simple blood test wasn't going to absolve her of any possible involvement.

"You almost done here?" Tobias asked Hooper's forensic expert.

The man shot Dylan a funny look, closed up his kit, and walked away. Tobias guided her over to the passenger seat and helped her in with diligent care, as if conscious of her internal fragility. Then he rounded the front of the vehicle and climbed behind the wheel. Using the keys, which lay on the dashboard, he started up the vehicle and studied the display.

"Check the gas gauge and the mileage," he requested. "Have they changed since yesterday?"

Dylan leaned closer and saw that her tank was nearly empty where yesterday it had been closer to full. "I don't remember my mileage, but I had much more gas than that." A shiver shook her frame. "What's going on?" she demanded a second time. "Who drove my car?"

He swept a reluctant eye over the busy parking lot. "Let's go somewhere more private." Backing them out of her reserved spot, he sped them toward the highway.

Dylan sat frozen in her seat, sick to her stomach. As she closed her eyes, her thoughts went back to the previous night. Remnants of memories floated in her mind like bits of confetti, too scattered to form any kind of coherent picture.

Tobias laid a warm hand over her fisted one. "Did you eat anything yet?" His concerned tone, which was meant to be consoling, had the opposite effect.

"I had orange juice and a donut when I got my blood drawn. I need to know what's going on," she demanded, a quaver in her voice. "Obviously, while I was drugged someone helped themselves to my car, and that's why the police went through it, but there's more to it than that, isn't there?"

"I'm going to pull off up ahead, and then we'll talk about it." His assuring tone ratcheted her adrenaline higher.

Ten minutes from the hospital, they neared a vacant scenic stop designated as an overlook for its stunning view. Toby swerved into the empty lot and parked the vehicle. Turning off the motor, he twisted in his seat and looked at her. The lines of concern carved into his face made him look like a different person, entirely. Where was the easygoing drifter who'd charmed his way into her heart? Only his navy blue eyes, filled with tenderness, struck a familiar chord.

"Dylan, do you remember those anti-war essays I asked you about?"

She thought back and nodded. "Yes, but I told you I never wrote anything like that," she insisted.

"I know." He reached for her hand and squeezed it, offering her the comfort she craved. "Sweetheart, someone is trying to frame you. Something happened last night, and right now it looks like you're the one responsible."

His words fueled her heart into a painful trot. "What happened?"

"Last night, a member of the Joint Chiefs of Staff, General Treyburn, was shot to death leaving a Halloween party."

She reeled at the awful news. Sorrow for the man's anguished loved ones competed with sudden, clawing anxiety. "Oh, my God, it's happening again, isn't it?" Her kindling panic brought on a cold sweat that bathed every pore.

"Yes." His lips thinned with equal parts regret and

determination. "Did you notice something different about your gun when you handed it over?" he asked her.

She had put it reluctantly into Sheriff Hooper's hands, loath to let it go. "I don't think so."

"What about the box of ammo?"

She thought back, and it came to her with a stab of horror. The sticker on the once tightly sealed pack of Speer bullets had been pulled off. At the time, she'd been too dazed to wonder why.

The look on her face must have betrayed her thoughts, for Tobias nodded. "Someone used your gun last night, Dylan, and some of your bullets."

A metallic taste filled Dylan's mouth. Adrenaline released an onslaught of fight-or-flight hormones that stirred visions of her vaulting over the railing at the edge of the mountain.

"Easy," Tobias crooned, as if privy to her thoughts. "Just stay calm." He held a warm palm against the side of her face, anchoring her for the time being next to him. "I'm right here. I'm not going to let anything happen to you."

"Someone is trying to frame me."

"Yes."

She remained rigid in her seat fighting to stay calm, to *think*. What if she'd done it and she just couldn't remember? With a gasp, she looked at Toby. "You don't think *I* shot General Treyburn?" she demanded.

"I know you didn't." His certainty, radiating through the timber of his voice, quieted the fear that she'd finally lost her grip on reality.

I'm not crazy, she assured herself. "I need an alibi," she said out loud. "The urine and blood tests might prove toxicity, but everyone responds differently. Some people pass out on benzos; others remain conscious but can't remember what they did." Closing her eyes, she covered them with her fingers, searching in the darkness for clues about what had happened to her. The barest scraps of a memory floated through her mind. She tried grasping at them only to have them melt away like snowflakes under a baking sun. "I can't remember last night at all!"

"Shhh, stay calm." He leaned in until his forehead touched hers, grounding her in his strength. "Hopefully, the results of the blood test will cast more light on the situation than the urine tests."

As he stroked the back of her head until her runaway heart slowed. Dylan groped for his other hand and held it tightly. "Thank God for you." What would she do right now without him? She would surely lose her grasp on reality, that's what. Her PTSD would get the better of her. "I love you," she blurted, too afraid of her circumstances to care about the risk her words carried. Tears welled in her aching eyes. Without Tobias, her life would scarcely be worth living, especially now, with this going on.

Yes, admitting her feelings for him stripped away the last layer of her protective shell, but she wanted him to know what a blessing he'd been to her, should the worst happen. She searched his stunned expression, wondering what his reaction would be.

Toby drew a startled breath. Dylan's confession spread through his consciousness to his extremities, warming him like a swig of brandy. Ah, Christ, she'd picked a hell of a time to admit to her feelings for him! And in a matter of days, after she learned who he really was, she was going to regret those unguarded words of love. All the same, he savored them for the momentary bliss they brought him.

"I love you, too, babe," he whispered, astonishing himself. The irony of his circumstances curled his upper lip. It had taken a feisty revolutionary, whose questionable stability made her an enemy of the state to win his heart. "And I'm not going to let you take the rap for this," he swore.

Determination roughened his voice and elevated his pulse. He squeezed her hand harder. Before she could react to his declaration, he prompted, "Try to remember what happened last night. Start with the last thing you recall."

Her brow furrowed, and her eyes slid off to the left. "I remember meeting with my last patient and grabbing crackers from the machine so I wouldn't be hungry working so late. Then I stopped by the nurses' station, and I checked in with Leigh. After visiting the restroom, I walked into my office and saw a cup of coffee on my desk with a note from the nursing staff."

Toby groaned as the source of her debilitation became apparent. "You drank a beverage you didn't get yourself?" he asked, marveling at her naiveté.

"The nurses bring me a mocha latte every morning," she explained. "It never occurred to me to hold it in suspicion."

"Then either one of the nurses laced it," he reasoned, "or whoever brought it to you knows about the nurses' habit. What happened after that?"

"I started reviewing my patients' records and looking for trends when my eyesight gave out." She fell quiet.

"And then what?" he prompted.

She struggled to remember. "I think I tried to stand up, and I couldn't. I remember reaching for the phone to call for help and…I knocked over my cup. That's it." She shook her head. "That's the last thing I remember."

"That's good, though," he said, encouraged that she remembered at least that little bit.

"Next thing I knew, I woke up at my desk all confused. And that's when I called you."

Toby scrubbed a hand over his face. God, if she could only remember more.

"Wait." A haunted look entered her eyes. "I think I remember dreaming that same dream..." Her voice faded off on a note of horror.

"What dream, beautiful? Did you dream about your boys?"

"No." Her pupils shrank to pinheads, as if a bright light of fear suddenly shone on them. "I dream that I'm in an insane asylum," she whispered, and a shiver ascended Toby's spine. "I'm in a straight jacket and people are poking me with needles."

Christ. "How many times have you dreamt that?"

"A lot."

"And you had that dream last night?"

Awareness entered her eyes, as if she'd just put together the first two pieces of a scattered puzzle. "Yes, but—then it was real."

His scalp prickled. "What do you mean it was real?"

She looked down at her fingers, curling the tips of them as if recalling some action. "I could feel carpet under my hands and something that felt like a candy wrapper. I was curled up in an enclosure of some kind. And I thought I could hear your voice in the distance," she added, cutting him a startled look.

Toby squeezed her hand. "That's good," he encouraged, both horrified and elated that she was remembering. "What else?"

She went perfectly still, but after a moment, the corners of her mouth drooped, and she shook her head hopelessly. "That's it. I can't remember any more. My next memory is waking up with my head on my desk and the sun in the window." Her face crumpled with sudden misery. "You believe me, don't you, Tobias?"

The depth of his own helplessness made him want to howl. "I believe you, Dylan," he assured her gruffly. Wrapping his arms around her, he held her tightly to him and rocked her from side to side. "I'm sure the blood test is going to corroborate your story. You'll be fine."

Providing the FBI couldn't find some clever way to dismiss the evidence she presented; after all, they were bound and determined to bring a perpetrator to justice, and she was already a suspect for a similar crime.

But for now, the best and only thing he could do for Dylan was to get her home so she could rest. Considering her mental-emotional fragility, not to mention the shock to her body, she'd suffered as much punishment as she could handle for one day.

As for himself, he wanted to savor her confession of love for as long as possible. All too soon she would learn the truth about him. Kissing her cheek, he worked his lips closer to hers. Her clenched jaw slowly relaxed. At last, she turned her head and trustingly touched her mouth to his.

"It's going to be okay," he reassured her.

She lifted tear-stained eyes to him. "You love me?" she asked, as if doubting his earlier confession.

Illogical joy buoyed his heavy heart. "Yeah." He laughed aloud at how ludicrous it was that he'd fallen in love with the FBI's top suspect. They were like two sappy kids so overwhelmed with their feelings for each other that the daunting odds against them could scarcely darken their joy. In all likelihood, Dylan would be charged with a crime she hadn't committed. Her life was going to hell in a hand basket, but—right here, right now—what they'd found in each other made them happy beyond measure.

Determined to make her smile, he started to sing his

confession to the tune of the Happy Birthday Song. "I love you, I do. I love you, I do. I love you, dear Dylan. I love you, I do."

By the time he finished, she was laughing and sobbing at the same time.

Toby's eyes stung as he regarded her. Framed by an autumn sea of undulating mountains and touched by a sun that turned her hair into a flame, she was the most beautiful woman he'd ever met. If there were any way to keep her smiling through the hours and days to come, he would do it, but it wouldn't be easy.

"Wake up, beautiful."

A feather-light kiss on Dylan's cheek roused her from a deep, dreamless sleep. Snapping her eyes open, she lifted her head to find herself stretched out on her own bed—not in Terrence's room where she remembered being last. Tobias stood over her, cloaked in the mellow tones of dusk that shone in her three narrow windows. Even in the muted light, she could read his concern.

"Did you move me in here?" she asked, still feeling disoriented.

"Sure did."

"When? I don't remember."

"Hours ago. You fell asleep in Terrence's chair," he said, sitting on the edge of the bed next to her hip. "The benzos are still in your bloodstream, making you drowsy."

Pushing herself into a sitting position, she encountered Milly snuggled against her other side. "What time is it now?"

"Four thirty in the afternoon."

"Did the results come back from the hospital yet?"

"As a matter of fact, they did." He sent her a lopsided smile. "I had to charm the nurse into sharing the report with me. And, by the way, Leigh swears that neither she nor any of the night nurses brought you coffee last night."

"Then who?" Dylan asked. Who, besides, Wesley Hendrix hated her enough to drug her?

Tobias shrugged. "If the cup and the note hadn't disappeared, we could analyze the handwriting. Whoever it was, they picked up the spill, all except for a small stain on the carpet. Do you want to hear the results of the blood test?" he pressed.

She swallowed heavily. "I don't know. Do I?"

"I think you do." He sent her an encouraging smile. "There were high levels of—" He glanced at a word he'd written on his hand, "—flunitrazepam," he said carefully.

"Rohypnol," she breathed, supplying him with the brand name.

All trace of his smile fled. "That's the date rape drug."

"It's one of them," she confirmed, experiencing a peculiar mixture of relief and outrage. What had seemed more like a dream than anything else was fast becoming reality. She really *had* been drugged.

Tobias reached for her. "Are you sure you weren't—?"

"Raped?" She rolled her eyes at him. "Honestly, that's the least of my worries with potential murder charges looming over my head."

"Christ, Dylan. Who would do this to you?"

She spread her hands. "Hendrix?"

"I already checked out that possibility. He was admitted to Jefferson Regional Hospital last night and held for observation until this morning."

The reference to last night's mission had her sitting up taller. "So you did it? How did it go?" In all the fuss surrounding her disappearance, she'd forgotten all about Tobias and Sheriff Fallon's mission last night.

Tobias grimaced. "Let's just say he'll think twice before prescribing Elypsia again. But if Hendrix didn't drug you, then who did?"

She blew out a breath. "Well, the director doesn't care much for me, but I can't imagine him murdering a general, let alone framing me for it."

"Both Nolan and Treyburn advocated military involvement in Syria. Who do you know that's opposed to war—besides your priest?"

She gasped at his implication. "My God, Tobias, you don't think Father Nesbit could have anything to do with this!"

He squeezed her thigh apologetically. "Honey, I don't know what to think."

"No!" She pushed his hand off her thigh and struggled out of bed, forcing Tobias to get up and disrupting Milly's slumber. "I've known him all my life," she railed, pacing toward her dresser and back. "He and Cal Fallon were my father's closest friends. He would *never* do anything to harm me."

Tobias held up both hands. "I'm not saying it's him. I'm just asking you if you know anyone else opposed to our involvement in Syria."

She whirled on him. "Well, who wouldn't be? No one in their right mind wants a war."

"You're right." His voice fell into a more soothing cadence. "No one wants war, but sometimes taking action is the only ethical thing to do. If we'd stopped Hitler early on in his career, six million Jews might have been saved."

Dylan couldn't argue with logic like that, but it was warring individuals like Hitler who spawned aggression in the first place. She dropped her throbbing head into her hands. "It's complicated," she admitted.

Tobias closed the gap between them. Pulling her hands from her face, he drew her into his embrace. "Hey, I'm right here," he assured her, holding her close.

Dylan burrowed her face gratefully into his shoulder and leaned into his strength.

"Sheriff Hooper's reviewing the footage on the hospital's security cameras," he added, "so if you never left the building then you have nothing to worry about."

She swallowed against the knot of fear in her throat. "But what if I did leave the building, and I just can't remember?" she whispered.

A knock at her partially open door prevented him from answering.

Tobias abruptly released her.

Gil Morrison poked his round head through the opening. "A couple of cars just pulled up outside," he warned. "They look official."

Dylan sucked in a frightened breath. "It's the FBI, isn't it?" she guessed, observing Tobias's grim reaction. "They're here to arrest me."

"No." He reached for her hand. "They'll just want to ask you questions. Just tell them what happened to you. Tell them about the results of your blood test."

Her stomach cramped. "What makes you think they'll believe me?"

"If they don't, they'll conduct their own tests. They won't arrest you, Dylan, not until they build a stronger case, and we're going to keep that from happening." He drew her gently toward the door.

She resisted briefly, forcing him to look back. "You still believe me, don't you, Tobias?"

"I'll always believe you," he affirmed.

That was all that mattered. He believed her, and he

loved her. How could anything go wrong when she had all that going for her?

CHAPTER 15

Dylan entered her command room on knees that jittered. No less than three men in suits awaited her, two of whom had paid her a visit a month ago when they'd questioned her about the bombing of Secretary Nolan's car. Under the suspicious and hostile gazes of her NCOs, the special agents milled about the room, eyeballing the maps and the easel and anything lying about, but not touching anything—yet.

At Dylan's entrance, they turned to face her. In the glow of several lit lamps, she could read suspicion in their alert gazes. Tobias's hand at her elbow gave her the courage to lift her chin and acknowledge each agent individually.

The one with the bristling moustache approached her first. "Charles Palmer, special agent in charge," he reminded her with a nod in lieu of a handshake. "You remember Tibbs, and this is Special Agent Maddox." The new man, Maddox, was a handsome mixed-race man in his thirties.

"Three of you this time." Dylan smiled bitterly. Was she such a dangerous entity that she merited three special agents?

"Plus a forensics team outside," Palmer informed her, causing her palms to sweat.

"I see." She clung to her poise. "Well, I know why you're here." She swallowed against the fear tightening her throat. "You think I'm involved in the shooting last night, just as you think I bombed the defense secretary's car. I assure you I did neither, and I'm happy to cooperate in your investigation, so you can find the culprit who did."

"Well…" Palmer looked bemused by her candidness. "We thank you for that." He withdrew a sheaf of folded papers from the lining of his navy blue jacket. "I have a warrant here to search your property and to seize anything of suspicious nature."

"Search away," she agreed. "But if you're looking for my gun, I've already surrendered that to the Martinsburg Police. They're investigating the matter of my disappearance last night. You'll have to confer with them."

Palmer shot his colleagues a startled and disgruntled look. He withdrew a pen and pad of paper from his breast pocket and scribbled himself a note. "What's this about your disappearance?"

Dylan gestured to the sofas and the armchairs. "Why don't we sit?" She suspected her amnesia story wasn't going to help her cause any. If anything, it made her appear even more suspicious. How could Tobias be so sure they wouldn't arrest her on the spot?

His steady hand led her toward the loveseat. The FBI agents dropped into various chairs around the room while the NCOs continued to hover. Hopefully, Terrence had fallen asleep and was oblivious to her circumstances.

As Tobias sat down beside her, Special Agent Palmer cut him a curious look. "Have I met you before?"

Dylan spoke up. "Oh, no you haven't. This is Sergeant Burke," she said, making introductions. "He's my...my senior operations NCO," she finished, lamely.

Something akin to comprehension flickered in Palmer's eyes before he looked fixedly down at his notepad. "You were saying that you disappeared last night?" he prompted.

The warmth of Tobias's knee where it touched hers gave her the courage to put her account forward. She explained what little she remembered of the previous evening, how she'd worked late at the hospital; how she'd found a cup of coffee on her desk as she did nearly every morning. "I didn't know it was drugged," she added.

Palmer's eyebrows, as bushy as his moustache, shot toward his hairline. "Drugged?"

"Yes." She described how her vision had failed her, how she remembered knocking over her coffee as she passed out. "I woke up later, still groggy, and it felt like I was sitting in a dark, confined space. There was something under my hand—a candy wrapper."

Palmer and the two other agents sent her blank looks, like they didn't know what to make of her story.

"I must have passed out again because the next time I came awake, I was back at my desk and it was morning." With her eyes, she invited Tobias to explain how she'd immediately called him, but he merely squeezed her hand and kept quiet.

She completed the tale herself. "I called home from my desk phone, and Sergeant Burke answered. When I told him what happened, he suggested I go straight to the lab to have my urine and blood tested. The first test came up positive for benzodiazepines. The latter specified high levels of flunitrazepam, better known as Rohypnol, the date rape drug—which explains why I don't remember."

When Palmer just frowned at her, she clarified, "Rohypnol causes anterogade amnesia. It induces dizziness and sleepiness. There's no way I could have driven a car, let alone operated a handgun."

The special agent scratched himself a few notes. "And you shared all of this with the Martinsburg Police?"

"Yes, I did. I also surrendered my pistol and the ammunition in my purse, and we noticed there were bullets missing."

Palmer's mustache twitched. "So, you're claiming you never left the hospital last night."

Dylan's heart beat faster. "I don't believe so."

He looked up at her sharply. "You don't believe so?"

Tobias ran a soothing hand up her spine. "I don't see how I could have walked," she clarified.

Palmer tapped the tip of his pencil on his notepad. "Would you be willing to submit a urine and blood sample to our own forensics team?"

She stiffened at the implication that she'd meddled with the tests already taken. "I don't see why not," she said slowly.

"Do you know whether the blood test indicates what *time* you might have been drugged?" Palmer inquired.

Dylan just looked at him. "What are you suggesting? That I ingested Rohypnol *after* I shot General Treyburn just so I'd have some type of defense?" Resentment rushed into her bloodstream, making her long suddenly for her revolver. It was starting to dawn on Dylan that, perhaps, she ought to have a lawyer present before she said anymore to these men.

Tobias laid a hand on her shoulder. "Easy," he murmured, clearly sensing her rising agitation.

The agent had raised an eyebrow at her vehemence. "Let me fetch the forensics team," he offered standing up.

In the following half hour, she surrendered a urine sample and three vials of blood. The forensics experts swept through her home, violating her sanctum and her psyche in one fell swoop. As she watched them raid her file cabinets, search her desk and bedroom bureau, and even poke their noses in her attic, Dylan could feel herself retreating into a remote corner of her mind where nothing touched her, not even Tobias's palpable concern as he hovered protectively near.

When the FBI finished tearing through the contents of her home, they turned their attention to the supply shed, just like the last time they'd been there looking for proof that she'd bombed Secretary Nolan's car. Tonight, they left the barn empty-handed. She supposed she ought to be relieved about that. Instead, what she felt was the return of the numbness that had retreated since Tobias first joined her militia. It was back, as dark and cold and joyless as it ever was.

Returning to the command room, Dylan sat stock still on the loveseat while Tobias and the other NCOs—all but Ackerman, who slinked off to sulk on his own—moved quietly about the room, putting items and papers back where they belonged. Above the exposed crossbeams overhead, she could hear Terrence struggling to make his way down the second-story hallway to the bathroom. A stab of concern roused her from her self-absorption. She got up to go assist him, waving off Tobias's offer to help.

She'd told him once that she didn't care about her future. But what would become of Terrence if she went to jail? And what of her and Tobias? The love they'd so recently declared would wither and perish if she found herself incarcerated.

Maybe she'd lied to herself, as well as to him. Maybe her future *did* matter.

A bitter chill seeped through Toby's militia uniform as he waited for Sheriff Hooper to sign the ledger and pick up a rifle at the front of the barn. The man had arrived early to the CPX, which—in spite of all that was going on in Dylan's life—was taking place as usual.

It can't be canceled, Dylan had told him just last night. We have to prepare for the protest at the fusion center on November 9th.

He hadn't tried arguing. She was better off having something to focus her attention on besides the FBI's investigation. He'd consoled himself with the fact that he could question Sheriff Hooper in person about the investigation. Had the man found anything important in the security footage? Had he been forced to surrender the investigation to the FBI already?

Hooper scribbled his name in the ledger, took the M-16 that Morrison issued to him, and joined Toby in the back of the barn. Out the corner of his eye, Toby saw Cal Fallon step up to the ledger and shoot Toby a glare.

Toby's scalp tightened with foreboding. Fallon's patience was obviously wearing thin. He had guarded the truth of Toby's connection to the FBI with forbearance, but the scowl on his face this morning warned Toby that he wouldn't keep his secret much longer.

Toby kicked himself for not telling Dylan the truth last night when they'd lain in bed. Hearing the facts from anyone besides himself would decimate her. But under the pretext of shielding her from yet another shock, he'd guarded his secret one more night, clinging selfishly to her devotion. He feared his cowardice had been a big mistake.

Hooper stuck out his hand, reclaiming his attention. "Morning."

"Hey." Toby searched his gaze. "Has the FBI approached you yet?"

The Sheriff of Martinsburg nodded gloomily. "Yep. They got me out of bed late last night. Had to give them everything I've got, right down to the swab taken of that stain on her carpet and the hair fibers found in her car."

Damn. But it was no more than Toby had expected. "What did you see on the security footage— anything?"

"A woman with long hair left the hospital by the door closest to her office at 9:45 that night and returned two hours later. But the quality of the footage is poor. You can't tell one way or another if it's Dylan."

The man's words crushed Toby's hopes. Even the security footage seemed to suggest her guilt. "Are you sure it was even a woman?"

Hooper shrugged. "Hard to tell. Could've been a man with a wig on. That camera's at least ten years old. Maybe the FBI can do more with it."

A sudden thought speared Toby's consciousness. "Could that hair fiber have come from a wig?"

"Doubtful," Hooper said, dashing his sudden hope. "More like hair from a stuffed animal."

That didn't make much sense.

Out in the yard, the bugle trumpeted, signaling the start of the CPX. Having agreed to take Lt. Ashby's place as acting XO, Toby excused himself and made his way toward the house, climbing the steps to stand on the fresh cedar planks of the porch and announce Dylan's arrival.

Shivering with a mix of cold and premonition, he surveyed the troops jockeying for position in the yard. The privilege of acting as the XO sat uncomfortably in his craw. Here he was, attached to the entity seeking to put Dylan behind bars while filling the large shoes of the one man whose loyalty could never be questioned.

As he gazed out at the men stamping their feet against the cold, their exhalations forming a misty vapor before their ruddy faces, he wondered if the rumors had begun to circulate about Dylan's potential involvement in Treyburn's murder. Then he imagined she was having second thoughts about running the CPX today, what with the worry that she might soon be arrested. He glanced at his watch. It wasn't like her to run even a minute late.

The door behind him wafted open, and he turned with a guilty start to snatch open the screen door. Dylan stepped through it, looking pale but somehow regal in her battle dress uniform. The burgundy beret sat regally upon her neatly braided hair. Her eyes caught and held the amber rays of morning as she cast him a wan smile that made his breath catch as it always did. Even in the face of adversity, she exuded dignity.

"I love you," he mouthed, chuckling when his words awakened color in her cheeks. And then, in a poor imitation of Terrence Ashby's ceremonial pomp, he presented Dylan to her militia before trailing her into the yard, walking just to her left and one step behind.

The dead grass crunched beneath their boots as they approached her now-quiet army. In the saluting soldiers' eyes, Toby read reverence and respect that came from their lifelong acquaintance, not to mention the respect her father had commanded and that she'd inherited.

"Stand at ease," she called, and the soldiers snapped their arms to their sides.

A moment of awkward silence ensued as she considered them with gravity. "The inspection and the march will commence shortly," she announced. "I know you are as eager as I to prepare for our protest at the fusion center in Woodlawn next Saturday. This being the final exercise of the year, I would like to share a word with you first." She glanced over at Toby, who pondered what she was about to say.

"As you all can see, Lt. Ashby is indisposed this morning. Most likely, he will not be joining us again. Your prayers for his health are requested." Her voice wobbled and she took a moment to tether her runaway emotions. Pressure descended onto Toby's chest as he considered how hard it was for her to watch her friend decline.

"I would like to remind you that my term as your captain ends this December," she continued, probably unaware that she wrung her hands as she spoke. "It has been an honor and a privilege to lead you." An air of expectancy hovered over the crowd. "However, I will not be running for re-election."

Murmured protests mimicked the sound of swarming bees. Dylan held up a hand. "Without the aid of my executive officer, whose health does not permit him to continue in his office, I would not be the kind of leader you deserve."

Once again, the soldiers objected, turning to their neighbors to voice their dismay.

Dylan raised her volume to be heard over the din, which promptly died down again. "*If* I am not in attendance at the fusion center protest next weekend, it must go on." A profound silence fell over the yard, as soldiers eyed her curiously. "You know what to do. Bring your signs from home and carry them peacefully."

"Where will you be?"

Dylan stiffened at the question that was called out from the back.

Toby pitied her. "You don't have to tell them," he murmured for her ears only.

In an admirably steady voice Dylan answered, "The FBI believes I'm responsible for the murder of General Treyburn, which occurred two nights ago."

A shocked hush emanated from the assembly.

"Those of you who knew my father," she pressed on, her voice gathering strength, "know that I was raised to value the sanctity of life. I had nothing to do with General Treyburn's murder."

Shouts of indignation erupted without warning, turning into a roar of solidarity.

"You will carry on without me," she shouted. "Until a new captain is elected, I am still your leader, and as your leader I command you to cooperate with the FBI's investigation. You may defend my innocence with your words alone and continue to trust in a justice system, which assures us that every man and woman is innocent until *proven* guilty!"

A roar of support followed her exhortation. With a nod of thanks, Dylan pivoted to inspect Toby's uniform through tear-bright eyes. Finding nothing out of place, she choked out, "Proceed with the inspection and the march," and retreated to a distance to collect herself.

Torn between wanting to comfort her and fulfilling his duties as the acting XO, Toby stepped forward to inspect the three sergeants, urging them under his breath to rush their own inspections. A brisk march to the firing range, followed by rigorous training, would give the militia an outlet for their rising resentment. He could tell by the speculative talk that, as a body, the militia saw circumstances only one way: their leader was being falsely accused by a government they already held in suspicion and contempt.

"Run them," he suggested to Dylan, who pulled herself together sufficiently to set a swift pace to the range.

But, even there, tension continued to ebb and flow. Toby worked hard to retain an air of normalcy. But with their ire and their anxiety levels raised, the soldiers were quick to quarrel. It was all he could do to keep brawls from breaking out.

At last, Ackerman sounded the retreat on his bugle. The soldiers slung their packs on their backs, hefted their rifles, and fell into line for the return march back to the house. Seeing Dylan move to the front of the pack, Toby quickened his pace to catch up to her.

"You hanging in there?" he inquired with a sidelong look.

"Sure." She tossed him a quick-to-fade smile. "It's weird to think that this is my final exercise."

They walked together, briskly, in comfortable silence.

"What are you going to do with yourself when you're no longer a militia leader?" he asked her, brushing aside the issue of her still having to defend her innocence.

She squinted off into the distance. "Well, I'll always be a doctor, but I was also thinking of farming the orchard again."

"Really?" He felt a grin split his face. "I think that's a great idea." The picture in his head warmed him from the inside out.

Some of the tension in her face disappeared. "You

think so?"

"I know so. You've got all the help you need to do it, too."

"Does that mean you'll help?"

Her question hit him like a right hook coming out of nowhere. He fought to keep his smile in place as regret vied with poignant longing for things to remain just the way they were. "We'll talk about it," he promised. "There's something I need to tell you first, as soon as the CPX is over." He'd put it off long enough. He wouldn't blame her, either, if she hated him afterwards and never wanted to lay eyes on him again.

The muscles in her face tightened all over again. "Why can't you tell me now?"

"I just can't." The phone hidden in the lining of his jacket emitted a sharp electric charge against his hip, distracting him. Why the hell would Ike be calling him now, when he couldn't possibly answer? His pulse kicked at the suspicion that there'd been a breakthrough in the investigation.

"Who's that?"

Dylan's sharp tone pulled him out of his preoccupied state. Following her stare across the swale separating two hills, he recognized the unmistakable form of two FBI-owned Tahoes pulling up to Dylan's front porch. The doors of the black SUVs popped open, and a total of six special agents sprang out of them, either blithely unaware or too arrogant to care that an army was about to come marching up over the adjacent hill.

Toby drew to a startled halt. What was the FBI thinking, showing up on Dylan's property while her militia was in training?

Suddenly, the screen door flew open, and Lt. Ashby tottered onto the stoop, his crutch under one arm and his rifle in the other. He heaved it upward, pointing the muzzle squarely at the approaching special agents. *Oh, shit*, Toby thought.

"No!" Dylan broke into a sprint, prompting Toby to give chase.

"Dylan, wait!"

"Terrence, it's fine," she shouted, racing ahead of Toby, who fought to overtake her.

Down the rest of the hill and up the long slope to the house she ran, her long legs keeping her in the lead. Two hundred yards narrowed to a hundred, then fifty. Toby sent a harried glance over his shoulders. More than a dozen civilian soldiers were just now cresting the hill behind them, confusion registering on their faces as they beheld the official-looking vehicles at the house and the stand-off taking place.

This is going to get ugly, Toby thought, with a burst of speed.

Suddenly, a rifle went off. The sound of it echoed off the surrounding hills followed immediately by the sound of a bullet punching through the windshield of one of the FBI's SUVs. "Get down!" Toby yelled. Dropping his own rifle, he hooked Dylan with his free arm and tackled her into the grass.

As he rolled to break their fall, he craned his neck for the source of the shot. It wasn't Lt. Ashby, who'd lowered his shot gun with a startled look. The FBI agents, seeing an army headed in their direction backed cautiously toward their Tahoes.

Dylan squirmed beneath Toby. "Stay down," he ordered, afraid that some random bullet might yet come their way. "Hold your fire, god damn it!" he bellowed at the soldiers running in their direction, looking more confused and angrier by the moment. "No one shoots. Put your weapons down, now!"

The sound of his own pounding heart drummed

within his ears as, one by one, members of the militia, recalling Dylan's earlier orders to them, rested the butts of their rifles on the ground. Standing shoulder to shoulder, they formed a wall of distrust. Eyes darted here and there as they sought to determine who had fired in the first place. A tense hush fell over the land, broken only by the cry of a hawk soaring high above them.

"Let me up," Dylan insisted. "I need to handle this."

Reluctance weighted Toby's limbs. He didn't want to let her up, didn't want to let her go, not now, not ever. The FBI wasn't here to talk to her this time. Armed with the evidence Hooper had gathered, they must have decided they had enough proof to convict her. Ike must have been trying to warn him with that phone call.

"Keep your weapons lowered," Toby repeated as he levered himself off Dylan and helped her to her feet. Everything was coming to a head faster than he'd thought it would.

Dylan pointed a finger at her soldiers. "Hold your fire," she repeated. Slapping the dirt and grass off her uniform, she adjusted her beret and started uphill.

Crack! Thunk! Another bullet shattered the tense silence, piercing the fender of the second Tahoe. Special Agent Palmer gave a roar of outrage, audible even from a distance.

Toby tackled Dylan to the ground a second time. Adrenaline juggernauted through him, making his head pound with frustration. *Jesus Christ! Who was firing on the freaking FBI?* He craned his neck trying to pinpoint the culprit. Whoever it was, his behavior was influencing the soldiers to do likewise. Two at a time, they came to a consensus, picking up their rifles and shouldering them in an effort to chase off the interlopers.

Ugly isn't the right word for this.

Lt. Ashby's booming voice reached Toby's ears. "If I were you, I'd leave right now," he cautioned the agents.

Toby agreed. Good idea. Get the hell out, now.

A brief discussion between the FBI special agents ended with the slamming of car doors and the revving of engines. Then the Tahoes took off, spinning up clods of dirt in their haste to hightail it off Dylan's property. Toby breathed a sigh of relief and rolled off Dylan to cast a grateful gaze at the robin's egg sky.

Her pale face reclaimed his attention as she kneeled next to him. "Talk about poor timing," she exclaimed in a shaken voice.

"Idiots," he agreed, drawing his knuckles down one side of her ashen face.

"You lying son of a bitch!" A rusty, furious voice intruded on their momentary interlude as Cal Fallon pushed through the line of soldiers to confront Toby.

Aw, hell, Toby thought. *Here it comes.* And he could only blame himself for putting off the truth when he should have come clean. He rolled to his feet, snatching up his rifle out of pure reflex.

"You liar," Cal roared. His face ruddy with fury, the Sheriff of Harpers Ferry barreled into Toby, shoving him hard. "You said you'd protect her, you son-of-a-bitch!"

Toby staggered back a step. "Easy, Cal. Don't do this, now." The odor of smokeless gunpowder clung heavily to the man's cammies, leading Toby to assume that he'd been the one firing on the FBI, but then, they'd all just come from the firing range. Fallon had tossed his rifle aside to free his hands, but he still had his side arm, a 9 mm pistol, in the holster under his arm pit.

Dylan scrambled to her feet and leapt between them.

Toby swept her behind him, out of harm's way. He clutched his rifle indecisively. Between Fallon's pistol and the roughly sixty or so armed soldiers standing behind him, he didn't stand a chance to defend himself with it.

"I've kept quiet long enough," Fallon snarled. "You want to know who he is?" he asked Dylan while pointing an accusing finger at Toby's chest.

"I was going to tell her myself, right after the CPX," Toby grated. "Don't make things worse."

"He's a god-damn Fed!" Fallon spat, ignoring Toby's words entirely and gesturing in the direction of the fleeing agents. "Just like them."

"What?"

The anguished question wrested Toby's attention from his accuser. He turned his head to plead for her understanding. "I work for the federal government, Dylan. But I know you're innocent, and I'm working with Fallon and Hooper to prove it."

The indignant mutterings of the soldiers gathering around them raised the hairs on the back of Toby's neck.

He held his hand out, palm up, entreating her forgiveness. "I would never hurt you, Dylan. You have to know that's true."

She staggered backward, her shock and horror utterly apparent. "You kept this a secret from me?" she demanded of Cal, all the while eying Toby like she'd never seen him before.

The click of a 9 mm pistol froze Toby's blood. He looked over to see Fallon staring down his sights at him, pistol aimed at Toby's chest. "He promised he would defend you," the sheriff explained through his teeth, "but that was obviously a lie. Drop it," he warned.

Reluctantly, seeing no way out of his predicament,

Toby set the rifle at his feet.

Fallon approached him and kicked it out of the way. With identical looks of incredulity and betrayal, Morrison, Ackerman, and Lee closed a noose around Toby as Fallon circled him. "Down on your stomach. Now," the sheriff commanded, his aim steady.

Following her initial outburst, Dylan fell mute.

Slowly, with a sardonic twist of his lips, Toby complied. Lying face-down on the cold earth, he wished he'd just bitten the bullet and told Dylan the truth the night before, back when he'd had the chance. If only she hadn't had so damn much to deal with already. If only he hadn't wanted to bask in her devotion a little longer.

Fallon's knee gouged his spine, sending shards of pain to his extremities. Sparing himself the indignity of being outnumbered, Toby let the sheriff cuff him roughly. Steel circlets bit into his wrists before he was yanked upright, back on his feet.

A disturbance on the fringes of the group announced Lt. Ashby's arrival. He had made his way off the porch and down the slope to join them. With a cry of consternation, Dylan rushed over to bolster up her friend, putting her shoulder under his free arm.

Lt. Ashby's dark, pain-glazed eyes alighted on Toby as he weaved on his crutch. "Is this true?" he demanded, laboring to catch his breath. "You work for the FBI?" he huffed with incredulity.

"Not exactly," Toby muttered, ashamed to cause the sick man any anguish. "I'm with a counterterrorist taskforce group that operates in support of Homeland Security."

"He's an informant," Fallon interjected giving the cuffs a yank.

"You think we're terrorists?" Ashby demanded with a visible shudder.

Toby let his gaze convey his deep regret. "No, of course not," he said gently.

"What do we do with him?" Ackerman asked, eyeing Tobias with malicious anticipation.

Lt. Ashby looked at Dylan, who stared down at the grass with a frozen expression. "What do you think?" the XO asked her.

She shook her head, unable to speak, unable to bring herself to even look at Toby. He knew he'd get no reprieve from her—not today, maybe never.

"I say we hold him hostage," Fallon suggested. "And we refuse to release him unless the Feds drop their charges against our leader."

A rousing huzzah followed Fallon's suggestion.

Toby looked back at Terrence Ashby, hoping to appeal to his common sense. "You'll have a war on your hands if you do that," he predicted. "A massacre along the lines of Waco. Just let me go. I can be a liaison between the local authorities and the FBI. I can help prove Dylan's innocence."

"We've trained for this," Cal Fallon continued as if Toby hadn't spoken at all. He spoke to the militia at large. "Are we going to let the Feds trespass on our leader's property?"

"No!"

"Strip her of her inalienable rights and arrest her for crimes she didn't commit?"

"No!"

"You know what I think?" Ackerman piped up, pinning Toby with a tightlipped glare. "I think the Feds faked General Treyburn's death just so they could frame Captain Connelly and shut us down. We're a threat to their tyranny!"

"Yeah!" Several in the crowd cheered Ackerman's paranoid conclusions while others like Dylan and Lt. Ashby just looked at him with their eyebrows raised.

At last, Dylan's brittle, disillusioned voice cut through the rabble rousing. "We're not taking anyone hostage," she declared, and Toby released the breath he hadn't realized he was holding.

"Ivan, collect Burke's possessions from the attic and his dog from the house," she said, removing the hair-trigger Ackerman from the scene. "Sheriff Fallon, kindly escort Burke off my property." Her voice wobbled slightly. She cut a concerned glance at the man leaning heavily on her shoulders before addressing her soldiers as a body. "If you all wish to keep the FBI from coming back, I give you permission to defend my property," she added. "But no one, and I mean *no one*, shoots to kill. Do I make myself clear?"

"Yes, ma'am!"

Look at me, beautiful, Toby willed, attempting to catch Dylan's eye. I'm so sorry. I didn't mean for you to find out this way.

But she studiously avoided his gaze.

As Ackerman stormed off to the house to collect Toby's things, Fallon swung Toby around and shoved him to get him moving. "Walk," he growled when Toby resisted.

He was hoping Dylan would look at him, just one more time, so he could convey his remorse with his eyes. But she turned her back deliberately to assist Lt. Ashby in making the long trek back to the house. Just like that, she had dismissed him from her thoughts, her life, her future.

With what felt like a gaping wound in his heart, Toby let himself be prodded toward the yard. A contingent of soldiers followed them. As they passed the front of the house, Milly burst through the screen door and streaked across the yard to join him, tail wagging, oblivious to his plight. Toby, with his hands cuffed behind his back, signaled awkwardly for her to heel. She flanked him as he and Fallon started down the long driveway.

"I've got it from here, fellas," Fallon told the stunned soldiers that still followed them. "Return to your NCOs to receive your orders. It's going to take all of us to hold off the OpFor."

In the distance, Toby could hear Morrison and Lee barking out orders to secure the perimeter, which would be all four corners of Dylan's vast property. For as long as the militia had been in existence, it had trained to deflect an invasion by oppositional forces. Today, in their minds, training had transitioned into reality.

Each man in the militia carried a three-day supply of rations; after that, they would have to rely on whatever Dylan's pantry had in store to keep them fed. Within a week, they'd all be hungry and tired and ready to go back to their real lives.

"Keep walking," Cal growled, shoving Toby to get him moving.

Every muscle in Toby's body balked at leaving. If only he could turn back the hands of time, he would tell Dylan about the amazing woman he had met on his undercover assignment. She wasn't the lunatic the government had made her out to be. She had done her best to turn her emotional anguish into something positive for others. She'd led the militia to uphold tradition and to combat her PTSD. She'd given both herself and others a sense of purpose. Dylan had integrity and compassion, and he admired the hell out of her.

He would tell her that, whether she forgave him or not, he would do whatever it took to keep her out of jail. Whoever the cold-hearted bastard was that was trying to frame her, *that* asshole was going to account for what he'd done.

Speaking of assholes, he could hear Ackerman running down the driveway to catch up to them, wheezing under the weight of Toby's duffle bag.

"Wait," Ivan called, and Cal Fallon jerked Toby to a stop.

"I ain't gonna carry his bag any further," Ivan declared, slowing his step. He threw the duffle bag at Toby, just like Toby knew he would. Of course, with his hands cuffed behind his back, it bounced off his chest and hit the ground. Startled, Milly scuttled out of the way.

"Love you, too, man," Toby said, just like he had the day Ackerman had lobbed his bedroll at him.

"Man, fuck you," Ivan countered, predictably.

Toby just rolled his eyes and then he started to grin as Cal Fallon shifted his aim so that he was pointing his gun at Sergeant Ackerman instead of at him.

"Pick it up and carry it to the head of the driveway," the sheriff ordered.

"What?"

"You heard me. If you don't want me telling the others that you lied about your past, then you'll do as I say."

When Ackerman blanched, Toby swung his gaze back and forth between them. "What do you mean, he lied about his past?"

Fallon curled his lip and mocked, "Figure it out yourself, wise guy."

With darting eyes, Ivan Ackerman snatched up Toby's duffle bag. Clutching it to his chest, he ran ahead of them with his awkward, loping gait. As Cal prodded Toby into motion again, he watched Ackerman drop his bag by the mailbox, send one last fearful glance in their direction, then hightail it through the orchard.

Well, I'll be damned, Toby thought, wondering what fact Fallon had unearthed and why he hadn't shared his information with Toby earlier.

Once Ackerman was out of sight, Cal Fallon shoved his pistol in his holster and started to take off Toby's handcuffs.

"Sorry about the rough treatment," he apologized, "but I did tell you I'd make your life a living hell if you let Dylan take the rap for Nolan's murder. And now there's this new case in which she's the suspect."

"You did warn me," Toby conceded, shaking out his arms. "And I intend to keep my promise. But you damn well didn't need to pull the rug out from under her feet that way," he railed, his resentment bubbling anew.

Cal's facial muscles flexed with sudden self-doubt. "Well, don't just stand there, bitching me out. Call your buddies in the FBI and tell them to pick you up. I know you've got some way to reach them."

The impulse to tackle Fallon to the ground and punish him for destroying whatever slim chance he and Dylan might have had tempted Toby briefly.

But in Cal's defense, he'd been protecting Dylan in the same way that Toby had been trying to protect her. Ultimately they were on the same team, only the sheriff didn't believe it yet.

"She's more vulnerable than ever without me. Just so you know, we love each other—or at least she did love me until you screwed that up. If she hurts herself now, then that's on you," Toby declared.

Snatching his duffle bag off the ground, he called Milly after him and turned his back on Dylan's farm, aware that he was leaving his heart behind him. The phone call could wait. He needed time to collect his mixed emotions—remorse, worry, anger, and loss—before calling anyone to pick him up.

Besides, if the FBI came anywhere close to Dylan's property right now, another Civil War just might break out.

CHAPTER 16

By the nightlight plugged into the socket, Dylan kept an eye on the rise and fall of her dear friend's chest as he slept. Outside his window, she could hear the occasional snippet of conversation as soldiers tramped across the dark yard. They'd been trained to rotate shifts every four hours, thus preventing boredom or risking the chance of anyone falling asleep on watch. Her radio, set to a new frequency every four hours, crackled softly on the bureau, its volume lowered so as not to interfere with Terrence's rest.

His confrontation with the FBI today had sapped what little remained of his strength. He'd refused to eat, to take his pain pills, to do anything but retreat into silence. Dylan knew he blamed himself for insisting that Burke join the SAM, only to have him turn out to be a traitor.

For the hundredth time that day, she closed her eyes and rubbed her aching temples. Her world—this carefully constructed reality that she had pieced together to give her life direction—was crumbling. It was just a matter of time, a week at most, before her soldiers weakened in the face of hunger, tedium, and the pressures of loved ones. Soon after that, they'd surrender their rifles and go home. And then the FBI would swoop back in to arrest her.

All that she could hope for was to be here at Terrence's side when his spirit went to rest. The prospect of him dying alone and miserable, while she languished in jail, was simply unacceptable.

The clock next to the bed blinked as the minutes turned to zero and a new day began. Time was running out already.

Get some rest, Dylan. The echo of Toby's advice sounded in her head, prompting such a sharp pang in the region of her heart that made her gasp out loud. She pressed her knuckles to her lips to stifle the sounds.

How could she have been so blind not to have realized who he was? The truth, in retrospect, was so terribly obvious. Tobias Burke had sought her out shortly after the FBI had questioned her in connection with Secretary Nolan's murder. Now she knew why she hadn't been able to get a read on him at their very first meeting: He'd been lying.

Frame by frame, she relived the previous three weeks with him in her home. *If you want to lean on me from time to time, that's okay, too*, he'd said the night Hendrix had covered her car in spray paint, and then he'd kissed her. And just a few nights later, he'd slipped into her room and brought her to a shattering climax in what amounted to magic for her, a calculated seduction for him. Her face flamed with furious chagrin.

Then there'd been that interlude on Jefferson's Rock when he'd sung to her so sweetly and freed the pins from her hair, saying, *This is who you really are.* He had blinded her with his smile, with the warmth of his gaze and the deep rumbling sound of his laughter. He had pried her broken heart wide open and sucked out her very soul.

Bitterness launched her out of the chair. She snatched up the radio and stalked from Terrence's room, leaving his door ajar just in case. Moving down the dark hallway toward her bedroom, she remembered how Tobias had sat outside her door the night that Terrence's condition worsened. Remorse burned like acid in her stomach as she recalled how she'd wept in his arms; how he'd held her so tenderly. *Don't apologize to me,* he'd growled when she'd told him she was sorry.

Confused by the memory, Dylan pushed into her room. Keeping her gaze averted from the bed they'd shared, she stormed to the window to search the dark terrain outside for signs of her loyal soldiers. The reflective tape on someone's uniform glimmered in the orchard. A flashlight winked on the horizon and turned off again. She pictured her followers huddled up for warmth on the cold ground and pitied them for their pointless efforts.

Protect them, Father, she prayed. It would be the saddest of ironies if a skirmish between federal forces and her militia broke out because of her. Her future meant nothing now. Her brief hope, her dream of starting a new life had been snatched away by an FBI informant, who'd resurrected her heart, only to murder it again.

Leaving the window sash raised, she turned blindly toward her bed and sprawled across it with her eyes tightly shut. Tobias's unique scent still clung to the sheets, bearing with it memories of unsurpassed pleasure, of tenderness, and of intimacy.

Don't cry, she commanded herself. *It wasn't real.*

But the floodgates parted, and the sobs that broke

free shook her entire frame.

She'd loved him, more than she had ever loved any man. To think that he had aroused her passions and aroused her affections—not because he had genuinely wanted to—but because he was being paid to do it! Beyond his deceit and outright lies, that betrayal stung the most.

God help me, she thought, *but I will never, ever forgive him.*

The Quality Hotel and Conference Center, situated two miles from historic Harpers Ferry, served a complimentary breakfast.

Tobias, who was used to waking up at the crack of dawn and couldn't sleep worth shit in a soft, queen-sized bed without holding the woman he loved, was the first patron to sample the breakfast items. Milly followed him down the food line, sniffing appreciatively, as he dished up scrambled eggs, bacon, and toast, and poured himself a tall mug of coffee. He sat down at one of the many empty tables, and Milly flopped down next to his chair, sighing hopelessly. Only Dylan ever snuck her people food.

Toby sampled the fare on his plate and tried not to think of what might go wrong in the stand-off between the SAM and the Feds. Fiascos like the siege at Ruby Ridge and the one at Waco had changed the way law enforcement handled extremists, which meant that Palmer and the superiors directing him from headquarters would proceed with patience rather than physical force. Dylan, who had not been seen since she'd escorted Terrence into the house, would not get hurt, he assured himself. Maybe if he kept telling himself that, it would turn out to be true. If he could just shake the foreboding that kept his shoulder muscles tense.

"This seat taken?"

The whip-crack syllables could not have been uttered by anyone other than Ike Calhoun. Toby glanced up with surprise. He'd neither heard nor seen Ike coming; in fact, he didn't even know the man had left D.C. He swallowed all the food in his mouth in one gulp. "Why don't you grab a plate first?"

"In a minute." Ike took the chair across from him, sat down, and stared at him hard.

It was all Toby could do not to squirm. "Is Hamilton here, too?"

"Exercising."

"Ah." The healthy color in Ike's own face suggested that he and TJ Hamilton had hit the gym together, something Toby probably should have done, considering how restless he felt.

"What's your frame of mind, Burke?"

Ike's unexpected words had Toby wanting to push his chair out and leave. He stared back at Ike, speechless. *Like I'm going to spill out my guts to a man with no feelings.*

But Ike was persistent. "Do you still believe that the suspect is being framed?"

Toby narrowed his eyes. "You mean Dylan?" Why did Ike continue to call her the suspect?

Ike's gaze dropped to the message on Toby's T-shirt. In a fighting mood this morning, he was glad he'd put it on. MY ANGER MANAGEMENT CLASS PISSES ME OFF.

Ike's mouth twitched. "I mean Dylan," he amended. "You still think she's innocent." It wasn't a question this time.

Toby wondered if he was imagining the subtle softening around Ike's acid-green eyes. "I know she is," he asserted.

The team lead gave a nod. "Okay, then."

Toby searched the man's enigmatic face. "Okay what?"

"Let's clear her name."

Toby set his napkin slowly on the table and looked around. The place was still empty. He could feel his eyebrows creeping toward his hairline. "Won't that pit us against the FBI director?" he practically whispered.

Ike shrugged. "Does that bother you?"

Toby just looked at him. He had never cared much for Ike in the past, but at the moment, he was tempted to lunge across the table and kiss the man.

"Just tell me where you think we should start," Ike invited.

Where to start? Toby's thoughts ran in a dozen different directions. There were multiple mysteries at play. In what way had Ivan Ackerman lied about his past? Who had published the anti-war articles in Dylan's name? Who had drugged her on Halloween night? "We need to research the backgrounds of some of her colleagues and question them in person." He started to list all the persons of suspicion, ticking them off his fingers. "There's Sergeant Ackerman, Father Nesbit, the Director of the VA Medical Center, Dylan's colleagues—"

"Today's Sunday," Ike reminded him. "Her colleagues won't be working today, and her priest will be busy leading mass."

Toby reined in his expectations. "Then we research today and interview tomorrow," he amended.

A commotion in the hotel lobby drew their attention to the swarm of FBI agents pouring in from the parking lot, including Special Agent in Charge Palmer. The weary slump of that man's shoulders and his heavy eyelids connoted that he'd spent all night watching Dylan's property. As they headed for the breakfast counter, Ike got up to share a word with them.

Toby picked up his muffin and peeled off the wrapper.

Ike came back with a single mug of black coffee and resumed his seat. "The press rolled in at the crack of dawn this morning," he reported.

Toby groaned.

"A command headquarters has been set up at the new Customs and Border Protection Training Center just up the road. First meeting is at noon. We'll be there."

"Yes, sir." The respectful term came out of Toby's mouth before he could stop it. Apparently, there really *was* a first time for everything.

"We'll hold our own meeting in two hours. See you in room 312 at o' eight hundred. Bring Jackson with you." With that, Ike got up and headed toward the buffet.

Toby stacked his silverware on his plate and left the table. Having a plan beat the hell out of moping around feeling helpless. He never thought he'd say this about Ike, but the man was looking out for him. With a grateful glance in his direction, he gestured for Milly to follow, and hurried back to his room to wake up Jackson and share the news: Fatherhood had improved Ike, after all.

"Ma'am?" Sergeant Morrison hovered just outside of Dylan's open bedroom door, distracting her from the phone call she was about to make. The time had come to call her priest.

She looked up at him in exasperation. "Yes, Sergeant?"

With fifty plus troops wandering around outside and the NCOs swarming in and out of her home to direct them, privacy had become a luxury of the past. The stand-off between the Second Amendment Militia and federal forces was barely twenty-four hours old, and she was already weary of the bustle and confusion taking place around her. At least morale was high. The troops had plenty of their own provisions, but Dylan got no pleasure out of knowing they risked their lives and their reputations by keeping her out of the FBI's grasp.

She'd made up her mind. As soon as Terrence passed away—and, sadly, it would not be long now—she would quietly surrender.

"I can't find Sergeant Ackerman anywhere. He didn't sleep in his bed last night. His squad members say they haven't seen him since yesterday."

And why wasn't she surprised to hear it? Dylan sent Morrison a bitter smile. After all she'd done for Ackerman, he was the first to turn tail and flee. "Looks like we've had our first desertion," she replied. And it probably wouldn't be their last. "Kindly assign the members of his squad to other NCOs." Sheriff Fallon had stepped into Burke's shoes as operations sergeant, so that even without Ackerman present, she still had three reliable NCOs to call upon.

"Well, good riddance," Gil Morrison declared looking like he might spit right there on the hardwood floor. "If I may be so bold, I never did like the man, regardless of what happened to him. He was a—"

Dylan cut him off. "If you don't mind, Sergeant, I was about to make a phone call."

"Oh. Yes, ma'am. Sorry, ma'am."

"Carry on, Sergeant."

Morrison scuttled out of sight, and Dylan drew a bracing breath. Lifting the receiver, she tapped out a number she had known all her life. It was only seven-thirty in the morning—funny how she'd already stopped thinking in military time. Her priest was probably heading toward the church right now to prepare for the eight o'clock service. She'd have to leave a message.

To her surprise, he answered on the third ring. "Hello."

All it took was the sound of his voice for Dylan's throat to close up. Averting her face from the still-open door, she clasped the receiver harder and choked out a single word. "Father—"

"Dylan, is that you?"

She dragged a breath into her convulsing lungs, struggling for composure. "Yes."

"Oh, my child. You must be beside yourself. The whole town is talking about it."

"Wh-what are they saying? Do they think I've gone crazy?"

"Of course not, my child. Everyone's on your side, even the local paper."

"I'm in the paper?" She'd been so caught up in Terrence's struggle that she hadn't given much thought at all to what was going on.

"The story broke on Fox 5 WTTG at dawn. You know, nothing escapes the media these days."

Dylan envisioned new journalists camped outside of her property along with the FBI agents. The story of the crazed militia leader and her loyal followers would sweep the country. She pushed the situation firmly out of her mind. It didn't matter anyway. Nothing mattered but taking care of Terrence's needs.

"That's not why I called," she said, pushing her request through an aching throat. "I'd like you to visit me as soon as possible." She struggled to articulate her next words. "Terrence is losing his battle, and I want you to give him last rites."

"Poor man." The priest clicked his tongue consolingly. "And my poor, sweet child having to go

through all this now. I would come this very
afternoon, but I have a meeting with the bishop that
cannot be rescheduled as he's headed overseas
tomorrow." The priest's tone conveyed sincere regret.
"But I can be there early Monday morning, if you
think he'll make it that long."

She swallowed hard. "I think so."

"Tomorrow, then. I trust the FBI will let me through
their roadblock."

She blinked. "They've closed the roads?"

"Since yesterday. It's all they can do to keep the
press as far away as possible. Under the
circumstances, I'm sure they'll let me through. If they
don't, I'll call you. We'll work something out."

She floundered like a sinking ship. "I need to see
you."

"I'm with you in spirit, darling. And soon, I'll be
there in person. Have faith, Dylan."

The phone clicked in her ear, and Dylan slowly
replaced the receiver. The premonition that the stand-
off between the SAM and the FBI would end
tragically kept her in a cold sweat. The famous words
of her ancestor, John Brown, recorded right there in
the book beside her bed came to mind, giving rise to a
shiver of dread.

*I, John Brown, am now quite certain that the crimes
of this guilty land can never be purged away but with
blood.*

God forbid that was still as true today as it was a
hundred and fifty-odd years ago.

Toby and Jackson knocked on room 312 at one
minute to eight. Milly sniffed the crack at the bottom
of the door and wagged her tail.

Not a sound preceded the door swinging open. TJ
Hamilton filled the opening. His raven, shoulder-

length hair appeared damp from a recent shower. Looking fit and obscenely tall, he raked his colleagues with his dark, all-seeing eyes before letting them wordlessly in the room.

Toby looked around.

Ike had checked into a two-room suite with a cushy office/living area in the middle. The team lead sat at his desk staring intently at his MacBook Pro. "Have a seat," he invited without glancing up. With his sleeves cuffed and his collared shirt unbuttoned, Ike looked more human than Toby could ever recall seeing him.

He and Jackson sank down on the couch. Hamilton folded his towering frame into the armchair. Tearing his attention from his laptop, Ike slid his wheeled chair to the edge of his desk to address them.

"So, we have an unprecedented situation," he began. "The FBI is engaged in a stand-off with the suspect— Dylan—" he amended, catching Toby's eye, "who allegedly murdered both Nolan and Treyburn. Burke, who knows her better than anybody, insists that she's innocent. And while we support the FBI, our primary mission is to promote homeland security, which—to me—means that we are obligated to find the real killer. Are you with me so far?"

The Taskforce team members murmured their agreement.

"Clearly whoever is framing Dylan Connelly works in close connection with her," Ike continued. "Close enough to upload documents at the hospital where she works, to plant evidence in her barn, to drive her car into Washington, D.C., the day before Nolan's murder. One possibility is Ivan Ackerman, her supply sergeant. I located his military file this morning."

Ike dragged his laptop closer, and consulted the screen. "Ackerman was a food service specialist in the U.S. Army. He was medically discharged after the mess hall in Camp Liberty was struck by a mortar attack last year. He returned to his home in Martinsburg, West Virginia, where he was treated for PTSD at the VA medical center. He would have met Dylan there."

Toby asked, "What's it say about his wife and daughter?"

Ike skimmed the document and found an answer. "Married in 1999 and divorced in 2002. No record of any dependents."

"What the hell?" Toby's outburst earned him startled looks. "The SOB told Dylan that his wife and daughter were gunned down by a shooter at the mall."

Jackson steepled his fingers. "A story guaranteed to elicit sympathy," he pointed out.

Ike pressed on. "According to Ackerman's file, he was expelled from high school for bringing a weapon onto school grounds. He took the GED and graduated early and the Army took him in. He may look fishy, but I don't see any motive on his part to target heads of state."

Toby had to agree. Ackerman didn't seem bright enough to know what was going on in the political arena.

"On the other hand, he might have been working at someone else's behest," the team lead suggested. "So we'll keep him on our radar."

Toby thought of something. "He gets counseling at the medical center every Tuesday. Maybe his doctor could give us some insight."

Ike crossed his arms and sat back. "About that," he said, "we don't have any legal right to solicit medical information, but we can canvas the staff and have a good look around. Palmer's going to realize what we're up to if we're not discreet." He nodded at Toby. "You and Jackson head over to the VA hospital tomorrow morning while Hamilton and I dig deeper on these suspects." His green gaze focused on Toby's smart aleck T-shirt. "Is that all you have to wear?"

Toby plucked at his casual garb. "I didn't know I'd be masquerading as an FBI agent," he apologized.

"There's a mall in Martinsburg," Ike informed him. "Opens at ten. Go buy yourself a suit. And hurry back in time for Palmer's briefing at the training center."

Minutes later, Toby, Jackson, and Milly squealed out of the hotel parking lot in Jackson's black Chrysler. Possibilities circuited Toby's brain. Had Ackerman done more than lie about his past? Had he planted the pipe and the copper wires on Dylan's property where the Feds were sure to find it? If he'd been working in cahoots with someone—then who? And why hadn't Sheriff Fallon exposed Ackerman as a liar earlier?

Something had to shake out tomorrow when he and Jackson panned the hospital staff. The FBI was tightening their noose around Dylan, and there was only so much time before they kicked the stool out from under her and strung her up for good. If the Taskforce was going to prove her innocence, then they needed to do it fast.

Dylan gripped the phone tighter. Her blood simmered at the way the FBI negotiators sought to manipulate her. When the first negotiator had called an hour ago, he'd played hardball. Unless her soldiers peacefully surrendered, he'd threatened, she was looking at life in jail, possibly the death penalty. Her PTSD had flared like dry tinder at his incendiary language. She'd lashed out at him and hung up the phone.

This second call came from a different negotiator, the one playing Good Cop. He apologized for his colleague's coarse manners and, on a more conciliatory note, asked if there was anything the FBI could do to assist her. Dylan rolled her eyes. "Listen," she commanded, "I don't have time to play childish games. Here's how the situation works: You stay off my property, giving me time to nurse my terminally ill executive officer, and my soldiers won't shoot anyone. Try trespassing on my land to arrest me, and you'll have a war on your hands. I give you my word that when my XO passes, I'll surrender."

Professing dismay and concern, the Good Cop negotiator promptly offered her medical assistance.

Dylan pictured an ambulance with a SWAT team hiding inside it. "I'm a physician," she reminded him. "Another doctor isn't going to make a difference in his case."

"How long do you think…?"

She cut him off. "Until he dies, you mean?" PTSD reared its grizzly head, causing her to counter attack. "Don't…don't talk about him like he's a temporary inconvenience!" she railed. "He's my friend, damn you!"

"I'm sorry, Dylan. I didn't mean to be disrespectful."

"Then address me as Captain Connelly. And tomorrow, when my priest comes to administer last rites, kindly see that he's allowed through the road block."

"Of course. No problem."

"Thank you," she bit out, slamming down the receiver a second time. In a vain attempt to ease the tension gripping her shoulders, she massaged the knots near the base of her neck. The phone jangled again, and her tension doubled. With a pulse of irritation tapping at her temple, she decided to ignore it.

* * *

"Come on, Dylan," Toby muttered. The rural highway conveying him and Jackson to the mall in Martinsburg took them through rolling pastures. "She's not answering," he groused, counting the rings over the sound of Milly panting in the back seat.

Jackson shot him a sympathetic glance. "Leave her a message," he suggested.

Dylan's voice barked suddenly in his ear. "What now?" she demanded.

The defensive question threw Toby off balance for a second. Had she been expecting someone else? "Hey, babe. It's me." He winced, regretting the endearment immediately.

She kept silent so long that he checked the bars on his cell to see if he'd lost reception.

"What do you want?"

Her belligerent tone offered no hope for forgiveness. "Um…I'm calling to apologize."

His words met with a bitter-sounding laugh. He forged ahead before he lost all courage. "I never meant to hurt you, Dylan. I'm so sorry."

"Do you really think an apology is all you owe me?" He'd heard that raised pitch before, signaling grave distress. "Every word you ever said to me was a lie."

If only he was there to soothe her with his touch. "That's not true—"

"It's not? You said you wanted to join my militia so you could serve your country."

"That's what I thought I was doing, but—"

"You said I could lean on you."

"Dylan, you can. I'm still here. I'll always be here for you."

"You've never been diagnosed with PTSD, have

you?" she demanded, throwing him a left hook.

Toby cringed. "No, I haven't," he admitted. "Milly's a bomb-sniffing dog, not a therapy dog." Two black and white heifers grazing peacefully alongside the highway stared at him, as if dumbstruck.

Dylan's bitter laugh raked over his conscience like claws. "Then everything you ever told me was a lie. *Everything.*"

He bristled. "Not everything. And I didn't lie to you to hurt you, Dylan. I had a job to do. What I said about my feelings for you—" he flicked an uncomfortable glance at his colleague and pitched his voice lower. "—that was absolutely true."

Cynical silence followed his humbling confession.

"Please believe me. Whatever it takes to—"

The line went suddenly dead. Toby's hand fell like a lead weight to his lap, and a vice clamped down around his chest. She'd hung up on him.

Milly, sensing his sudden upset, snuffled at his ear and delicately licked it.

Jackson cast him a sidelong grimace. "She just needs more time," he said encouragingly.

Toby stared straight ahead, seeing nothing but flashing white and yellow lines. Time was the one thing Dylan didn't have. He'd seen the signs of her emotional distress before. Without him there to reassure her, she'd start to fall apart, lashing out in ways that would make her seem as crazy as the FBI alleged she was. She was tumbling in a downward spiral, and there was little he could do about it—not on a Sunday, anyway.

Bastard! Dylan leapt from the bed to pace the length of her room. If only she could leave the house and run, she would take off running and never stop. How she needed that release, now more than ever! But a blind sprint across her property would inevitably result in her stumbling into edgy soldiers bearing loaded M-16 rifles. She'd end up getting shot, or worse.

How dare Tobias even speak to her after what he'd done? *Babe!* She was nobody's babe, and certainly not his! What a weak, easy conquest she must have seemed to him. A few slow smiles, a couple of laughs, and one mind-blowing kiss—that's all it had taken to lure her into his trap. And now he had the gall to tell her that it hadn't been a lie? How could he possibly have loved her while sharing her innermost secrets with the FBI?

Snatching a pillow off the bed, she hurled it to the floor. The relief it brought had her reaching for another pillow and then another. When she ran out of pillows to throw, she hauled open a dresser drawer and flung its contents across her room, one fistful at a time, unmindful of the mess she was making. Her elbow caught a lamp, and it toppled to the floor, the light bulb shattering. Her throat ached with the need to scream, except she couldn't, not without disturbing Terrence, not without alerting her men.

Blinded with tears and fueled by betrayal, she tore her room apart until she was left standing up to her knees in wreckage.

Only then, did she look around and realize that she was in danger of tipping over the edge into the dark abyss of insanity.

CHAPTER 17

Wilford Loomis, the silver-haired Director of Martinsburg VA Medical Center, responded to Toby and Jackson's visit with a look of annoyance. "I thought you were dropping by this afternoon," he groused, pushing aside the fat folder on the desk in front of him.

His statement betrayed the fact that Palmer's investigative team had planned to drop by later.

Toby seized the man's assumption and ran with it. "Sorry, but we're under pressure to build our case against Dylan Connelly."

The director's eyes brightened at the mention of Dylan's downfall. "Please, have a seat."

By the time they left his office, Toby had moved Loomis to the top of his suspect list.

"You think he could be the one framing her?" Jackson muttered as they made their way toward the wing where Dylan worked.

"He hates her enough." Loomis had made no secret of his contempt for Dylan, who'd used her militia to protest one of his new hospital policies. "If anyone has the power to make her disappear at the hospital, it's that guy," Toby whispered. "Maybe he enlisted Ackerman to help him." Except Ackerman had been home on Halloween night with the other NCOs, hadn't he?

En route to Dylan's office, they encountered Leigh, the same nurse who'd dealt with Toby twice before. She caught his eye and did a double-take. "What are you doing here?" Her gaze flickered over the smart navy blue suit he wore. "I thought you were in the militia." She gasped in horror, her eyes flying to his. "You're with the FBI?" she squeaked.

He was never happier to disassociate himself. "No, actually, I'm with a taskforce dedicated to proving her innocence."

Only a portion of Leigh's suspicion faded. "Well, thank goodness," she declared, still clearly wary.

"We need your help figuring out who laced the mocha latte someone left for her the other night."

She wrung her hands. "I've been thinking about that," she admitted. "I've tried remembering who might have approached her room, but I just can't come up with anything."

"That's fine," Toby assured her. "It's not your fault she was drugged."

Jackson motioned toward the short corridor where Dylan's office was situated. "Who else has offices on this hall?" he inquired.

"The names are on all the doors," Leigh answered, "and I believe every doctor is at work today, except for Dr. Connelly, of course." She glanced over her shoulder, stepped closer and whispered, "Have you questioned Dr. Hendrix?"

"We're keeping him in mind." Except that Hendrix had been hospitalized at the time of Dylan's disappearance, and the only way he could have been involved was if he worked in cahoots with someone else. "Who else holds a grudge against her?"

She spread her hands helplessly. "Director Loomis?"

"Can you tell us who she works with on a daily or weekly basis?"

Leigh provided them with a list of doctors, nurses, orderlies and staff. "Oh, and there's also Dr. Richardson, our resident psychiatrist, whom she sees professionally, if you know what I mean," she added under her breath. "I think he's in his office now, just down the hall from hers." A disruption along the main corridor captured her attention. "You'll have to excuse me," she said, rushing off to help the orderly coax a veteran back into his wheelchair.

Toby gestured for Jackson to follow him. "Ackerman's psychiatrist. We need to talk to him anyway."

They found Dr. Richardson's office two office doors down from Dylan's and across the hall. A peek through the open door revealed a cozy ring of comfortable-looking chairs, several potted plants, and a fountain bubbling over into a granite basin. "Not here," Toby muttered.

Jackson pointed toward the glass exit doors nearby. "Do you think that's him?"

A man in a white smock stood on the cement steps outside, hugging himself against the cold as he puffed on a cigarette. Toby started toward him. "Only one way to find out." But then, considering that Dylan might have described him well enough for Richardson to guess who he was, he drew Jackson in front of him. "You do the talking," he instructed. "Don't mention my name."

Jackson nodded his understanding. "Dr. Richardson?" he called, as they pushed their way outside.

The middle-aged doctor with a shock of salt-and-pepper hair turned to take stock of them. Hazel eyes widened behind his plastic-framed lenses. "Yes." He quickly snuffed out his cigarette in a nearby ashtray and turned to face them expectantly. "Let me guess," he said, taking in their dark suits. "You're with the FBI?"

"Special Agent Maddox," Jackson said, not bothering to introduce Toby, who remained on the step behind him. Jackson shook Dr. Richardson's hand. "I'd like to ask you some questions, if you don't mind."

"Sure, sure. You want to go inside or—"

"This is fine. What can you tell us about Ivan Ackerman?" Jackson asked.

"Ackerman?" Richardson gave a startled laugh. "I thought you were going to ask me about Dylan Connelly."

"We'll get to her," Jackson promised. "Ackerman first."

"Well, he suffers from PTSD like the rest of the vets I treat around here." He gave a helpless shrug.

"Did he tell you that his wife and daughter were murdered at the mall?"

Richardson's face reflected shock. "Good heavens, no. Were they?"

"No, they weren't. So, you know how he contracted PTSD?"

"Well, yes, he was caught in a mortar attack. Being a cook and not a war fighter, he took it harder than most."

"Any idea why he would lie to Dr. Connelly about his past?"

The lines strafing Richardson's forehead deepened. "To make her feel sorry for him?" he guessed.

"Hmm," Jackson hummed. "Dylan Connelly also

came to you for treatment, is that right?"

"Yes, yes, she did. Of course, I am bound by doctor-patient confidentiality not to disclose personal information, unless this is an emergency or you have a special warrant?" he lightly fished.

"You'll see the warrant soon. I presume you know she's been charged with the murders of Defense Secretary Nolan and General Treyburn, both staunch advocates of military intervention."

"Of course. I imagine everyone knows that by now. It's all over the news."

"Do you think her capable of committing those murders?"

Richardson hesitated. His forehead creased again. "She's a remarkable individual, very tough, but at the same time, extremely vulnerable," he replied, clearly loath to categorize her as a murderer.

It sounded as though Richardson knew Dylan as well as he did. Jealousy snaked through Toby unexpectedly.

"She's seen things far more gruesome than either you or I could even imagine," Richardson continued, his eyes darkening with sympathy. "I wouldn't presume to say if she was capable of murder, or not," he replied, meeting Jackson's gaze in a challenging manner.

Jackson slid his hands into his pockets. "I understand that you prescribed her a sleeping aid?"

"Yes, uh, Hipnosedon. She was in desperate need of sleep."

"Is that a benzodiazepine?"

Richardson blinked. "Yes, it is."

"And that's in the same class as Rohypnol, correct?"

Dr. Richardson looked confused. "Both are in the Benzodiazepine family. Why would you ask?"

Jackson grimaced. "I'm afraid that's classified. Dr.

Richardson, were you working on Halloween night?"

Richardson chuckled and looked away. "Well, yes and no. I was at my niece's costume party." He reached into the pocket of his smock and pulled out his cell phone. As he did so, a bit of cellophane from the wrapper of a cigarette box fluttered from his pocket onto the step where he stood. "Here, I'll show you a picture." He turned his body to show it to Jackson. "She's fifteen, now, and it's all my brother can do to keep the boys away, so he enlisted my help."

Toby crept one step lower to assess the photo over Jackson's shoulder.

"That's me there, obviously, wearing the big bad wolf costume," Richardson explained. "There's my niece, Maxine, impersonating some teen celebrity—Selena Gomez, I suppose."

"Who's that next to her?"

"My brother, Scott."

"He looks just like you."

"We do resemble."

"Who took the picture," Toby interjected, "your wife?"

Richardson cut him a curious glance, no doubt wondering why they hadn't been introduced. "No, no. I'm divorced," he admitted. "My brother's wife took this picture, actually."

Toby couldn't help asking one more question. "So, you wore the mask the whole night?"

"Oh, heavens, no. I get claustrophobic with a mask on. Most of the time I just wore it on the top of my head. It kind of loses its impact that way, but...," He shrugged as he dropped the phone back into his smock and stepped on the cigarette wrapper.

"Well, thank you for speaking to us, doctor. I'm sure you'll hear from us again," Jackson drawled, his irony lost on Richardson but not on Toby. Palmer's team would probably question Richardson that very afternoon. "Is there anything else you'd like to share with us—something that could shed light on Miss Connelly's motives?"

The doctor pushed his glasses higher up his nose as he considered the question. "Well, if you do arrest her, just make sure she's evaluated by a qualified psychiatrist," he begged.

Jackson cocked his head. "Why is that?"

What was he implying? Toby wondered.

Richardson heaved a sigh. "I'm saying that if she *did* commit those murders, then it's possible she didn't know what she was doing. Sometimes extreme trauma—like what Dylan has experienced in the past—gives rise to dissociative identity disorder. I thought I saw evidence of that earlier in her altercations with Dr. Hendrix."

Toby gripped the metal rail as Richardson's insinuation slipped under his skin. He thought she was crazy. *Admit it, Toby*, his common sense urged, keeping him in check. *You've had the same thought.*

"If you like," Richardson suggested, "I could continue treatment with her at her home, perhaps, or in a local institution and give you my own diagnosis. I'm sure she's in a very agitated state, given all that's going on. There's even a likelihood that she's suicidal at this point."

Concern plunged through Toby, supplanting his anger.

"We'll take your offer into consideration, doctor," Jackson promised. He shook Richardson's hand one more time while Toby swiveled on the balls of his feet and stalked back inside, heading to the hospital lobby to clear his head.

"She's not crazy," he insisted when Jackson caught

up to him. "I lived with her day in and day out for three weeks. Other than her bouts of PTSD, there's nothing wrong with her mental state." Except now he couldn't stop worrying that she might actually attempt to kill herself.

Jackson sent him a searching look. "Are you sure?"

Toby sucked in a deep breath and closed his eyes, counting to five. When he opened them again, Jackson was standing a yard farther away from him. A reluctant chuckle scraped his throat. "I'm not going to hit you, Stonewall—not in public, anyway."

"You never get tired of that joke, do you?"

"Nope." Toby closed the gap between them. "Listen, if she committed the murders herself, why would she have had benzos in her bloodstream?"

"Because of the sleeping pills her doctor prescribed?" Jackson raised his eyebrows.

"Right, those are benzos, too, and only a blood test can distinguish the two. But Dylan swears she wasn't taking any sleeping pills around the night of the murder, and why would she take one at work, anyway?"

"You're taking her word for it," Jackson pointed out. "Plus, you're assuming she was drugged first, and *then* Treyburn was shot. She may have drunk the coffee *after* shooting him so that she would have an alibi. That's Palmer's take on it. Or maybe it's like Richardson said, and she just doesn't remember anything because of a dissociative identity disorder."

Toby's temper rekindled. "That's bullshit, and we can prove it."

"How?"

It came to Toby suddenly. "The coffee stain. I saw it on her carpet when I looked for her the night of the shooting. Sheriff Hooper swabbed it, which means that FBI forensics has a record of it. If traces of

Rohypnol were in that stain, then her story's true. She drank the coffee and knocked over the cup while passing out. The real killer cleaned up the spill, which was why her desk was wiped down, but he missed the stain on the carpet. Then he dragged her from her office and stowed her somewhere nearby, in an empty closet, maybe."

"With a candy wrapper in it," Jackson added.

"Exactly."

Jackson regarded him in thoughtful silence. "I'll need to call forensics to see what kind of data they have on that swab. But you're right. If traces of Rohypnol were found in the stain, it would lend credence to her story."

Hope buoyed Toby's anxious heart. "Let's search for spaces where she might have been hidden."

They spent the next hour knocking on doors and peering into office closets, storage closets, and janitor's cabinets—all without a search warrant. The doctors and nurses cooperated fully. Toby searched high and low for a candy wrapper, but found none.

"Time to go," Jackson said, glancing at his watch. "It's a quarter to twelve."

Dejected that they were no closer to solving the mystery than they'd been earlier, Toby nonetheless clapped Jackson on the back as they headed through the exit closest to their car. "Thanks for your help, man. Love you. Mean it."

Jackson shot him a grin. "Do you have a T-shirt that says that?"

"No doubt."

Milly greeted their return to the car with a happy bark. Jackson unlocked the car doors and they climbed inside, both of them lost in thought. Jackson put the air on full blast to clear the windows Milly had fogged up. "I'm sorry we didn't find anything definitive," he said to Toby.

Toby grunted his acknowledgment. If anything, they had more suspects now than ever.

As Jackson sped them toward the Customs and Border Patrol Training Center for Palmer's noon briefing, Toby mulled over what they'd learned that morning. "What do you think of Richardson as a potential suspect?" he tossed out, more curious than serious. Was his sixth sense really talking to him, or was just annoyed with Richardson for thinking Dylan was so mentally unstable?

"Richardson?" Jackson frowned at the road ahead of them. "What would his motive be?"

Toby scrubbed a hand over his face. "No idea," he admitted. "Maybe he's tired of having to treat soldiers with PTSD. But there was something about him...I can't put my finger on it."

Jackson merged onto the sparsely populated highway. "Look, I know you doubt Richardson's diagnosis," he said gently, "but if Dylan is convicted, then dissociative identity disorder may be her best defense."

"She's not crazy," Toby repeated. He lapsed into worried silence. "But she may be suicidal," he finally muttered. "I don't know how she's going to handle Ashby's death."

"Perhaps Richardson should talk to her like he offered," Jackson suggested. "We could escort him through the roadblock and drop him off a little ways from her house. Her soldiers wouldn't shoot an unarmed man, would they?"

Toby swiped a hand over his eyes. "I don't know."

"Maybe you should try calling her again."

He'd called her six times since she'd hung up on him yesterday. "She won't answer." And who could blame her? The press had probably been hounding her for interviews, and the FBI had doubtless been in touch with her, as well, alternately threatening her and persuading her to surrender.

But Jackson was right. Regardless of how Dylan felt about him now, she needed to be reassured that she wasn't in this fight alone.

"I'll call," he promised, reaching for his phone. God forbid she should try ending her life without knowing how hard he was working to save her.

Dylan knelt on the hard floor at the end of Terrence's bed, hands clasped in prayer and pressed to her lips to keep her sobs locked inside. Her aching heart kept her oblivious to the fact that her legs had gone numb as she watched Father Nesbit administer last rites. Terrence lay against his propped pillows, too feeble to move. Watery sunlight filled the open windows making his pallor all the more apparent.

The priest smoothed sacramental oil into the shape of a cross on Terrence's forehead. "Through this holy anointing, may the Lord in his love and mercy help you with the grace of the Holy Spirit," he prayed.

"Amen," Dylan whispered for Terrence, who was in too much pain to speak.

Next, Father Nesbit smoothed the oil onto the patient's palms. "May the Lord who frees you from sin save you and raise you up."

"Amen," she whispered again.

Her priest then prayed for a painless death, and Dylan added her own silent petitions. He reached for the plate he had placed on Terrence's bedside table. "I have brought provisions for your journey," he informed him. "Is he able to eat?" He glanced at Dylan for permission.

She swallowed the painful knot in her throat. "It's up to him."

Terrence made a wheezing sound and nodded.

Laying his hand over the bread, the priest blessed it, broke it, and fed a morsel to the patient, who obligingly chewed and swallowed. The priest did likewise with the cup of wine. Terrence choked and sputtered as it went down his throat. He immediately caught Dylan's eye as if to reassure her, and a helpless tear coursed Dylan's cheek. *Please don't suffer long.*

"May the Lord Jesus Christ protect you and lead you to eternal life." Nesbit sat back, squeezing the patient's hand. Then he began to put away his belongings. "I'd like to speak with you before I leave," he murmured to Dylan. "But stay with him a moment."

As Father Nesbit left the room, Dylan struggled from her knees to sit on the side of the bed. Terrence had closed his eyes. His peaceful expression alleviated some of the weight on her chest. He slit his eyes to look at her. Then his vocal chords vibrated and he spoke up unexpectedly. "Go talk to him," he exhorted.

"Hush. I will. In a bit."

"Don't grieve." His words slurred together. "I'm ready to go."

Scalding tears flooded her eyes. "Well, I'm not ready," she retorted, blinking them back.

"Forgive…Burke."

A tide of confusing emotions swept through her. "Don't mention his name to me. Why are you talking when you should be resting?"

"Be happy."

Happiness was a state of the heart so far removed from where she was at the moment that such a request seemed ludicrous. Tears of frustration rimmed her lashes. She sprang up before Terrence could see them. "I'll be back," she promised, fleeing his room.

On the landing, she encountered Father Nesbit sitting at the top of the stairs. As she neared him a helicopter skimmed over the house, so low it set the tin roof humming. The press had been circling like vultures, no doubt filming the movements of her soldiers and hoping to capture something of interest to relay to the American public. Those stations sympathetic to Washington, she was sure, were portraying her as a dangerous and radical extremist.

"Sit," he called over the din and patted the space next to him.

As she sank down beside him, the priest looped an arm around her. That single act of comfort broke the dam keeping Dylan's grief contained. She dropped her head into her hands and sobbed. When the flood abated, he patted her back, and she straightened self-consciously, wiping the wetness from her face.

"When it rains, it pours," he sympathized. "Too much is happening at once."

A welcoming numbness filled her. She nodded her agreement.

"Have you spoken to Kevin Richardson, Dylan?"

She leaned away from him, surprised.

"I know he's your counselor," the priest admitted with a self-deprecating smile. "It's one of the privileges of being a priest; we know more than we'd probably like to."

"Has he talked about me?" Dylan asked, thoroughly discomfited.

"Only to say how much he admires you. I think you should give him a call." He patted her hand and shook his head. "I'm just a priest, Dylan. I don't know how to make this better for you other than to assure you that God will get you through it, if you lean on Him."

"You've already made it better," she insisted. "Terrence is at peace, thanks to you."

He squeezed her hand and searched her gaze. "I'm not worried about Terrence. He'll soon be in a better place. It's you I fear for," he admitted, letting her glimpse his deep concern. "Kevin has helped others in your situation. He's the one you should turn to, now."

A bitter smile tugged at Dylan's mouth. Her priest thought her suicidal. Maybe she was.

"Call him," Nesbit repeated.

"I'll be okay," she insisted, telling both herself and him that.

Looking sad, perhaps because she wouldn't make him any promise, he added, "You know, I gave your father last rites when he was ill."

"I remember."

"I promised him I would look after you." His chin wobbled unexpectedly. "I feel as though I've failed him miserably in that regard."

"No." She vehemently shook her head. "No one could have protected me from what's happened. And no one can fix what's happening now." *Except possibly Tobias.* The unwelcome thought skittered through her mind.

"God can fix it," the priest insisted, lifting wet eyes to her. "Let's pray together."

Over the sounds of raised voices outside and the distant clatter of the helicopter, they prayed that Dylan would be relieved of the burden of persecution and free to live her life fully, once and for all.

"Amen," she murmured. Resignation weighted her shoulders.

Nesbit sighed. "Now, there are some earthly matters that I need to attend to. Do you know where Terrence wishes to be buried?"

Dread filled her at the prospect of having to make arrangements. "He wants to be cremated, his ashes spread across my land."

"I'll take care of it," the priest promised, patting her hand. "It's the least I can do. We'll have a lovely memorial for him when it's time."

"Thank you." His offer took a weight off her shoulders until she remembered the negotiator's warning that the FBI would arrest her the instant she stepped off her property. In that case, she wouldn't get to attend Terrence's memorial, at all.

"You're not alone, Dylan," Nesbit assured her. "In spite of all that's happening now, there's always hope."

The words reminded her of something Tobias had told her. She nodded numbly.

"Call your counselor," he repeated, pushing to his feet.

Dylan trailed him down the steps toward the front door. She watched through the screen door as he slipped into his car. It came as almost a surprise to realize it was an overcast November day. The muted sun shone feebly through the clouds to illumine the dozen or more tents pitched in her front yard. Her soldiers had set up a permanent camp, while Sheriff Fallon occupied Ackerman's old bedroom. Those who'd been relieved of their watch were either sleeping in their tents or standing about small fire pits trying to keep warm.

Beyond the barren apple trees, other militiamen kept the federal agents from trespassing on her property.

How do I get out of this?

Tobias had promised he would prove her innocence. But how could he, when all the evidence pointed to her guilt? She led an anti-government militia. She suffered from clinical PTSD. Her revolver had fired the bullets that killed General Treyburn. Either she had killed him, and she couldn't remember, or someone had methodically set her up to be their scapegoat.

A chill spread on the top of Dylan's head. Who did she know who could be so coldly calculating? It had to be someone close to her, someone she trusted. Yet, for the life of her, she couldn't imagine who would use her as his sacrificial lamb.

Father Nesbit had said there was always hope. But what hope was there that Tobias could save her now? And what made her think, after all the lies he'd told her, that she could put any faith in him at all?

With a heavy heart, she turned and plodded back upstairs, ignoring her phone as it began to ring. *Not again*. She tried to guess who was calling her. Was it the Fox News Channel or CNN this time, with a new angle to entice her to interview with them? Or perhaps the FBI negotiators had some clever new tactic up their sleeves. None of it mattered. She let her message machine take the call.

The sound of Tobias's voice had her halting on the landing. Her heart leapt up her throat.

"Hey, Dylan, it's me."

Just the sound of his voice filled her with a poignant longing to believe in him. If only he hadn't lied to her.

"Just listen to me and believe me when I tell you that I'm going to get you out of this mess. In fact, I made some headway this morning that I wanted to tell you about—"

Cynicism overtook her weak impulse to dash to the nearest phone and pick it up. Turning a deaf ear to the rest of what he had to say, Dylan plodded up the rest of the steps and turned toward Terrence's bedroom, shutting the door.

Tobias couldn't save her now. No one could.

"Okay, I've done background checks on Loomis and Richardson," Ike said to the Taskforce team, once more crammed into his hotel suite early the next morning.

The television, broadcasting the latest situation on the "Harpers Ferry Stand-off" with the volume lowered, vied for Toby's attention. News that seven of Dylan's civilian soldiers had surrendered to the FBI the previous night had taken top story. One by one, the deserters were being interviewed. With a pinch of disappointment, Toby recognized Nathan, the waiter, as one of those who'd walked out on his leader.

"Here's the bad news," Ike announced, reclaiming Toby's attention. "I've dug up every bit of dirt I could find on Dylan's colleagues, and they all come out squeaky clean. Director Loomis was a UDT diver back in 'Nam. He voted for Bush in 2000, and his stance on Syria is pro-intervention, giving him no motive to kill Nolan or Treyburn. You can scratch Loomis off our list."

Toby glanced at the television in time to hear Nathan say, "The only reason I gave up is because my wife just had a baby, and she needs my help at home."

"Then you still believe in the militia leader's innocence?" asked the reporter interviewing him.

"Hell, yes, I believe in her innocence," Nathan shot back, regaining a portion of Toby's respect. "Ask anyone around here if they think she's a murderer, and they'll tell you you're crazy. The Feds are framing her because they think the SAM threatens national security. Just what are they afraid of, that's what I want to know. If you think we're anti-government extremists, then Santa Claus must be a pedophile."

"Then there's Dr. Kevin Richardson," Ike continued, unaware of Toby's difficulty focusing. "Listen to this quote from an article in *Army Magazine*, written back in '06, when Richardson received a bronze star.'"

Ike leaned toward his laptop to read out loud. "'During the bloodiest months of the Iraq War, Captain Richardson worked 60 to 70 hours a week counseling soldiers who struggled with insomnia, nightmares, shock, and grief. Risking his own life, he boarded helicopters and joined convoys in order to reach the hundreds of shattered soldiers needing his help. Colleagues attribute his success to the instant rapport he established with the troops. Though planning to resign his commission, Richardson intends to continue comforting and healing veterans returning from war.'"

The team lead leaned back in his chair and looked at Toby. "He doesn't sound like the type to go murdering heads of state."

Toby had to admit that he didn't. But he couldn't ignore the suspicion niggling inside him. Maybe it was that bit of cellophane that had fallen out of Richardson's pocket yesterday. Every time he thought about it, he wondered if Dylan hadn't mistaken a wrapper off a box of cigarettes for a candy wrapper.

What if pack-a-day Richardson habitually stuck his wrappers in the pocket of his smock and hung them in his office closet at night? What if one of those wrappers had fallen out and Dylan held felt it when he'd stuck her in there, while helping himself to her purse and her car keys? It was totally possible.

Toby sat forward. "Bear with me for just a sec," he enjoined the others. "Imagine what it must be like to be a man in Richardson's shoes."

Ike narrowed his eyes at him. "Go ahead," he offered, giving Toby the floor.

He drew a deep breath. "Okay. Imagine that, for the past fifteen years, you've treated hundreds of soldiers whose lives have been torn apart by war. You do your best to put them back together, but they *never stop coming*. One war leads to another, first Iraq, then Afghanistan. You're exhausted trying to give these vets some kind of quality of life when along comes the threat of more urban warfare, more IEDs, more trauma. You start to wonder if there'll ever be an end to it and who will help these soldiers when you retire."

The room fell quiet with the exception of the chipper allergy commercial on TV.

Hamilton spoke up in his calm, bass voice. "But the man has an alibi."

"That's right. He was chaperoning his niece's party," Ike reminded Toby.

"Wearing a mask," Toby pointed out. "How could anyone tell if it was him or his brother, who looks just like him?"

"We ask his brother's wife," Jackson proposed, and they all turned to look at him.

Ike reached for his keyboard. "Easy enough. I'll find the brother's address right now. With a little luck you could question her this morning."

"Have we tracked down Ivan Ackerman yet?" Toby asked. "Richardson treated him for PTSD. He could have used him to plant the evidence."

Ike started sifting through his notes. "The state police haven't found him, but I came across his father's address in Martinsburg. Maybe Ackerman senior knows where his son is hiding. Why don't you drop by there after questioning Richardson's sister-in-law?"

Feeling encouraged for the first time in days, Toby entered the two addresses Ike gave him into his phone—Scott Richardson's and Ivan Ackerman Sr.'s. They had three and a half hours before Palmer's daily briefing. Wars had been won in less time, he reminded himself. With a little luck, maybe they'd find proof of Dylan's innocence, and her persecution would be over.

"Hey!"

A distant shout startled Dylan out of a light slumber. She found herself in her own bed, lying on top of the covers, having sprawled there in exhaustion toward the wee hours of the morning. The brightness of the light in the windows had her turning her head to her clock with a stab of alarm. It was 8:05 in the morning, and Terrence hadn't yet had his medicine.

Snatching up her bathrobe, she flew barefooted down the hall toward his bedroom. She was still threading her arms through the sleeves when she barreled through his door. The absolute stillness beyond drew her to a sudden stop. The way the sunlight sparkled in the suspended dust motes had her drawing a frightened breath, and the faint but unmistakable odor of death hit her nostrils.

For a brief moment, the world funneled to black and she was staring down at the mangled bodies of her boys. But then the image dissolved, giving way to the brilliance of the morning sun and the gentle coo of a dove sitting on Terrence's windowsill.

Keeping her gaze averted from the bed, Dylan watched the bird bob behind the glass. At the same time, she absorbed into herself the reality that Terrence was no longer in the room. Only his broken and diseased body remained, but he himself was as free as the bird, which lit abruptly off the sill and flew away. It had been there just long enough for Dylan to see it.

Oh, Terrence. She closed her eyes, savoring the vision and the certainty that he'd wanted her to know that he was happy. He hadn't died the way her boys had. He'd been ready to go. And though her heart felt utterly hollow and she lacked the desire to do anything but turn around and crawl back into bed, she knew she would be all right.

The realization had her opening her eyes. They slid slowly toward the bed, where she absorbed the details in as detached a manner as possible. She took a wary step closer. Terrence's eyes were closed. His jaw hung open, but there wasn't any sign that he'd struggled in his last moments. Her prayers for a peaceful death had been mercifully answered.

It's over, she thought, with a hitch of foreboding. *What happens now?*

CHAPTER 18

"Mr. Ackerman?"

"Who's wantin' to know?"

Leaning against the cold stone wall at the rear corner of the Ackerman residence, Toby overheard Jackson introducing himself and Hamilton to the individual answering their knock at 18 Piney Knob, one of two dozen mobile homes occupying a tract of forested land.

Toby, meanwhile, kept an eye on the humble abode's rear exit. The Rangers had a term for cowards who fled the scene whenever there was a confrontation—squirters. If Ivan Ackerman happened to be in his father's house, he'd go running out the back, for sure.

"He ain't here," Ackerman Sr. asserted.

"Any idea where we might find him?"

Toby rolled his eyes. Jackson was always so freaking polite. He had to be hearing the same thumps and bumps that Toby could hear as someone inside the trailer scurried around frantically. If luck was with the Taskforce members—which it had certainly been when they'd questioned Sally Richardson earlier that morning—then Ivan Ackerman was right here in his father's house panicking over the thought of being apprehended.

Toby's blood bubbled with anticipation. *Come out, come out, wherever you are.* They didn't have a warrant, which meant they couldn't break the door down. But a tip to the state police, who hadn't managed to locate Ackerman on their own, even though he owed them several outstanding fines, just might persuade Ackerman Sr. to hand his son over. Either that, or Ivan would pop out on his own, and *then* they could call the state police.

"I haven't seen my son in years." The father's belligerent lisp told Toby they wouldn't get any cooperation from him.

Toby could hear the doorknob on the back door squeaking. Anticipation whipped his muscles into a state of readiness. The hinges groaned, and he peeked around the corner of the house, only to tamp down a full-throttle charge as a middle-aged woman with frizzy hair stepped outside to light a cigarette.

Damn. Toby sagged against the corner of the house, doused in disappointment. Just then he heard the woman whisper, "All clear, honey. Hurry!"

In the next instant, Ackerman, Jr., wearing the same militia uniform he'd worn on Saturday, went streaking across the small back yard toward the cover of the pine forest, some fifty feet away. Toby let loose a whoop of relief and lit out after him. "Squirter!" he called, alerting his colleagues and praying the woman didn't produce a weapon and shoot him in the back.

The startled look on Ivan's face as he cranked his head around was one that Toby would savor for days. With a burst of speed, he barreled into Ivan, knocking him down onto a bed of pine needles that crackled and popped as they rolled. Ivan struggled but proved no match for a former state champion wrestler. Within seconds, the deserter lay face down, one arm and one leg bent up behind him, completely immobilized.

Hamilton materialized out of thin air to back Toby up, leaving Jackson to keep the residents subdued. "Police are on their way," TJ relayed.

"I've got a question for you, Ivan," Toby growled, taking advantage of the time they had to themselves to clear up certain matters. "Did Dr. Richardson give you that pipe to put in the barn?"

Ivan blanched. "Man, I told you, I found it next to the driveway," he insisted.

"You're lying. Someone told you to plant it on her property. Was it your psychiatrist? Did he also tell you to drive Dylan's Suburban into D.C. one night in September?"

"I don't know what you're talking about."

Damn it. "Are you going to play dumb with me?" Toby asked, tightening his hold.

Ivan howled in pain. "Please! Please, don't hurt me. I don't know anything, I swear."

"Then why did you desert the militia when your captain needed you, you backstabbing, weak-willed son-of-a-bitch?"

The gentle hand landing on Toby's shoulder eased the compulsion to make Ivan suffer.

"He'll spill the truth soon enough," Hamilton assured him.

The DEA agent's calm energy flowed down Toby's spine, prompting him to loosen his brutal grip. Hamilton was right. After all, Ivan was a classic squirter, the first to turn his back on his teammates. With a little persuasion from the state police, he would eventually blurt the secret he was keeping. But would he do it before the siege turned ugly? And would his words have any effect on the charges staring Dylan in the face?

Sally Richardson had told them that she'd gone to bed before the party was over, leaving her husband and her brother-in-law in charge of the party. Scott had complained the next morning that Kevin had taken off for a couple of hours, forcing him to handle the dozen or so teens on his own. Toby's theory appeared to be gaining ground. If the fur fiber found in Dylan's car matched the fur on the mask Kevin had worn that night, Dylan's good name might be cleared. But a warrant was required for that to happen, and only the FBI could get it now that they'd laid claim to the investigation. Furthermore, getting a judge to sign off on a warrant took time—twenty four hours at least.

The odds of keeping Dylan out of jail were dwindling by the moment.

Dylan startled at the slamming of the ambulance doors. Terrence's sheet-draped body had just disappeared from view. The need to ensure that he received the same care and consideration she'd bestowed on the fallen back in Afghanistan had her taking a step toward the vehicle as it pulled away. Sergeant Morrison caught her back by her elbow.

What if I never get to say good-bye? Scalding tears blurred her vision. She'd attended every one of her boys' funerals. But with her arrest now imminent, chances were she'd be deprived of that deeply symbolic experience. She'd never get to honor Terrence the way he deserved to be honored.

The lights atop the ambulance sparkled all the way down the driveway—now flanked by notably fewer cars and trucks. Its siren remained respectfully quiet. A cold chill seemed to rise from the gravel under Dylan's feet to ascend her legs and spine like mercury rising up a thermometer. It was over. Another Chapter of her life had ended.

Rousing from her self-absorption, she forced herself to consider her remaining militia members, many of whom appeared to have abandoned their posts to witness the solemn occasion. Their grimy faces reflected defeat. They had sacrificed their time and risked their lives to defend her innocence from a misguided and presumptuous federal government. Some may have lost their jobs because of their devotion to her; others had jeopardized their relationships with loved ones. She refused to ask anything more of them. The time had come to surrender.

Clearing the phlegm from her throat, she turned to tell them it was over.

"Wait." Sheriff Fallon stepped in front of her, cutting her off. "We've held out this long," he insisted, having accurately guessed her intentions. "We can hold out a little longer."

She shielded her eyes to study him incredulously. "What for, Cal?" she demanded. "They're ready to go home." She gestured toward the yard. "Look how few of them remain."

The scar hashing Fallon's upper lip whitened as his face hardened. "The whole town is behind us," he insisted. "They're protesting in the streets. The entire nation is divided! We can't quit now. This is history! This is where the people check the power of the federal government once and for all."

Dylan drew a tight breath. The legacy of being descended from John Brown was something she could not escape.

Fallon stepped closer. His slate-gray eyes burned with emotion as he added intently into her ear, "All you have to do is talk to the media and protest your innocence. When the nation sees and hears you, they'll know you've been wrongfully accused, and they'll rise up in protest of federal tyranny!"

"Stop it, Cal." She'd heard enough. "If you want to start a revolution, you can do it on your own turf. But this is *my* land, and I will not have any blood spilled on my account. Marshal the troops. Have them clean up this yard and gather their possessions. We're surrendering today."

Whirling, she marched proudly into the house to wash up and dress. If her capitulation was going to be aired on national television, then she would do it with as much dignity as she could muster.

Eastern Regional Jail in Martinsburg lacked adequate heat to warm the cinderblock maze of rooms and hallways. Even so, when Toby stepped out of the low-security corridor into the waiting lounge and realized what he was seeing on the television, his soaring hopes took a nose dive, and he broke into a cold sweat. "No fucking way."

Suddenly, it no longer mattered that Ivan Ackerman had just buckled under the threat of a lengthy jail sentence or that he'd confessed on tape who the real killer was and how he'd been paid by him to divert suspicion onto Dylan Connelly.

"We're too late," a stunned Jackson concluded, having followed Toby's horrified stare.

Ike and Hamilton joined them in the room, saw what was happening live on television, and stared in silent dismay. As a unit, they drew nearer to the wall where the TV hung to watch the unfolding news story.

Following a three day stand-off, Dylan and her militia appeared to be surrendering of their own volition.

Frustration roared through Toby as he took in the

aerial view of three dozen or so militia members marching toward the head of Dylan's driveway. They kept their hands behind their olive berets, fingers interlocked to communicate the intent to surrender. Dylan, with her burgundy beret, stood apart from the rest as she led them toward her mailbox and the wall of black SUVs lining the other side of the road. A hundred yards in either direction, border patrol agents fought to keep the press at a distance, behind a line of yellow tape.

Toby rounded on Ike. "Damn it! Why didn't Palmer tell us this was happening? Call him. Tell him what we know."

With a hard look, Ike showed him the cell phone that was already plastered to his ear. "*Obviously*, he's not answering," he bit out.

"Shit!" Toby wheeled away from the television unable to watch. Grinding the heels of his palms into his eyes, he told himself this couldn't be happening. They'd been minutes away from tipping the scales of the investigation in Dylan's favor, only to run out of time.

He'd failed her. He'd promised himself he would spare her the indignity of being arrested while a nation watched. Now, the most that he could do was get her charges dropped before she slipped off the deep end and was lost to him forever.

The Fox 5 news helicopter hovered over Dylan's orchard stirring the leaves that carpeted her estate. It would have sent the beret flying off her head if her hands weren't locked at the back of her braid, holding the hat in place.

The tramping of boots on the gravel behind her reminded her of the beat of a drum, such as the one she imagined had accompanied her ancestor to the hangman's rope.

In a solemn procession, her army marched toward the end of her driveway, where the FBI had instructed her to surrender. She'd been promised that her followers would face no charges; that she, alone, would be taken into custody.

The sight of a half-dozen black Tahoes made her stomach ache, especially when she spied the heads bobbing behind them, and the automatic rifles of at least three sharpshooters trained on her and her hesitant soldiers. At either end of the FBI convoy, media vans jammed the road as far as the eye could see. Their logos—WTTG, WJLA WUSA—marked them as stations from the metro area, all of them sympathetic to the government. Where was the local representation?

Sweat gathered at the base of Dylan's spine. *So, this is what defeat feels like.*

She cast a wary glance back at Cal Fallon, who, unlike the soldiers that had all turned in their weapons at the barn, still carried his service pistol tucked inside his shoulder holster. If Cal fired on the Feds this time, they'd end up like victims of a firing squad, all mowed down at once.

"Hands above your heads, all of you!" a voice shouted, and Dylan jerked to a stop, signaling to her soldiers to do the same.

With his pistol trained on Dylan, Special Agent in Charge Palmer crept out from behind his Tahoe and ventured warily into the road. A cadre of agents crept into the open after him, and Dylan's knees quaked as they fanned out, forming a U-shape around her and her men.

"Captain Connelly, approach the road in the company of your leaders," Palmer barked. "The rest of you boys hang back."

Dylan's boots felt like lead as she and her NCOs stepped forward. They now stood a mere twenty feet from the FBI contingent, close enough to see the mistrust tightening the agents' faces, the whites of the knuckles crooked over their triggers.

"Step slowly into the road," Palmer added.

With a sense of finality, Dylan crossed the invisible boundary of her property line.

"Sheriff, remove your weapon, now," barked Palmer, waving his pistol at Cal Fallon. "Lay it on the ground, nice and easy-like."

The resentment blazing in Cal's eyes made Dylan's heart skitter. For one terrifying second, she was certain he was going to shoot Palmer dead on the spot. But then he laid his sidearm on the street and kicked it across the asphalt at the agent.

Relief gusted out of Dylan's lungs.

"All four of you, keep your hands behind your heads and kneel," Palmer shouted.

Dylan looked sharply up at him. "But you said—"

"I know what I said," he retorted, cutting her off. Without a word of explanation, he gestured for his men to pounce on her three NCOs, forcing them to lie spread-eagle on the street and submit to a search.

"You coward," she hissed as Palmer bore down on her. "You're nothing but a god-damned liar."

"Down!" Palmer grated, pushing her prone onto the cold asphalt. Awash in humiliation and rage, she watched her leaders being patted down and cuffed, in the same way that she was.

Anger boiled in her veins, most of it self-directed for having ignored her own instincts. The damn Feds had lied to her—just like Tobias had. Were they all cheats and liars, then, making whatever false promises it took to ensure their adversary's capitulation? Of course they were. She ought to have expected that her leaders would be apprehended. Steel bit into the tender skin at her wrists, but she scarcely felt the bite, enraged as she was.

"Stand up," Palmer ordered, hauling her off the ground. No sooner had she staggered to her feet than he pushed her toward the open door of a waiting Tahoe. The sound of running feet and of her name being shouted startled her attention to the journalists rushing toward her. The throng had found a weak link in the perimeter, or—as Dylan suspected—had been allowed in by one of the agents.

"Bastards," she muttered under her breath.

Humiliation brought a flush to her cheeks as the media horde descended on her like a pack of wild animals. Camera operators zoomed in to film her being thrust into the back seat of Palmer's Tahoe. At the same time, the low-flying helicopter swooped over the crowd, snatching the beret off her head just as she was being thrust into the car. As it sailed out of sight and the door slammed shut behind her, the words of John Brown, uttered to the jury at his final hearing, reverberated in Dylan's head: *I submit. So let it be done.*

And, yet, she felt anything but complacent.

"Why the hell did you leave us out of the loop?" Toby demanded, elbowing his teammates aside to attack Palmer the instant he emerged from the high-security wing at Eastern Regional. Dylan had become a temporary inmate there, just a wing apart from Ivan Ackerman.

Ike rounded on him with a warning look, and Toby backed off, leaving Ike to handle Palmer. He was the team lead, after all.

"You had better have a damn good reason for pulling me from my prisoner right now, Calhoun,"

Palmer groused, ignoring Toby's verbal attack. "What is it? And why the hell have you been leaving me voicemails all morning?"

Ike held up the digital recorder with Ackerman's confession on it. "Listen," he said, thumbing the play button. Ackerman's sobbing declaration echoed off the cinderblock walls.

He told me to leave the pipe out where someone might see it. I swear to you, he didn't tell me why or I wouldn't have done it.

And what did he give you in exchange? Hamilton's gentle voice sounded almost sympathetic.

Prescriptions for pills—Xanax and Klonopin. I used to sell them for money so I could pay off my fines.

And you never suspected what the pipe was for?

Not until the FBI came and seized it. And then I was afraid I'd be in trouble if I said anything.

Did you ever drive Dylan Connelly's Suburban into Washington D.C.?

He told me to do it, Ivan blubbered. I never knew why.

"Who...who is this talking?" Palmer sputtered. A red tide had crept out of his collar to rise up his thick neck.

"Ivan Ackerman," Ike replied. "One of the suspect's NCOs, until he deserted on the first day of the standoff."

"Well..." Palmer's deep-set eyes darted toward all four members of the Taskforce. "How do we know he's telling the truth? He might simply be defending her."

"You want proof?" Ike countered. "That's easy. All you have to do is request another warrant."

The slate-colored walls, the absence of windows, the thin mat for a bed, and the crazed voices of the inmates in the high security wing at Eastern Regional—Dylan's temporary cell until she was moved somewhere closer to the capital—combined to threaten her sanity. With no means of running, no way to dispel her agitation, Dylan paced in the crude space for hours. She slammed her hands against the walls, bruising them, until exhaustion finally overcame her.

When the lights blinked on, signaling that it was morning, Dylan rose stiffly off her mat. A breakfast of cold oatmeal and reconstituted orange juice came sliding under the bars into her room. She ignored it. Terrence's memorial would take place in a couple of hours or so, as promised by her priest, and she would miss it. Since the initial process of being stripped and searched and fingerprinted yesterday, she hadn't been visited by a soul, not even a lawyer.

Is this normal? Had she been forgotten so soon and by everyone—even Tobias?

Averting her gaze from the orange jumpsuit that encased her body, she helped herself to the cold, steel toilet, stepped up to the sink and splashed cold water on her face. Dispensing toothpaste from the tiny tube, she brushed her teeth with a flimsy toothbrush.

If this is going to be the new normal, she told herself, *then I need to deal with it.* Laying down the brush, she scraped back the tendrils that had escaped from her braid, and turned to regard her cell. The Bible she'd spied lying on the shelf above her mat seemed to beckon her. Returning to her mat, she sat down and flipped idly through the pages, seeking consolation.

Her gaze fell on two lines from Psalm 124. She read them over and over again. We have escaped like a bird from the fowler's snare, the snare has been broken, and we have escaped.

God, if only that were true.

The tread of footsteps in the hallway had her looking up. She expelled her held breath as Special Agent Palmer sidled up to her door in the presence of a security guard. Resentment made her heart pound. *The lying bastard.* The time had probably come to be moved to a different facility.

He said nothing, just stood there hefting a plastic sack as the guard unlocked her door.

Dylan closed the Bible and set it warily aside.

"There's been a change of plans," Palmer informed her, slipping into her cell. He extended the plastic sack. "These are the clothes you wore yesterday. You may put them on to attend your executive officer's memorial."

The four walls of the room seemed to rotate. "Why?" If they thought her a murderer, why would they risk the liability of letting her out in public?

Palmer's fleshy face remained utterly inscrutable. "Let's just say that your presence ought to subdue the protesters."

Was the situation that bad? Gratitude toward the people rallying on her behalf eradicated her sense of abandonment. She hadn't been forgotten, after all.

"I'll be right back for you," Palmer said, swiveling on his glossy shoes and disappearing. The door clanged shut, and she was left alone.

Shrugging out of the orange jumpsuit, Dylan fumbled her way into her own clothing. As she laced her boots, she started to feel like her old self again. "I'm dressed," she called, but no one came. Surely they weren't playing a cruel prank on her. The opportunity to honor Terrence was more than she'd expected—nothing short of a gift, really.

To her relief, Palmer reappeared five minutes later, bearing a device that resembled a cell phone, except for the narrow wire poking out. "You're to wear this at all times," he instructed, sliding it into the breast pocket of her camouflage jacket. "Anything you say and do can be used against you in a court of law. All set?" he asked, ignoring her bemused look.

Dylan just stared at him. Weren't they going to cuff her or at least place some kind of security anklet on her before leading her out into the world? She couldn't help wondering if instead of just a sick joke, this was something more sinister, like an abduction followed by a quiet murder. Surely the FBI had ways of making people simply disappear.

Keeping a tight grip on her fears, she followed Palmer out of her cell, where he took hold of her arm. The guard escorted them through the brightly lit high-security wing. Cat calls chased them all the way to a steel door. The guard used his thumb print to pull it open. They swept Dylan down one more deserted hallway to a door marked with an emergency exit sign. Cold, moist air greeted them as the guard pushed that door open. Just outside, in what looked like a loading area with walls on three sides and no witnesses, Palmer's black Tahoe, with three more agents in it, idled quietly.

Dylan drew a tight breath. This couldn't be normal. She'd never heard of a prisoner—certainly not a murder suspect—being released for a special event, not even for a funeral. Why, then, were they secreting her away? She didn't dare ask, didn't even want to know. It was easier to hope that Palmer would be true to his word and that she was headed to Terrence's memorial.

As she slipped into the back seat trapped on either side by two broad-shouldered agents, the verse she had just read from the Bible returned to her. Had she, in fact, escaped the fowler's snare? Or was she being taken into a situation from which there was no return?

CHAPTER 19

"Park right here," Toby said, pointing out a grassy area on a knoll not far from the church. In a town where parking was already scarce, not a single legitimate parking spot remained, especially on a day like today, when a respected member of the community was being honored. Terrence Ashby's memorial promised to be packed, with every member of the militia, their families, and townsfolk in attendance.

Jackson eased the four tires of his Chrysler onto the grass and killed the engine. "Would you look at this mob scene," he marveled.

"Crazy," Toby agreed. The town of Harpers Ferry probably hadn't seen this much excitement since the Civil War. On streets below the bluff where they'd parked, he could just make out the heads of the locals continuing to protest Dylan's arrest. Marching in a circuit around town, they had been carrying posters and displaying banners for forty-eight hours now, decrying First and Second Amendment violations. Toby could make out one such sign hanging between third-story windows with a message in bold, red letters stating that Uncle Sam was a bully.

Made identifiable by their olive berets, members of the militia began to part from the crowd as the bell within the bell tower tolled. Like salmon swimming upstream they swarmed up the steps to the church to honor their fallen leader. Spying Gil Morrison's girth, Toby surmised that Dylan's NCOs had been charged with violating the peace and then released. The local media, sympathetic to Dylan's cause remained present while the larger metropolitan stations went back to D.C. Positioned in strategic locations here and there, journalists sympathetic to Dylan's cause continued to broadcast the ongoing drama. Anti-government sentiment brewed like the dark clouds squatting over the mountaintops, portending rain.

Jackson slanted Toby a worried look. "Are you sure this is a good idea?" His light-colored eyes lowered to take in Toby's outfit.

"Probably not," Toby conceded. The last time he'd worn his militia uniform, he'd been exposed as an informant and led away at gunpoint. Members of the militia weren't exactly going to welcome him with open arms—not with their leader, whom he'd supposedly informed against, in prison. "But Terrence was the man. I have to try."

"Do what you have to do," Jackson said on a resigned note. "I'll stay here with Milly in case I'm told to park somewhere else."

"Coward," Toby ribbed, taking off his seatbelt. "Text me if you see anything strange, like Richardson showing up."

For all they knew, Dr. Kevin Richardson was sitting in FBI custody somewhere. Palmer kept the Taskforce intentionally out of the loop for having thrown a wrench into his open-and-shut case. Ike, who was confident that Palmer would pursue the match between the fur fiber and the big bad wolf mask, had departed the area that morning, taking Hamilton with him. As far as Toby knew, he and Jackson were the only Feds still brave or stupid enough to stick around, given the current atmosphere.

"Wait." Jackson shot out a hand just as Toby reached for the door handle.

Toby twisted in his seat to follow Jackson's startled gaze. The sight of Palmer's SUV braking on the narrow road behind them made his stomach lurch. "What now?" he exclaimed, astonished to see the FBI on the scene, especially considering the present atmosphere.

Three doors popped open, and several agents in dark suits jumped out, including Palmer, who turned to help someone out of the back seat. Toby blinked and looked again. "Dylan!" he cried, nearly falling out of the car in his haste to get to her. "Hey!" he yelled, leaving his door ajar as he rushed over to intercept Palmer's path. Behind him, Milly gave a joyous bark.

"Tobias!" Color bloomed in Dylan's waxen cheeks. She looked equally astonished to see him. "What are you doing here?"

Before he could reach for her, Palmer blocked his path. "Step back, Agent Burke. You've meddled in my affairs enough as it is."

Toby didn't even spare him a glance. "You okay, sweetheart?" he asked over Palmer's shoulder. He searched her puzzled gaze, wondering what they'd told her, if anything about the state of the investigation.

"She's fine," Palmer retorted, cutting off Dylan's murmured affirmative. "What the hell are *you* doing here?" he demanded.

Toby waved a hand at the church. "Honoring the XO, of course. I think a better question is what the hell are you doing here? Don't you have something more pressing to do? Like arresting the real killer?"

Palmer thrust a warning finger in Toby's face. "Not another word," he threatened. "We are handling this case, not you. So step aside and let us handle it."

The *click-click* of a round being chambered snatched Toby's attention to the pistol being brandished by one of Palmer's agents. "Back off," Tibbs advised with a jerk of his head.

Toby took a healthy step backward, but he couldn't contain himself as the agents continued toward the church, drawing a stunned-looking Dylan with them. "Didn't they tell you what's happening?" he called, trailing them at a distance. The baffled look she threw back at him confirmed that Palmer had kept her in the dark, the son-of-a-bitch. "Ackerman planted that evidence in the barn; he confessed to everything!"

Dylan jerked to a startled halt. He could read her lips. "Ivan?"

Tibbs wheeled on Toby a second time, driving him back, as the rest of the entourage urged a resisting Dylan down a set of stairs to the piazza in the front of the church.

Toby found himself with his hand outstretched, like a love-sick school boy. Feeling foolish, he immediately lowered it and watched with throbbing jealousy as the crowd in front of the church swallowed Dylan. Amazed militia members flocked to her like disciples to the Messiah, and the four FBI agents slinked off toward the south side of the courtyard, keeping to themselves. Journalists, attracted to the chorus of happy greetings, turned their cameras from the protest to the reunion taking place in front of the church. Toby could see them speculating, pulling people out of the crowd to ask them what was going on.

Puzzled by Palmer's intentions, Toby slipped back into Jackson's car and slammed the door hard behind him. "What the hell's going on?" he raged.

Jackson rubbed his jaw with the tips of his fingers. "No idea," he admitted.

Together, they considered the four agents, now standing with their arms folded next to the wrought iron fence that kept visitors from plummeting off the edge of the mountain. Toby's thoughts churned. "It's got to be a publicity stunt," he concluded. "The Feds want to placate the crowd by bringing her around."

"I think there's more to it," Jackson suggested.

"Like what?"

"Like maybe they're hoping Richardson will show up?"

"Christ." Toby strafed a horrified gaze over the crowd. "Why wouldn't they just arrest him?"

"On the basis of a single fiber?" Jackson shrugged. "Maybe they're hoping for more."

Toby blew out a long breath. "He'd be a fool to show up. Surely he knows by now that he's a suspect."

"Not necessarily. They might be stringing him along."

Toby sought Dylan's bright head in the crowd. Concern vied with poignant longing as he saw her smile wanly at Sergeants Morrison and Lee. "She's glad to be here," he surmised, happy on her behalf. As she moved into the church, bookended by her NCOs, he watched Palmer separate himself from the other agents to follow her. But a short time later, the man emerged from the church, escorted by a stone-faced Sheriff Fallon.

Toby chuckled. "Check that out."

"Palmer doesn't look too happy," Jackson noted.

And given the tense situation and the fact that the

agents were immensely outnumbered, Palmer didn't dare assert his authority either. "Serves the bastard right," Toby muttered, secretly relieved that Fallon was an elected official and, as such, Palmer couldn't get him replaced for his insubordination.

"It's not like Dylan would try to run," Jackson noted. "Would she?"

"Impossible. There's only one way out of that church, and it's through the front door. It's a firefighter's nightmare."

The sound of organ music carried through the slightly lowered window. Jackson waved him away. "You'd better get in there."

With a deep breath, Toby pushed out of the car a second time.

Flipping up the collar of his jacket, he managed to avoid being seen by the agents as he shadowed another latecomer toward the church doors. Shuffling up the steps to the church, he kept his chin ducked, his eyes fixed on his boots. He had just crossed the threshold into the nave, when a firm hand landed on his shoulder, making him glance up into the cold eyes of his nemesis.

"Not you," Sheriff Fallon growled, ejecting him back onto the stone stoop.

"Oh, come on, Cal. You've persecuted me enough. I just want to pay my respects."

"Bullshit. You're a lying son-of-a-bitch. You—"

"Language, Cal," Toby scolded, putting a wrestler's move on Cal that reversed their positions and gave him the upper hand. "Jesus, man, you're in church." He slammed Cal's back against one of the stoop's thick pillars. "Yesterday, Ackerman confessed to planting the evidence in Dylan's barn," he hissed in Cal's ear. "Why didn't you tell Dylan the truth about his past?"

"Ackerman?" The sheriff's stunned reply made Toby ease up on his grip. "I just assumed he was ashamed of the truth." The sheriff stared at him intently. "Who told him to plant the evidence?" he demanded.

A thundering chord on the organ yielded to absolute silence. Toby breathed the name quietly in Cal's ear, then pulled back to witness his reaction.

Cal appeared thunderstruck. "He goes to this church."

"Did you see him inside?"

"I don't think so."

"Now, can I go in?" Toby asked him.

The sheriff straightened his jacket with a jerk. "You can stand in the back with me."

Together they eased into the sanctuary, and Toby saw that it was packed—standing room only. Sliding his shoulders along the rear wall, he fixed his attention on the back of Dylan's head. Her gaze was riveted to the jade-green urn holding Terrence's ashes. As she lifted a hand to wipe away an errant tear, sympathy constricted Toby's chest. Given all she'd endured in the past week, it was a marvel that she hadn't come unhinged. God, how he loved her!

Why hadn't Palmer told her that half the charges had been dropped in light of Ackerman's confession? And if the fur fiber found in her vehicle had proved to match that of the big bad wolf mask, Palmer already had himself another suspect. So why wasn't he out questioning Richardson even now?

The priest's thoughtful words, echoing in the vaulted chamber wrested Toby's attention.

"Those who knew Terrence Ashby recognized in his presence that he was an old soul. Life had not been kind to him. But rather than grow bitter and disillusioned, he allowed himself to be smelted, beaten, and shaped into something useful—a vessel of wisdom and patience. God was the blacksmith, and Terrence Ashby was his iron, forged in the refiner's fire, and made pure."

Toby gave up on second-guessing Palmer's intentions and tuned his thoughts toward remembering a great man.

A river of tears flowed down Dylan's throat over a lump that made it difficult to swallow. The priest's every word strummed her heartstrings making her long for the company of her dear friend, whose absence, coupled with Toby's betrayal, had left such a gaping void. Even so, she had managed to keep her grief locked within. A leader, in her opinion, didn't have the luxury of bawling. She would keep up a front of strength until such time as she was alone again—a prospect that would occur all too soon.

Not even her overwhelming emotions could distract her from her awareness of Tobias, standing at the rear of the church, watching her. His presence brought her unexpected comfort, just as his words, spoken outside, gave her reason to hope that he might, in fact, prove her innocence. What evidence had Ackerman confessed to planting—the pipe found in her barn? And had he become involved in a plot to frame her?

Between her grief and her fractured thoughts, it was all she could do to follow the priest's elaborate metaphor as he built upon it, reading aloud from scripture, "Behold, I have refined thee, but not with silver; I have tempered thee in the furnace of affliction."

As the eulogy came to a close and the service moved into Eucharist, the sharing of the bread and the wine, Dylan glanced toward the rear of the church, her spirits diving to see Tobias retreat into the nave. He had never taken communion during Sunday services, why should today be any different? Still, in her heart, she had hoped he'd come forward, if only so they could be closer to one another for a few moments.

She had sworn to herself she would never forgive him, but that was a sin, wasn't it? And here he was, just as he'd sworn he would be, honoring Terrence and working to acquit her of her charges. What if she'd been wrong about Tobias? What if he wasn't the traitor she'd judged him to be but, rather, an agent who'd honestly fallen in love with her and now risked his career to prove it?

Her knees shook as she rose to approach the altar rail, kneeling as close to Terrence's urn as possible. Father Nesbit briefly blocked her view of it as he stood before her. "The body of Christ. The bread of heaven," he murmured, placing a wafer in her cupped hands. His robes rustled as he moved to the next parishioner.

The urn's clean lines and simple design were elements Terrence would have approved of, Dylan mused. Father Nesbit had made the perfect selection. But what were the odds, she wondered, that she would get to disperse the contents herself, on her own land, as Terrence had wished? Again the tantalizing hope at the prospect of being set free—regaining her privacy, her reputation, possibly more—pulsed through her.

Forgive Burke. Terrence's words echoed in her head.

If his efforts resulted in her freedom, then of course she would forgive him. Clinging to her resentment these past few days had been hard enough.

"The blood of Christ. The cup of salvation."

As Dylan sipped from the goblet, the priest took a scrap from the pocket in his robe and pressed it into her hand. Startled, Dylan read the note as she withdrew from the railing. *Dr. Richardson is in the sacristy. Please speak to him while you have the chance.*

As she looked up, the priest caught her eyes over the head of the next parishioner and, with a nod, urged her toward the tiny room at the back of the church, accessed via a door beside the pulpit.

Dylan glanced back at her empty seat, then at the rear of the church where Tobias had abandoned his post. Cal Fallon's attention had wandered. With the federal agents right outside, it wasn't as though she were doing anything wrong or trying to escape. After all, she wouldn't even leave the building. And she knew it would ease Father Nesbit's mind if she spoke with her psychiatrist, even briefly.

Whispering to Sergeant Lee that she'd be back shortly, Dylan cut through the line of people waiting to kneel and slipped through the door into the room where the altar cloths and priestly robes and sacraments were stored. The Spartan room had been furnished with a throw rug, a sofa where the priest was known to catch a nap between services, and a narrow desk and chair. Kevin Richardson leapt from the sofa as Dylan approached him.

"Kevin," she exclaimed, noting that his unkempt hair appeared even more disheveled than usual. He wore a button-up shirt that looked like it had been slept in and a wild-eyed expression she had never seen on his face before. "What are you doing here? Why aren't you participating in the service?" she asked him.

"Oh." He huffed a nervous laugh and waved his hands to ward off the invitation. "Too many people. I tend to get claustrophobic. But it's good to see you, Dylan." Wiping his hand on his slacks first, he extended her a moist handshake.

"Well, it was good of you to come."

"Of course. Terrence was a wonderful man. I didn't want to miss it. But, actually, I'm here for two more reasons."

"What reasons?" she asked.

"Well, first, Father Nesbit has expressed grave concern about you. He's been asking me to visit you for days now."

"And the second reason?"

He drew a strained breath. "The FBI have asked me to evaluate you, as well," he somberly admitted.

Dylan's hopes plummeted. If the FBI wanted Richardson's evaluation then that had to mean she was headed back to jail. Not only that but, considering the wire tap in her breast pocket, Palmer was probably listening to whatever she might say. *Anything you say or do can be held against you*, he'd warned her. How could he expect her to be forthcoming while wearing a wire tap?

"I watched you surrender on television," Richardson volunteered. "I can't believe how well you've held up. How are you...?" His Adam's apple bobbed. "How are you doing, really?" he asked.

He struck her as obviously uncomfortable with the task the FBI had foisted upon him, and no wonder. So was she. They weren't exactly sequestered in his cozy office. Nor was their conversation a private one, though Richardson didn't know that, and she saw no reason to tell him. "I think I'm fine, really." She resolved to say as little as possible, to thank him for his concern, and promptly excuse herself.

"I'm sorry, this isn't the best place for us to talk," he admitted, casting his gaze around the room almost nervously. He gestured at the couch. "Would you care to sit down?"

"No thanks." If the FBI had spoken with him,

perhaps he knew more than she about Ackerman's confession. "Did the FBI tell you the latest news?"

"No, what news is that?"

"Sergeant Ackerman confessed to planting evidence on my property."

Richardson sent her a frozen stare. "Ivan? He confessed to that?" He started patting down his pockets in an obvious and frantic search for a pack of cigarettes.

"I think that might absolve me of Nolan's murder, don't you?" she asked.

"Yes it might," Richardson muttered, looking deeply distracted. He found the pack that he was after, pulled it out, and tapped loose a cigarette. "Would you step outside with me while I have a smoke?" he begged. "It's been over an hour, and I'm a wreck without nicotine."

The reason for his edginess became suddenly clear. Dylan's tension eased. "No, thanks." She looked around. "Besides, there's no door."

"There is," he said, "just down those stairs." He pointed to a door leading to the basement.

She balked at joining him. "I really ought to go back to the service."

"In a minute, Dylan. I promised the FBI that I'd evaluate you. It'll only take a sec. Come with me." He started down the basement steps without waiting to see if she would follow.

Dylan hesitated. If Palmer had ordered this evaluation, then she might as well get it over with, she decided. With a tisk of her tongue, she chased Kevin down the steps into the dark cellar carved into the shale mountain and found him unlatching an iron door. Its hinges gave a grating sound as he swung it open, admitting a blast of damp, chilly air.

Dylan's eyes widened as she beheld the south side

of the mountain. A shallow ledge was all that separated them from the boulder-strewn slope that dropped a hundred feet or more to the rooftops of houses built below. No wonder she'd never seen the door before.

Richardson ignored the drizzle to put one foot on the slick-looking ledge and light his cigarette. His shaking hands riveted her attention. Closing his eyes, he took several deep draughts that made the tip of his cigarette glow red.

"Nasty habit," he apologized, exhaling a cloud of smoke. "Just give me five minutes, Dylan. Then you're free."

Dylan gave another thought to the device in her breast pocket. Should she tell Kevin about it or just be mindful of her own words? "Five minutes," she agreed as the organ upstairs began to play softly. "What do they want you to ask me?"

Toby peeked out the front of the church, only to draw back into the nave when he spied all four FBI agents on the church steps, hiding from the rain. Palmer had one hand clamped over his earpiece. The other agents eyed him intently. Toby had a hunch they would cart Dylan off as soon as the service was over—leaving him no opportunity to talk to her.

The organ music thundered out a closing hymn. In the next instant, Father Nesbit pushed into the narthex. Catching sight of Toby, he shot him a forced smile as he propped the doors, then turned to greet the first parishioner.

Toby looked for Dylan over the heads of the exiting swarm. His gaze plumbed every corner of the crowded space without lighting on her. And with every second that he expected to see her burnished head and fair face and didn't, his worry increased.

Sergeants Morrison and Lee hovered next to the urn holding Terrence's ashes, but no Dylan.

He tried to slip past the priest, but Father Nesbit caught him by his sleeve. "Not now," he pleaded, unexpectedly.

"I have to talk to Dylan, Father. Where'd she go?" Toby demanded, searching the crowded room again. She couldn't have vanished into thin air.

"She's getting help," the priest replied.

Whatever that meant. Tugging free, Toby ignored him, squeezing back into the sanctuary, only to run straight into Cal a second time.

"Out," the sheriff insisted. With one hand on Toby's shoulder, the other on the butt of his service pistol, he forced Toby backward.

Finding himself on the receiving end of several glares, Toby realized he'd have to take on the entire militia to speak to Dylan in the church. Conceding defeat, he stormed outside to confront the agents. "I don't see her in there," he informed Palmer. "Where'd she go?"

Palmer, still listening to his earpiece, threw him a distracted glance and didn't answer. His three subordinates ignored Toby completely.

The inkling that Palmer was listening to Dylan—where ever the hell she might be—sent Toby's thoughts into overdrive. What the hell? They must have wired Dylan in advance of the memorial, but why, and for what, unless...The suspicion that they'd manipulated a meeting between her and Richardson knifed through him. That meant Richardson was here and Dylan was with him, somewhere in the building, since the agents hadn't left.

Vaulting off the steps, Toby stepped into the spitting rain to circle the exterior of the church.

From up on the hill, Jackson's voice floated down

through the car's lowered window. "Hey. You need help?"

"Dylan's missing!" Toby called back, only to curse his actions when a curious journalist took note of his reply and started following him.

Waving Jackson around the front of the church, Toby passed the line of stained glass windows to approach the attached building in the back. Once there, he drew to a frustrated halt, aware that the journalist was now filming him. It was just like he'd told Jackson earlier, no rear door existed.

So where could Dylan be?

"I suppose I should ask if you've had any more memories about the night General Treyburn was murdered." Richardson's dark eyes pinned Dylan through the lenses of his glasses. The tremor in his fingers seemed to subside as he drew deeply on his cigarette.

"No." She shook her head, unwilling to discuss what little she did remember. "None at all." Was it her imagination or did he look a bit relieved?

Richardson hesitated. He sucked on his cigarette and exhaled. "I'm sure you've heard of dissociative identity disorder," he said finally, gently.

"Of course." He'd mentioned it to her once before, quite tentatively.

"You'll need other clinicians to confirm or deny it, but—whether you agree with my diagnosis or not—I'm telling you right now, dissociative identity disorder is your best defense." He sent her a pitying look while exhaling through his nostrils. "Without it, you'll be sent to a traditional prison if convicted. If you go with the disorder, you'll be put into a mental institution and treated well, as you should be."

Dylan's heart began to thud. The blood in her ears

gave a muted roar. "That's your diagnosis?" she asked him stiffly. She couldn't believe what he was telling her. He'd all but consigned her to a lifetime of incarceration.

"Yes, it is," he said after the slightest hesitation.

"Why didn't you tell me this before?" She would never have gone to him in the first place if he had so little faith in her sanity.

He stopped puffing, started to say something, then changed his mind with a shake of his head.

"This discussion is over," Dylan declared. Stepping into the doorway and braving the immense drop only feet in front of her, she pushed her face into his and hissed. "I will never plead insanity. Do you know why? Because I *know* I'm innocent!"

He abruptly ground his cigarette butt into the wall, snuffing it out. "Are you certain?" he asked, his expression completely unreadable.

The suspicion that he'd told the FBI that her amnesia was due to a psychological disorder filled her with betrayal. "I was *drugged* that night," she insisted, balling her hands into fists.

He shook his head almost pityingly. "In the same way that you were framed?" he scoffed. "Who would do that to you Dylan?"

Doubt briefly shook her confidence. "Ackerman confessed to planting evidence," she said stonily.

"Oh, come on. That pipe could have come from anywhere."

The words echoed in her head, prompting a horrifying realization that spurred her heart into a gallop. "I never said it was a pipe," she whispered.

Richardson's expanding pupils betrayed the realization of his error. Without warning, he grabbed her with both hands, hauling her toward him.

Shocked by his strength, Dylan resisted. "Let me

go!" she cried. The heels on her boots caught a moment on the threshold before sliding across the wet shale as he dragged her out into the spitting rain with him. "It was you!" she blurted, praying now that the FBI was listening and that they would save her before Richardson did something rash. "You drugged me," she added, hurling accusations at him, one after the other. "You knew that Leigh always brought me coffee, so you laced some with Rohypnol and left it in my office!"

He shook his head in pity and denial; only the tension gripping the muscles in his face was unmistakable. "Oh, Dylan, listen to yourself," he scoffed.

The pieces all crashed together to form a clear and perfect picture. "You prescribed me those sleeping pills which were also benzodiazepines, thinking that would negate the claim that I was drugged. Only you didn't count on me taking a blood test to find out which kind, did you?"

Richardson's tense countenance crumpled unexpectedly. "Stop!" he pleaded, sobbing and shaking her at the same time. The sharp drop loomed in her peripheral vision. Adrenaline screamed through Dylan's bloodstream as the extent of her peril hit her in the face. *He's going to throw me over.* The terrifying certainty had her straining to free her wrists from his strong grasp.

"Kevin, don't! Don't kill me, too!" She started to knee him in the groin, only the slippery surface made her traction slip, and she quickly put her foot back down.

He hushed her wildly. "Don't say that, Dylan. I could never kill you. I swear I never meant for this to happen." A wail of frustration tore from his throat as he tossed his head back. Tears streamed from his eyes, gathering just above the lower rim of his glasses like a scuba diver whose mask was filling up.

For a moment, pity overcame Dylan's fear.

"Can't you see?" he cried. "I had to do it. Those men would have tipped the scales in the president's decision to send troops to Syria. Because of their influence, thousands of innocents would have been shipped to the other side of the world to endure the very same hell you've been though. It would happen all over again. Is that what you want—more young people to end up maimed, their lives destroyed?" His lungs convulsed on a sob. "My God, they'd be lining up at my door, expecting me to fix them, to give them drugs so they could sleep, so they could leave their houses without fearing for their lives. Don't you see why I had to stop it?"

He rattled her with both hands now, shaking her until her neck felt in danger of snapping. "Your life was already ruined. It's not like you would ever go to jail—not if you plead insanity."

Dylan gaped at him. "But I'm not insane," she protested. *You are.*

CHAPTER 20

The sound of an agitated male voice caught Toby's attention. It seemed to come from below him on the side of the church that teetered on the mountain's edge. Curiosity and fear of what he would find drew him toward the rear corner, trailed by the journalist. The hair on Toby's nape rose straight up as he peered down the southern wall. Standing on a narrow ledge at the church's foundation, Dr. Kevin Richardson gripped Dylan's arms with both hands, shaking her as he railed. Only one of her feet touched the ground; the other flailed in the air as she clung to him in absolute terror.

"Dylan!" Toby's shout startled Richardson into nearly dropping her.

Putting his back to the wall of the church, Toby picked his way down a rocky embankment toward the narrow ledge as quickly as he dared. Panic threatened to overtake him, making him reckless in his quest to reach her. His training kicked in, urging him to remain sure-footed. He'd seen the look on Richardson's face on other cornered individuals—the look of a man with everything to lose. Cursing his lack of a weapon,

Toby edged closer.

"Let her go, Richardson!" he called, raising his voice to be heard over the patter of rain. "It's over. Everyone knows you tried to frame her."

The latter might have been an exaggeration but the word "Freeze!" shouted from somewhere inside the basement confirmed that Palmer had been listening to Dylan and Richardson's conversation all along, and he'd finally decided to intervene. *About time, motherfucker.*

And now Richardson had nowhere to go. He was, quite literally, a man on the edge. *My God, don't throw her,* he prayed, catching sight of Milly and then Jackson at the front corner of the church, barred from helping by a wrought iron railing and a sheer drop. The look on Jackson's face as he absorbed the situation mirrored Toby's terror. Spying Dylan below her, Milly started to bark which, in turn, drew the attention of people leaving the church. Cries and exclamations of horror added an audio component to the already ghastly scene. Kevin Richardson held Dylan's fate literally in his hands.

Dylan's life panned through her mind, from her earliest years to this terrible unforeseen moment. She could see it in Richardson's tormented expression. It would all end here and now, shaping her brief life into a pointless melodrama.

In terms of her professional life, she harbored no regrets, but what about her personal life? Richardson's fingers bit into her wrists. His chest seemed to expand as he prepared to hurl her off the ledge to her death. And out of the corner of her eye, she glimpsed the camera man bracing himself to film whatever happened. She was going to die. The anguish and regret on Toby's face told the same story.

At the same time, it communicated just how much he loved her. He'd told her the truth about that. He hadn't lied!

From the recesses of her being, her spirit protested. Why should she be forced to leave this world and the resurrected life she had found in Toby's arms. "No-o-o!"

Her visceral protest cleared the haze from Kevin's eyes replacing it with sudden clarity. His eyes jerked left, center, then right, absorbing the presence of agents in the basement and on every side; townsfolk gaping; the media filming; even Milly, all poised in positions depicting dread as they waited for him to act. When he looked back at Dylan, the realization of what he'd done and what he was doing registered on his face.

"Oh, Dylan. Please forgive me," he rasped. The crushing grip on her wrists abruptly eased. His eyelids sank shut with an air of resignation He folded his arms across his chest and pitched backward, in slow motion, off the ledge into nothing but space.

"No!" Dylan lunged for him instinctively. Her own scream filled her ears as she lost her balance, her arms wheeling in an effort to recover. In the next instant, a powerful grasp snatched her back, suspending her shrill cry as she watched Kevin's body strike a projection, bounce, flip, and plummet some more.

"Don't look." Tobias crushed her to him, blocking her view and banding her in the safety of his arms.

"Oh, God, oh, God!" she cried in a high, frightened voice.

"It's over," he crooned. "Shhh." His soothing voice and the sound of his heart galloping under her ear suspended her outburst as he guided her to safety. A number of hands reached out, hauling them out of sight of the crowd and back into the cellar. From there she was swept up the steps into the warmer sacristy where Tobias drew her down on the sofa next to him. Palmer and his three subordinates, even her priest, formed a tight circle around them.

Too overcome to speak, Dylan hid her stricken face against Tobias's shoulder. His warmth fended off the icy coldness that made her shiver uncontrollably. The sweet assurance of his embrace mingled with her recollected horror, keeping her detached from the storm breaking loose around her, as Tobias thundered, "Palmer, you son-of-a-bitch, you used her as bait!"

"Now, calm down, Burke," Palmer warned, pointing a finger at him. "We had her monitored the entire time. Nothing would have happened to her."

"That's bullshit. Richardson could have thrown her out that door, and you couldn't have done a thing to stop him." Patting her down with gentle hands, Tobias found the recording device in her breast pocket. He drew it out and waved it accusingly. "Is this how you were monitoring her?"

"Give me that," Palmer snapped. "Do you seriously think we could've convicted Richardson on the basis of a single, synthetic fiber? Wake up. We needed more proof than that."

"At Dylan's expense?" Toby slapped the wire tap into Palmer's hand. "Here's your goddamn proof. And now your suspect is dead, having nearly killed Dylan in the process. I can't believe you threw her in this room with him without checking first if there was a basement door."

"Er…I'm afraid that was my idea."

Father Nesbit's timid confession pulled Dylan's face out of Toby's shoulder. She looked over to find the priest hovering at the door.

"I'm so sorry, Dylan," he cried, meeting her eyes and shaking his head to forestall her suspicions. "I swear to you, I had no idea what he intended. Richardson and I often discussed the tragedy of war and what it's done to veterans like you. But I had no idea he was willing to kill to keep another war from breaking out. My God!" He wrung his hands in obvious distress. "Who would ever have guessed that he could murder in the name of peace, especially when he expressed so much concern for others—and for you." Nesbit broke into a sob. "I was so afraid you might hurt yourself! I arranged for him to meet you, thinking he would help, never suspecting…"

"It's okay." Relieved that her priest hadn't betrayed after all, Dylan crossed the room to console him. "It's not your fault." Glancing back, she impaled Palmer with an accusing gaze. "It's exactly what the FBI hoped would happen."

Tobias glared at Palmer also. "Since you now have what you came for, I'll be taking Dylan home." His tone brooked no argument; nor did it allow for a return to jail to process papers. "I assume she's no longer a suspect."

No longer a suspect. The words blew through Dylan's mind like a warm, spring breeze. She felt compelled to pinch herself. Was it truly over?

Palmer flicked her a dismissive look. "We may have questions for her later, but—yes—she's free to leave."

A bitter laugh worked its way up Dylan's throat. "That's it?" She narrowed her eyes at the agent. "No apology? No statement to the press?"

"Our public affairs officer will issue a statement in time," Palmer promised. "As for an apology, I spent three nights hunkered on the cold, hard ground making sure your trigger-happy soldiers didn't open fire on federal agents. Count yourself lucky you got off as easy as you did," he retorted.

"Lucky? Is that what you call it? I have every right

under the American Constitution to defend my own land."

"That's our cue to leave," Tobias interjected firmly. "You have a body to collect," he coldly reminded Palmer. "Come on, sweetheart."

With a hand under her elbow, he escorted her past the priest into the now-empty sanctuary, where she broke away to collect the urn from its pedestal. Carrying it reverently, she marveled that she would, in fact, get to disperse Terrence's ashes, after all. The events of the past twenty minutes replayed in her mind, subjecting her to shivers that would not subside, not even when Tobias took her other hand and led her to the exit.

The doors had been bolted shut, presumably to keep the public from reentering. As Tobias opened them and drew her out, the crowd hovering on the portico and in the piazza before it erupted into exclamations of victory.

Unable to push past them, Dylan acknowledged the well-wishes with a strained smile. A journalist, forcing her way through the crush of bodies, stuck her microphone into Dylan's face and barraged her with questions. Dylan turned with relief to Milly, as the dog wriggled through the crowd, planted her front paws on Dylan's chest, and licked her face with exuberance.

"No comment. Let's go." Tobias and the light-skinned agent who'd once worked for Palmer used their athletic frames to carve a path through the crowd toward the parking area on higher ground.

The tenacious journalist pursued them. "Who was the man who just fell to his death?" she demanded. "Is it true that he tried to kill you?"

Another journalist shouted from the crowd. "Are you still the primary suspect in the Nolan and

Treyburn murders?"

Halfway up the steps, Dylan halted. "I have to say something," she told Tobias. Here was her chance to reclaim her reputation as an ordinary citizen with God-given rights, not the fanatic the federal government had portrayed her as.

Tobias gestured for her to go ahead.

Facing the crowd, Dylan raised her voice to thank the town of Harpers Ferry and her militia members for supporting her. "In the famous words of my ancestor, John Brown," she called out, raising her voice so that everyone could hear her, "'This is a beautiful country.' We may all have our differences, but ultimately, we are all united and protected under the American Constitution, which guarantees us the right to bear arms against tyranny and corruption. Today, my good name has been restored, and the charges against me dropped."

Her announcement elicited a roaring cheer. With a final wave for the crowd, Dylan allowed Tobias to guide her up the remaining steps to a waiting vehicle.

"I want to sit with Milly," she insisted when he tried putting her up front.

Before he could protest, she dove into the back seat where she wrapped her arms around a supremely happy dog. Milly's warmth eased the shivers that continued to wrack her. The memory of her horror on the ledge replayed through her mind as she processed what had happened.

Tobias's colleague drove them away, but moments later, they were idling at a standstill in the congested, narrow street. The *whoop-whoop* of a siren startled Dylan into looking up. Sheriff Cal Fallon circled their vehicle on his motorcycle. With a wave of his hand, he signaled for them to follow him, using his lights and his imperious gestures to part the traffic before them.

Dylan closed her eyes with relief. Soon the town of Harpers Ferry and the chaos that had surrounded her for days would be a thing of the past. Opening her eyes again she found Tobias studying her over the back of his seat. His protective gaze cloaked her in warmth.

"You okay?" he inquired.

Dylan drew a shuddering breath. "I thought he was my friend," she whispered, stating out loud what disturbed her most about the recent tragedy. Despite her efforts to stem them, tears of betrayal and dismay welled in her eyes. How could such a well-meaning man have turned into a murderer? Not only that, how could he have lived with himself for making it look like *she* was guilty of the crimes he'd committed?

"He *was* your friend, sweetheart," Tobias assured her. Reaching through the seats, he laid a hand on her knee. "If he weren't, he would have thrown you over that ledge and told everyone that you'd committed suicide. I'm sure he was tempted, but he didn't do it. He took his own life, not yours."

The memory of Kevin's body bouncing like a rag doll down the side of the mountain made her stomach pitch. She swallowed down her sudden nausea. "He said he never meant to hurt me," she relayed. "The way he figured it, my life was already ruined, so what difference did it make if he framed me? I could plead dissociative identity disorder and live like a queen in a mental institution, and it wouldn't make a lick of difference."

"That's not how you feel about your life, is it?" Tobias asked, giving her knee a gentle squeeze.

Tree branches flashed past the windows followed by open pastureland. She would soon be home. With Tobias's steady hand on her knee, she could feel her shock and disillusionment falling away behind her. The fact that she was free, no longer a suspect, filled her with giddy relief. "Not since I met you," she dared to admit.

His slow smile drove away her shock, once and for all. "Sweetheart, this is my colleague, Jackson Maddox," he said, making introductions.

Jackson sent her friendly glance through the rearview mirror. "Nice to meet you, ma'am," he said, in a voice suggestive of the Caribbean Islands.

"Likewise," she replied, wondering how much Tobias had told him about her. "Thank you for your help today. I'm...I'm not usually this much trouble," she added by way of apology.

Tobias snorted at her outright lie.

"No, it's true," she insisted. "I like to just keep to myself and do my own thing."

"Right. And that's why I am always rescuing you."

"About that," she said, laying her hand over his and threading their fingers together. "Thank you. I would have died today if not for you."

His smile faded, yielding to unaccustomed gravity. "I would never have let that happen," he swore, as they swung into her driveway.

Sheriff Fallon veered to one side, gesturing for them to stop, and Tobias was forced to turn his attention out the lowered window. Cal peered into the car, cast Dylan a respectful nod and speared Tobias with a hard look. "Guess I owe you an apology, Burke," he bit out.

"None needed, Sheriff," Tobias assured him. "I would have treated me the same way. Friends?" he offered sticking his hand out the window.

Dylan was fairly certain Cal's handshake would have crushed a lesser man's hand. With a parting nod, Cal sat back and roared off, freeing them to proceed up the gravel drive toward Dylan's home.

"If it's all the same to you," Jackson told Tobias, "I think I'll head back to the city. Lena's been texting me."

Tobias flicked Dylan an uncertain glance. "You want me to stay, beautiful?" he asked. "Or leave with Jackson?"

"Stay," she said, trying to keep her tone breezy and impersonal and failing miserably.

He rewarded her with a grin, and heat suffused her face.

The instant the car stopped, Dylan leapt out, freeing Milly to bound across the yard to her favorite elm tree. As Dylan watched her go, her gaze lit with dismay on the mess her militia had left behind.

"Don't even look at it," Tobias advised, shutting both their doors. Several tents lay strewn across her grass. Trash littered the lawn, fluttering in the wet breeze. "I'll help you clean it later," he promised.

As he turned his attention to seeing Jackson off, Dylan headed up the porch steps. Using the key she kept under a flower pot, she let herself inside. Her footsteps echoed in the quiet hallway as she carried Terrence's urn into the command room. She paused a moment by his desk, recalling snippets of the previous year and how loyally he had supported her radical efforts to heal by heading up a militia. The house had never felt so empty as it did without him. Approaching the unused fireplace, she set the urn on the heavy mantle where it dignified the space. One day soon, when she was ready, she would scatter his ashes on her land.

The screen door creaked open and then thudded shut. Milly padded into the room to bump Dylan's hand with her head. Sensing Tobias, but not hearing him, Dylan turned her head to find him standing at the threshold, just watching her. She wasn't so alone, after all.

"It's so quiet without him," she commented.

"Too quiet," he agreed.

They stood for a moment simply regarding each other. Dylan's heart thudded out the seconds. What happens now? she wondered. How did they move beyond the past, the lies, the betrayal, their many differences?

"Let's start over," Tobias proposed, answering her unspoken question as he took a step in her direction, and then another. "My name's Tobias Avery Burke. I'm thirty-three years old." His crooked smile spanned the distance between them like a beam of sunlight. "My dad's a career Army Ranger, who works at the Pentagon. My mom does charity work. I grew up on bases all over the world. I have three older sisters who spoiled me rotten. I like singing, working out, training dogs, and wearing obnoxious T-shirts."

She searched his eyes as he stopped in front of her. "You don't have to do this, Tobias. I understand why you lied to me. I just don't understand why you would let the government tell you what to do in the first place."

He sighed and stuck his hands into his pockets. "Because I thought the government had good reason to suspect you. And it's my job to stop people from building bombs or owning firearms to kill people," he added reasonably.

His words panged her. "Do I look like a killer to you?"

His gaze drifted over her, lingering first on her lips and then her breasts. "Not at all," he admitted. "And that did throw me, at first. At the time, you seemed to fit the profile of a terrorist—that is, until I got to know you better," he added, warding off her indrawn breath.

"I have to confess it worried me that I was so attracted to a potential enemy of the state."

Folding her arms across her chest, she studied him through narrowed eyes, not knowing whether to be offended or pleased. She tapped a toe. "And what about now?"

"Now, I'm just worried that you'll never forgive me," he said with a vulnerable look in his eyes. "Believe me, once I saw the real you through the smoke and mirrors, I knew you hadn't killed anyone."

Like a high tide washing footprints out to sea, his words eradicated her lingering resentment. Abandoning her defensive stance, Dylan dropped her arms and bit her lip, instead. "Just like that? You knew?" she asked, lapping up the desire and willingness to commit that blazed in his eyes.

"Just like that." He stepped closer. "I meant it when I said I love you. I fell hard for you, Dylan. Your passion, your commitment to everything you believe in impresses the hell out of me. I need you to understand that I was just following orders, just doing my job. Once I knew you were innocent, I pulled out every stop I could think of to prove it. I want to be part of your life. Please don't put up barriers to keep us apart."

Shimmering warmth spread from Dylan's core to every extremity. Throwing caution to the wind, she rolled up on her toes, tossed both arms around his sturdy neck and kissed him with abandonment.

This, she thought, savoring the sweet, languorous melding of their mouths. *This is what we have in common.* The hardwood floor beneath her boots seemed to tip as if the entire house was falling over. Pressing closer, she encountered irrefutable proof of Tobias's devotion.

But was it enough? Practicality dragged her lips

from his. "I'm terrified," she whispered.

He pulled his head back to frown down at her. "Of what, baby? What's to be afraid of?"

"Come on, Tobias. You know we're complete opposites, from different ends of the political and religious spectrum. You grew up in a military family; you work for the government. I'm an individualist. You're a statist."

"Love can overcome our differences," he replied with certainty.

The conviction shining in his eyes made her long to agree with him. "But you're an agent of the federal government," she reminded him, trying to mask her disgust. "Why would you waste your unique skills working for an entity that stifles your creativity and regulates every aspect of your being?"

"How can you ask me that when you used to be a military officer? Why'd you join the military?"

"They paid for medical school."

"That's not the only reason and you know it."

"Fine. I wanted to serve my country. That's my reason for leading a militia, too."

"Well, there you go. We're not as different as you think. I work for the ATF to keep citizens of this country safe. I believe in its mission. But at the end of the day, I can take off my gun, and climb into bed with you and it won't matter that you don't agree with me."

At the mention of a bed, Dylan's knees turned to mush.

"Listen," he added, "you said it yourself when you addressed the crowd earlier. This *is* a beautiful country. What makes it beautiful is that we're entitled to have differing opinions. I can respect your political philosophies if you can respect mine."

She doubted her ability to do that. "You make it

sound so simple."

"That's because it is simple. We compromise." He gathered her closer, sparking goose bumps as he nuzzled her ear. "Come on, sweetheart. Let me show you how it's done."

Anticipation powered through her, making it impossible to resist. "Okay," she agreed with a sigh of surrender.

As he nipped and licked her neck and ear, he skillfully let her hair down, much like he'd done on Jefferson's Rock. Sliding his fingers through her unwinding hair, he cupped her head, holding her perfectly still to receive his kiss. His lips warmly covered hers, plying them apart. His tongue swept in, coaxing a response. The breath left her lungs, and her mind melted into a languorous stupor.

As the buttons of his jacket parted under her nimble fingers, Dylan scanned the message on the underlying T-shirt from beneath her lashes.

IF YOU CAN'T TAKE THE HEAT, DON'T TICKLE THE DRAGON.

Laughter bubbled up her throat, shattering their kiss. "Oh, Tobias," she gasped, "you're too much."

"You think that's funny?" he said with mock-seriousness. Drawing her hand over the bulge now straining the fabric of his crotch, he growled lecherously, "I would say you're in very serious danger, ma'am. This dragon is particularly ornery and large."

Her eyes widened in feigned dismay. "Did you say horny and large?"

"Close enough."

"But you'll save me won't you?"

"Of course. It's what I do."

"My hero," she crowed, throwing her head back. "Now, take me upstairs and help me to forget this entire week," she commanded.

"Oh, you'll forget it, all right." Extracting out another shriek of laughter, he scooped her off her feet and headed for the stairs. "My God, you're heavy," he huffed, halfway to the second story. "How much do those boots of yours weigh?"

She play punched him in the chest. "Stop it. I'm not that heavy."

"They must have fed you nonstop in jail," he groused, panting up the past few steps. "Not you," he added, preventing Milly from darting into the room with them. "Three is a crowd. Out." Turning sideways, he edged into the room with Dylan and shut the door with his foot.

"Poor Milly," Dylan lamented.

"Poor Milly, my ass. She went from a working dog to the most coddled Lab on the planet. Plus, I'm sure you'll make it up to her later," he added, lowering her gently onto the bed. "But right now, I want you all to myself, with no distractions. This is our time." He lowered his mouth to hers.

Dylan went to kiss him back then changed her mind. "I'm sorry, I have to shower first. All I can smell is Kevin's cigarette smoke and…" Pressure descended without warning on her chest.

"Sweetheart," Tobias exclaimed, immediately contrite. "Baby, I'm sorry. I'm pushing you too fast."

"No, I want this. I want you. Trust me. I just need to…" She sat up swiftly, tearing at her clothing in her haste to take it off. "Help me," she demanded.

He kneeled before her to divest her of her boots and socks. Then he pulled her to her feet and stripped off the rest of her clothing until she stood in her bra and panties.

Suddenly shy, Dylan bolted to the adjoining bath, tossing a flirtatious glance behind her. Waiting for the water to warm and for Tobias to join her, she slipped off her undergarments. "Are you coming?" she called him.

He peeked around the door jam, his shoulders bare and feasted on her naked figure. "Are you inviting me?" he asked, "Because I can wait if—"

"Now," she said firmly.

A grin split his face, and he stepped into the room, completely naked, his *dragon* fully evident. "I love it when you order me around," he admitted.

"Well, then, get into this tub with me and scrub the smell of smoke off."

"Yes, ma'am."

They stepped into the tub together. Hot water sluiced over them as their bodies met, mouths feverishly locked. With a whimper of relief, Dylan yielded to the tide of passion rising up in her. Tobias's sure hands swept over her body as he shampooed her hair and soaped her from heel to shoulder, ignoring his own, very obvious appetites to put her in the right frame of mind first. Arching her back, she invited his hands to linger on her breasts.

"So beautiful," he whispered, ducking his head to suckle the pert tips, even as he donned a condom.

Dylan moaned. Behind her closed eyelids, the world became encapsulated in this perfect place and time. With a trembling hand, she reached between them, encircling his velvety erection.

Tobias lifted his head to consider her. "Better now?" he asked. Water droplets clung to his lashes. His hopeful expression made her smile.

"Much better," she agreed, lifting a knee to coil a leg around him. Heat flared in his eyes as she signaled her desire to make love right there under the shower's caress. Lifting her in his powerful arms, he pinned her between his larger body and the cool, tiled wall. Their breaths mingled and their gazes locked. Over the drum of water, Dylan could hear her heart thudding in her ears.

"I love you," she declared, bracing herself to receive him.

"We're going to make it, Dylan," he promised, filling her with his certainty, as he filled her with his body.

Joined to repletion, she had to admit she could not imagine a life without his teasing smile, his positive presence. She needed him like she needed the air she breathed. In spite of their differences, she had to believe they would thrive together.

EPILOGUE

Dylan's ears pricked at the sound of Milly's happy bark. She'd left the dog sniffing at the fresh spring grass in the yard, while she, Gil, and Chet worked inside the barn, setting up the cooling unit that would keep their first harvest of apples crisp this coming fall. The faint crunch of gravel on the driveway suggested that a car was crawling up her driveway. Her heart gave a leap of hope. *Tobias?*

It couldn't be. After their last, heated argument, he wasn't ever coming back.

Pain lanced her chest at the memory that had ended in his departure a week ago. Hours of cell phone silence had turned into days. And she'd been too proud, too ashamed to call him first. It was her fault that he'd left in the first place. Despite the passion that kept them breathless and laughing and delighted with one another's company, she hadn't been able to accept his upcoming assignment. Not only would it take him away from her for a month or more, but he'd been ordered to operate undercover, to use his wiles on the girlfriend of an arm's dealer in the Washington Metro area. Her stomach had twisted at the thought of him flirting with another woman, perhaps kissing her or…worse, all in the name of doing his job.

"You're just Uncle Sam's puppet," she'd yelled at him. "And I can't stand the thought of you in my bed if you take this assignment!"

And he'd stormed out.

Not a day had passed in the long week following that she hadn't regretted her harsh words. What she ought to have said, instead, was the truth: that she feared he would fall in love with this other woman, the way he'd professed to falling in love with her. It wasn't their differing political views that had driven a wedge between them. It was her insecurities and jealousy.

"You expectin' someone?" Gil Morrison asked, setting aside the wrench he was using.

"Nope." She waved Gil back and headed toward the barn doors herself. "You two keep working. I'll check it out."

Shading her eyes against a bright April sun, she gave a soft gasp as she glimpsed Tobias's neon-green Jeep fording the driveway under endless boughs of blooming apple trees. Milly raced alongside it, barking in joyful welcome. Tears of relief moistened Dylan's eyes as it drew steadily closer, then slowed to a stop, just yards away. Toby's window lowered. The sight of his wind-tussled hair, dark blue eyes and broad shoulders had her biting her bottom lip to keep from bursting into tears.

Without a word, he pushed out of the driver's seat, crossed to where she was standing and spun her in a circle while Milly pranced around them. "God, I missed you," he grated in her ear.

His hoarse confession and the familiar scent stealing over her freed the sob that she was holding in. "You came back," she cried softly against his neck. "Thank you. Thank you for coming back."

Milly moved away to sniff around his car.

Tobias pulled away just far enough to assess her emotional reaction. "Sweetheart, don't get upset," he begged, putting her down to cup her face in his warm hands. "Of course I came back," he chided. "You think I'm that easy to get rid of?"

Dylan tried to blink away her tears. "But you said the assignment would last about a month, and it's only been a week."

He sent her a crooked smile. "I didn't take the assignment."

Confusion assailed her. "But you said you didn't have a choice. Either you took the job or you...you quit." Her voice trailed away as remorse dropped in her belly like a rock down a well. My God, he'd chosen her over his career?

"I didn't quit," he added, baffling her further.

"Oh." So where had he been this whole last week?

"After our blow out, I did some serious soul searching about who I am and what I'm passionate about."

Her heart thudded with mixed hope and trepidation. "And?"

"And I'm passionate about us and keeping my country safe—in that order. Honestly, I couldn't stand the thought of cozying up to some other woman. And you deserve better than a husband who's going to take off to God-knows-where at any given moment. That means no more undercover jobs for me."

Overwhelmed by the messages bombarding her, she jumped on the latter statement. "No more undercover work? Then, what will you do? What about the ATF?"

"Don't get ahead of me." The twinkle in his eye belied his stern tone. "I still have to feel like I'm contributing to the general welfare of the population. It's who I am. I'm still going to work for ATF, and even for the Taskforce, if they need me."

"And you should," she countered earnestly. "I should never have called you a puppet of the government." She clutched his sleeve. "Tobias, I'm so sorry."

Her apology rendered him mute for a second. A slow grin split his face. "That wasn't so hard, was it?"

Not nearly as hard as she thought it would be. Not when it meant having Tobias permanently in her life, in her bed. "Not really, no."

"So, do you want to hear the solution my supervisor and I came up with?"

A whine and a yelp coming from inside the back of his car provided her with her first inkling. Stepping around Tobias, she neared the car to see what held Milly's interest. Two bright sets of eyes gazed back at her out of crates stowed in the shadowy interior.

"Puppies?" she exclaimed, reaching in to let them lick her fingers through the bars. They appeared to be slightly older pups, perhaps six months old, almost fully-grown.

"Future bomb-sniffing dogs," he clarified, joining her at the window. "I'm going to train them the same way I trained Milly. That's my new job description."

"Really?" Dylan tore her attention from the puppies to eye him in astonishment. "You're giving up the Special Response Team?"

"I'm specializing. We're not all about snuffing out the fireworks, you know. We train dogs, too."

Tears of gratitude stung her eyes. She shook her head in amazement. "Puppies," she breathed.

"Trust me, it's not all games and slobber. It's going to take consistent, hard work on my end to turn these pups into absolutely reliable working dogs. No feeding them treats on the sly," he cautioned.

"Oh, I won't. I promise."

"And this way, I'll be right here on the farm, so I can help you run the orchard."

It seemed too good to be true. "Milly wants to meet the puppies," she observed. Then she gasped and whirled around to face him. "Husband?" she cried, a wave of pleasure rushing over her. "Did you say husband?"

"Whoa, lady, you are long on the uptake. I thought you'd either forgotten I said it or purposefully left it hanging because the thought horrified you."

"Horrified! Tobias Avery Burke, are you asking me to marry you or not?"

"Damn straight." He stepped back, opened his jacket and let her read the message on his T-shirt: KEEP CALM. AND WILL YOU MARRY ME?

She stared at the message, letting the full implication of it steep in her brain a while, before meeting his eyes again. Her heart beat at twice its usual rate. She could have sworn her feet were floating off the ground. God, what this man could do to her! In a matter of five minutes, she'd gone from utter despair to euphoria.

Hurling herself at him, she caught him off guard, managing to knock him flat. "Oooph." They rolled and tussled for a moment in the cool, tender grass until Tobias gained the upper hand, pinning her beneath him.

"That was anything but calm," he pointed out.

"You caught me off guard."

"Should I take this as a yes, or what?"

"Definitely. Take it—and this," She lifted her head to claim his lips in a tender, love-filled kiss, "—as a yes."

THE
TASKFORCE SERIES

The Protector
The Guardian
The Enforcer

Turn the page for an

excerpt from

DANGER CLOSE

The Echo Platoon Series
Book One

———◆———

Marliss Melton

She whirled and stared at the door in stupefaction. *Sam?* How could Sam be here? Her gaze darted to the rum still sitting on the counter. She had to be hallucinating.

"Open up. I want to know if you're okay."

That had to be Sam. No one else was so infernally bossy. She retraced her steps to unlock the door with uncertain hands. The light from her condominium fell on Sam's rugged beauty—crooked nose and all—his broad shoulders and long legs. Without thinking, she launched herself at him, hugging him with a whimper of relief.

"Whoa, hey, hello to you, too," he exclaimed, clearly not expecting such a warm welcome. With a glance over his shoulder, he maneuvered them both inside of the building and shut the door with his heel, all without releasing her.

Maddy held tight, absorbing reassurance from the breadth of his chest and mustering the strength to stop digging her fingers into his camouflage jacket. She couldn't afford to look weak in front of him. Collecting her composure, she released him and stepped back. "What are you doing here?" she demanded.

He didn't answer right away. Jungle green eyes raked her pale face, sliding down her rigid torso to the fingers she was curling into fists. "What's going on?" he countered.

"What do you mean?" A sudden suspicion had her clapping a hand to her forehead. "My father sent you here again?" she railed, anger driving back her fear.

"No."

His immediate assurance only confused her more. "Then he sent you here to spy on me," she concluded, still bristling.

"Wrong again. I just met your colleague, Ricardo."

"Ricardo?" What did Ricardo have to do with any of this?

"He mentioned what happened at the lab today."

An image of Enrique flashed before her eyes.

"Are you okay?" Sam continued. "You seem…," he angled his head with suspicion, "you don't seem like yourself."

She tore her gaze from his all-seeing eyes and fixed it on the bottle sitting on the kitchen counter. "I think I'm drunk," she said seizing the first excuse she could think of.

He glanced over at the bottle. "The bottle's still full. You sure you're not just scared?"

Maddy lifted her chin a notch. "Of course not." She ruined that assertion by all but jumping out of her skin as Sam laid a hand squarely over her thumping heart.

"Tell me what happened today," he exhorted.

Maybe she was dreaming him. That was all she seemed to do lately. She couldn't wrap her mind around the fact that he was here in the flesh, in a place where she'd never expected him to be, regarding her with concern. Part of her longed to share her terrifying experience, but she couldn't. Sam would have her packing and on a plane headed for home by sunrise tomorrow.

"Nothing," she said with a shrug.

"You found the body of the guard at the lab," he stated.

"Right. But nothing else happened." She winced the instant the words passed through her lips because they so obviously sounded like a lie.

He cocked his head a second time, suspicion brightening his eyes. "You saw the men who killed him," he immediately guessed.

Maddy shook her head. "No." She forced the denial past her tongue.

He stepped closer, using his height and breadth to impose his will on her. "Were they foreign soldiers?" he interrogated, ignoring her denial. "Lebanese, maybe?"

Surely he could see the pulse galloping at the base of her throat. "I don't know. I never saw them," she insisted.

"Then why are you so terrified right now?"

"I'm fine." She cast a longing glance at the bottle of rum. Maybe another shot or two or three would convince her of that.

"Maddy." Sam's large hands rose without warning to capture her face between his large, warm palms. A frisson of awareness arced clear to her toes. "Those men have been identified as terrorists. If you know anything about them, anything at all, we could use that information."

"That's why you're here," she realized, putting two and two together. He hadn't chased her to the Southern Hemisphere just to be close to her again. Of course, not. Why would she even think that when he'd left her home in McLean without so much as a fare-thee-well?

He released her with a grimace of annoyance. "I

can't talk about that," he told her flatly. "Our presence here is top secret. No one is supposed to know, not even you. Promise me." He held up a warning finger.

Maddy glared at it. She hated when he pointed his finger at her. "I know how to keep secrets," she averred, flinching inwardly as she realized she was keeping one from him now.

Doubt reared its grizzly head. If the Lebanese soldiers were terrorists, then shouldn't she tell Sam everything she knew? But then she would have to admit that her life had been threatened, and Sam would insist that she leave the country.

Besides, what could she tell him that might possibly be useful?

He flipped his wrist over to glance at his watch. "I have to be going," he said. Looking back at her, his gaze centered on her mouth.

Craving a kiss, Maddy touched her tongue to her parched lips. "I can't believe you're here," she marveled. "It's almost like you're following me," she added, laughing self-consciously at her wishful thinking.

"Pretty amazing coincidence," he agreed. Cynicism curled the edges of his upper lip. "I'm not supposed to have contact with any civilians in the area," he added, putting a damper on her expectations.

"Oh." Her giddiness evaporated. "I see." He would leave without another backward glance, just like the last time.

But he didn't. Instead, he stood there taking her in with such brooding intensity that it dawned on her that he didn't really want to leave. The pleasure that bloomed from that realization emboldened her. Seizing the front of his BDU jacket, she jerked him closer and stole the kiss she'd been craving.

The feel of Sam's supple lips made her groan in

remembered pleasure. He responded with initial restraint, his body tense with self-control. But then his control crumbled suddenly, dissolving into an avalanche of desire as he palmed her head, cupped the curve of her bottom and plundered her mouth like a man starved for the taste of her.

Behind closed eyelids, Maddy's world tipped off its axis. A shimmering heat spread to her extremities. She could feel Sam's heart thudding beneath her palm, his sex swelling against her hip. Would he stop? Did she even want him to?

Then, with a frustrated growl, he raised his head and gazed at her beneath hooded eyes. Breathing harshly, he brushed her cheek with the pad of his thumb and reluctantly released her.

"Stay out of trouble," he ordered, turning to the door. He flicked off the light before stepping through it—to keep anyone outside from seeing him, she realized—and shut the door firmly behind him.

Maddy released a whimper as her expectations drained abruptly away, leaving her feeling deprived. She drifted to the door, locked and bolted it, and then went to peek through her kitchen window, hoping to catch another glimpse of Sam, but he had disappeared. There was nothing to see except the sandy front yard, a scraggly cactus plant, and an empty street. Would he even come back? she wondered, or would he keep away like he said he had to?

She reached for the bottle of rum and tossed back one more swig. One thing she was grateful for, she wasn't so terrified anymore. By some miracle, Sam Sasseville, her unlikely guardian angel, had followed her to Paraguay. And oddly enough, his assignment was to get those men who'd almost killed her today— the men who had murdered Enrique and terrorized her.

Once they were dealt with, Maddy wouldn't have to worry that the leader might change his mind and come looking for her. God, she hoped Sam and his SEALs dispatched those men quickly!

◆

DANGER CLOSE
The Echo Platoon Series
Book One

available in print and ebook

Marliss Melton is the author of ten gripping romantic suspense novels, including a seven-book Navy SEALs series and continuing with The Taskforce Series. She relies on her experience as a military spouse and on her many contacts in the Spec Ops and Intelligence communities to pen heartfelt stories about America's elite warriors and fearless agency heroes.

Daughter of a U.S. foreign officer, Melton grew up in various countries overseas. She has taught English, Spanish, ESL, and Linguistics at the College of William and Mary, her alma mater. She lives near Virginia Beach with her husband, tween daughter, and four young adult children.

You can find Marliss on Facebook, Twitter and Pinterest. Visit www.MarlissMelton.com for more information.